THE BESTOWED BRIDE

BOOK THREE
LORD DERE'S DEPENDENTS

CHRISTINA DUDLEY

Cover design: Kathy Campbell, www.kathryncampbell.com

PROLOGUE - 1801

And then I swore thee, saving of thy life,
That whatsoever I did bid thee do,
Thou shouldst attempt it. Come now, keep thine oath.
—Shakespeare, *Julius Caesar* (1599)

It was seven full months of captivity before the first letter reached him, and in the hard Spanish sunshine Horace Langworthy squinted at its cover, which had been addressed and re-addressed and re-addressed. It was a miracle it had reached him at all, considering the many emendations, the Spanish postal system, and the countless ships and hands involved in its passage. And the leaping excitement which flooded him when the officer first held the letter up and called out a mangled version of his name gave way to disappointment when he saw the unfamiliar hand.

It was not from Mary, then.

They were only recently engaged, to be sure, but it should have made all the difference! Before, when they could not openly correspond, she had always found ways around such rules. She had made her mother write to him, for instance, more than once, to which she would add greetings and illustrations in the margins. And she had always, always, written the direction with her own sweet hand.

This was not from Mary.

What was the reason for her silence? Horace had blamed his Spanish captors to this point, attributing to them all manner of offenses, ranging from bureaucratic incompetence to outright malice. Because clearly they wished him to die of loneliness and *ennui.* But now here was positive proof that such obstacles had been purely imaginary. Letters were indeed getting through, but Mary Pence had not sent one.

After the first wave of chagrin passed, he told himself that, still, here was a letter. A tangible piece of home and familiarity, whoever might have sent it.

Breaking the seal he found two sheets, the outer cover enfolding another sealed note. And the inner note was addressed in a hand he *did* recognize, the sight of which made him straighten and his breath catch.

Quickly he turned to the writing on the cover sheet.

> *Mr. Langworthy, I regret to inform you that your friend Mr. Sebastian Barstow died yesterday of infection, following injuries sustained in the action of 31 March off Malta. While his goods have been sent to his wife and son, the enclosed letter addressed to you was found among them, and I have taken the liberty of forwarding it to you directly, to spare his widow the task.*

> *Yours, etc.,*
> *Wm. Wold, Chaplain Royal Navy*

The letter was dated May of 1800, and here it was, nearly a year onward. Which meant, in all the intervening time, the missive bounced from Malta to ship to ship to the Admiralty, and from there again outward, from ship to ship, to where Horace Langworthy sat a prisoner of war near Ferrol, Spain.

He found himself sitting on the rickety plank which served as a bench in his quarters. Sebastian Barstow dead? *Dead?* Good old Barstow? Lively, humorous, daring Barstow? They had known each other for years as young midshipmen and then lieutenants in the same fleet. Seen half the world together. It would not be an exaggeration to say Barstow had saved his life—for when Horace joined the Royal Navy at fourteen, he had not known how to swim, and when a forty-year-old, bullying third lieutenant pushed him overboard, it had been Sebastian Barstow who leapt in to save him. No small feat, considering how undersized Barstow had been as a youth. And it had been Sebastian who taught Horace the splashing, lolloping stroke which, if not graceful, would at least improve his chances of not drowning.

And now, his erstwhile rescuer and dear friend was no more.

Chance alone had prevented Langworthy himself from participating in the Malta action—he had fallen off a roof (long story) on leave in Palermo and remained there while his broken leg mended. Though slated to rejoin the HMS *Lion* the next time she put in, before that could happen, *Contre-amiral* Decrès and his *Guillaume Tell* attempted to sneak through the blockade of Valletta, only to be discovered by the patrolling HMS *Penelope*. The result? a glorious action for the Royal Navy, but one costly on both sides.

Costly especially for Sebastian Barstow, it turned out.

And to think, all through his captivity Horace had been envying him! He'd heard of Barstow's injury, yes, but he'd imagined that after Barstow recovered he would once more be out there in the thick of things. Not trapped in a prison camp doing nothing all day long, every day. For months therefore Horace had been envying his friend the glory of it all.

Who knew but that Barstow had envied Horace in return, seeing him whole and free to sail away in search of excitement and prize money while he lay in hospital. Langworthy's reality had proven altogether different as well, however. For a short month after Valletta, the little sloop *Fiat* under acting commander Jones had been ignominiously captured, having blundered in the fog into the midst of three Spanish ships.

And here Langworthy had been penned, ever since.

The wrapper letter falling unheeded to the floor, Langworthy emerged from his narrow quarters to the fenced yard, feeling the heat rising as the sun climbed.

There had been ninety-seven men taken on the *Fiat* that unfortunate day, a few dozen of whom had since died of wounds sustained in the capture. Of those captives, Jones the commander had his freedom on parole in the town, while his remaining crew, both officers and seamen, occupied themselves however they could manage, but usually with dice, cards, and sleep. The officers kept themselves apart from the humbler seamen, though after such protracted, enforced idleness, Langworthy thought there was little enough difference between the groups. They were now uniformly tired of each other, uniformly surly, and uniformly combative, and it was just as well none of them knew their captivity would last another full year.

Having made two circuits of the yard, he paused at the corner where a gap in the boards permitted a slice of the water to be seen. This would be as good a place as any to read Sebastian's last message, Langworthy supposed. Bracing himself, he slid a finger under the wax and squinted at the shaky writing.

> *Horry, old boy, things are looking grim for me. They had to take my leg below the knee, and while that might have been got over, it's the splinter in my hip that will do me. The area begins to suppurate and I to shiver, fit to break myself apart.*

It's not leaving this life that eats at me, my friend. It's abandoning my dear Sarah and my boy, whom I have not yet even seen. Sarah has no family of her own, and while I trust she will have a home with mine, there is hardly any money, and I dread to think what will become of them all, if anything were to happen to my father.

Horace, I know you haven't any more to your name than I have, but I am dying, while you may yet make your fortune in this war. I know as well your attachment to Miss P. But I beg you on bended knee—will you look Sarah and Sebastian up? Will you, to the extent of your power, do what you might for them? There has never been a better, dearer wife than my Sarah since all the world began, and if I were my old self I would call your Miss P pitiful in comparison, whatever her charms and graces might be. But I have not many jokes left in me, I'm afraid. I will only say, if anything ever were to prevent your marrying your Pitiful Miss P, you could not do better than to transfer your affections to my poor Sarah. How I wish you might! How I wish I might imagine her cared for by someone who has proven the best of friends and best of men. I would bestow her upon you with my blessing.

This is all I can manage now. I will write more if I can. –
Barstow

Langworthy found himself leaning his head against the boards, one eye staring through the gap at the outer world. But it was not the sliver of the glittering Ria de Ferrol he saw, but rather a gallery of memories. His throat was tight, and the spring sun radiated its heat with heartless indifference. Ah, confound this war and this prison! Confound death, confound Napoleon Bonaparte, and confound all of Spain, from top to bottom. Confound even Mary herself, for not writing when he needed more than ever to hear from her!

Confound *everything*.

He did not dwell overmuch on Sebastian's feverish imaginings that day—of course he would pay a visit to his friend's widow and infant son, if ever he were delivered from the everlasting monotony of captivity. He would pay a visit—or he and Mary would together, once they were married—and he would tell the Barstows some stories to make them smile. And should he find the family out of pocket as well as grieving, naturally he—they, rather—the Langworthys—would spare what they could, without grudge or stinting. Why, he would have eventually gone to see Mrs. Barstow in any case, for his old friend's sake, just as Barstow would have called upon Mary, had the situation been reversed. Indeed, Barstow might have saved his breath there.

But as for *marrying* Barstow's widow instead of his own beloved Mary...well, old Bash must have known the request was a long shot. And had he made his suggestion in person, doubtless they would have had a good laugh over it and made some competitory jokes about their sweethearts' relative perfections.

So much for that.

Still.

Whenever he should be sprung from this maddening limbo—whenever he should be given his first leave home, not only would he lead Mary Pence to the altar with all possible rapidity, but he would find a few days to run up to Twyford in search of Mrs. Sebastian Barstow, that he might speedily fulfill his obligations to her husband.

"Consider it done, old boy," muttered Langworthy to the air about him. "And who's to say? When this war is over, Mary and I might give up Portsmouth and its environs and settle nearer your kin. I'll look after your little son and do what I can for your Sarah—making sure she neither starves nor throws herself away on some worthless fellow. Or, at least, no more worthless than you were."

But there was no Sebastian Barstow to laugh at this jest, and the lack gave Langworthy another pang.

With a sigh, he delivered an idle kick to the walls of his prison and one last curse, though with little heat. Then he turned on his heel, lips pursing to whistle a boat song, and went looking for a game of dice to join.

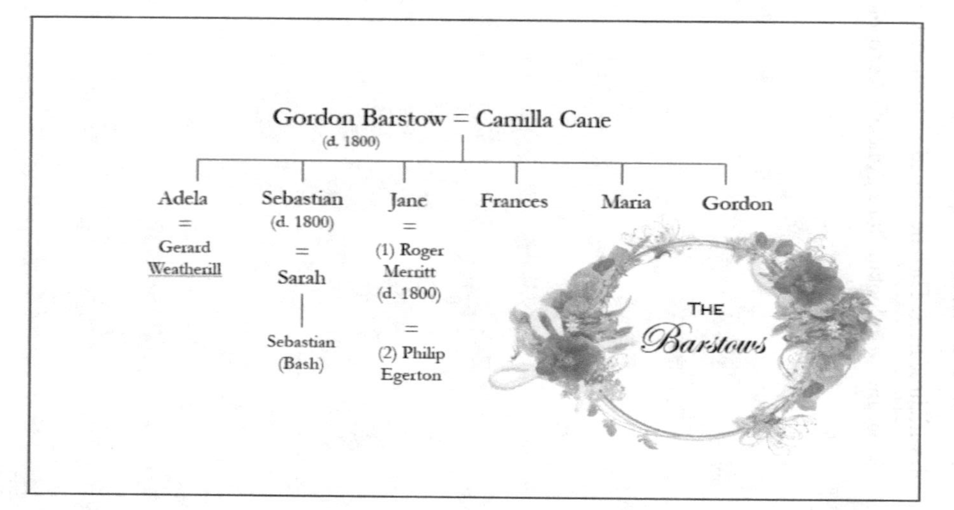

Gordon Barstow = Camilla Cane
(d. 1800)

Adela
=
Gerard
Weatherill

Sebastian
(d. 1800)
=
Sarah

Sebastian
(Bash)

Jane
=
(1) Roger
Merritt
(d. 1800)
=
(2) Philip
Egerton

Frances

Maria

Gordon

THE
Barstows

CHAPTER 1

January 1803

**These Refflexions draw after them others
that are too melancholy.
—Lady Mary Wortley Montagu, *Letter,* 22 August (1716)**

G ood-bye! Good-bye!" The landau provided by Lord Ranulph Dere of Perryfield rolled away from the great house with a crunch of gravel, carrying off to Oxford the happy bridal couple of Mr. and Mrs. Philip Egerton, as well as Mrs. Egerton's sister and brother-in-law the Gerard Weatherills.

No sooner was the vehicle down the drive, however, than a depression of spirits swamped the bride's nearest relations. Or, at least, the two eldest remaining. The bride's mother Mrs. Gordon Barstow pressed the hand-kerchief she had been fluttering to her lips to hide her efforts at fighting back a sob, while her daughter-in-law Sarah sighed, "I wonder how long it will be before we see her again."

"I lay odds at less than a fortnight," said the third Barstow daughter, seventeen-year-old Frances, with irksome cheer. "After all, the Egertons might walk from their new home in St. Lawrence to Oxford in an hour, and riding would be even quicker. It's not as if they were setting out in search of the Northwest Passage."

"But we are not in Oxford," spoke up Maria, the fourth sister. She was nearly twelve but looked younger because she was so diminutive. "It is a half-hour walk from our house to Della's, so if Jane already walked for an hour to reach Della at Keele's School, coming all the way on to Iffley would require an hour and a half altogether, and then she would still need to return."

"You need only say the word, and I will send a carriage wherever and whenever you like," their kindly benefactor Lord Dere reminded them. "You might see Mrs. Egerton every day of the week, if you cared to."

"Why, uncle, that would be very inconvenient for you, never being able to call your vehicles or your time your own," his niece by marriage Mrs. Markham Dere protested, her brows rising up her alabaster forehead. "Not to mention, the servants would resent the unpredictability of such an arrangement. I think it better if the Barstows and the Egertons visit at set times, scheduled with appropriate notice. Once a month, perhaps. Or twice, if need be. But I'm sure Mrs. Egerton will be so busy setting up her new household that she might prefer to be left alone at present."

"Mama," called the youngest son Gordon, from where he and his friend Peter Dere had been leaping back and forth over the hedge, "if Jane is gone, what if I were to have a bigger room? You said yourself I have grown."

"Do say yes, Mrs. Barstow," Peter urged in his piping voice, "because Gordy sleeps in a cupboard." Though the boy laughed as he said this, and though he was Mrs. Markham Dere's son and heir to the Dere baronetcy, there was only good-natured raillery in the declaration.

"At least Gordy has his own space," countered Maria. "So lucky to be a boy! The rest of us, being girls, must be crammed together: Frances and me in the green bedroom, and Sarah and Jane and little Bash in the room leading to the cupboard."

"I never asked for special treatment," her brother protested. "And Bash and I could probably share now. Though he isn't breeched yet, he isn't a girl, at least, and he sleeps to beat us all hollow. But I doubt you could fit both of us in my cupboard, so it'd better be a bigger room."

"You aren't suggesting we put Sarah in the cupboard, just because Jane is gone!" cried Frances, aghast. "And her a married woman—or used to be married!"

"Why not Maria, then?"

"But Gordy, I'd be scared by myself," his sister reproached him.

"How could you be, you ninny, with Bash and me just on the other side of the door?"

"Children," murmured Mrs. Barstow, raising her hands to silence their bickering. "How unseemly this is, with Jane barely gone from us." But at least their squabbles made her forget her lowness, and she almost twinkled at the baron. "You must pardon them, sir. One would think they were raised by wolves."

The silver-haired peer made her a bow. "No one acquainted with you, my dear cousin, could possibly think such a thing. I, for one, like to see lively and opinionated young people."

Putting light fingertips to her brow, the mistress of Perryfield grimaced at this nonsense, so typical of these burdensome Barstows, the family of poor relations Lord Dere had taken under his wing. But at least Mrs. Dere was soon relieved of their presence for the day, for Mrs. Barstow refused the baron's invitation to return inside, and in minutes the Dere coach rolled up to carry the whole brood away.

"Sarah, my dear," said her mother-in-law in her soft voice, shortly before they reached the cottage, "I hope you will not take it amiss if I *do* offer you the cupboard bedroom—Mrs. Dere's erstwhile dressing room, that is. I mean it as a compliment, you see. To offer you a little privacy, after these past few years. You have been so very, very good to us, sharing not only a bedchamber, but indeed a *bed*, with first Adela and then Jane. And that was not all you have shared. I do not know what we would have done without your widow's pension."

"Oh, madam," breathed Sarah, feeling her throat tighten, "the obligation goes entirely the other way! You know little Bash and I have no family remaining but you Barstows, and I only wish I had more to give, when you have shared with us a home and the warmth of your companionship and—and everything. And I will of course sleep wherever you like."

"Don't be polite," scolded Frances. "This is your chance to sleep wherever *you* would like, and if I could be rid of Maria I would leap at it, for she kicks fearfully in her sleep."

"And *you* steal the covers," retorted her younger sister.

Again Mrs. Barstow raised her hands to hush them. "I have good news, children, but I did not want to say anything before Mrs. Dere because it would only annoy her. But Lord Dere has anticipated us. Before you even thought to quarrel about how we would arrange ourselves with Jane gone, the baron thought of it, and he has given us a little money for—"

"Money!" whooped Maria and Gordy, causing the coach to bounce and little Bash to kick his legs in excitement.

"—A little money," she repeated, too glad to reprove them, "for furniture and what not, because he said a house with three grown people and three young people was altogether different from a house with *four* grown people and three young people."

"He said that?" marveled Frances. "It is like mind-reading. He ought to tell fortunes!"

Sarah smiled at this. "I think it more likely that he seizes on all possible occasions to be generous."

Ruefully Mrs. Barstow chuckled. "I agree with Sarah. I suppose he thought this the most plausible excuse for a gift. But what would you say if we replaced the beds? The rooms are not large, but I daresay two narrow beds could be squeezed in the place of the one larger bed in both the green room and the one attached to the cupboard."

Which is how, not three days onward and for the first time since her girlhood, Sarah Barstow found herself sole occupant of all she surveyed, a realm composed entirely of the tiny chamber which had once served as Mrs. Markham Dere's dressing room.

The limited space barely held a narrow bed, dressing table, chest of drawers, and washstand, and Sarah might have sat upon the coverlet and reached any other piece of furniture by simply rotating in place. But small as her new quarters were, they were hers alone. Even her little son Bash had delighted to leave her, removing across the passage to share the green bedroom with his nine-year-old uncle Gordon.

Dim light filtered through the casement, falling in a beam across the dressing table, and Sarah moved like an automaton to pull open the second drawer and draw out the packet of letters it contained. It was something she could have done in her sleep, having made the motion so frequently in the past two years. The letters were soft now with overhandling, the creases in the paper in danger of tearing, and the ribbon binding them fraying at the ends. And not only could her hands seek the packet unerringly, but she knew as well the letters' contents nearly by heart.

Sarah, my dearest, I write with my mind and heart full of you. We saw a rare sunset, the rosy, lambent sky recalling the rush of blood beneath your skin when you blush, and the warmth of the declining sun caressing me as your hands and lips once did...

My heart's own, do you remember our first walk together, after we were engaged? There was so much to say, but who could take the time to say it when my leave was so short? Every moment not spent with my arms about you was a moment wasted. I told myself there would be time for words when we were apart, when I had no ardent, vibrant creature to hold, her glowing eyes raised to mine and her lips waiting for my kiss...

Yes, indeed, Sarah had read passages such as these so many times she required no aid to recollect them, but still she gently unfolded the letters because she loved to see the words written in his spiky hand and to run her finger over the lines, if she could no longer run her finger over the writer himself.

Though the news of his death had fallen heavily upon her, and though at the outset she almost believed she could have lain down in her grief and never risen again, mercifully she had her infant son to bind her to the living world. Her son and her husband's family, with whom she had come to live when Sebastian was assigned to the HMS *Penelope*, his last posting. And when Sebastian's death proved only the first in a series of blows to those she loved, there had been neither time nor breath to wallow in despair. Sarah picked up her burdens, therefore, and marched on.

The passing months became a year.

The one year became two.

And little Sebastian grew into a solid, healthy little boy with his father's blue eyes and hearty laugh and affectionate nature—the joy of his mother's life. Every day she thanked God that, though her boy had no father, he had a half dozen relations eager to pet him and play with him and transfer to him the love they had borne his father.

Thus had the memory of her lost husband slowly, imperceptibly faded to a wistful glow, like dying embers which occasionally still flared, but less and less often, and with diminishing strength.

Though Sarah would have said she loved her departed husband as much as she ever had, the truth was that the healing effects of time and circumstance could not be entirely withstood. And perhaps there was something on that particular morning—her sister-in-law Jane's blissful expression as she was joined to her beloved Philip, or the stolen kiss Sarah saw Adela's husband give her when he thought no one was looking—which niggled at her, something which in another person Sarah would have called restlessness.

Whatever it was, on this hundredth or thousandth time when she took up Sebastian's packet of letters and untied the ribbon, she passed over the most familiar and timeworn passages to linger on those she usually skipped. His descriptions of nautical minutiae, for instance. His expenses. His anecdotes of political wrangling aboard the *Penelope* or in the larger navy. His more unsettling tales of foreign shores and shore leaves.

The penultimate letter she ever received from her husband came from Palermo, in the Kingdom of Sicily, and truth be told, Sarah had only read it in its entirety once, the day she opened it. For one of the stories it contained had so annoyed her she refused to read those particular paragraphs again—and then his next letter, his final one, came from the hospital some weeks later.

She almost smiled now, remembering her earlier vexation. What had been the incident described? Would it still have any power to move her?

...in the Albergaria near the palace, making our way back to the ship. You know how buoyant Langworthy's spirits are at all times, how irrepressible, and on this occasion even a far soberer fellow would be forgiven 'a madness of frolick and

intemperance.' To have his own Miss Pence pledge herself to him! Though this Miss P can be nothing in comparison to you (as I have told him on more than one occasion, when he would weary me with her praises), you are mine, and the rest of the world must shift as they might.

In any event, we had been toasting the good lady's decision with likely more diligence and loudness than you would approve, and in doing so, it seems we also overtaxed the goodwill of the citizens and local gendarmerie. In short, the early hours found Langworthy drunk as a wheelbarrow and myself not much better. (You will frown, darling, and how I wish you were at hand to punish me!) We were expelled from our cozy tavern in Via Porta di Castro and forced to take flight. He and I lost sight of each other in the darkness, and I was nearly to the Scrigno Tower when I heard him cry out. The fool had climbed to a rooftop to make his escape, but, not being in perfect command of mind or limbs, he had fallen and broken his leg. It was just as well, Sarah, for then he was taken to the Ospedale "Grande e Nuovo" (how's that for a name?) instead of being arrested, and I, being also in uniform and having some little Italian, must accompany him.

It's bad luck for Langworthy, for the Penelope *sails tomorrow. You may imagine Captain Blackwood's disgust with the whole situation. It has been all I can do to make explanations and compensate for my friend's absence. Horace himself is as sorry and remorseful as a man newly engaged can be, for he fears what he will miss. What adventure and what possible prize money. But Blackwood says...*

Not caring to read more, she refolded the letter with a grimace.

"Exactly," said Sarah aloud to her little chamber. "No wonder I never read that bit again. It was all Horace Langworthy, doing Horace Langworthy things." As pleasant as it had been to rediscover Sebastian's little compliments to her, the sensation gave way to crossness.

Horace Langworthy!

Time had done its work during Sarah's mourning, and like all good, loving wives, she had gladly let it blur and then obliterate the few faults her husband had possessed. Sebastian Barstow *emeritus* retained all that was sterling, like a monument in a church, the rest left unrecorded.

But this brief excerpt on this January morning operated as a key within a lock. Its creaking lid giving way with a protest, the chest of truth was opened once more, and from its depths emerged things long disregarded. Other passages in other letters which she had read once and never again.

The time the two lieutenants were thrown out of the Blue Posts in Portsmouth because Langworthy "had words" with one of the older midshipmen. That one shore leave in the West Indies where "a number of them had their eyes blacked during a scuffle where some tempers ran high." The trick played on a seaman whose talk had grown too big for the officers' taste.

Sebastian made light of the episodes, laughing them off as "boys being boys," but it had never escaped Sarah that the chief boy always being a boy was her husband's boon companion. Was Horace Langworthy.

"Sebastian wasn't perfect, of course," she said softly to the dressing-table mirror, in which her troubled reflection gazed back at her, "but he would have approached much nearer that state, had it not been for that one particular, regrettable friendship."

She realized her heart was pounding irregularly, and she flattened a hand against it. And it was in this attitude she was caught when a rap came at the door, followed at once by its opening and the appearance of Frances.

"Has Bash woken from his nap?" asked Sarah, blushing guiltily as her hand fell back to her side. She hoped the discontentment which she was certain lingered on her face had gone unnoticed, but judging from Frances' curious expression that seemed doubtful.

"He's still asleep," answered her sister-in-law. "Do forgive me for surprising you. I should have given you a minute to collect yourself. I suppose it was a very trying morning for you."

Sarah swallowed. "Why so? Here I am, spoiled with my very own room."

But Frances wasn't fooled. She sat beside Sarah and tapped a finger on the letters spread across the coverlet. "I meant because of Jane getting married. I thought it might make you sad about Sebastian." Her brow knit as she peered more closely at her. "Though you don't look sad—you look...I would say 'cross,' if you were anyone else. But you are never cross."

"Of course I am cross on occasion," Sarah said with a rueful grin. "I would not be flesh and blood if I were not."

"If you say so," answered her sister-in-law dubiously, "but why should today be one of the occasions, if I might ask?"

Ordinarily Sarah would have put the younger Frances off with some neat evasion, but perhaps the peculiar mood which impelled her to read the Palermo passage in the first place gripped her still. All she knew was that, in the resuscitation of her dislike of Horace Langworthy, she wanted to complain of him to someone.

"It's this," she said, snatching up the letter and thrusting it at Frances, a fingertip marking the offending paragraphs. "Look here. If I am cross, it is because I was reading this."

Frances needed no further urging. Sebastian had been quite a few years older than she, and he had passed the last of those years mostly away at sea, but she still remembered the glow his dashing, infrequent presence imparted to her childhood home and the excitement his letters brought. He had been generally admired—adored, even—and though Frances was proud of him, she could not say she truly knew him. And certainly she had never heard any story of Sebastian like the one she now read.

Before she knew what she was about, she gave a low, unladylike whistle. "Fancy that!" she marveled. "Nearly being arrested in Palermo for drinking and making a row! I wonder if Mama knows."

"I suspect she does not," Sarah replied crisply, gathering the other letters into a neat stack.

"Arrested!" repeated Frances.

"*Nearly* arrested."

"Chased by the gendarmerie for drunkenness and—and riotry!"

"He didn't say he was drunk!"

Frances merely raised a skeptical brow, her lips twitching. "He was, in his own words, 'not much better,' in any event. Did he—write to you of such things often?"

For a moment Sarah was silent, but when Frances did not retract the question, she reluctantly replied, "...Sometimes. Not *too* often, mind you." As if a veil might be drawn over a handful of occasions. And indeed it might, though in truth each instance had pained her.

Now Frances was forced to repress a smile, accurately translating "not *too* often" as "more than I would ever like known." Eyes alight, she murmured, "So he did, then. You know, Papa and Mama always did speak of Sebastian as if he were at least as much saint as he was sailor. It was always, *Your brother is so good and brave and honorable—*"

"And so he was, all those things," insisted his widow.

"Of course he was," agreed Frances cheerily, "but I daresay I like him the better now for learning he was no angel. One can't have one's older siblings too perfect, you understand. So good old Sebastian got up to mischief and malfeasance, did he?"

"Not 'malfeasance,'" Sarah objected. "Mischief perhaps, but not 'malfeasance.'"

Frances shook this off. "Well, I don't know. Look at when Jane's Mr. Egerton was arrested for disturbing the peace in Oxford. Would you call that mere 'mischief'? For it is precisely what they were chasing Sebastian for in Palermo—"

"They weren't only chasing Sebastian, Frances," cried Sarah, seizing upon this. "In fact, they were also—*primarily*—chasing his fellow officer—this Horace Langworthy. If not for Horace Langworthy, I doubt Sebastian would ever have found himself in such circumstances. In fact, those—few—times when he ever…mentioned…things of this nature, Horace Langworthy was without fail always at the bottom of it!"

"Oh, do tell me more, Sarah," urged Frances. "I am old enough to hear such things now, and I promise I will say nothing to Mama, though Gordy might like the—escapades—too. Was there more drinking and carousing in foreign places? More disturbing the peace? Perhaps a little gambling?"

Sarah stared at her, telltale color flooding her face.

"I've nicked it!" whooped Frances, waving the letter she held like a victory banner.

Plucking the sheet from her sister-in-law's grasp, Sarah began to fold it up, pressing the creases more firmly than was strictly necessary. "There were indeed other incidents he told me about—and possibly even others he spared me, knowing they would put me out of countenance. I suppose such is the case for all navy men. But I persist in believing that, if not for fate placing him in the constant company of the…less-principled Mr.—"

"—Mr. Horace Langworthy. Yes, I caught the name," Frances finished for her dryly. "And yes, I suppose this person was Sebastian's preferred confederate. But surely Langworthy could not always have been the instigator! That would make my brother his spiritless lackey; whereas I am certain so dashing a fellow as Sebastian was entirely capable of getting up to no good on his own. Come now—let's have it."

But Sarah had reached her limit. Tying the ribbon around the packet, she stuffed it back in the drawer and rose. "You have guessed it all already."

"But I want details!"

"Another day, perhaps, you greedy girl."

"Do you promise?"

Sarah arched an eloquent eyebrow of her own, and Frances' shoulders drooped. Clearly she would have to be cleverer about this, if she ever hoped to learn more.

CHAPTER 2

Do not think, that I am slack in coming for to reap.
—Jane Lead, *A fountain of gardens,* 304 (1696)

Post for you, Mrs. Barstow," announced the maid as the family sat at breakfast.

"Thank you, Reed," answered Mrs. Barstow, indicating where it might be placed beside her dish.

"Pardon me, Mrs. Gordon Barstow, but I meant for Mrs. Sebastian Barstow."

That got everyone's attention, for no Barstow could remember Sarah receiving any letters, she having no family outside of them. While little Bash instantly bounced in his chair, holding out a plump hand and demanding, "I see! I see it, Mama," the others did their best to feign indifference. This courtesy lasted throughout the time she spent frowning over the direction and the design of the seal but was abandoned at once when, upon finally unfolding the sheet and glancing at the signature, Sarah gave a loud gasp.

"What is it?" cried Frances and Maria in unison, while Mrs. Barstow said, "Is it bad news, my dear?"

But Sarah had embarrassingly choked, and it took her some moments to stifle her coughs and recover the power of speech, by which time the others were tempted to snatch the correspondence from her. And surely it was discomfiture at her outburst which caused scarlet to wash over her as she read, pressing a napkin to her mouth.

At last, however, she lay the napkin aside and looked up.

"It is—an old naval comrade of Sebastian's," she rasped. "Ahem. He—er—writes to say he will come to Iffley this week to call."

"Now?" marveled Mrs. Barstow. "Who can it be? Sebastian has been gone over two years."

"He must have been too busy fighting to come before," suggested Gordon, picturing broadsides, ships on fire, blasted masts with their rigging tangled, and everywhere wounded men lying about, moaning.

"That can't have been," said Maria, with the scorn only a slightly older sister could heap upon a younger brother, "because we've been at peace for months and months now."

"He was a prisoner of war," explained Sarah, the color only now beginning to recede from her face. "So he says it took some time for him to be released by his captors and returned and paid off. But now he comes."

"Hurrah!" shouted Gordon. "A naval man coming to call! Hurrah!"

Bash at once took up the cheer, beating his spoon upon the table.

When order was restored, Mrs. Barstow repeated her question in a trembling voice. Because—a friend of her son's! What might he share with them of Sebastian?

Sarah's eyes briefly met those of Frances. It was a warning, lest Frances screech or jump or blurt something regrettable when she learned the name.

"It's a fellow officer from the *Penelope,* madam," she answered her mother-in-law. "You will surely remember the name from Sebastian's letters when I tell you. One Horace Langworthy."

"Of course I remember that name," breathed Mrs. Barstow in delight, entirely failing to notice Frances clapping a hand to her mouth. (It need not be stated here that, however much Sebastian Barstow had softened his stories when writing to his wife, he did so even more when writing to his mother.) "Does Mr. Langworthy say how far he is coming from? Surely he must intend to stay in Iffley or in Oxford for a few days, at least. I hope he will! For a mere fifteen-minute call will never suffice. Yes—perhaps he could be persuaded to pass a week in Iffley. Lord Dere had always said surplus visitors who could not be accommodated at the cottage were welcome at Perryfield—"

To Sarah's relief, the clamor of the children's suggestions provided time for her to collect herself, though she wished she might have done so without Frances observing her. Heaven help her! Had she somehow summoned Horace Langworthy by the power of thought? A case of "talk of the Devil, and he's presently at your elbow"? What could he possibly have to say to her—to any of them? Stories of Sebastian, most likely, but were they likely to be stories the children or Sebastian's mother should hear?

Well, Sarah sighed inwardly, whatever the reason bringing the dreadful man down upon them, at least she had a week to prepare.

But even as she thought this, some sixty miles away in London, a stocky man stumbled over a trunk in a passageway and hurtled through an open door.

"What the deuce?" cried the room's occupant Horace Langworthy, as he stood at the washstand shaving. He eyed the intruder, taking in the man's downy white hair, luxuriant whiskers and sober attire. "You're not Conklin. Have you mistaken your way, sir?"

"Mistaken my way? Indeed not," blustered the whiskered man. Struggling to his feet he straightened his black coat and dusted off his knees. "I tripped over your luggage in the passage—luggage most inconveniently placed, I might add—and fell. If you object to receiving unexpected visitors in this manner, I suggest you move your trunk to one side and shut your door firmly."

Langworthy's half-lathered face cracked in a grin, which would have further stoked the priest's indignation, had it not been followed with an affable "We share a common enemy, then, my good sir: Conklin, the inn servant, who has proven sadly deficient though I tipped him respectably. To add insult to injury, whatever is obstructing the passage does not belong to me, as you see my trunk here." He nodded toward where it lay still open. "Nor have these latest bungles of his been solitary examples. But if it comforts you, I will not be in your hair much longer, for I take the Oxford coach within the hour."

"You're going to Oxford!" The whiskered man straightened to study him, while Langworthy proceeded to slap water on his clean-shaven face and then to rub it vigorously with the greying, frayed inn towel. Though it was midwinter and his sunburn mostly faded, yet enough of his former ruddy bronze remained to make the clergyman appear pale as paste, and the latter soon ventured, "But you're a navy man, aren't you?"

Langworthy threw the towel aside. "I am. Do I still look so weatherbeaten?"

With a plump finger, the parson indicated the uniform coat, neatly brushed and buttons gleaming, draped over the trunk lid. "I've seen many paid-off sailors with the peace, but you are the first who is headed for Oxford, as I am. Clerics such as myself go there by the score, of course, but sailors...Do you hail from there, originally?"

"Not a bit. Can't you hear my accent? In Sussex we don't prance and bleat like you Oxford sorts." But he removed the barb from the jibe with a wink. "I stray so far from shore because I have a duty to discharge to a fellow sailor, whose widow now resides in Iffley."

"Iffley!" echoed the parson, his whiskers quivering in amazement. "Why that is precisely my destination! If you will allow me to introduce myself, I am Dr. Septimus Rearden, and I go to take up the duties of an old Oxford colleague who is in Italy now for his health. I am fortunate in having appointments which obviate the need for a living of my own, leaving me free to do little favors such as these."

"Honored to make your acquaintance," replied Langworthy with a bow and a twist of his lips. "Mr. Horace Langworthy at your service." A note of self-mockery tinged this declaration, which Rearden could not interpret, but which other navy men would have understood. To wit, while captains might be given their rank even when limping along onshore at half pay, lowlier lieutenants dwindled once more into mere "misters."

"Will the discharging of your 'duty' keep you long in Iffley, Mr. Langworthy?"

A pang rippled through the sailor at this, and he shifted restlessly before giving the question the go-by. "Hard to say. Will yours, Dr. Rearden?"

"I expect to be there at least through the summer. Terry and his wife will not want to exchange the mellow glory of Rome for our wet, dank springtime, and then it will take them some weeks to return, if they choose to return."

With a mechanical clearing of its throat, the mantel clock arthritically chimed the half hour, and Langworthy began to gather his remaining belongings, tossing them into a gaping valise. "Well, let us hope it stays dry for our journey at least, for I'm up top."

Where nine out of ten men would have excused themselves at that point and withdrawn from the room, Dr. Septimus Rearden proved the tenth man. In truth, having been widowed twenty years earlier, and being childless and of no interest to his remaining youthful relations, he seized upon this encounter with the younger man. In place of hours of silence, confined to the coach with a variety of mismatched companions, he pictured a cozy chat with a social equal. Doubtless Mr. Langworthy had a store of stimulating experiences to share, and perhaps he would ask questions in turn, which Rearden would be happy to answer. His heart beat faster just imagining it. What if, instead of arriving in Iffley travel-stained and alone, he descended with a spring in his step and a new friend in his pocket?

Emboldened, Rearden tugged on his side whiskers and advanced a step. "Up top, you say? Ah, I could never travel so, for my balance is not what it was, and I fear I would doze and tumble off. But I suppose you navy men are indifferent to peril."

"Let us say my pocketbook is indifferent to it," said Langworthy dryly, fastening the straps of his valise.

"Right, right," agreed the parson to himself. "Half pay, after all. Say—as we will both be residents of Iffley for whatever length of time, what would you think, Mr. Langworthy, of taking a seat within the vehicle for the journey? That is, I would consider it a great service to me in whiling away the hours and would therefore insist on treating you. Your only duties would be to stay awake and indulge an old man with some conversation."

Now it was Langworthy's pulse which sped. He demurred of course, as courtesy required, but even to his own ears his protests sounded half-hearted. For if Dr. Septimus Rearden was a lonely man, Horace Langworthy was a disheartened one. And the thought of spending hours and hours teetering far above the ground, clinging for life to the roof of a jolting coach—to which he would be less securely attached than the luggage which shared the space—held no appeal.

And would it be so bad to arrive in Iffley already on good terms with the resident clergyman? Why, he might be standing before the same doctor a month hence, to be joined in marriage to Mrs. Sebastian Barstow! There was nothing to be lost in beginning to lay a foundation now. Surely he could listen to the fellow and ask appropriate questions without having to share much himself.

After a decorous interval, therefore, he yielded, and when the Oxford coach lurched from the innyard of the Bull and Mouth in St. Martin's le Grand promptly at nine, both gentlemen were seated within. Not alone, to be sure, but they were beside each other on the rear-facing bench, and opportunities for confidences arose while their fellow passengers dozed and the elderly couple opposite fell into hissed arguments.

Thus, by Ealing, Langworthy had heard all about Rearden's childhood and years at Christ Church. By Uxbridge, he knew of the late Mrs. Rearden's disposition, constitution and early demise. By Beaconsfield, he was fully acquainted with the clergyman's sundry appointments, all of which required little in the way of work, but which taken together paid handsomely.

Not that Dr. Rearden was the sort to prose on and on about himself. On the contrary, he made several attempts to turn the conversation back to his companion, but so great did the young man's interest in him seem that it was too easy to veer away again.

Only when they reached Stokenchurch did anything shift. Fortifying themselves with tea and bread while the horses were changed, Rearden contemplated the dry portion in his hand with a sigh. "There is a cook at the Iffley rectory—one Mrs. Winching—and a maidservant Polly, Terry says, but I confess I am a trifle uneasy about them. Since I lost Mrs. Rearden I have kept only one manservant and always had my meals from the nearest inn or chophouse. And now to have two women about! I only hope Terry's pupils will be persuaded to return from the school in Oxford to which they removed when my predecessor departed. Two boys. I would be more comfortable with more people in the house."

The parson's whiskers trembled at the horrors which lay ahead, and Langworthy might have grinned, had Mary Pence's perfidy not continued to weigh heavily on his heart. Indeed, something of his own burden must have shown on his face for Rearden straightened, venturing, "See here—I've done it again. Talked and talked of myself, and you've let me. Nay—encouraged me. But now that we are over halfway to our journey's end, I insist you say something of yourself, Langworthy. To begin, where will *you* be staying? In Oxford or in Iffley?"

"Oxford," he replied, though in truth he had made no arrangements in either place. "It is less than an hour's walk to Iffley, I believe. Just long enough to awake the blood and determine what must be accomplished."

"And...what must be accomplished? You spoke of discharging a duty...?"

But the driver marched in at that point to bellow, "All is ready!"

Wearily, the passengers climbed once more into the coach and took their places, the elderly couple openly bickering and the others settling themselves either to listen or to sleep again or both.

"I needn't have married you," grumbled the woman, jabbing her husband with a gnarled finger. "Clem Hawes would have had me. The poor man bawled his eyes out when I jilted him for you."

"The more fool he," her spouse retorted. "If he weren't dead these forty years I'd send you back to him yet."

Perhaps it was this interchange, or perhaps it was that, after so many hours and so many miles and so much candor on the parson's part, Langworthy felt his reticence much diminished. His companion was kind enough. And had their positions been reversed, Langworthy might have resented someone who absorbed all one's confidences while sharing none of his own.

Therefore, when they were again underway and jolting over the rutted road toward Wheatley, and when the elderly couple were deep in rehearsing each other's part in some ancient wrong, he said in a low voice, "To return to your question, sir, the duty I mentioned to you involved a fellow sailor. More than that, he was a dear friend and comrade, of whom it is not an exaggeration to say I owe my life. He was injured in the action off Malta and later died, when I myself was a prisoner of war in Spain."

"Spain, you say!" breathed Rearden, tempted by that little titbit to ask a dozen questions. With difficulty, however, he refrained, lest Langworthy retreat again.

"During my captivity," the young man went on, "a letter from this friend at length reached me, written from his deathbed and asking me to...look up his widow and young son and ensure they were...all right. I suspect he hoped I would live to make my fortune with prizes taken. Indeed, he might never have made the request, had he known how soon after I left him I myself was put 'out of action'! Now here it is, two years onward, and I am only now carrying out this task, not only because there was considerable delay in returning from Spain, but also because I had first to see my own...family and friends."

"After so long a time, they must have been very, very pleased to see you, Langworthy, for doubtless they were on tenterhooks during your imprisonment."

In response, Langworthy's brow darkened and lines appeared to flank his mouth, making him appear altogether a different man.

"My uncle was well," he answered vaguely, "and took my reappearance as composedly as he had my departure." He gave himself a shake. "You must not think me ungrateful. It was he who fitted me for the navy, a debt which took me years to repay. And if not for him using what influence he had, I would never have made lieutenant."

Though no deep bond seemed to join Langworthy to his relations or vice versa, Rearden surmised the gloom did not stem from this lack, but having finally succeeded in making the young man talk, he knew better than to press.

It was a wise strategy, for Langworthy now felt the temptation to relieve his spirits after the last wretched month.

"I...had a sweetheart," he confessed. "With whom I grew up and to whom I was engaged, only waiting until I should have made my fortune."

Guessing where this was leading, the parson shrank in anticipatory sympathy.

Langworthy cleared his throat once. Twice. Scratched at a corner of his eye as if dust had flecked it. "When I returned at last from Spain, I learned she—well—in short, she...released me from our engagement and—and—promised herself to another."

"Ah."

Another pause. Langworthy's lips parted as if he would say more, but then he took himself in hand, color flooding his face. He had already admitted to Mary Pence's defection—there was no need to advertise every detail of why he came to Iffley. Not that the parson looked like a blabber, but still—

When, after a few minutes, it was clear his companion would say no more on the matter, Rearden gave vent to his feelings by boldly administering a bracing, *chin up!* sort of thump on the young man's shoulder (an awkward move, as they sat side by side, but one appreciated nonetheless), before falling into his own brown study. It was only when they drew near at last to their final destination that the clergyman offered up what he had been mulling over during the intervening miles.

"Langworthy, I have a proposal to make and ask you to hear me out."

Then his companion did grin. "Do I have an alternative, locked together here as we are?"

"No, but you might run for it the minute the coach stops at the Angel Inn. Look—if I will be living in Iffley in a rectory too large and too female-occupied for my comfort, and if you have business in Iffley for a few days or weeks, or even months, why should you walk over from Oxford in all weathers to conduct it? Why not simply lodge at the rectory with me? You would be more than welcome! You would be doing me a favor. After I have, by virtue of our circumstances, seized you by the button for hours, so to speak, you know more of me than my own shadow, and I know enough of you to suspect we would get on. What do you say to it, Langworthy?"

It was the offer to treat him to an inside seat all over again, only more so.

And Langworthy had even less reason to refuse it. Strained in pocket, homeless, nigh friendless, and embarking on a stern fulfillment of duty—whyever should he look a gift horse in the mouth? Fate, all unsought, had sent Dr. Septimus Rearden stumbling into his life (literally), offering answers to several of his problems, and he found he could not bring himself even to pretend decent reluctance.

Thus, by the time the steps of the coach had been lowered and the tired passengers clambered down to go their various ways, the bargain had been struck.

CHAPTER 3

**...He hath some offences in him
that thou wouldst discover if thou couldst.
—Shakespeare, *Measure for Measure* (c. 1604)**

For the first time in her long career, Mrs. Lamb, postmistress of Iffley and landlady of the Tree Inn, failed in her self-appointed role of town-crier. For though she—and indeed everyone in the village—knew of and looked forward to the arrival of the new temporary curate of St. Mary the Virgin, she—and everyone in the village—was caught thoroughly napping by the simultaneous arrival of Mr. Horace Langworthy.

She blamed herself. If she had not been so thoroughly distracted the morning the unusual letter arrived for Mrs. Sebastian Barstow, she would have remarked its uniqueness and never rested until she learned its contents. But she had indeed been distracted. As a marriage gift to the departing Egertons, she had too generously agreed again to employ the rapscallion Harry Barbary as an errand boy, only to discover him, that precise crucial morning, scrawling mischievous postscripts to the outside of several outgoing letters! As a result, the unprecedented letter to the younger Mrs. Barstow was bundled with the other Iffley Cottage correspondence without a second glance.

Mr. Langworthy, therefore, slipped into Iffley unheralded, sitting beside Dr. Rearden as the wagon from Oxford's Angel Inn conveyed the two gentlemen to the rectory after nightfall.

And so it was that, when he paused at the front gate of Iffley Cottage the following day, that was the first the Barstows knew of him being anywhere about.

"Look, Mama," said Maria from her favorite seat at the window, "it's some strange gentleman."

"Oh, yes?" asked her mother absently. The three older Barstow women were absorbed in inspecting a recent issue of *The Lady's Magazine* for ideas to refurbish their wardrobes.

"Must be the new curate," said Frances. "What about this for the spotted muslin?"

"I don't know if there is enough," Sarah frowned. "See the gathers at the shoulder? That would require—"

"He's coming up the walk!" cried Maria, bouncing.

"Oh, bother," sighed Frances, slapping shut the magazine as Sarah swiftly wound up the muslin and stuffed it in the nearest workbasket.

By the time the maid opened the parlor door, every Barstow stood neat, trim, and idle as you please, but their assumed tranquility received a blow when Reed announced, "Mr. Horace Langworthy!"

Mr. Horace Langworthy!

Today?

Sarah felt her blood turn to ice. But—but—*here? Now?*

Even as her knees wobbled, she carefully wiped all trace of horror from her features and took advantage of his first attention to Mrs. Barstow to study him beneath her lashes. She saw a surprisingly tidy man of medium height and pleasant features—a straight nose, high cheekbones, candid blue eyes, reddish-brown hair with a slight wave to it. She had always imagined he would be a disheveled person (a looser life, in her mind, entailing looser comportment), but he was cleanly enough in his plain blue coat, white frilled shirt, and trousers. Her experienced eye noted the shirt and trousers were likely the ones he had worn for daily work on board, having sewn several of the like for her husband, and she found confirmation in the minute, nearly invisible repairs at places of common wear and tear.

For his part, Langworthy proved equally sly in his surveillance. Even as he bowed to Mrs. Barstow and murmured apologies if his call came as an intrusion, and even as Mrs. Barstow demurred, saying she was only too glad to meet and welcome any friend of her late son, etc. etc., he was gathering data on Mrs. Sebastian Barstow in a series of glancing glances.

His friend had never stinted in his praise of his wife. According to Sebastian Barstow, his wife was peerless. "A pearl in both character and appearance." Langworthy had taken this with the requisite grain of salt, however, and now he congratulated himself on his good judgment. That is, while he knew nothing yet of her character or personality, he thought Mrs. Sebastian's appearance far inferior to Mary Pence's. Mrs. Sebastian was—pshaw!—mild as milk. Smooth, light-brown hair, eyes somewhere between grey and blue, a small nose and chin, a quiet air. Whereas Mary sparkled, from her crown of red-gold hair, to the flashing looks she threw from her warm eyes, to the dancing feet which carried her light figure.

But the comparison brought pain, and he shied from it.

Forget Mary.

As she has forgotten you.

"—Mrs. Barstow, Mrs. Sebastian Barstow, Miss Barstow, Miss Maria." With a bow toward each young lady as he repeated her name, he claimed the chair the elder Mrs. Barstow indicated for him.

"My younger son Gordon is at school at present, so that introduction must wait," his hostess continued, "but here is my grandson—Sebastian's son—also called Sebastian. Though we have nicknamed him Bash." She gestured at the plump little boy stumping around in his frock, holding a wooden toy aloft.

"A fine, healthy boy," Langworthy said politely. "I see why Barstow was so proud of him." For this he was rewarded with smiles from all around, with the exception of the child's mother, whose expression remained impassive. She had curtsied to him, and possibly her color rose a degree, but otherwise he might have been a new yarn sample, for all she betrayed.

Irritation pricked him. She might show a *little* interest in someone who had come quite a way and who might as easily have spared himself the inconvenience. Did she not realize he could simply have written a letter full of heartwarming anecdotes accompanied by a few banknotes (not that banknotes were thick on the ground of late), and considered his duty done?

Miss Barstow, at least, who looked to be a fine young girl of perhaps seventeen, regarded him blushingly and said, "We didn't expect you yet."

"I am relieved to hear my letter reached Iffley, in any event," he answered. "I should perhaps have been more precise about when you might expect me." But precision had been impossible. That is, he left Portsmouth precisely when he could bear it no longer.

An awkward little silence fell, broken only by Bash making experimental *b-r-r-r* sounds with his lips as he now dragged his toy over the sleeping housecat.

Rarely at a loss, Langworthy was at one now. Should he launch into a few of those heartwarming anecdotes? Or should he come straight to the point of his visit and ask to speak to Mrs. Sebastian alone?

Mrs. Barstow helped him through the difficulty, eager as she was to draw him out. Indeed, she regarded him with such wistfulness that he felt his discomfiture ebb. "Mr. Langworthy," she began, "I believe you served with my son under Captain Blackwood on the *Penelope*?"

"Yes, madam, I had that pleasure. Your son was my friend and comrade from the time we were midshipmen. I am certain he must have told you how he fished me from the sea nearly the first week of our acquaintance and saved my life?"

He had not. As much from modesty as a wish to hide from his family the cruelties of the lieutenant who caused the incident. But the chorus of gasps and questions which met Langworthy's declaration obliged him to tell the story now. He did so with as jaunty an air as he could, but instead of causing his listeners to beam with pride, the eyes of all the ladies save the youngest filled alarmingly with tears.

"Oh, my boy. My dear boy," choked Mrs. Barstow, dabbing at her eyes. "Thank you for sharing that, Mr. Langworthy. My lost boy. How very...good and brave he was." Miss Barstow openly wailed. And Mrs. Sebastian—Langworthy saw her swallow and hunch lower on the sofa, as if she had received a blow.

Unexpectedly, his own throat constricted—not for grief over Sebastian Barstow, though it was there, but rather because the sight of Barstow's wealth of relations openly mourning his loss, even two years onward, gave Langworthy a hollow feeling. If the earth were to swallow *him* up when he left Iffley Cottage that day, would anyone in the world notice, much less weep?

Another silence fell, but Mrs. Barstow was quicker this time in mastering herself.

"Do forgive us," she said at last with a watery smile. "Such a display will make you afraid to tell us anything else! But you mustn't hesitate—we promise not to dissolve again, Mr. Langworthy. Don't we, girls?" They nodded apologetically, and she cleared her throat. "No. We know your time is valuable as well. Are you long in Iffley or Oxford?"

"Er—I don't know how long I will be here," he confessed, "but for the time being the new curate Dr. Septimus Rearden has invited me to stay at the rectory." This led to questions, naturally, and gladness—at least on

Mrs. Barstow's part—and he gave a brief version of his meeting with the clergyman at the Bull and Mouth in London.

"Fancy that!" laughed Miss Barstow. "You already know the new curate better than we do. You ought to have brought him along."

"I did ask, but Dr. Rearden said he thought it better if I—met you all first myself."

"Quite sensible," agreed Mrs. Barstow, "for now we need not be shy about talking Sebastian, Sebastian, Sebastian. Tell me, sir...were you too involved in the Action of 31 March, where my son was wounded?"

"I was not," he replied, in the same moment as Mrs. Sebastian said, "He was not."

This being her first contribution, their simultaneity startled them into looking directly at each other, and at last she showed signs of awareness, color flooding her face. His curiosity piqued, Langworthy made an *after-you* gesture and sealed his lips.

Lowering her needlework to her lap, she said quietly, "Mr. Langworthy was in the hospital in Palermo at the time and could not rejoin the ship. Sebastian told me so in his—penultimate letter."

Though her voice was sweet and attractive enough, the coolness of her manner made his eyebrow lift. She was aware of his hospital stay, then? That meant she was likely also acquainted with what landed him there—the night's elation and carousing, the wild flight from the authorities, his unfortunate fall. Well, there had been no reason for Barstow to keep mum about it. But why should she be so cold about it? Whenever Horace regaled Mary Pence with his escapades, she would giggle and declare she wished she had been there. (*Forget about Mary Pence!*)

Perhaps Mrs. Sebastian held herself aloof to avoid breaking down. She might be sad or bitter or both over her husband's bad luck. God knew, if Barstow had also had the good fortune to fall off a roof and break his leg that fateful night, he would likely be alive today, and Langworthy would not be sitting in this parlor in his place.

Aloud he merely said, "Indeed, so I was. In the hospital. Where Barstow kindly saw me deposited in a bed before he took himself off to rejoin the ship. I cursed my fate, then, imagining myself deprived of who knew how much action and prize money, but alas, we neither of us were fortunate in that respect. Though he, of course—though he—that is, I am sorry for what happened to him. I did not mean to make it sound—"

"Mr. Langworthy," breathed Mrs. Barstow, "you must not apologize for being alive, though my son is gone. One has nothing to do with the other, and I would hate to be so selfish to wish you harm or misfortune simply because you were spared. Please. It is so kind of you to come."

"It *is* kind," Mrs. Sebastian murmured, as one who worked to convince herself. "You are from Portsmouth, I believe, so this journey has cost you not only money, but also time away from your friends and family."

"Oh—" He gave a vague, deprecating shrug because he could hardly say, *To what friends and family do you refer, madam?*

"I imagine we are to congratulate you on more than your survival, sir," she went on, taking up her sewing again. "For I believe Sebastian said two years ago that you were engaged to be married. In your own letter, you said you were delayed from returning to England because you were held prisoner in Spain until the Peace. Now that peace has come and you have your liberty, you must also have married. Therefore please thank Mrs. Langworthy as well for letting you come."

Sarah made her speech with all goodwill—indeed, she had been reproaching herself for ingratitude after hearing her mother-in-law's sincere gladness—so her surprise was great when their visitor's brow knit and his eyes darkened.

"Thank you, Mrs. Sebastian Barstow," he replied, cool as cool. "But I am not yet married."

"Oh!" Stricken, she wondered if something had befallen his intended bride, and she had cruelly rubbed upon the sore. The other Barstows must have feared the same, for they were careful to avoid each other's eyes, despite their curiosity.

Though there was nothing in all the world he would less like to discuss, Langworthy said gruffly, "Miss Pence has engaged herself to another. Therefore, I am...entirely free to go where I please." To forestall any pitying remarks, or, worse, any wild attempts to change the subject, he did it himself.

"Speaking of—er—ladies," he resumed hastily, "did Barstow ever tell you of the time when Captain Blackwood was charged with bringing a Mrs. Dulles from Portsmouth to Southend? No? Well, then. The crew thought conveying female passengers a task beneath our dignity in time of war, but she proved a most interesting figure..."

His attempt to distract them succeeded, though not, perhaps, for the reason he imagined. Frances would say later, "It was all I could do, to keep my mouth from hanging open, when he told us Mrs. Dulles had been an actress on the stage and was the admiral's 'special friend'!" (This, with a sidewise glance at her younger sister Maria.)

"Mrs. Dulles was the only true woman ever carried aboard the *Penelope*," Langworthy told them, "but there were other temporary ones."

"What can you mean, 'temporary'?" asked young Maria. Quite captivated by their new acquaintance, she had crept closer with the lapdog Poppet in her arms, until she was nearly at his feet.

"Did your brother ever tell you of our first time crossing the line?"

"What line?"

"You ask me 'what line?' And you, a sailor's sister?" he teased. "I refer to the equator, of course."

"Certainly he did," said Mrs. Barstow.

"He said there were frolics and pranks, and the first lieutenant Beeton dressed up as King Neptune to 'baptize' the newer sailors," said Sarah.

"I suppose one might call them frolics and pranks," he conceded, "but I was right glad Barstow and I were in it together, along with perhaps another score of the crew. And because we were members of the Gunroom, we got off more easily than the landsmen and ordinary seamen. *They* were the temporary ladies I mentioned, for a few of them were made to wear ladies' clothing for the ceremonies. Four of Neptune's constables came for us all and locked us on the lower deck, and with the hatchways battened down it was dark and hot as—as a place you would rather not be. Barstow and I were let out first, however. They blindfolded us and led us along, everyone tossing buckets of water over our heads. Then we were made to lie along a plank, where they proceeded, with far more water, lather, and vigor than strictly necessary, to shave us, before tilting the plank up and dumping us in the sea. Just to press the point home, a couple men bobbed in the water to administer one final ducking, and then the 'frolic' was ended. Let me just say, I had reason that day to be glad again that Barstow had taught me to swim."

He gave a hearty laugh, slapping his knees, before noticing the utter astonishment, not unmixed with dismay, on the ladies' faces. Prodigious! Clearly his comrade's letters home had been watered with vagueness and euphemisms to make them more palatable, for his womenfolk stared at Langworthy as if he had just described to them the alien customs of South Sea islanders.

His laugh broke off, and he felt his face warm. Belatedly he recalled that Barstow's father had been a clergyman, though, by gum, Langworthy would never have called his friend strait-laced.

Maybe the family saved all the strait-lacing for the female members.

For her part, Sarah was conscious of a peculiar fluttering in her mid-section which she did not like one bit because she knew from experience it presaged a thought she had never thought. A realization she had never realized.

On this occasion, that her dear husband had more sides to himself than he had revealed to her. Those stories in his letters which she had read once and no more, thinking them too rackety, too Horace-Langworthy for her taste—those were not even the worst of it!

There had been more. Who knew how many! More riotry and whatnot, which he had withheld from her.

It was one thing for Sebastian to excise incidents like the voyage of Mrs. Dulles the admiral's mistress from correspondence with his mother and sisters, and to dilute the crudeness of "crossing the line" to spare them concern, but why should he not have told her, his wife? Why tell her stories which were a degree milder, but not tell her all? Had he meant to protect her? Or had he thought (with good reason) that she would not like such things and therefore should be spared them?

But—she did not want to be spared! She loved him! She was his wife, meant to share the entirety of life with him and to be told of those experiences for which she could not be present, whether she liked them or not. He had known she would disapprove of admiral's mistresses and naval traditions which bordered on violence (were the perils of war not enough to be going on with?), but that did not mean she did not want to know of such things.

But he had never told her.

Had chosen not to tell her.

Indeed, who knew how much he had withheld over the years? The few disconcerting episodes Sebastian elected to share all included the man now seated across the room, and she had naively assumed there was no more to tell. Had naively assumed that what few there were could all be blamed on Horace Langworthy in any case.

Dismally she thought of the letters she had written to *him*—letters which held nothing back, brimming with the concerns and color of her days. She wondered now if Sebastian had found them tedious. Humdrum.

"My goodness," Mrs. Barstow was saying, having recovered her composure again. "I am not sorry I did not know all the details before of such a...custom, or I would have been quite anxious to know that my son must face it. But he did face it and...survived, so there is that."

"I hope you have a hundred more stories like that to tell us," said Maria greedily, and Sarah could tell from the light in Frances' eyes that she thought the same but was trying to be grown-up about it.

"Yes," agreed their mother, her voice growing in confidence. "I admit I was a little taken aback, but it was silly of me. So no more of that, either. The most generous thing you can do now would be to tell us more of your adventures with Sebastian. He wrote to us, of course, but, as you now understand, he did not tell us *everything*. Therefore, whatever you might have to share will add immeasurably to our little trove."

"Yes, yes!" cried Miss Barstow and Miss Maria, and even little Master Bash bounced on his chubby legs in sympathy, but Langworthy could not help but notice Mrs. Sebastian remained subdued. Her closed lips smiled, but the smile did not involve her eyes.

Faced with this reminder of drawing-room manners, some men might have hung out the white flag, defeated by the company of so many genteel ladies, but rebellion stirred in him. Amplified, perhaps by Mrs. Sebastian's continuing aloofness. Where the rest of the family threw off ceremony, eager for what he might share with them, she alone kept her distance? She alone did not trouble to hide her displeasure?

Well! She was not the only one that day facing what was not altogether delightful to face. Look at the task he had set himself, for instance—or the task Barstow had set him, and which he had accepted!

So that's how it's going to be, he thought resentfully. *If she will not pretend to what she does not feel, neither will I. If she will not assume a role, neither will I.* He would be himself, come what may.

If anything, truth be told, Horace Langworthy was a little *more* than himself in the minutes that followed. Having begun with the harsh customs associated with crossing the line, he was reminded of other shipboard pranks, some harmless and others making the Barstows catch their breath. Maria's and Frances' questions about the names he mentioned led to further tales of fellow officers, and it being a rare ship not burdened with some bullying lieutenant frustrated in his attempts to rise, Beeton's name was heard several times, arousing indignation in the Barstows.

"That Lieutenant Beeton better beware of meeting me!" declared Frances. "Imagine using one's superior rank to vent one's ill feeling! I don't see why he harassed poor Sebastian, however. With no great connections, my brother had no more chance of advancement than he."

"I suppose he spread his unpleasantness evenly about," suggested Mrs. Barstow.

"He did." But even as he said this, a shadow settled on his features. Langworthy had always suspected Beeton was especially beastly to Barstow and himself because he envied their closeness. Funny, that. If Beeton had got his wish and been Barstow's bosom friend, would it now be the *Penelope's* embittered first lieutenant sitting in this crowded parlor?

He glanced at the mantel clock. He had been there nearly three quarters of an hour and must now either take himself off or do what he came to do.

Seeing the direction of his look, Mrs. Barstow clasped her hands together and said, "Mr. Langworthy, I should have asked sooner, but would you have leisure to stay for dinner? We keep country hours and never dine later than two."

But he was determined now and was shaking his head before she finished speaking. "Thank you, Mrs. Barstow. I am not certain—"

"Or tomorrow, if today will not be convenient?" she pressed. "Surely having come so far from Portsmouth you do not intend to turn right around and go back?"

"I have not yet decided on the—er—length of my stay here. Yet. That is—"

"Must you go already today?" wheedled Maria, now using Poppet's paw to pat the visitor's knee.

"Er—there is just one more thing before I go," he answered, giving the dog's head an absent pat.

They turned expectant faces to him, prepared to grant whatever he might ask, and he felt his palms dampen.

"Mrs. Sebastian Barstow, if I might have a—private—word with you?"

CHAPTER 4

The very first Time he came a Courting.
—Jacob Hildebrand, *Happy Constancy* (1738)

Sarah felt her pulse speed. He wanted to speak with her aside? Could he possibly, at this late date, when two long years separated her from her lost husband, have some final message from Sebastian to impart?

Her family were so swift in their desire to grant Langworthy's request that they nearly stumbled over each other to escape the room, Maria hitching a protesting Bash on her hip and Frances throwing back a *you-had-better-tell-me-all-about-it-the-instant-he-leaves* look so obvious she might as well have spoken aloud.

And then they were alone. Or alone with the dog and the cat. Sarah fought an urge to take Poppet or Outlaw upon her lap to hide behind or to occupy her, but there was no time because Mr. Langworthy picked up his chair and carried it to place nearer hers. Facing her.

She saw now the fine lines the sea and sun had etched in his still darkened skin. And while she had earlier deemed him "pleasant" in appearance, she amended this to "pleasant at a distance." It was not that he was bad looking, by any means, but his nearness flustered her. When he was a mere foot away, she could see his eyes were not simply blue, but rather blue at the centers, deepening to violet at the edges. And his hair was not simply reddish-brown, but rather a mix of brown and red with occasional strands of gold, untamed by pomade into orderly waves. He had removed his gloves at some point, wadding them up in his hands, and Sarah could not help but observe that he did not have the typical hands of a gentlemen. His were neither white nor smooth nor slender nor perfectly manicured; instead they were as tanned as his face, square and strong. Why, hands like that might do anything.

At the moment they clenched in slow fists, and Sarah raised wondering eyes to see a new expression settle on his features...uncertainty? That seemed unlikely in one so comfortable with himself, but otherwise she could not classify it.

"Mrs. Barstow," he began at last, his voice more muted than it had been when engrossing the family with rollicking tales, "I am certain you must be wondering what has brought me to Iffley, beyond courtesy and the sharing of some idle stories."

There was no use in beating about the bush.

"I can imagine only one reason," she said, fitfully crumpling the sewing in her hands before she could prevent it. With an effort, she swallowed and stilled herself. "I—suppose Sebastian asked you to come."

Her guess must have relieved him, for some strain in his bearing slackened. "Yes. That is exactly it. Then perhaps he already told you what he asked of me?" The thought flashed through him: Was this what lay behind her *froideur*? Feminine modesty?

But when she answered earnestly, "Mr. Langworthy, I haven't an inkling," he heard the ring of truth.

Blast.

Well, now for it.

Briefly he recounted his receipt of Barstow's letter whilst in prison in Ferrol and the anxiety for his family's welfare it contained, concluding, "He asked me to come and look you up, and as he was my dearest friend in the service, he would have done as much for me, had I asked."

"I don't doubt it," murmured Sarah. "And I thank you for heeding his wishes." She then unbent another fraction. "Indeed, I am certain he would have been honored by such a commission from you, for he spoke often of you in his letters." (No need to mention her own response to those particular passages.) "And—you say Sebastian asked you to...ensure Bash and I were well?"

"Yes." He cleared his throat, glancing away at the front windows, which had darkened as rain began to lash them.

"Well," she tried again, when he made no further reply. For a man who had spoken with such jolly ease only a few minutes earlier, the contrast was remarkable. "Thank you again. I hope Sebastian would be...relieved and even pleased, to see how well provided for Bash and I am. Between my husband's dear family, of whom you have only met a fraction—for there are two other married sisters—and the generosity of Mrs. Barstow's cousin the baron, Lord Dere, who allows us to live in Iffley Cottage, you see how comfortably we are situated. We lack for nothing. It is a quiet life, but one I would be ungrateful to—to—find fault with."

At this he grimaced, inexplicably, but said nothing.

She gave him another moment, but if not for the rain, the little parlor would have been totally silent. Any eavesdroppers must be fidgeting with annoyance, wondering what they were missing, Sarah expected. The thought made her press her lips together to hide an unexpected smile.

But this could not be allowed to drag on thus, or who knew what everyone would think? Not to mention, if Sebastian had some secret message for her—

"Sir," she tried once more. "If this was not all, ensuring my son and I were provided for and safe from the workhouse, may I ask what you wanted to say to me which could not be said in front of the others?"

Blowing out a breath, he slapped his palms on his knees, his lips parting. Sarah waited again.

And waited. But nothing emerged.

What *was* it? Now impatience seized her, touched with vexation. *Out with it, man!* What could Sebastian possibly have told Mr. Langworthy, that the latter hesitated to speak it? What other sort of thing might her husband have kept back, unwilling or unable to tell his own wife? And, equally important, *why* should Sebastian leave those final words with this person? Why entrust them to another, if they were ultimately intended for her? Only look how long it had taken his chosen Mercury to deliver his message—over two years!

Unless—

Fear opened like a trap door beneath her.

Unless—dear heaven!—it were a confession of some sort. Something Sebastian had not dared to tell her while he lived. Something more disturbing than those selected stories edited for her eyes. But—but if it were such a thing, a revelation of some hideous, unknown act of which she was ignorant, why would he not then take it to the grave with him and leave her in peace?

There is another child.

Another family.

In seconds, fear blossomed into certainty, and Sarah could wait no longer for this Mr. Langworthy to collect himself.

"Tell me at once," she commanded, shooting to her feet. "You must. Whatever he charged you with. Please. Do not keep me in suspense but let me know all."

It was her sudden motion which finally jogged him from his paralysis. Noting how she wrapped protective arms about herself, he sprang to his own feet, extending a hand which almost, but did not quite, touch her elbow.

"Mrs. Sebastian, do not distress yourself. I will make a clean breast of it."

"Dear Lord," she breathed, her hands moving to take hold of her throat.

But then, to her astonishment, he collapsed against the mantel with a bark of laughter. "Confound me for a blundering fool! No, no—don't look like that, Mrs. Sebastian. It's nothing like that! Nothing of *that* nature. Oh, mercy."

"Then speak!" she cried, flushing crimson. Her hands fell to her sides, but she was horrified to find she would have liked to hit him for laughing at her discomfiture. Worse—for guessing immediately where her thoughts had tended. How could she have wronged Sebastian so, even in thought?

Her unspoken anger must have communicated itself to him nonetheless, for his brows rose in mock dismay, and he held up placating palms. "I will obey. I had better, if I hope to return to the rectory unharmed. In short, the matter is this: Sebastian asked me not only to discover whether you and his son were cast 'homeless, hopeless, friendless' on the world, but also to do what I could to ensure you never would be."

"Yes, so you have said, and so I have reassured you," she said tightly. "Which part of my answer do you still not understand?"

"Oh, pardon me for being unclear," he replied. "I understand you. That wasn't the difficulty. And I hope you will understand me, once I stop talking in circles. Which I will this very instant. Ahem. That is, in a word, Mrs. Sebastian, will you marry me?"

"Wh-what? Will I *what?*" she choked, certain she must have misheard him.

"Er—marry me."

The turnabout was so unforeseen, so precipitate, that Sarah could only stare at him. And so astonished was she that her mouth hung agape for a full five seconds before she became aware of it and snapped it closed. If he had indeed announced that Sebastian had shamefully fathered a child in Spain, Sarah did not think she could be more amazed.

"What—? Is this—one of your pranks, Mr. Langworthy?" she asked, breathless.

"Pranks?"

"Yes. Pranks. Such as you would often involve my husband in. Is it a joke?"

"Do people often joke with you, Mrs. Sebastian, by proposing marriage?"

"I—I—*no!*" she sputtered.

"And I don't know what you mean, saying I would involve Barstow in pranks, as if he had not been himself the fomenter half the time."

But she was shaking her head and not even listening. "Keep to the point, I entreat you, sir."

"Certainly. Though if it were not beside the point, I would make the point that you were the one who led us astray."

This little raillery proved too much for her, however, and she went up like a rocket, Langworthy would recall later. Like a whizzing firework. Her mild eyes sparked, and she glowed with indignation. He could not even say why he was teasing her, except that her nun-like air made it impossible to resist.

See? he demanded of no one in particular. *She is not as perfect as Barstow boasted. If I am not deceived, a mighty temper lies under that smooth surface.*

"Mr. Langworthy," she bit out, spinning on her heel and resuming her seat, "do you or do you not have any particular message from Sebastian to me?"

"But I've just delivered it," he said meekly.

"What can you possibly mean, sir?"

With the same assumed timidity, he crept back to his own chair. "I asked you to marry me, didn't I? Er—which part of *my* answer do you still not understand?"

Sarah's hand flew to press against her chest, for incredibly she had the feeling that if she did not physically hold herself together, she would explode. Her breathing was so rapid and her temper so high. And she had considered Mr. Langworthy irksome even when mentioned in her husband's letters? In person he was a hundred times more so! What sort of company had Sebastian been keeping? Lucky for her husband he was dead, or Sarah would set him straight on a matter or two, beginning with his fondness for Horace Langworthy!

"That cannot possibly be the task Sebastian set you," she said, when she could do so without breathing fire on him like a dragon. "Asking me to marry you."

"I beg your pardon. It was exactly that."

"And I say it *cannot* be!"

His maddeningly cheerful face creased in a grimace of mock helplessness. "I don't know what to say, then, Mrs. Barstow."

"He cannot have," she insisted, hardly hearing him over the roaring in her ears. Her foot twitched, so badly did she want to stamp it. "What would he have been about, assigning me another husband? *He* was my husband!"

"But he—knew—he was dying."

"He would better have spent his energies in trying to stay alive, then," she muttered, "than in making ridiculous, unwanted, unnecessary, un—un—unacceptable, impossible arrangements for my welfare!"

"I daresay he thought it best."

"'Best'?" she seethed. "I'm not a—a—a—parcel of goods to be handed off on the first passerby."

His eyebrows lifted. "I think there's an insult aimed at me in that last analogy. My good Mrs. Sebastian—"

"I am not your good Mrs. Sebastian."

"Er—Mrs. Barstow, then, though that will be confusing, with your mother-in-law about. But perhaps she would submit to being called by her husband's name? Unless he was also a Sebastian. Then I might have to resort to Mrs. Sebastian Barstow, Senior and Junior. In any event, try and see it from his—Junior's, that is—perspective—"

"He is not a 'junior.' His father's name was Gordon Barstow."

"Hurrah! What a relief, and so much simpler," he said, beaming. "Try and see it from Sebastian's perspective, then. He is dying; he knows you have no relations left to you, save those he brought to your marriage; he knows you will be reduced to whatever piddling pension the Chatham Chest allots you; and he knows you will have your son to raise, without, so far as he knew, connections or benefactors to look kindly upon him. For these reasons, I daresay his—er—'handing the parcel to me' thus struck him as the best straw at which to grasp. I was a friend; I was an officer with the possibility of advancement and fortune ahead; and I was still alive. Barstow could not guess I would be taken prisoner and left to molder for two years, nor that the war would end—at least temporarily—casting me ashore and reduced to half pay myself."

"But he did know for a fact that you were already engaged!" protested Sarah, almost desperately, as she conceded to herself the logic of his words.

"Yes, he did." A note of coolness entered his voice. "Which is why he only asked me to offer for you if I somehow remained single. Had I—married—my obligation would have ended, I suppose, with simply keeping you and Master Bash out of the workhouse."

"Ah." She bit her lip.

He regarded her levelly, waiting.

Waiting.

"...Well?" he prompted.

"Well, what?"

"Well, since I stand before you—or sit, rather, if you have no objection to me sitting again—Where was I? Oh, right. Since I sit before you a single man, clearly something became of my engagement to remove that obstacle. And don't you wonder what it was?"

"I'm sure it's none of my concern," she returned primly.

This drew a slow grin, though one which had not a trace of humor. "Indeed? Mrs. Barstow, I cannot hit upon anything which could concern you more. Had I married Miss Mary Pence, you would have been spared the most arduous part of this morning's parley. Unless I am mistaken in guessing you mean to refuse me?"

"You are not mistaken." Sarah could have kicked herself for how missish she sounded, especially when his grin widened.

"Just so. You might have a little pity on me, for this makes two rejections of me in as many months."

If you proposed to Miss Mary Pence in the manner you proposed to me, you should not be at all surprised to be rebuffed, she said inwardly, and again he replied as if he read her thoughts. "It must be my delivery. Or my appearance. Or my shabby prospects, unless war breaks out again. Or all three together. Do help me, Mrs. Barstow, if you cannot marry me. How might I improve my chances of acceptance in the future?"

"Sir, I would not presume—"

"But you must. Don't you see you must? In common humanity you must. Nay, I believe it is even common manners to give a reason for refusing an offer of marriage. Even Miss Pence did me that courtesy."

When Sarah said nothing, merely taking up her needlework again and beginning to whip tiny, furious stitches, he went on. "Mary—er—that is, you will understand if her Christian name slips from me on occasion—we have known each other from childhood—Mary grew weary of waiting for me while I languished in Ferrol. Indeed, she grew weary of me altogether because she told me she no longer believed we should suit. In short, she gave me my freedom, just as the Spanish did, eventually, after the treaty was signed and word of it reached them. In my place she has chosen a captain who invalided out. A one-legged captain even, to add injury to insult. But one-legged or not, there's no denying a captain's half pay beats a lieutenant's all hollow."

"Surely Miss Pence did not give his larger pension as a reason for her defection," she murmured, fighting a twinge of sympathy for him.

He considered. "Not in so many words, perhaps. But, again, we have known each other from childhood. So there you have Miss Pence's reasons, Mrs. Barstow. Would you say yours are the same? General weariness with me, along with an irresistible one-legged captain?"

In spite of everything, Sarah could not repress a smile. "Having known you one mere hour, sir, if I already found you wearisome, that would reflect more upon me than upon you. On the contrary, I do not know you well enough to judge." As soon as the words left her lips, however, she straightened with sudden awareness. Without meaning to, she had just lied, she realized. For had she not made up her mind about Horace Langworthy years ago, on the basis of her husband's stories? Stories which, she understood now, had not presented a complete and candid picture of either young man. (Not that Mr. Langworthy had said or done anything this day to make her think differently of him.)

For fear he would see through her again, however, she added quickly, "Nor is there a captain I prefer, whether one-legged or whole. But you have no need of my pity, Mr. Langworthy. You have discharged your duty to my husband admirably, however I might feel about Sebastian laying such a charge upon you. My son and I are well and well-provided for, and your offer of marriage in this instance being surely above and beyond what he could have demanded in this situation, you may go your way in peace."

His eyes widened, and he gave a low whistle. "Well!" he exclaimed. "Well, well, well. That's sending me to the right about. I asked for reasons, and you have them at your fingertips: you don't know me; you don't care to know me, you're doing marvelously, thank you very much; and you bid me go in peace." He told these off on his own fingers before heaving a sigh and pulling his crumpled gloves from a pocket to don once more. He took his time, but they did need to be smoothed out first.

It struck her suddenly that he must welcome her refusal, his facetiousness notwithstanding. After all, he knew her no better than she did him, and given his own circumstances, he probably wanted to be saddled with another man's bride as little as he would wish to be saddled with another man's debts.

Had it all been a ruse, then? Had he made his offer in this repellent way, so that he might do his duty, while at the same time ensuring he would escape any consequences? Indignation surged through her once more, though why she should be indignant Sarah couldn't explain. She should be glad—glad all through—that he didn't want her any more than she wanted him.

But I would rather he came out and admitted as much. It would be the nobler thing to do. Supposing I had accepted him! Then where would we have been?

"I am relieved we understand each other," she managed. But there! She had done it again. Lied! No, no—she *was* truly relieved. But she was also annoyed. Could she then fault him for not speaking in bare truths, if she herself could not? When courtesy and propriety dictated they perform this ridiculous minuet of manners?

"And now I think you had better go," she added.

"Certainly, certainly," he agreed, looking about for his hat. "Only—what about the elder Mrs. Barstow's dinner invitation?"

"Her what?"

"She asked me to dinner," he reminded her patiently. "And I gave her no firm answer. Do you think I had better make my excuses?"

Courtesy had its limits. Or, at least, Sarah Barstow had her limits.

"As a matter of fact, I don't think it would be at all agreeable to sit across the table from each other pretending nothing has happened," she said in a burst of candor.

A glint of pure mischief shone in his eye and vanished the next instant. "So...does that mean don't stay to dinner?"

"No! That is—yes. Yes, don't stay to dinner!"

He nodded, plopping his hat upon his head and rising to his feet. "You know the consequence of today's business, then, in all likelihood, Mrs. Barstow?"

She waited, her lips pressed together, and he was forced to continue.

"It means we will never see each other more." With a precise bow, he turned, pausing a second at the door without looking back.

"Good day to you."

CHAPTER 5

**You had better let her alone, you will but provoke her.
—Danel Defoe, *Family Instructor* (1715)**

The rectory stood a stone's throw from Iffley Cottage, a distance Horace Langworthy should have covered with a hop, step, and a jump reflective of his lightened load, but anyone who chanced to see him would have thought him a perplexed, rather than a triumphant, man.

He could hardly account for himself.

He hadn't *wanted* to marry her, of course. Despite his friend Sebastian Barstow's boasts and brags, Langworthy didn't think Mrs. Sebastian held a candle to Mary Pence, lacking altogether "the sparkle of spirit and the languish of tenderness." As soon as he pronounced this, however, the image of Mrs. Sebastian's barely suppressed fury returned to him, and he almost laughed aloud.

All right, then. Mrs. Sebastian had spirit enough, he supposed, beneath her quiet exterior, but there remained nevertheless a vast divide between Mary's spirit of liveliness and wit and Mrs. Sebastian's spirit of bad temper. As for whether the latter had any "languishing tenderness," he could not say, but certainly he had seen no hint of it.

How would Mary Pence have responded to such a situation, for instance? He could see her in his mind's eye and knew without a doubt she would have been delighted. Delighted to receive an offer of marriage, whether she expected it or not, and whether she intended to accept it or not. Because it was a feather in her cap, was it not, be the suitor ever so humble? Mary Pence aside, how could *any* young lady possibly regard a proposal as an affront? As an insult?

Yet Mrs. Sebastian had done precisely that.

No, he hadn't wanted to marry her, but that didn't mean he would not have appreciated a sign of...gratitude, for heaven's sake! A bare acknowledgment that his offer came at a cost to himself. Did it not require him to lay down his own desires for life and to take up, with attendant expense and inconvenience, another man's burden? That alone should have elicited a sense of obligation. Not to marry him, of course, but at least to be courteous and gentle in refusing!

Doubtless an out-and-out acceptance of his proposal would have been a remedy worse than the disease, he recognized, but a softer refusal would have been a balm on the wound Mary Pence dealt him. As it was, Mrs. Sebastian's indignation and coldness had compelled him to act as if the whole question were a matter of supreme indifference, almost a joke.

He unconsciously came to a halt where the wall enclosing the churchyard began, steadying himself with one gloved hand and feeling his own anger rise.

That's right. Would it have been too much to ask of her, that she simply *pretend* a minute's hesitation? The merest pause, to indicate she gave it due consideration?

But no.

It was, No, thank you. It was, Heavens, what a farfetched idea. It was, Good-bye and best of luck.

Barstow's "perfect pearl," indeed!

With a grimace he tugged at a tendril of moss. Why, there wasn't a thing perfect about her! Not one single thing.

She was cold, insipid, inert, and very nearly plain. That is—she was all those things, except when one roused her temper. When in a temper, Langworthy had to admit Mrs. Sebastian Barstow was made passionate, quick, and very nearly beautiful.

"What of it?" he muttered. "Who wants to spend life leg-shackled to a woman who is only beautiful when she is beating and berating one?"

It didn't make a jot of difference in any event. He would never see her again, as long as he lived. He would take the first coach to Newbury on the morrow and be in Portsmouth before the week was out.

Portsmouth.

Langworthy's runaway reflections jarred to a halt here.

And what would he do in Portsmouth, an inner voice jeered, besides wear a path from the back bedroom at his uncle's house (where he knew himself to be *de trop*), to the docks, to the Clerk of the Cheque to collect his half pay, and thence to the Long Rooms, where he would gamble away that same half pay? There would be nothing else to do, nowhere else to go. Now that Mary had renounced him, there would be no days spent walking with her, nor evenings passed in the bosom of her family. All must be avoided. *She* must be avoided.

No, the only advantage of Portsmouth would be, should hostilities recommence, Langworthy would be on hand when ships were commissioned and placed on a war establishment. But even that required luck and a delicate balance. It would be no use to be on hand, if one had been too long there, doing little beyond developing a peacetime reputation as a penniless idler.

Ah, but if war did come again, wouldn't Mary be sorry! To have thrown in her lot with her shore-bound, one-legged captain, when he, Langworthy, would again have the opportunity to go to sea, to rise, and to capture untold amounts of prize money.

The vision warmed him, but however the newspapers rumbled with rumors that neither side perfectly observed the terms of the Treaty, that revenge must wait. And if he could not return to Portsmouth with an imminent appointment to dangle before Mary, he had better linger in Oxfordshire.

"I will stay," he decided, now brushing the dirt from his gloves and tugging on his coat to smooth it. "Why should I not? Rearden has invited me, and I may as well save a few shillings and have a look about me." That his continuance in the village would irk Mrs. Sebastian Barstow now only added to its appeal.

Yes—if he could not yet make Mary Pence's heart burn with regret, he could at least bide his time retorting Mrs. Barstow's disdainful dismissal with disdain of his own. His eyes lit at the thought of it, and had his old comrade Sebastian Barstow been alive to witness it, he would have recognized at once the spark presaging one of Langworthy's famous larks.

"Oh, sir," cried the maid Polly when she opened the rectory door to him. "We are all in uproar, we are. The boys have returned, you see, and then some!"

Indeed the passage was crowded with trunks and baggage, through which they had to pick their way, while a clamor of voices reached them from the parlor.

"Look here, Langworthy," Rearden greeted him, his extravagant whiskers trembling with mirth. "From an empty rectory to an embarrassment of riches. Not only have Mr. Terry's two pupils returned, but they are accompanied by other schoolmates from their time at Keele's. Come, come, lads, settle down and meet my new friend."

There were four boys called to order, the oldest and tallest an adolescent of perhaps thirteen or fourteen, and the younger three closer in age and fidgetiness.

"Langworthy, may I present Terry's pupils, the so-called Tommies? The elder Tom Ellis and the younger Tommy Wardour. And these other two are Iffley neighbors and Keele's School pupils, Peter Dere of Perryfield, great-nephew of the local grandee Baron Dere, and Gordon Barstow of Iffley Cottage."

Langworthy gave the last of these a sharp, appraising look, noting his dark brown hair and clear green eyes. The coloring was different, but something about his carriage and expression recalled the boy's elder brother.

"And boys, this is Mr. Horace Langworthy, a navy man. A lieutenant, in fact. Now ashore because we are at peace. Langwor—"

"My brother was in the navy and a lieutenant," interrupted young Gordon. "He died, though."

"Now, now, Master Barstow," chided Rearden, laying a hand on the boy's shoulder. "Manners."

"Sorry, sir."

"Yes," interposed Langworthy. "I knew your brother."

"Did you?" Gordon's eyes widened. He had been only six years old when Sebastian Barstow died, and though his memories of him had dimmed, his curiosity about him had not.

"I did. A fine fellow. I suppose you want to be a navy man yourself?"

The boy colored, and Langworthy belatedly remembered how Sebastian said it had taken every penny his family could scrape together to send him to sea as a midshipman; now there were no more pennies to scrape, even if Gordon's mother could be persuaded to let another son go.

But that was not what discomfited the boy.

"I—don't especially want to, sir," answered young Barstow. "Because I think I would prefer to be an explorer like my teacher Mr. Keele who traveled in Egypt. Or an ambassador to foreign lands, like Macartney, who went to China." There was a hint of defiance in his voice, as if he expected Langworthy to ridicule his ambition.

"That's something!" cried his new acquaintance, however. "I've never seen either myself. We were far off in the West Indies and altogether missed the Battle of the Nile. And as for China—that might as well be the moon."

"Yes, that's what my sister Sarah said," sighed Gordon.

Instantly Langworthy's back was up, and he came to the right about. "She did, did she? Then don't you listen to her, young man. For she looks like the timid, whey-faced sort, and we all know that fortune favors the bold."

While Gordy was flattered by the dashing lieutenant including him among the world's valiant, this *lèse-majesté* against his beloved sister-in-law made him uneasy. Gallantly Gordon screwed up his courage to pipe, "She *is* quiet, sir, but I don't think Sarah is any more pigeon-hearted than other ladies."

"No?" Langworthy injected just a hint of doubt. "Well, I suppose you would know, as you live among a fair lot of them."

This drew another sigh from the boy, but it made him forget the slight to Sarah. "So I do. It's just Bash and me and the servant Irving against all those girls, but of course Bash is so little he hardly counts, and Irving spends most of the day out of doors. But really, sir, they're not so very bad, even if they're all female. Only Maria who is nearest in age to me causes me much grief. Frances is all right, if you do what she says, and Mama, of course. And Sarah is nicest of all."

"So many Barstows!" put in the curate. "I hope I will be able to keep them all straight. Did you meet many of them besides the—er—possibly timid one when you called, Langworthy?"

"Indeed I did. All the before-mentioned."

"Splendid. And were you...able to complete your business there?" Rearden asked delicately.

To his surprise, the navy man reddened under his tan. "I...that is...there remains some still undone."

"What business?" asked Gordon, his smooth brow gathering in a little furrow. He might only be nine, but he considered himself the man of the Barstow house.

Langworthy hesitated. "Hm. Well. Your brother asked me to make sure Mrs. Sebastian and your nephew were not—er—lacking for 'food, raiment and the like.'"

"You needn't have bothered," piped up Peter. "Because my great-uncle Lord Dere looks out for them. All of them. My mother Mrs. Markham Dere says the baron never saw a pauper he didn't like."

"They're not paupers!" Gordon scowled at his friend. But it must have been a familiar argument between them because Peter only shrugged. "Well, they're not rich, at any rate."

"Goodness!" The curate coughed to hide a chuckle before quickly turning the subject. "If you have business yet to do, Langworthy, that means you will stay longer. You simply must!" He beamed, rubbing his hands together as he surveyed the company. "Look at us all. And to think I feared it would be only me, the maid, and the cook!"

In the face of this eagerness, Langworthy's demurrals were even feebler than they had been at the inn. It was too easy to fall in with wishes which coincided with his own, and he surrendered with, "All right then, Rearden, if your invitation still stands, I'll trespass on your hospitality a little longer."

"What nonsense, 'trespass'! One hardly notices visitors before a month is gone. Ah, what a merry household we will be, don't you think, Tommies?"

The Tommies nodded and muttered fitting phrases, finding it equally impossible to dislike the jolly man who welcomed them all.

Langworthy did not accept without a twinge, however, being fully aware that his own liking for Rearden was matched, if not outweighed, by the twin desires to economize and to vex Mrs. Sebastian. But it was settled, in any case, and he dismissed his qualms with a shrug. If he were guilty of using Rearden for his own ends, he would compensate by doing what he could for the curate, providing agreeable company and alleviating the man's fear of the female servants. Besides, it would only be for a short spell, most likely. A few salvos directed at the widow to break down her offensive pride, a few pennies saved, and with any luck the war would start up again and he would be off.

"We must celebrate," declared Rearden, "with whatever Winching can produce upon the moment. Likely only sandwiches, for whatever goodies she might have made for my predecessor Egerton will be long eaten."

"You could all come to Iffley Cottage," suggested Gordon, with the ease of a boy who thought nothing of the effort required to feed six unexpected male guests. "My mama is sure to have some cakes or biscuits on hand."

"Or to Perryfield," put in Peter Dere, not to be outdone. Though at least Perryfield's housekeeper Robson could be depended upon to have treats at all times, given the baron's sweet tooth.

"Oh, dear," Rearden chuckled, "though it sounds tempting, I had better wait to be introduced to your families myself before I show up with a hungry troop in tow." Winking at Langworthy he added, "No, no, I will screw my courage to the sticking place and speak with Polly."

With the assistance of several cups of tea and slices of spicy gingerbread, the boys soon grew less shy of their new acquaintances, enough to fall into their usual ease with each other.

"One time we were with Denver—that's an old pupil of Mr. Terry's, Dr. Rearden, sir—who tried to show Tommy and me around Oxford," Tom Ellis was saying at one point (his mouth not entirely empty of food, but with no ladies present to reprove him for it), "but he has no instinct for direction, and once outside the walls of Christ Church he was as lost as if you set him down in the steppes of Tartary."

"It's fortunate your schoolmaster found you, or who knows how long you might have wandered, or in what shabby part of town you may have got to!" exclaimed Rearden.

"Has this unfortunate Denver any head for mathematics?" asked Langworthy. "For his own safety and the safety of others he might be taught then to navigate by the stars on clear nights, instead of relying on instinct or memory."

This observation led to the boys wanting to hear more about navigating by the stars, of course, which led Langworthy to telling them about learning from the master of the ship when he was a boy not much younger than Tom Ellis, and from there to him taking up a slate on which to draw figures.

"Ah, Langworthy," said the curate, a half hour later, when nothing was left of the gingerbread but crumbs, "I daresay if any press-gang had ventured this far inland today, it might have taken four young recruits with little trouble."

"But Gordy here doesn't want to be a navy man," said Langworthy dryly.

"No, sir, but I wouldn't mind learning to navigate by the stars. An—explorer or a traveler to distant lands would still find it a useful thing."

"So he would!" cried Rearden, snapping his fingers. "What would you say to it, Langworthy? I confess I haven't a brilliant head for mathematics beyond arithmetic. Suppose you were to teach the Tommies a little celestial navigation?"

"But what about Gordy and me?" complained Peter Dere. "We still have to go to school at Keele's, where Mr. Weatherill teaches us mathematics, but he doesn't know a thing about selectual navigation."

"Ah. I forgot," Rearden frowned. "But I am not here to stir up trouble, lads. Keele's is a good school, and in truth, you—all—have more pressing things to learn at your age."

Remembering his decision to aid the curate where he could, Langworthy considered. The proposed task, practical or not, would provide an excuse for him to remain as long as he liked. And beyond his continued presence, would it not annoy Mrs. Sebastian further, to think her brother-in-law beholden to him for anything?

"I might teach on a Saturday morning, for an hour or two," he suggested, "for any boys willing to give up a little of their winter leisure time. Not *this* Saturday, to be sure, for we must all settle ourselves in this new place, but the next?"

This met with instant acceptance and enthusiasm so great they might have wheedled him into beginning at once, had Polly not come back into the parlor to collect the dishes. Clicking her tongue, she gave the mantel clock a significant look.

"Master Peter, didn't Harker say he would come again to fetch you home before two o'clock, knowing them at Iffley will eat their dinner then? You and Master Gordon had better be on your way, if you don't want to keep the coach waiting. And only see! Not a scrap of Winching's gingerbread left. You boys have spoiled your appetites, to be sure."

Groans met this, but Rearden was sufficiently cowed by the maid to apologize for letting them eat so much and for losing sight of the time, and he added his urging to Polly's.

"One moment, Gordon," said Langworthy in the bustle. "If you are going home now, perhaps you might carry your sister-in-law a note for me. Something I forgot to say while I was there." Striding to the desk he took up a sheet of paper and a pencil. Scribbling hastily, he folded it up and handed it to the boy. "There you go. We'll make a lieutenant of you yet."

Grinning up at him, Gordy made his best attempt at a salute and an "Ay ay, sir!" before he and Peter hurried away.

Excusing himself to go and unpack, Langworthy did not get much beyond flipping open the trunk lid before he threw himself across the old-fashioned curtained bed and stared up into its high canopy.

Am I behaving as befits an officer and a gentleman?

He wasn't properly in the navy at present, he retorted inwardly. Never mind that Old Simes in his military guide declared, "Politeness should exceed authority, and the Officer subside in the gentleman."

What happens on shore stays on shore, he insisted, just as he had often told himself when he had mischief in mind. Mrs. Sebastian's aloof, dismissive face presented itself again in his memory, and he took a long look at it, to harden his resolve. And why should he not be resolved? Was she not just another in the sisterhood of her sex, a sisterhood to which Mary Pence belonged? Another who did what she pleased without regard for what it did to a fellow.

One thing was certain: jousting with Mrs. Sebastian had roused him from his general gloom, if nothing else, and while he would not have called it pleasurable, it was so near to pleasurable that the word sufficed.

CHAPTER 6

I can be secret as a dumb man.
—Shakespeare, *Much Ado about Nothing* (1600)

W ell?" demanded Frances as she led the other Barstows back into the parlor. "What did he want to say that was so secret? Tell us!"

Sarah swiftly stowed her handkerchief, but there was no disguising her high color. Her mother-in-law noted it in one glance and stepped between her and her daughters.

"Frances, for shame. Let Sarah have time to ponder what she has heard." With the discipline of her years, Mrs. Barstow added firmly, "You needn't tell us, dear. Now or ever. Private sentiments between husband and wife are precisely that: private."

"It *was* private, then?" asked Maria, disappointed.

"Yes, I'm afraid so," Sarah answered, hardly audible. It was not another lie, was it? For what could be more private than the ridiculous marriage proposal Sebastian had just subjected her to, from two years beyond the grave?

Frances huffed out an equally disappointed breath, looking not much older than Maria. "Well, then. Of course you needn't say anything. But if it was just to say he loved you he loved you he loved you, I don't see why he needed to send Mr. Langworthy to do it. I would be mortified to be given such an errand."

"Yes," Sarah said again, vaguely.

"I wish someone would tell me he loved me he loved me he loved me," cried Maria.

"And we would have to hide you away in a box if someone did," her sister retorted, "for you are only eleven, and it wouldn't be at all appropriate."

Reluctantly the ladies picked up their work again. Sarah considered fleeing to her closet room—everyone would only think she meant to have a good cry—but she refused to give Mr. Langworthy that satisfaction, even if he would never know of it. He had said his piece and was gone, and she need never think of him again. From this moment onward.

But though Mrs. Barstow and Frances sewed and Maria worked at her lessons, and though an embargo had been placed upon Sebastian's "secret message," nothing prevented them continuing to discuss Mr. Langworthy, and soon Frances remarked, "I am sorry Mr. Langworthy did not stay for dinner, at any rate."

"I too," agreed her mother.

"I three," said Maria.

Sarah said nothing.

"What stories he told!" resumed Frances. "I had no idea young men had such...goings-on. Or, if I did suspect it, I did not know my brother...participated."

Mrs. Barstow pressed her lips together, glancing again at Sarah. "Your brother was as lively a young man as any other, and I suppose in the navy, where there are no ladies present to...dampen their excesses..."

"I would have thought it would be the officers who kept everyone to the straight and narrow path," Frances mused, "but it seems the officers themselves are guilty of all sorts of things. That 'ceremony' he told us about, when they crossed the equator! And that lieutenant Boston or Beatty or whatever his name was—he was worst of all."

"Sebastian was never a Beeton, I trust," her mother answered.

"Beeton, yes, that was it. However 'lively' Sebastian might have been, he cannot have been cruel like Lieutenant Beeton."

"Of course he was not," replied Mrs. Barstow and Sarah in unison. But Sarah twitched as she said it. Was it not a tiny bit cruel to have sent such a one as Horace Langworthy to her, to make such a proposal as he had made? Clearly Langworthy himself thought so, or he would never have done it in the manner he did.

"Will we see Mr. Langworthy again?" asked Maria after some minutes. "Did he say, Sarah?"

"I believe he was returning soon, if not at once, to Portsmouth."

"Oh, no! What a shame," Mrs. Barstow mourned, echoed by her daughters. "I would have liked Gordy to meet him."

"He can hardly catch the Newbury coach today," Frances observed. "It's far too late, unless he goes via London and takes the last coach. I'll warrant he won't leave until tomorrow at the earliest. Maybe we should send a note saying he could ride with Gordy and Peter to Oxford tomorrow. There's no reason Lord Dere's men couldn't leave him at the Angel Inn before they go on to Keele's."

"There's an idea!" agreed Mrs. Barstow, only to have Sarah say, "Oh, madam, it might seem very...pressing of us. If he had not time to stay to dinner, chasing him with notes might feel like desperation. He would have to accept, even if he did not wish to."

It was rare that Sarah was insistent—she who was usually so amenable—that this exception left the Barstows with no alternative but to abandon their plan and hide their chagrin. It also had the effect of dampening further talk of Mr. Langworthy (at least when Sarah was present, though Frances fully determined she would talk more to her mother of him and of Sarah's odd behavior at the nearest opportunity), with the result that they fell silent. More rain fell. Bash teased the dog and dragged a string for the cat and begged Maria to tell him a story, but that was all until an hour had passed and they heard the sounds of a carriage drawing up before the house.

"That will be Lord Dere's landau, delivering Gordy home," said Mrs. Barstow, rising to open the door.

The rain had slowed to a dribble, and voices carried clearly to the rest of them in the parlor.

"In you go, Master Peter," called the Perryfield footman.

"Oh, can't it wait a minute, Ogle?" came Peter Dere's protest. "There's new people at the rectory, and I want to go with Gordy and tell his family about them!"

"It's more than my head is worth, lad. You know when it rains or snows or even blows too hard, your mother can't rest till you're safe inside and bundled up."

"It's ridiculous," the boy grumbled. "I'm nine years old, and she treats me as if I'm made of spun glass."

"Up you go, Mr. Sickly Constitution," said Ogle.

"It was my father who died of pneumonia, not me!" Peter muttered. He must have climbed in, though, for his voice grew fainter.

"Ay," Ogle agreed. "And if he'd died of taking a splinter in the leg like Master Gordon's brother, she'd never let you join the navy. That's mothers for you."

"Did you hear him, Gordy?" shouted Peter. "The navy! I could never join the *navy*."

Then the landau door banged shut, and Peter submitted to being carted off in warm, dry comfort, while Gordy took a run to vault over the low gate.

Frances was beside her mother in the doorway in time to see his boot slip on the wet stone path, landing him in a heap.

"Gordy, what on earth?" accused his sister Frances. "Now Reed will have to dry and brush your trousers before you can go to school tomorrow."

"Mama," he cried, ignoring Frances, "Peter and I met the navy man!"

Clenching her jaw, Sarah steadied herself to listen to another burst of talk about Mr. Langworthy, and Gordon did not keep her waiting.

"The new curate has come to the rectory, so when the Tommies were removing there again, I asked Della if Peter and I could go, and she said yes, so we all piled into the Tree Inn's wagon! And there was the new curate Dr. Rearden, and what a jolly fellow he is, all chuckly and whiskery, but we weren't there more than a few minutes before Mr. Langworthy comes in, and he said he'd just come from here!"

"He did," his mother answered, taking his hat and helping him hang his coat.

"So you've all met him too! Isn't he something? Polly brought us tea and gingerbread, and we ate and drank and listened to his stories about Sebastian and the navy and mathematics—"

"Mathematics?" interrupted Frances and Maria.

"—And not just mathematics, but *navigation!* How you use mathematics and the stars to find your way—all because I'd told him how Denver got us lost in Oxford—how Denver always gets lost because he doesn't pay attention—and Mr. Langworthy said he could use the stars—Denver, that is. So I will have to teach him—Denver."

"For pity's sake, Gordy, take a breath," Frances scolded.

"How will you teach Denver?" asked Maria. "You don't know how to navigate yourself."

"I don't *yet*," he retorted. "But I will."

"Did he recommend a book?" asked Mrs. Barstow.

"No, but he is going to teach us—the Tommies and Peter and me—himself!"

"What?" gasped Sarah, speaking for the first time. "When? How?"

"At the rectory on Saturdays. Not this one, of course, because everyone must settle themselves, he says. But next."

"But how can he possibly teach you at the rectory on Saturdays, Gordon, when he will be *gone back to Portsmouth*?" she demanded awfully.

Her young brother-in-law gazed at her in perfect innocence. "Going back to Portsmouth? He didn't say anything about that. Maybe he means later. Because he is certainly staying in Iffley for the present, or he wouldn't have made arrangements to start next Saturday. Oh—and he said he forgot to give you this." Gordy dug in his pocket for the message he was meant to deliver and thrust it at her.

Sarah stared at the crumpled note as if it were a serpent poised to strike. *What under heaven could the man have left to say to her?*

Maria shook eager fists. "I know what that is! It's more 'I love you I love you I love you'!"

"Hush, dearest," said her mother.

Gordon made a disgusted face. "Why should Mr. Langworthy tell Sarah he loves her?"

"Not Mr. Langworthy," his sister replied with maddening superiority. "*Sebastian*. Mr. Langworthy is passing along another secret message from *Sebastian*."

When Sarah still did not reach to take the note, Gordy tossed it in her lap, where it fell with more weight than a simple sheet of paper. She thanked God that, after the discussion which had taken place earlier, no one would ask her to open it now; nor would anyone ask about the contents later. They would all assume, as Maria did, that it was more of Sebastian's posthumous endearments. Therefore, with an unsteady hand, she slipped the message into her pocket for later perusal.

"I cannot think what made him change his mind about going," she murmured. "He told me quite clearly that I—that we—would not see him again."

But Mrs. Barstow was too pleased by this turn of events to question or criticize. "How delightful! And how very kind of him to offer to teach you boys, even if only for a fortnight or two. Did he say he thought of staying at the Tree Inn? Lord Dere did say once that any houseguests of ours were welcome at Perryfield, and I suppose we could ask..."

"He's staying at the rectory," replied her son. "Dr. Rearden likes him as well as we do and insisted on it."

"Well, isn't that kind of the new curate? I look forward to meeting him as well. And even if Mr. Langworthy only stays a little longer, that will give him time to meet the Deres, and surely he will be able to dine at Iffley Cottage now."

"Yes, yes," crowed Gordon. "And don't forget Della will want to meet him too, because he was Sebastian's especial friend. Why, even Jane might come from St. Lawrence."

"You're right about that," Mrs. Barstow said, a hand flying to her bosom. "I will write to them directly after dinner. Oh, isn't it lovely that things could turn out this way?"

The general family elation lasted through their meal, and if anyone noticed Sarah said not a word throughout, they attributed it to too much excitement. Mr. Langworthy's postscript had been forgotten, moreover, by everyone at the table.

Everyone except Sarah.

It was not until Bash was laid down for his afternoon nap that she could retreat to her little room unaccompanied and unremarked, and by that time the note might have been a volcanic rock in her pocket, growing hotter and heavier by the minute.

The weather had cleared, allowing winter sunlight to penetrate the window, and she sat on the corner of the bed where it fell brightest.

Being unsealed, the note required only a twist to unfold, and the moment she did so, out bounced a silver coin, rolling along the coverlet to fall ringing to the floor. That explained the weight!

Perplexed, Sarah bent to retrieve the crown and set it on the dressing table. Then her eyes dropped to the page enclosing it, and though it was only the second specimen of Horace Langworthy's hand she had seen, she recognized its characteristics already: hasty, forceful, the letters of each word not always connected.

"'Madam,'" she read under her breath, "'Have no fear that I write to renew my repulsive attentions. Rather I do so to inform you that my stay in Iffley will now extend an indeterminate length. Moreover, having heard your family referred to as "paupers" for whom Lord Dere "looks out," and remembering the solemn trust placed in me, I enclose this donation to your maintenance. Yours, etc., H.L.'"

"*Paupers*"?

And he enclosed a "*donation*" toward her maintenance? One equivalent to five piddling shillings?

Sarah hardly knew whether to laugh or to march straight over to the rectory to fling the coin in his face. What in the world sort of person was this Horace Langworthy? The coin could not have been given in any sincere wish to do good; rather, it must have served simply as the excuse to send this message, warning her of his change of plans. But why should his plans change? Why should he remain in Iffley for who knew how long, instead of taking himself straight off, as he had assured her he would?

There was no point in wondering about his reasons, though wonder she did. One thing was certain: if she was to meet him again and perhaps repeatedly, she must master herself, inure herself. She could not again lose her temper and behave as she had that morning. It was almost unbelievable now, when she thought of her fit of anger. What did it matter if she had never liked him, or if his manner of carrying out his obligation was offensively flippant? He had nevertheless carried it out, at least as regarded the letter of the law. Added to this, he had been Sebastian's boon companion. Whether he would have been the friend Sarah chose for her husband did not matter; the friendship had existed in any case. Could she not, now, let bygones be bygones and show herself gracious for a fortnight or two?

I will, Sarah vowed. *If it kills me.*

Picking up the silver crown again, she tapped it on the surface of the dressing table. What to do with this "donation," however?

She was almost certain now that it had not been given in earnest. Had she and little Bash truly been "paupers," five shillings would not have sustained them even a week. The coin was simply a makeweight and another example of his general lack of respect. He sent it to vex her. But to hurl it back at him would only make him think himself justified in acting as he did.

No, she decided. Two could play at this game. The only way to vex a vexer was not to be vexed. Let him find all his weapons blunted in his hands, and he would soon leave off. And when he did, her own displeasure with him might fade.

They could not be spouses, not even to please the mutually loved Sebastian Barstow, and it was doubtful they could even grow to like each other. But perhaps, for Sebastian's sake, they might learn to see what he had seen in each of them and even, just possibly, to appreciate it.

CHAPTER 7

But the most common appellation of such men was that of...parasites...a name of reproach for those who, by flattery and other mean arts, used to insinuate themselves to the tables of other men.
—John Robinson, *Archæologia Græca* (1807)

Though Mrs. Lamb had been caught unawares by both the advent and the stealthy arrival of Mr. Horace Langworthy in Iffley, she quickly made up for lost time, and after the rectory maid Polly walked up to the Tree Inn for the post the following day, all that could possibly be known had been pumped from her. Nor was the postmistress alone the wiser, for while she questioned Polly, her errand boy Harry Barbary stood by, polishing the gleaming wood of the bar with unusual diligence.

"My word," said Mrs. Lamb to no one in particular, when Polly was finally released. "My, my word. A navy man in Iffley! Friend of a dead husband!" She clicked her tongue, meditating how best to spread such delicious news. "Yes, indeed. For sheer interest and entertainment those Barstows are worth their weight in gold."

A thump which she instantly recognized as an empty jug being knocked over on the wooden counter recalled her attention. "Harry Barbary, you mischief of a child, what are you doing over there?"

"I haven't had any schooling since Mrs. Egerton and Miss Egerton went away," he answered sullenly.

"You learned your letters, didn't you?" she threw back at him. "Certainly enough to make my life difficult, what with you scribbling on things which don't belong to you."

"But I didn't learn any mathematics besides sums. No sensual navigation at all," he persisted.

The post- and tapmistress gasped. "Don't let the new curate be hearing you say such things! 'Sensual navigation,' indeed! It was 'sequential navigation' or 'essential navigation' or some odd. And you shouldn't be eavesdropping on what doesn't concern you but learn to mind your own business. Now—don't you stick out your lip at me, my boy! Take this broom and sweep the passage and the step, or I'll apply it to you, I will. I've got work of my own to do."

While Mrs. Lamb proceeded to her tasks with her usual diligence, seizing all by the button who came in for their post or to wet their whistle, that her learnings might be shared, Harry took advantage of her preoccupation to steal away after the most cursory of sweeps.

It was true that Mrs. Egerton (Mrs. Merritt that was) and Miss Egerton had taught him to read and write, but it was equally the case that after Mrs. Merritt married the former curate, both Harry's teachers left Iffley, abandoning the little parish school, and trusting Harry to the tender mercies of Mrs. Lamb to prevent him falling again into idleness. Having never known an idle moment herself, Mrs. Lamb had no difficulty in coming up with a hundred tasks to keep him busy, but she had no patience for his awakened curiosity. The morning's conversation had gone no differently than a dozen others. Whenever he asked, *Why* or *What about*, Mrs. Lamb would retort some version of, "Never you mind. 'It is the glory of God to conceal a thing.' Especially from children. Keep your head down, Harry Barbary, and do what you're told."

"But *you* ask questions all the time, Missus, concealed or not," he would point out. "You want to know everything about everybody."

That one earned him a fierce look. "It's my duty, child, to know things. I am the hub of the wheel in Iffley. When I ask things, it is from neighborly concern. When you do, it's from devilish curiosity."

Devilish or not, Harry Barbary found himself wanting to know more about the new navy man, and as soon as Mrs. Lamb forgot to watch him, he leaned the broom against a wall and took himself off. He might have no more friends or acquaintances at the rectory, but one remained at Iffley Cottage.

Appearing in the parlor door, Reed announced disapprovingly, "That Harry Barbary is at the kitchen door, wanting to see Miss Barstow. I told him she was out with Mrs. Barstow, calling at Perryfield, but he says he'll wait. That's all I need, Mrs. Sebastian, is that boy staring at me while I salt the pork."

From her seat beside Maria, where she had been hearing her lesson, Sarah made a little face. "I can't say I want Harry Barbary staring at me either, but perhaps I could hear his message and send him on his way. You may ask him, Reed, if he would be comfortable seeing me instead of Frances."

"I already did, ma'am," the maid answered promptly, "and I'll send him straight in."

Having the feeling she'd been managed, Sarah repressed a sigh, and within moments the ragged boy with light hair and pale eyes slouched in, hat in hand.

"Mrs. Sebastian, Miss," he began, executing a jerky bow, an uneasy scratch at his midsection betraying nerves.

"Welcome, Harry. I hope you and your family are well."

"Mm-hm. Well enough."

"And I'm sorry Miss Barstow isn't home at present, but perhaps I could answer your question or tell her your message?"

His gaze traveled over the table drawn up before Maria and the open book and slate thereon. "You're giving lessons," he said.

"Yes."

"Mrs. Merritt that was used to give me and Jimmy and Anna Cramthorpe lessons."

"So she did. I know she was sorry to have to leave off with them when she married Mr. Egerton."

"Sometimes, when Mrs. M couldn't be at the rectory, she sent Miss Barstow in her place."

"That's right," agreed Sarah, wondering where this rehearsal was tending. Did he want Frances to start another little school? Frances had never said she enjoyed teaching as Jane had, and she would surely ask Sarah to help her if forced to do it again—

"We don't know the new curate," Sarah rejoined. "Or what he might have in mind, but if—if he shows any interest in starting another parish school, shall I tell him you would like to attend?"

To her surprise and relief, the boy shrugged. "If you like, Missus. But—but I wondered if you could do some-odd else for me. I was going to ask Miss Barstow because she knows me better, but you're really the one I want."

"I?" repeated Sarah.

"I mean ter say, she met him too, but it's you he came to Iffley for."

Something fluttered in the pit of her stomach. "To whom do you refer? You can't mean the new curate Dr. Rearden."

"No, ma'am. I mean the navy man. He came here for *you*, so says Polly from the rectory."

"What would Polly know about it?" demanded Sarah, turning pink with indignation.

"She got it from the navy man hisself, Missus," he explained patiently. "That he came to Iffley because Mr. Sebastian asked him, to make sure you and the little one weren't starving in the streets."

Sarah shut her eyes.

Well? And what had she expected? That both Mr. Langworthy's coming and his reason for doing so might be kept from the world at large?

She was old enough to know better. Indeed, she ought to thank Providence word had not got out (yet) about his ill-starred proposal.

"What do you want with the navy man, Harry?" she asked.

"I want to meet him!" he declared. In justice to the boy, his heart was likely pounding as hard as hers. "Polly said he was going to teach the parson's pupils s—sensu—centennial navigation, and I wanted to learn too. I don't have to sit in the room, but if I could sit in the passage—and maybe I could, Missus, if you would innerduce me to him and—put in a good word."

For a minute Sarah made no reply. Perform introductions between that man and the village rascal, who stood before her wringing his cap in his hand? What would Mr. Langworthy think she meant by it? That she thought he owed her a favor?

Harry's brow darkened as the silence stretched. "I could ask Miss Barstow, if you don't want to do it. She knows me better anyhow."

Contrarily, Sarah said, "Why, Harry, other than the few lessons where Miss Barstow took Mrs. Egerton's place, I suppose she knows you the same amount I do. I've visited your home as many times as Fr—Miss Barstow has, if not more."

"You'll do it, then?" he asked eagerly. "You'll innerduce me to him?"

Suspecting she had been "managed" for the second time in half an hour, she sighed. "I hardly know Mr. Langworthy myself. But—yes.

If—when—I meet him again, if opportunity affords, I will mention you and your...interest. If he is amenable to some sort of arrangement, then I will send a message to you. Either way I will, that is. Give me a few days. Perhaps he might be in church on Sunday."

But the opportunity arose sooner than expected, for when Mrs. Barstow and Frances returned, they brought the news that the Deres' intended to call at the rectory and meet the newcomers that very day.

"And Mrs. Markham Dere said that, if they found Mr. Langworthy to be the 'right sort of person,' she would invite him and the new curate to dine tomorrow," Frances reported. "To which the baron replied that, even if Mr. Langworthy were very much the wrong sort of person, as he is staying at the rectory, they could hardly invite Dr. Rearden without including him. Mrs. Dere was put out by this, you may imagine, so she said we Barstows better be invited, then."

"What do we have to do with Mr. Langworthy being the right or wrong sort of person?" asked Maria, puzzled. "And is he the right sort or the wrong sort?"

"The right sort," answered her mother, at the same time that Frances said, "The wrong sort."

Putting an arm about her youngest daughter, Mrs. Barstow explained, "Maria, what Frances means to say is that he is a good man, at heart, but he might be a little...rumbustious for Mrs. Dere. And what Mrs. Dere means, though she would never say it, is that, if it is the Barstows who brought Mr. Langworthy here, it is the Barstows' duty to soften his presence. That is all."

Maria only sighed. "I suppose it does not matter. *I* will not be invited either way, but made to stay home with the 'babies.'"

Poor Maria guessed correctly that she would be left out, but Sarah could spare no pangs for the girl, being too occupied with her own concerns. For too soon the expected invitation arrived from Mrs. Dere, and far too soon she was seated in Lord Dere's coach beside Mrs. Barstow and Frances to be carried over the hard, frosty ground to Perryfield.

"My uncle wanted to have Harker and Ogle stop at the rectory as well, to pick up Dr. Rearden and Mr. Langworthy," Mrs. Markham Dere informed them, when they had greeted each other and were warming themselves before the fire, "but I reminded him that you Barstows had not yet been introduced to the new curate, so it simply could not be done."

"Therefore my coachmen must make another trip to fetch them," added the baron in his gentle voice.

His niece by marriage stood alongside him, her golden hair gleaming beside Lord Dere's silver head and one hand placed on her son Peter's shoulder. While Mrs. Dere was always an impressive woman, handsome, immaculate and well-dressed, Sarah was especially struck by her that afternoon in the vast Perryfield drawing room because she imagined how different this reception would appear to Horace Langworthy after the Barstows and their crowded parlor. Here everything shone: Mrs. Dere's hair, the ormolu sconces and mantel clock, the polished wood furniture, the scattered porcelain pieces. Enough winter sunlight filtered through the windows to throw bars of light and dark across the heavy carpet and figured plasterwork.

"How did you like Dr. Rearden?" asked Mrs. Barstow, thinking to approach the subject of Mr. Langworthy's acceptability by indirection.

The baron smiled. "He—"

"Quite unexceptionable," declared Mrs. Dere, "though he had little to say to me. He is perhaps Mr. Terry's age and more accustomed to academic duties than such as our parish will require."

"Jolly fellow," observed Lord Dere. "What do you think, eh, Peter?"

"I like his whiskers," said Peter, with a flat air unusual to him.

Mrs. Dere rolled her eyes. "Peter was disappointed not to be taken to Iffley Cottage this evening."

"He does usually get to, whenever we come to Perryfield to dine," Frances said. "And Reed makes them something tasty and interesting to eat, like—what was that Gordy said you had last time? Icicle sandwiches? It was really shavings of white carrot and roast pork." She gave the boy a playful nudge. "Today you must stay here with the dull grown-ups."

As ever, when Frances exerted herself to ease matters with Mrs. Dere, the mistress of Perryfield thawed. "Well, Peter, you may think furthering your acquaintance with the curate dull, but you did like the sailor, I believe. You had enough to say about him later."

Here was the opening they had been waiting for, and Peter gave an outright bounce on his toes. "I did like him, Mama, and you must must must let me take navigation lessons with Gordy and the Tommies! I will die to be left out!"

"Now, now," she murmured, her frown returning. "I have told you I will make up my mind soon on the matter, though I still cannot see what earthly use such a skill would be. *You* are not going to be a navy officer, after all, any more than Gordon or the Tommies, and I cannot think what the man was about, putting such an idea into all of your heads." Her disapproval swept from her son to fall upon Sarah. "Honestly, Mrs. Sebastian, it is one thing to invite your late husband's friend to pay his respects, and quite another for him to *take up residence* with our new curate and make a stir."

Despite having known Mrs. Markham Dere for over two years now, Sarah was caught off guard by this charge. Indeed, of all the Barstow ladies, she was most used to being ignored when at Perryfield, having neither entangled herself with the baron (Adela), shamed the family with a sordid history (Jane), or won Mrs. Dere's favor with hard work and flattery (Frances). Sarah had always imagined Mrs. Dere considered her a younger version of her mother-in-law: quiet, proper, and harmless—apart from wearisome poverty and dependence, of course.

Here was a new development! And how unjust to be attacked for something which was none of her own doing. She bore up to face it, however.

"Madam," she replied, her voice a touch higher than its usual register, "before Mr. Langworthy wrote to announce he would be coming, I had no more notion of it than you. Nor did he come at my request, but rather he was asked to do so by my late husband Sebastian, and altogether without my knowledge."

When Mrs. Dere made no answer, only lifting a questioning brow, Sarah was forced to go on. "You see, he was Sebastian's fellow officer and good friend, and he asked him to make sure Bash and I were...provided for, in case of his—Sebastian's—death."

"And if you were not? What was Mr. Langworthy to do in that instance?"

Feeling herself blush, Sarah said, "Share what he could spare, I suppose. Navy men are inclined to look out for each other that way. But—because of Lord Dere's goodness to us, Mrs. Barstow's income, and the pension afforded me from the Chatham Chest, no more was required."

Mrs. Dere knew very well the baron hated to have his generosity held up for all to see, and as his generosity was no favorite subject of hers either, she moved on. "That's all very well, Mrs. Sebastian, but seeing, as you say, that your needs are met and more, why should he then stay? That is my question."

"In truth, I do not know."

"For my part," interposed Mrs. Barstow, "I am glad he will stay longer, for talking to Mr. Langworthy of my son gave me a little piece of him again."

"Yes, how fortunate for our little community," spoke up Lord Dere. "Even if we have no future sailors among our young boys, it can do them no harm to learn of the danger and sacrifices such men have made in these times."

"Yes, sir, exactly!" cried Peter again, and if he had asked Frances for advice, she would have told him he was in danger of doing it too brown, but Mrs. Dere easily ignored him.

"That may be true of navy men in general, Uncle," she resumed, "but we know nothing of this *particular* person, as even Mrs. Sebastian admits. I have nothing to say against him, you understand, having only met him yesterday, but I confess to a…slight uneasiness as to how quickly he has insinuated himself into the community. Lodging at the rectory! Offering to teach Dr. Rearden's pupils and the foremost young man of the parish!" (Gesturing to Peter, in case no one knew whom she meant.)

"We do know, however, that my son not only approved of him but considered him an intimate friend," spoke up the elder Mrs. Barstow stoutly, "and that is the only endorsement of Mr. Langworthy we require, is it not, Sarah?"

"Sebastian did—certainly—he—Mr. Langworthy, that is—was certainly Sebastian's intimate," Sarah floundered. How could she possibly please both these important women in her life? While she shared Mrs. Dere's suspicions of Mr. Langworthy, siding with Mrs. Dere against her own mother-in-law was out of the question.

As usual, when one tries to please two widely separated camps, Sarah's reply pleased neither. Mrs. Barstow regarded her with a hint of reproach and Mrs. Dere with clear vexation at her wheyishness. But finding her the weakest link in the chain, the latter pressed harder upon her.

"Mrs. Sebastian, you are perhaps best positioned to speak to Mr. Langworthy's character, if your husband confided in you. Did Mr. Sebastian Barstow ever characterize his friend as…impulsive? One inclined to…take advantage of the liberality of others?"

"He—er—"

"Mrs. Dere," Mrs. Barstow interjected again, now seeing she must do battle alone and drawing herself up, "my lost son not being present to mount a defense of Mr. Langworthy, I must speak." She held up deprecating palms. "I am sure, if Mr. Langworthy took a liking to Dr. Rearden and had no other matters pressing upon him at present, there is no reason to suspect him of any other motive beyond a wish to show us kindness, for Sebastian's sake. I must admit I took to the young man instantly for that reason and was quite candid in saying I hoped we might have more opportunities for conversation—"

"You do not suspect him, then, of also hoping to stretch his limited means?" uttered the relentless Mrs. Dere.

"I do," blurted Sarah, her pulse speeding. "If—if he was anything like my Sebastian. Having never been a poor lieutenant yourself, Mrs. Dere, you will have no idea how nearly all of them must 'stretch' as you say, until their luck turns and they come into some prize money. How much more when the Peace has put them ashore on half pay! If—if Mr. Langworthy was quick to accept Dr. Rearden's invitation, I can only say Sebastian would likely have been just as quick, in his shoes."

The speech won back some of Mrs. Barstow's favor, at least, though Mrs. Dere's lips pressed into a line.

But there was no time for more. The footman Wood flung open the drawing room doors, announcing, "Dr. Septimus Rearden and Mr. Horace Langworthy!"

CHAPTER 8

A pardon Sir? 'Till I am conscious of an offence
I will not wrong my innocence to begge one.
—Philip Massinger, *The Maid of Honour* (1632)

Horace Langworthy had last seen such a collection of conscious, guilty faces when a bottle of Captain Blackwood's finest wine went missing, and Beeton assembled the crew for questioning. And as with the incident on the *Penelope*, the trespass appeared to have been a group affair.

They have all been talking of either me or Rearden or both, he thought. *And I don't suppose I'm too conceited of an ass to guess it was more likely to be of me.*

Alone of those gathered, Mrs. Markham Dere held her head high, making her curtsey with perfect ease. Mrs. Sebastian, on the other hand, was crimson as a poppy, her movements jerky, and he felt his mettle rise. Had she been the chief perpetrator?

"You are welcome at Perryfield," said Mrs. Dere before the baron could open his mouth. "And Dr. Rearden, I believe you have not yet met the Barstows?"

The introduction of the new curate provided a welcome distraction from whatever came before, and the Barstow ladies seized upon it, smiling and making little courteous comments while Langworthy held back, keeping mum while continuing his observations.

When the baron and his niece by marriage had called at the rectory the previous day, five minutes sufficed to make all plain. Whatever pre-eminence his title, sex, and age should grant Lord Ranulph Dere proved but a hollow crown, for the orb and scepter were gripped by Mrs. Dere. Nevertheless, with a military man's understanding of rank, Langworthy guessed the best way to flatter the woman was to respect her uncle.

For the moment, however, he was more interested in determining how the Barstows related to their benefactors. Would they fawn and cringe, or would they struggle to hide resentment of their dependence? They were not so easy to read. Both Mrs. Gordon Barstow and Mrs. Sebastian Barstow had recovered from their embarrassment and wore expressions of studied calm. Younger Miss Barstow was more straightforward, keeping her bright gaze trained on their hostess—alert, without being obsequious.

"—Our thanks for sending your coach, my lord," Rearden was saying. "Langworthy and I, being hale and hearty, were quite prepared to walk, but our cozy ride was a treat."

"A nuisance for your coachmen, though," put in Langworthy, "making two trips."

"With your leave, sirs, now that you are all acquainted, in the future we may fetch and deliver you all in a blow."

Of course this was agreed to, and the company took their seats, arraying themselves at appropriate distances from Mrs. Markham Dere like planets about the sun. She in turn shone the beams of her attention first on the new curate, questioning him about his connection to their rector Mr. Terry. Being already deeply familiar with Rearden's story, having shared the coach with him from London, Langworthy sat impassively through the clergyman's talk of his university days with Terry and the fellowship and sinecures which followed. It was astonishing, really, the inequalities of the universe. Here sat Rearden, single, with no one to support but himself, and yet he had four discrete sources of income, by Langworthy's count. Rearden's acceptance of his friend's temporary curacy was a favor done for Terry, and not the other way 'round. Yet the blessed parson shared the drawing room with the penniless Barstow women, who had five mouths to feed and not a whole income among them!

If they had any sense, they'd try to catch him. The mother ought, for Rearden doesn't need children at his age, and he'd likely be frightened of the younger ones. A slow grin tugged at one corner of his mouth. *Though it's Mrs. Sebastian who has the most to gain by it. I ought to make the suggestion to her. It's my duty, after all, to see to her welfare.*

"—Was it not, Mr. Langworthy?" Mrs. Dere's voice penetrated his musings.

Having no idea what she had just said, he bowed his head in agreement and murmured, "Indeed."

"And how do you find your charges?" she asked, nodding toward Mrs. Sebastian, who was seated beside her mother-in-law. "They lack for nothing, I think you must agree."

Picking up the thread, the expected response would have been some comment about how the Barstows were living in clover thanks to the baron, but Langworthy still had hold of his own thread, and he said instead, "Yes, madam, Mrs. Sebastian and her son have a comfortable roof over their heads and lack for no material thing, but I daresay my comrade Barstow would have liked Bash to have a father."

A tiny gasp escaped Mrs. Sebastian as every eye flew to her, but they were all too polite to stare and just as quickly looked away, to be relieved the next instant by the entrance of Wood announcing dinner.

A bustle followed, Lord Dere offering his arm to his niece and Rearden to Mrs. Barstow. When Langworthy realized he must escort Mrs. Sebastian, he almost laughed. Her hand did not so much rest on his proffered arm as hover above it, and her features might have been carved from marble, if not for the rush of blood beneath her skin.

"I didn't mean *me* as a father, it goes without saying," he muttered, scarcely moving his lips. "As I said, I will not trouble you with that business again."

She said nothing. He might have been the wainscoting, for all the notice she paid him.

At the table Mrs. Dere had placed Langworthy on her left and Mrs. Sebastian on his other side, and it was soon apparent their hostess's mind turned still on her guest's last remark.

"Mr. Langworthy," she began, once the soup had been served, "you must indulge me, for I confess I know little of the navy or navy life."

"Madam."

"Such fellow feeling among comrades!"

"Long hours—even years—of duties shared, I suppose."

"Not to mention dangers," put in Mrs. Barstow, leaning forward from the other end.

"Indeed," agreed Mrs. Dere. "All such things. They must often lead to promises of such sort. 'You look out for mine, and I will look out for yours.'"

"Perhaps. It did for Barstow and me."

She gave an unreadable *hmm*. "But when you struck this bargain, he had a wife and child and you, I believe, were not yet a family man...?"

"Nor still am not, as far as I know."

This brought a chuckle from Frances, which she quickly smothered when she saw Mrs. Dere's eyebrow lift.

Softly, Langworthy told himself. Clearly he was on trial here, and though he did not give a fig for the worthy lady's opinion, there was no sense in making an enemy of her with questionable jokes. Doing so, in fact, would make life harder for both Rearden and the Barstows, besides complicating his own situation.

Therefore, when his soup was removed and fish placed before him, he said, "You are right to find the obligation placed on me curious, Mrs. Dere. Having only one living uncle and one married cousin, and no wife or children myself, the burden placed upon Barstow would have been lighter, had our situations been reversed. But beyond our comradeship, I owed him a greater debt to begin with." Once more he told the story of Sebastian fishing him out of the sea and threw in Sebastian accompanying him to the hospital in Palermo for good measure. "He was a noble and generous fellow, you see, so to strive to repay him is as much as I can do."

"Quite so." She lifted two fingers from the cloth, and the footman hurried forward to move the sauceboat down the table.

"And now that you will be staying in Iffley a little longer," Mrs. Barstow spoke up again, "we Barstows certainly hope to see much of you. We must apologize in advance, Mr. Langworthy, for the claims we will make on your time. In addition to wanting to hear you speak of Sebastian, my Gordy tells me you have offered to teach the boys some mathematics, as it relates to celestial navigation."

"Oh! Oh!" burst out Peter. Forgetting himself to the point that he fidgeted in his chair, he threw his mother a pleading look.

"The Tommies showed far more eagerness for Langworthy's subject than for Latin and geography," said Rearden with a smile. "He will be a boon to me, for as long as I can persuade him to stay."

"And how long will that be, Mr. Langworthy?" persisted Mrs. Dere, one stern glance at her son serving to quiet him.

"It depends," he answered lightly.

"On...?

Langworthy sensed rather than saw Mrs. Sebastian stiffening beside him. Biting back a grin he said, "On France, I suppose. On when hostilities between our nations resume."

"You believe they will resume, then?" asked the baron.

Langworthy turned to regard him. "Sir, I am not certain they ever entirely ceased. I do believe *open* war will break out again at some point, however, and possibly soon."

"Are you frightened?" breathed Peter, this time earning a throat clearing from his mother.

"Quaking in my boots," he returned, unable to prevent the quip. "But a navy man ashore is not exempt from fears of other kinds, Peter."

"Really? What kinds, sir?"

"Oh...fears of general unemployment, shiftlessness, vagrancy... dread poverty and such like."

The boy's eyes widened, but his mother's contrarily narrowed, and Langworthy pressed back a grimace. *Softly, you idiot! If there is a humorous bone in her body, she has not discovered it.* And yet what had he done except give voice to the fears expressed in every newspaper, with so many discharged soldiers and sailors now wandering the country in search of employment?

After a mere few days' acquaintance Rearden had taken Langworthy's measure, and his whiskers were already quivering as he chuckled silently. "Well, my good young man, until you may earn your bread again in harm's way, I will do what I can to keep you employed, shift-ful, housed, and, if not rich, at least not poor."

"I applaud you, Dr. Rearden," said the baron, to his niece's further dismay. "It seems not too much can be done for those who have risked so much." He beamed down the table at his two new acquaintances. "In fact, I would like to do my part as well."

"Y-Your part, Uncle?" squeaked Mrs. Dere.

"You must not be expected to teach the Iffley boys gratis, Mr. Langworthy," he continued.

"Nothing of the kind, sir," Langworthy replied. "I do it in return for my keep at the rectory."

"Pshaw," protested the curate. "How dare you make mincemeat of my boasts of hospitality and selflessness? You do not teach in order to repay expenses, as if the rectory were some—some Bush Inn—no—was it—as if it were some Shrub Inn—!"

"*Tree* Inn!" Peter shrieked with laughter. "Not Bush or Shrub. It's the Tree Inn, sir."

The parson rapped the table and winked at the child, "That's right! The rectory is no Tree Inn. Langworthy, if you did not stir a finger you would still be welcome under my roof."

Mrs. and Miss Barstow were hiding smiles at this point, but the baron was not deterred from his intent. "Mr. Langworthy, surely you will need certain appurtenances to give your lessons? Books, instruments, wide open spaces to see the horizon?"

"Well, as we are on land, sir, and plan but an hour or two every Saturday, I thought we might merely learn terms and make imaginary calculations on a slate. Nothing so grand as you picture."

"Very sensible!" struck in Mrs. Dere, trying to regain control of the conversation and fearing whatever purchases the baron might be contemplating. "No need to be carried to extremes for what might only be a fortnight's exercise."

"Then I may participate, Mama?" asked Peter with another bounce.

She gave what might, in another woman, be called an apprehensive groan. "Oh, I suppose so, if the Tommies and Gordon will—don't shout, Peter. An hour or two at the rectory once per week, if it must be. Though if we were going to add to your schoolwork, in my opinion other lessons would be more pertinent for you than navigation. Dancing, say, or a modern language."

Her son was too pleased with her concession even to make a face at these latter suggestions, but the baron straightened, setting down his fork. "I say, Alice, you make a point."

"Of course I do," she sniffed. "I know Keele's school is a favorite project of yours, but you must admit, for all Mr. Keele's and Mr. Weatherill's academic excellence, they neglect other parts of a gentleman's education."

"Ah," mourned Rearden, "when you find fault with the school there, you show me my own shortcomings as well, madam. For I could no more teach the Tommies to dance or speak French than I could embroider a screen."

"Do you remember how Mrs. Terry once wanted to have a children's ball at Perryfield, Mrs. Dere?" interposed Miss Barstow. "It was precisely because Mr. Terry could not teach the Tommies or poor George Denver to dance. You are not the only one to see the lack."

"I remember," answered Mrs. Dere, softening at this nod to her perspicacity. "But it never came off because that George Denver broke his ankle or some such."

"Let it come off now," said the baron, and Langworthy wondered if he seized upon the idea so eagerly because he too wanted to soften Mrs. Dere. "Why should the boys not learn a little dancing, along with their navigation?"

"Dancing?" she echoed, as if she had not just put the thought in everyone's head. "However would that come about, and who would teach them?"

"If you are proposing me as dance master, sir, I must decline," grinned Langworthy. "Though I will take my part in the set if another body is needed."

"It had better be you, then, Alice," Lord Dere said slyly. "And perhaps we might prevail upon all our dear Barstows to swell our number?"

"But, Uncle—"

"Do say yes, Mrs. Dere," urged Miss Barstow. "What fun it would be to dance again, and you were such a pleasure to watch last November at the Greenwood Ball. Moreover, if it were a children's ball we practiced for, my youngest sister Maria would be beside herself with gratitude, for she has only ever danced with us at home, you know." Seeing Mrs. Dere weaken, she hurried on. "I would be happy to provide accompaniment on the instrument. And only imagine Mrs. Terry's pleasure when she and the rector return to find what we have done in their absence!"

"Pardon me, Miss Barstow," Rearden spoke up again. "I don't mean to be a wet blanket on this delightful idea, but I'm afraid the rectory drawing room would never allow for four couples to stand up and move with any ease, even if they were all children and the furniture taken out."

And here the baron's straight, slim figure swelled with anticipation, to see the pieces of his plan fit together so neatly. "You're right, Dr. Rearden. Which is why both the navigation lessons and the dance lessons had better be at Perryfield. We have the old schoolroom for the mathematics—I will gladly order whatever you think necessary, Mr. Langworthy—and our drawing room would allow for more than ten couples at once."

Mrs. Dere drew a sharp breath, but when Miss Barstow and the curate burst into happy applause, and all heads turned back to her for her approval, she could see no gracious escape from the trap she had unwittingly laid for herself. Therefore, with a little shrug, she murmured, "As you wish, sir."

Her concession led to an outburst of delight and eager conversation, and Miss Barstow further smoothed her feathers with a combination of praise and appeals to her for how matters should be managed, so that by the time the ladies rose to withdraw Mrs. Dere was quite content to let the baron indulge his new hobby horse.

Only one guest had said not a word in either approbation or protest, but when the drawing room door closed behind them, Sarah steeled herself to follow Mrs. Dere.

"May I help you prepare the tea, madam?"

This was usually Frances' task, but Mrs. Dere politely made room for her on the sofa. "Thank you, Mrs. Sebastian. Frances, then perhaps I could prevail on you to play for us?"

Welcoming the cover of music, Sarah waited for her sister-in-law to select a sheet and play opening scales and arpeggios to limber her fingers before speaking again. "Thank you again, Mrs. Dere, for agreeing to both the navigation lessons and the dance lessons. I know they will give my family much enjoyment. Only Gordy may care about the mathematics, but all the Barstows dearly love to dance."

"And does that include you, Mrs. Sebastian?"

"It does," Sarah admitted, "but I do not mind sitting out."

Mrs. Dere favored her with astonishment. "Sit out? Whyever would you sit out the dance lessons, Mrs. Sebastian?"

"I—er—I have my little son. He is too young to take part, and I will stay behind at Iffley Cottage to watch him."

"What nonsense!" Mrs. Dere dismissed this. "Of course you must come. Reed can watch the boy for a few hours once a week, or you may bring him and leave him to one of our maids if he does not want to watch the dancers. No—no argument, Mrs. Sebastian. By my count there are the four boys and possibly Mr. Langworthy and my uncle and even Dr. Rearden—seven gentlemen! We will need every partner we can find for them, especially if Frances or I must play. Absolutely you cannot be excused. I'm very sorry, but that is how it must be. Besides which, this whole enterprise could be laid part and parcel at your door, for how would any of it have come about, if not for your late husband sending Mr. Langworthy to see to your welfare? No, indeed. Let us hear no more of you sitting anything out."

"No, madam," uttered Sarah, hiding her dismay.

She had to work even harder the next moment, when Mrs. Dere added, "Do permit me one word of caution, however, Mrs. Sebastian. You heard Mr. Langworthy before we went into dinner: he declared that he thought your son in need of a father. I do not presume to know what is in the man's mind, but if he, a penniless officer with uncertain prospects, thinks to trade upon your higher connections and pay his addresses to *you*, I cannot approve of it. What would you live on? Therefore, a word to the wise. The baron is a generous man—generous to a fault—and he already seems to like Mr. Langworthy, but to accept a man who has nothing and no better hopes than to marry into dependence and parasitism—"

"Mrs. Dere," choked Sarah, "I beg you. Please—say no more. I understand you, and there is no danger of such a—situation—coming to pass, even if it ever entered Mr. Langworthy's mind. Please—be at ease—"

"Mm."

Her hostess regarded her steadily but found nothing to doubt in Sarah's anguished face.

"Very well, then," she conceded. "I will forbear, since it pains you. Ah, here comes Wood with the tea things."

Sarah could have slumped then with relief, but for one last little word which Mrs. Dere said as much to herself as to her companion: "Dr. Rearden, though. That's another matter."

CHAPTER 9

Stay, Sir, I must have a word with you in private.
—Ben Jonson, *Bartholomew Fair,* III.v.45 (1613)

S arah had not forgotten Harry Barbary's request, though after Mrs. Markham Dere's interfering remarks, she was even less desirous of seeking Mr. Langworthy out.

The gentlemen soon emerged from the dining room to join them, and having offered to help with the tea, it fell to her to carry everyone his cup. Dr. Rearden accepted his with a gracious nod which set his whiskers waving, but Sarah only smiled at the top of his waistcoat, determined not to show him anything which could be construed as favor.

With Mr. Langworthy she was even more remote, holding the cup a good foot away and fixing her eyes on the plastered tracery ornamenting the wall behind him. "Tea?"

No answer came.

Edging an inch nearer, she said a hair more loudly, "Tea?"

Nothing.

Frances was playing a lively march, but it was impossible he could not have heard her. And even if he had not, what would she be doing, holding a full teacup to the empty air?

"I said, *Tea,* Mr. Langworthy?" she hissed.

He gave an exaggerated start, which surprised her into looking at him directly.

"Oh, pardon me, Mrs. Sebastian," he said, taking the cup from her. "I thought you were addressing the wall sconce."

"Wall sconce—fiddlestick," she muttered, her eyes dropping again. "You were deliberately ignoring me."

"In my defense, how could I know you were talking to me, when you have been determined not to see me this evening," he explained dolefully.

Her reply was quick. "You did promise me when we parted that I would likely never see you again. Though that promise was soon broken. More milk or sugar?"

He took a tentative sip. "No, this is perfect. A little bitterness can be stimulating, you know."

If his words had a double meaning, she refused to acknowledge it.

But she could not stand there forever, not with Mrs. Dere's gaze drifting their way. With a grimace, she gave in. "So—I must ask: why are you still here, Mr. Langworthy, after what you said to me about going?"

"Dear me. Did you not *hear* me this evening either? If you had, you would have known our hostess thoroughly canvassed that subject. Shall I rehearse my reasons again for you?"

Sarah threw him another astonished glance. "I thought your answer to her a sportive one. You mean to say you were not teasing her when you said you stay in Iffley to avoid 'unemployment, shiftlessness, vagrancy and dread poverty'?"

"Don't forget 'and such like,'" he reminded her. He took another slow sip of his tea. "You were listening, then."

"With only eight of us at table, I could not help but hear."

"Then did you not think those excuses persuasive enough?"

Twitching, she took a step away from him before halting again. "Mr. Langworthy, if you were indeed speaking bald truths, I—I marvel at your honesty."

A sigh escaped him. "There are two ways to take such a statement. One: you marvel that I should be so honest as to 'tear off reserve and bare my swelling heart' to people I have just met. Or, two: you find truthfulness unlikely in me and therefore marvel at it."

Her lips parted to say the polite thing, only to hesitate before any words emerged. Why should she not say what she really thought? He might mock and trifle if he pleased; it should make no difference to her. It was as if their conversations took place in a world apart, where the usual feints and dodges of courtesy could be dispensed with.

Raising her eyes again, she was unsettled to find his own locked on her, alert and penetrating. *Like a man who lights a fuse and waits for the explosion!* And indeed, some *frisson* rippled through her, but she waited for it to pass before saying frankly, "I suppose I meant a little of both, sir. But if you truly are so poor as you told Mrs. Dere, I ought to return your five shillings, for you have the greater need."

At this he laughed aloud, causing heads to turn, and Sarah felt her color rise. But he read her resentment, and his rescue of the situation came at once. "Yes, please, Mrs. Sebastian," he said in a voice for those nearby to hear, "I did drink that tea quick as lightning. It's the best I've had in ages. If I could trouble you for more...?"

"You had much to say to Mr. Langworthy," observed Mrs. Dere when Sarah returned with the cup.

"Just small talk," she answered. She bit the inside of her cheek. Why—she was becoming a frequent liar! Not to Mr. Langworthy, to be sure—with him truths seemed to burst from her unchecked—but to others.

Mrs. Dere's brows lifted eloquently, but she refilled the cup without another word, and Sarah retraced her steps across the drawing room. She would make Harry Barbary's request, but she would do it with all speed. No more being drawn in by the man. No more unintended confidences. *Keep to the point, my girl.*

"Your fresh cup, Mr. Langworthy."

"If I might return to our topic, Mrs. Sebastian," he said, lifting the cup but pausing before it reached his lips, "I rejoice to tell you that, though it was fear of unemployment, shiftlessness, et cetera et cetera which impelled me to remain in Iffley (as I told Mrs. Markham Dere and reiterated to you), my decision has paid off handsomely."

"Yes. Dr. Rearden has given you both a task and a roof over your head," she agreed quickly, anxious to introduce her own item, "and those two boons will, in turn, allow you to stretch your half pay to the utmost. I see."

"So you do. Most perspicacious of you, madam—"

"And therefore you can well spare the five shillings you gave me," she interrupted again. "Never mind them, then."

"If you insist. Thank you. But it gets better, even."

That checked her. "How so, sir?"

"After you ladies left us in the dining room, Lord Dere—er—availed himself of the resulting... slackening of supervision."

He did not need to glance toward Mrs. Dere for Sarah to catch his meaning, and though in the privacy of Iffley Cottage the Barstows openly decried that lady's domination of the poor baron, Sarah felt it was not the place of a newcomer to mark such things, much less to comment on them.

Seeing her stiffen and her chin lift, a smile tugged at his mouth, but he repressed it and went on. "Having already offered the use of the schoolroom, Lord Dere insisted on knowing how we were taught navigation at sea. Then nothing would convince him it could possibly be done without a sextant and the latest nautical almanac. And then, added to that, nothing would convince him it could be taught if the—master—was not given a fee for his services."

And then she could not help staring at him. "How—how you do manage to fall on your feet, Mr. Langworthy!"

"I have, haven't I?" he asked with boyish pleasure, reminding Sarah of the cat that got the canary. He rocked on his heels a moment, his lips pursing as if he might begin to whistle, but thankfully he did not. After a moment he said, "That is, things have turned out well for me, apart from the one, crushing blow."

Her brow furrowed. "What crushing bl—?"

She broke off suddenly, flushing. Did he mean the girl who had jilted him? He must, because surely, surely he wasn't referring to his recent preposterous proposal to *her*—

But he was.

Because he placed a hand to his breast and whispered like an actor in a melodrama, "What devastates me, leaves her untouched! 'What crushing blow?' she asks! I refer to your devastating refusal. Unless you've changed your mind, Mrs. Sebastian?"

Sarah's response, whatever it might have been, was drowned by the final chords of Frances' piece, played with a flourish, and the subsequent applause of the gathering. Later she would be glad of it, though it meant she still had not fulfilled her word to Harry Barbary, for she would surely have blurted something regrettable in the heat of provocation.

As it was, she turned on her heel and walked away, resuming her seat beside Mrs. Dere. And when that lady rose to take Frances' place at the instrument shortly afterward, Sarah joined her mother-in-law and Lord Dere, who were discussing boys' education in general.

Only hours later, as she lay in her tiny chamber, did she groan and give herself over to uncomfortable meditations. For the first time she was almost sorry to have a bed all to herself, for it would have been welcome to confide in Adela or Jane under cover of darkness.

How *could* she let that man nettle her?

Was it not obvious—had it not indeed been *glaringly* obvious from their first meeting that Mr. Horace Langworthy had a streak of mischief in him? One so wide it might be more accurate to say it characterized him from end to end?

"It did not begin with our first meeting," she amended aloud. "I knew it before. From Sebastian's letters. Because Sebastian was so often led in his train."

Therefore, if she had always and ever known this fact about Mr. Langworthy, why did she nevertheless allow him to surprise her? To get in his little quips and scoffs? To let him keep her continually at a disadvantage?

And to think he was only here—lodged in the Iffley rectory like a burr in sheep's wool—because Sebastian had sent him!

But if Mr. Langworthy was mischievous, it was equally true that he boasted a certain charm. Whatever misgivings Mrs. Markham Dere or Sarah herself might still harbor, they seemed to be the only ones in doubt. The new curate liked him enough to invite him to share his home. The boys liked him enough to caper with delight when told they might learn from him. Lord Dere liked him enough not only to outfit him for teaching, but to pay him a wage to do so. Mrs. Barstow liked him enough to press him to come to Iffley Cottage whenever he liked. And Harry Barbary—Harry liked even the rumors of him enough to beg for an introduction.

"You must face up to it," she counseled herself. "He is here for the time being, and you must do better. It cannot go on, that your only defense is to retreat and pretend to ignore him." This was precisely what she had done for the remainder of the time at Perryfield and during the coach ride home, when Mr. Langworthy chanced to sit directly across from her. But it had been an awkward business, and Mrs. Barstow had even asked, "Are you tired, dear Sarah? You have been very quiet."

Shrinking under the blankets and counterpane now for warmth, she curled on her side and shut her eyes. All was not lost. The strategy she had formed at the tea urn was good, if she could only stick to it. If she could not be rid of his company (and that did not look possible at present), she must take care not to be his most interesting source of amusement.

Oh, and one last thing, she remembered sleepily. She simply must mention Harry Barbary to him on the very next occasion, or the child's importunings would be added to her burdens.

"I think that's Harry Barbary who keeps peeping over the gate," said Maria the next morning as they put on their cloaks and hats for the walk to church.

"Whatever could he want?" asked Frances. "It cannot be that he wishes to go to church with us. Maria, come away from the window and let me button your coat properly."

"He wants to talk with me," spoke up Sarah. "I—forgot to mention it, but when you all were out, he came by to ask—us—to introduce him to Mr. Langworthy. It seems he's heard about the celestial navigation class."

"*He* can't be in it!" cried Gordon. "He's only a baby!"

"I don't believe he's more than a year younger than you and Peter," said Sarah, "but of course he can't be taught alongside you because—"

"Because only imagine what Mrs. Markham Dere would say!" Frances whooped. "Harry Barbary in the Perryfield schoolroom, sitting beside her precious Peter!"

"But Sarah," murmured Mrs. Barstow, "if you make the introduction, won't Mr. Langworthy perhaps feel obligated to...do something for Harry? It might put him in a difficult spot with Mrs. Dere."

"I'm not sure he *would* feel obligated," answered Sarah dryly. "And surely he is astute enough to know which way the land lies. No, I have told

Harry I would make the introduction, so I will. But then everyone must fend for himself."

The harum-scarum boy danced from foot to foot as they emerged into the street. Scraping his cap from his head, he bared his rumpled light hair and nodded cursorily at each Barstow until he came to Sarah. "Well, Missus?"

Sarah shut the gate behind her, letting Frances take hold of Bash's hand. "Good morning, Harry. I haven't asked him yet."

"Haven't asked him!" he protested. "But you all were at Perryfield yesterday."

"So we were, but—everyone wanted to talk to Mr. Langworthy." She gave the smallest shake of her head—*another partial untruth, Sarah Barstow! When will this end?*

"If he is in church today, I will look for my chance," she assured him (and herself). "You might—er—come in with us."

His mouth popped open like a fish's. "And sit in Lord Dere's pews? What would Mam say? She doesn't go to church in the mornings with the Quality, but in the afternoon, and I try not to go at all. Nosir, I won't go in with you. Not on your life!"

"Oh, heavens," Sarah almost laughed, imagining Mrs. Dere's face, were she to file in with Harry Barbary in tow. "Of course I didn't mean to suggest you should sit with us. Listen—if I get to speak with Mr. Langworthy, I will send a note to your house later. Will that do?"

The boy gave a disgusted grunt, slouching away without another word and leaving Sarah to hurry after the others.

The little church of St. Mary the Virgin was full that morning, the parishioners eager to see the new parson read in. After the good-looking young curate who had preceded him, there were a few sighs among the women over Dr. Rearden's age and heavier person, but all in all he seemed perfectly amiable, and at least, being neither young nor handsome, he would be less likely to marry and run off as Mr. Egerton had.

With one of the congregation, however, Dr. Rearden made an immediate hit, for no sooner had Sarah taken her seat in the second Dere pew than her little boy crawled over his aunt Frances' lap to whisper loudly in his mama's ear, "Who dat?"

She followed his stubby pointing finger before gently pushing it down, and she was glad to see it was not Mr. Langworthy Bash indicated.

"It's our new priest, dearest," she whispered back. "Dr. Rearden."

"I like him," declared her son, holding up both his hands to slap his own cheeks and then to wave his fingers alongside them. "He has fur."

"Hush, darling."

"Fur like Pawpaw." *Pawpaw*, Bash's version of "Poppet."

At this, Frances glanced over, her lips pressed together and her eyes crinkling with mirth. Not so Mrs. Markham Dere's eyes, as she turned from the pew in front to give Bash a quelling look, which he failed to see because Sarah was trying to get him to sit on his bottom.

He was quiet enough during the service, doing no more than kicking his legs and rubbing the side of his head against Sarah's sleeve, but she thought it would have been hypocritical to scold him, when she was just as restless inside. Bash might be fascinated by Dr. Rearden's wagging whiskers, but now Sarah several times had to shut her eyes, when the resemblance to Poppet became too striking. Her gaze wandered to the back of Mr. Langworthy—a broad back and a straight one. She supposed it was his military bearing. The stripe of darkened skin above the collar.

Shifting in the pew as if he sensed the observation, his head turned a few degrees short of profile, revealing the cut of his cheekbone and the square of his jaw, and heat flooded her cheeks as if she had been caught.

She did not look at him again.

When the service ended an hour later, the curate swooped past them down the aisle toward the south door. Bash tugged on her hand. "Pawpaw," he said again. "Pawpaw."

"Dr. Rearden, dear. His name is Dr. Rearden."

"Tocktoe Weird," repeated Bash. "Tock Weird."

"Now you've done it," Frances said with twitching lips. Though Sarah wanted to giggle herself, she gave Frances a fearsome frown. If Bash's bungled attempts at the curate's name made his family laugh, they would never hear the end of it, for he would quickly add them to his arsenal of capers and tricks.

The churchgoers rose to file from their pews, waiting for the baron and Mrs. Markham Dere to lead the procession. But instead of following them, Bash toddled across the aisle to clamber into Dr. and Mrs. Lane's pew, giving his little gown a jerk when it caught beneath his knees. Once freed, he leaned on the pew back before him with one hand and prodded Mr. Langworthy with the other. The latter looked down, grinning. "Good morning to you as well, Master Bash."

Hastening after her son, Sarah threw the Lanes an apologetic smile and gestured for them to precede her into the aisle. Then she snatched Bash up—or would have, except he had taken hold of Mr. Langworthy's top waistcoat button, and her effort only served to jerk her toward the man.

"Goodness me," she gasped, her face veering so near his that they might have kissed.

"There it is," he mused. "Newton's Third Law of Motion."

"Hep!" came Bash's muffled voice from between them. The boy released the button and shoved Mr. Langworthy with what force he could. Not that force was necessary, for the latter retreated a step, his eyes alight, unreadable.

"Pardon us," murmured Sarah, hoping he could not see the pulse jumping in her throat. Had her breath brushed him, as warmly as his did her, in the instant before they separated? Might something more have happened—something more have been said—if the Lanes had not been by?

It did not matter.

It should not matter.

Mustering what dignity she could, Sarah hitched Bash on her hip and marched away.

Chapter 10

Those two massie Pillars...
He tugg'd, he shook, till down they came.
—Milton, *Samson Agonistes* (1671)

N o sooner had she turned away, however, than she remembered yet again her neglect of Harry Barbary's request.

Mercy. Can I possibly make Frances do it? I should have asked her at once.

Nor were her trials ended that morning.

The new curate had wisely chosen to stand in the yard outside the door to the church, lest the people wanting to meet him prevent all egress. When Sarah emerged with Bash in her arms, the Deres and Lanes had just paid their compliments and were stepping aside to allow Mrs. Barstow to introduce the remaining members of her family.

"Ah, there you are, Sarah. Dr. Rearden, I hope you will meet my oldest daughters and their husbands someday, but here is my youngest, Maria, and here is Sarah's boy, my grandson Sebastian."

"What fine, healthy children the Barstows boast," declared Rearden, raising benedictory hands.

Maria dropped a curtsey, but Bash turned in his mother's arms to regard his new acquaintance. Then, before Sarah realized what he was about, he extended a plump hand to indicate the clergyman's lush whiskers.

"Pawpaw."

"Now, dearest, his name is Dr. Rearden," Sarah reminded him, pushing his arm down and trying to move along before anyone could ask what her son had said.

"Pawpaw," repeated Bash, spinning in Sarah's hold to keep his eye on his quarry.

"'Papa'? Does Dr. Rearden...resemble your late husband, Mrs. Sebastian?" asked Mrs. Lane innocently.

Sarah could not hide her amazement at the ridiculous idea—how could Bash possibly remember what his dead father looked like, when he was not even three years old? And how could her dead husband be older than his own mother Mrs. Barstow?

Nonetheless she gathered her wits to make a polite demurral, only to be forestalled by the reappearance of Mr. Langworthy over Mrs. Lane's shoulder.

"Come to think of it, madam," he said thoughtfully, "there *is* something there."

Mrs. Lane not being acquainted with him, a series of introductions followed as the gathering around Dr. Rearden swelled, but when they had been got through, the amiable matron took up the thread again.

"Mr. Langworthy," she said, "I have done some calculations in my head, and it wasn't very kind of you to humbug me when we had not even been introduced. I see now it was silly of me to ask if Dr. Rearden might have resembled the late Mr. Sebastian Barstow. After all, his mother Mrs. Gordon Barstow is not old enough to have a son Dr. Rearden's age."

"Tocktoe Weird," agreed Bash.

Sarah quickly put him down, hoping he would run off and play, but instead he took hold of her skirts. "Uppy. Uppy, Mama."

"I will hold you," offered Frances, but he shook his head and scowled at his aunt.

"Mama uppy," he insisted.

Stifling a sigh, Sarah uppied him and was rewarded with him repeating, clearly and with greater emphasis, "Tock—toe Weird."

"Indeed, Master Sebastian," interposed Mr. Langworthy smoothly, "it *is* weird. In the sense of 'odd.' For while Dr. Rearden bears little physical resemblance to your late 'pawpaw'—who was somewhat younger and clean-shaven—he undoubtedly shares Barstow's ability to garner and hold attention."

"What nonsense," chuckled the curate, but he beamed with pleasure. Leaning forward, he wagged his own finger in Bash's face, saying amiably, "Talkative little fellow. I am glad to make your acquaintance, Master Sebastian, and hope to see much more of you."

Seeing the glorious whiskers hovering so near, the temptation proved too great for the boy, and with another crowing "Pawpaw!" his hand flew out to snatch hold of the clergyman's lavish side wings.

Sarah gasped and instinctively pulled him back, but Bash's grip was tight, and it was a case of Mr. Langworthy's button all over again, this time with poor Rearden stumbling forward and crying "O-o-o-o-ooh!"

"Let go, Bash!" cried his mother, shrinking to avoid colliding with the parson. Scrabbling at her son's fingers to pry them open she scolded, "You mustn't hold his whiskers—let go at once!"

"Oosker," Bash insisted, pushing at his mother with his elbow while maintaining his hold. "Oosker." He might as well have plucked Rearden's hairs with tweezers, the way he pinched a few strands between each of his fingers, and their new shepherd gave another involuntary yelp, his eyes beginning to water.

While everyone clamored around them with advice and urgings, calling Bash's name or otherwise trying to distract him, it was Mr. Langworthy who rescued the situation. Extending a fingertip under Sarah's uplifted arm, he gave Bash's side a tickle. The little boy shrieked and instantly released the parson in order to bat away this attack, squirming and giggling until Sarah nearly dropped him.

Clapping his hands to the sides of his mistreated face, Dr. Rearden retreated at once, backing into Dr. Lane and having to beg his pardon.

"Oh, Dr. Rearden," Sarah almost wailed. "I am so sorry. I hope Bash didn't injure you. I cannot think how he could be so naughty."

"No harm done, no harm done," he assured her, but he kept a careful distance. "I will be more cautious in the future. Thank you, Langworthy, for your quick thinking."

The latter gave a short bow, not bothering to hide his amusement, and Sarah would have been resentful if she had not been so grateful for his intercession.

"Yes, I imagine you navy men are all practiced in quick thinking," spoke up Dr. Lane, whose one wisp of a beard threatened to draw Bash's eye next. "What would we do without you all?" No sooner did he speak than his wife jabbed a not-very-subtle elbow into his ribs and hissed, "Husband, can you possibly have forgotten Mrs. Sebastian's situation and how she lost—er—"—a well-intentioned action which only served to make uncomfortable everyone in hearing distance.

Again it was Langworthy who got them through the difficulty. "It is because of Mrs. Sebastian's late husband that I am here," he announced, and whether those around already knew this or not, they welcomed the chance to ask him questions and to let the widow recover.

Sarah was tempted to march straight out of the churchyard, sparing any more gentlemen from having their buttons or whiskers pulled and herself from further discomfiture, but before she could do more than look over the churchyard, a movement behind one of the stones distracted her. Light hair under a shabby cap. A glint of pale eyes. The head popped up, sunk back down, popped up again.

Oh, right.

Harry Barbary was wise to suspect Sarah would forget yet again the task he had assigned her. Clearly, if she ever wanted to be left alone, she should defer it no longer. But how could she draw Mr. Langworthy aside?

Reaching to tap her youngest sister-in-law, she whispered, "Maria, would you keep an eye on Bash? He might like to play peep-bo with the other boys among the stones." She thrust him at the surprised girl, but Maria took him willingly enough, leaving Sarah free to concentrate her efforts.

"—Offered to teach the Tommies and a couple local boys the wonders of celestial navigation," Dr. Rearden was explaining, to general approbation. Even Mrs. Markham Dere favored them with a chilly smile and murmured something about Peter participating.

Here was an opening!

"—Dr. Rearden—did you know there once was a little parish school for the poorer boys?" blurted Sarah. In courtesy everyone turned toward her, and she swallowed but pressed on. "That is—not a parish *school*, really, but more of a little class where the former curate's now wife—my sister-in-law Jane—and the former curate's sister once taught a few of the village children their letters and sums. One of them turned out to be rather clever. He's an errand boy for Mrs. Lamb at the Tree Inn now. One Harry Barbary."

The curate assumed an expression of polite interest at this random contribution, but Mrs. Dere sniffed, "'Clever,' indeed. 'Mischievous,' more like. As Mr. Pope has said, 'A little knowledge is a dangerous thing,' and so it has proved for Harry Barbary. I believe he has given Mrs. Lamb a great deal of trouble, writing—actually *writing things!*—on some people's post on one occasion. I would advise you, Dr. Rearden, to keep clear of him."

"Goodness," he said inadequately.

"I didn't mean to suggest you should start a parish school again, Dr. Rearden," Sarah added, clasping her hands together so hard it might have been called *wringing*. "Only that—I suppose you will meet the Barbarys—all of them—soon, and—and—other struggling families in Iffley—and you too, Mr. Langworthy—and it so happens I think I see Harry himself...over there...and thought I might as well perform the introduction." Raising a hand she pointed, and all turned in time to see Harry's blond head whip down and out of sight, as if he were dodging sustained musketry fire.

"Harry!" she called, "Come here a moment."

"Whatever are you doing, Mrs. Sebastian?" demanded Mrs. Dere.

Too addled to think of another explanation, Sarah told the truth—or very close to it. "It is not a whim of mine, Mrs. Dere. It is actually an obligation of sorts. You know how Mrs. Lamb is, how she discovers everything. Harry no sooner heard of—the newcomers—from her than he came by and asked me to make them known to him."

"But why on earth should he ask *you?*"

Hoping to avoid further questioning, Sarah replied, "He meant to ask Frances because he knows her better, but Frances wasn't at home. That left...me. Oh, Harry! Yes, you—come over here."

No one would believe he had made any such request, the way he ducked down again and tried to pretend he wasn't there or didn't hear. Only when Sarah fairly bellowed, "I know you're there, Harry!" did he straighten, shoulders still hunched and face scowling, to drag himself thitherward.

"Are you *quite* certain he wanted to meet us, Mrs. Sebastian?" asked Mr. Langworthy mildly.

"Quite."

She suspected Harry's disinclination stemmed from the gathered crowd. He certainly had not asked her to make a public event of it all, and this slinking approach was the result. When the circle parted to admit him, it reminded Sarah of the Gospel of John, where the woman taken in adultery was "put...in front of the crowd," and a good stoning anticipated.

"Harry, may I present you to our new curate Dr. Rearden and his houseguest Mr. Langworthy?"

"How do you do, my lad?" Rearden accosted him with hearty warmth.

Harry dragged a toe in the dirt, eyes lowered and nothing more than a grunt emerging.

"Look up and speak up when you're spoken to, child," commanded Mrs. Dere.

(Sarah could have pinched him herself—and Mrs. Dere, for good measure—for shyness had never been one of Harry's traits, and this was an unfortunate time for it to appear. Moreover, one feature she was certain he possessed in abundance was contrariness, and who knew what he would say or do when thus chided?)

"Oh, yes," she struck in hurriedly, addressing the adults with forced gaiety. "When Jane and Miss Egerton taught Harry and the Cramthorpes, they insisted on clear enunciation, but I suppose when school ends, a holiday mood prevails."

Still Harry said nothing and still he rolled a pebble beneath the sole of his worn boot, but the sympathetic baron touched his niece on the arm. "There is the carriage, Alice, Peter. Good day to you all."

It was the signal for the gathering to disperse, and Sarah too wanted to wash her hands of the matter, but something in Harry's discomfiture kept her beside him. With a grimace, she leaned down and whispered, "Well? After all that fuss, have you nothing to say to anyone?"

"I didn't want all of *them*. I didn't ask for any of *them*."

"Fair enough," she conceded. Straightening, she would have tried to catch Mr. Langworthy's eye, only it was already upon her, one brow arched in maddening fashion.

I will not let him get the better of me.

Taking a deep breath, she let the others drift farther away before saying, "It so happens, Mr. Langworthy, that it was you Harry was most interested in meeting."

At her words, Harry's head bobbed up as if they had planned it this way, and he gave Langworthy a straight look. "I can do figures," he announced. "Sums. As good as—better 'n—others. Faster."

Langworthy regarded him with unfeigned surprise. "Is that so?" He took in the boy's shabby clothing and challenging expression. "What an...interesting fact."

"It's more 'n interesting," insisted Harry. "It's God's truth!"

A twitch of the man's lips. "But why are you telling me this?"

Harry glanced at Sarah, but she said nothing.

"I want—I want to learn to navigate too," he confessed, scarlet burning his cheeks. He was more used to telling people what he *didn't* want or wouldn't do. "But I know that woman—" (pointing toward Mrs. Dere at the churchyard entrance, being assisted into the carriage) "—won't want me near."

Langworthy's grin broke out. "It looks like it's not only numbers you're clever with."

"But I could sit outside and—and listen through the winder, if you'd leave it cracked," Harry suggested. "Jimmy and Anna and me used to learn in the rectory schoolroom, and it had an old casement that opened."

"Ah. But I won't be teaching the other boys in the rectory, but rather at Perryfield, and I believe the schoolroom might be on the first floor, out of reach."

"Worse," murmured Sarah. "It's on the second."

"Worse indeed, then," Langworthy said. "On the second floor I could throw the window wide and speak at the top of my voice, but I daresay you wouldn't see or hear a thing, Harry."

The boy's narrow face contracted in perplexity. "But—but—" And then suddenly his features cleared, and he threw out an impulsive hand to pluck at Langworthy's sleeve. "But supposing I work for you, and—and—and you give me my own lessons some other time, instead o' brass for it?"

"Harry!" exclaimed Sarah.

"Work for me?" Langworthy repeated. "Doing what, may I ask? How old are you?"

"I don't know," answered Harry. "Can't you think of nothing for me to do? I'm seven or eight, I s'pose, and strong and quick. For Mrs. Lamb I take messages and deliver things and clean and carry and what all. I—I could be a footboy. At the rectory there ain't but Winching and Polly to do all the work, not now that Mrs. Terry and Miss Egerton are gone. Just Winching and Polly, with all you fellers to look after. They're crying in their aprons about it, like as not."

Mr. Langworthy was amused and therefore wavering. Sarah could see it. But ought she to say something? Heaven knew Mrs. Lamb considered Harry Barbary her cross to bear, but might he be a better worker when he wanted something very badly from his employer?

Horace Langworthy is a grown man, she decided. *If he chooses to take on Harry Barbary, that's his lookout, as Gordy would say.*

This figurative washing of her hands would not serve long, however, for the next minute Mr. Langworthy said, "Well, Harry, your point is a persuasive one. Winching and Polly might indeed consider themselves overworked at the rectory with four of us to see to and no womenfolk to help them. And if Mrs. Sebastian vouches for you, that's good enough for me."

"Oh! But I never said—" began Sarah, startled. Then she found her own sleeve plucked and Harry Barbary staring up at her with pleading blue eyes which she had never once seen before. For heaven's sake!

"—I never said I would countenance stealing you away from Mrs. Lamb," she finished lamely. "And—and—certainly Dr. Rearden had better consult Winching and Polly before you hire them an assistant, Mr. Langworthy."

He shrugged. "That sounds sensible. Allow me a few days to give you an answer, Harry. And now run along, so I may speak with Mrs. Sebastian."

"About me?" asked Harry.

"Ah." The navy man held up an instructive forefinger. "Setting aside the secrets of celestial navigation for now, here we would at least have Lesson Number One in becoming a footboy: you must hide all curiosity about your employers and learn what you want to know of them by other means. No bald questions."

With difficulty, Harry Barbary nodded, stuffing down his curiosity and backing away with nods and bows which would have been comical if they didn't make Sarah feel guilty. Dear, dear—the boy's heart really was set on it!

"Should I have accepted him straightaway?" asked Langworthy. "I wanted to, you know, Mrs. Sebastian, for any friend of yours is a friend of mine."

The mocking note had returned, but she was prepared for it. "Mr. Langworthy, I will be honest with you. By introducing Harry to your notice, I have fulfilled my promise to him in its entirety. What you choose to do with your new acquaintance is up to you. I can only say that Mrs. Lamb will surely tell you that he is as exasperating as he is clever, and not only you, but also Winching and Polly might find his mischief burdensome."

Instead of appearing disturbed by her revelations, Mr. Langworthy only contemplated her impassively, measuringly, and it was all Sarah could do to bear it without flinching. Then he clicked his tongue softly. "It is the mischievous who always row against the stream in life, do you not think?"

She returned him nothing but a wary gaze.

"Unlike the majority," he pursued, "who are content to be carried by the current wherever it tends, be the surrounding banks ever so high and narrow. The mischievous find the thought of such a journey confining, however. Less like floating, and more like drowning."

She did not miss his meaning, and her own reply held a touch of asperity. "You make it sound as if rowing against the stream of life—and I assume by 'life' you mean something more like 'convention'—were always a noble thing, sir. But is it not the case that sometimes mischief is no more than mere perversity? That is, sometimes mischief is done not because the perpetrator might find convention stifling, but rather simply for the *fun of the thing*."

If she thought this near-reproof would silence him, she was disappointed, for he laughed. Not in a sneering way, but with sincere enjoyment.

"You have me there, Mrs. Sebastian. There is no defense against your charge for I recognize myself in it, if not Harry Barbary. But come—if I choose to do the boy a good turn—to thrust my hand in the fire, as it were, and see how long I can hold it there before it burns—you will not try to oppose me, will you?"

"Oppose you? How would I do that, sir?"

"Why, I am sure you could think of something," he replied amiably. "I could, if I were you. I would drop a word in Mrs. Markham Dere's ear, or tell Winching and Polly how much *additional* work Harry's presence will cause, or convince Mrs. Lamb that she cannot spare the boy, unsatisfactory though she thinks him. There are a thousand ways you might thwart me, if you chose."

He hid a smile to see her bosom swell.

"I shan't do any of those—mean things," Sarah retorted. "I have said my piece, and whatever you do now is your own business."

"Ooh!" With a wince, he pressed a hand to his heart. "How you do tend to bear upon a sore spot, Mrs. Sebastian, with these constant reminders that my business is my business and only my business, and your business is your business and not at all my business, world without end. When you know how I longed for your business to be my business and my business your business, but you sent me about my business, did you not?"

To this nonsense Sarah made no reply, however, for she had already walked away.

CHAPTER 11

**The greatest fault of a penetrating wit is not
coming short of the mark but overshooting it.**
—*The English Theophrastus: or, The manners of the age*
(1702)

A full week passed before Sarah saw Mr. Langworthy again, yet the hiatus would have been much briefer, had she happened to be at home the two times he called at Iffley Cottage. On the first occasion, however, she was at Perryfield practicing the pianoforte with Frances in advance of the dancing lessons, and on the second she and Maria had been taking a basket to the Cramthorpes. Still, to be spared the sight of Mr. Langworthy by no means spared her the sound of his name.

"Dr. Rearden and Mr. Langworthy called," reported Mrs. Barstow the first time. "And while the new curate is everything one could wish for, I was still glad when he went away and Mr. Langworthy remained, so we could have a comfortable coze about Sebastian."

"It was also good that he went away because Bash would not leave him alone," Maria put in, keeping her voice low, even though her nephew was in the kitchen having a snack of bread with jam and butter.

"Oh, dear," fretted Sarah. "What did he do to the poor man?"

"He brought him Poppet to admire and kept saying, 'Pawpaw'—"

"But we explained that was his way of saying 'Poppet'—"

"Thank heavens!" Sarah interrupted. "At least now Dr. Rearden will know Bash wasn't calling him 'papa.'"

"Though he may yet wonder why Bash was saying 'Poppet' when he saw him at church," Frances observed.

This stopped them for a moment, but no ready rebuttal coming to mind, Maria went on. "Perhaps he didn't remember. At least, he didn't ask or mention it. In any event, everything seemed all right until Dr. Rearden leaned down to pet Poppet—"

"Oh, no!" breathed Sarah. "Did he learn nothing on Sunday? Bash didn't grab his whiskers again, did he?"

"No," Maria assured her, "but he dumped Poppet straight off and threw his fat little arms around the parson's knees and just about *swooned* up at him, crying, 'Oosker! Oosker!'" To demonstrate the scene, Maria seized her tall sister Frances, but Frances began laughing so hard Maria could hardly hold her.

"The child is in love!" crowed Frances, placing a hand to each side of her face and waving her fingers like fins. "Oosker! Oosker!"

Even Sarah had to giggle over this nonsense, though it made all the talk of Mr. Langworthy which followed come almost as a relief.

Not an enduring relief, however, for it seemed that if Bash now doted upon the new curate, Mrs. Barstow and Maria felt much the same for Mr. Langworthy.

"I brought out the atlas Lord Dere gave us, and Mr. Langworthy showed us everywhere he and Sebastian sailed!"

"Mr. Langworthy told us of a time when that bullying Mr. Beeton was making one of the poor young midshipmen miserable, and Sebastian devised a plan of distraction!"

Of course Sarah wanted to hear the story about Sebastian—all the stories about Sebastian—but in every case, where Sebastian was, Mr. Langworthy was also found, and she ended in hearing as much of Mr. Langworthy as she did her lost husband. Nor could she let her impatience show, or she would have to make up an acceptable reason for her dislike—a dislike no one else would countenance.

"I wish we had been home to hear him, Sarah," Frances sighed at last, "because hearing such things makes me quite prepared to adore Mr. Langworthy myself!" Slyly she added, "Of course, I might have given Dr. Rearden the preference initially, but it seems Bash has already earmarked him for *you*."

"Pooh," said Sarah, blushing.

"*May* I marry Mr. Langworthy if he offers for me, Mama?" Frances asked. She took Mrs. Barstow by the hands and twirled her on the carpet, narrowly missing two chairs and a side table.

"Foolish girl," scolded her mother without heat. "What would you live on? Though I would be happy to have such a son."

"Mrs. Dere would probably pester the baron into giving me a portion, if she could be got to approve of Mr. Langworthy," Frances answered blithely. "Oh, don't frown like that, Mama. I'm only jesting, though he is quite attractive, I think. Perhaps not so handsome as Adela's Mr. Weatherill or Jane's Mr. Egerton, and he hasn't Dr. Rearden's magnificent whiskers, but beggars must not be choosers."

Frances was more fortunate in being at Iffley Cottage when Mr. Langworthy made his second call (and then it was Maria's turn to sigh and complain about her bad luck), and more stories and praise and joking ensued, but at last Saturday and its dancing lesson arrived, and all the Barstow ladies were promised their share of the gentleman.

Whether we want it or not, Sarah told herself.

It had been agreed that the Barstows would walk to Perryfield, barring rain or mud, and Gordon having gone ahead for his mathematics and navigation lesson, Sarah knew there was no danger of falling in with Mr. Langworthy. The sight of the ladies passing the Tree Inn was too much for its landlady, however, and Mrs. Lamb raced out to greet them.

"Good morning! Good morning! Saturday already, is it? Fine day for a walk and nearly warm as April, wouldn't you say? I wish you the best for your dance lessons. What a to-do! I suppose I should be grateful Harry Barbary has no interest in learning to dance, or he would have abandoned me altogether."

Since Mrs. Lamb had done nothing but complain of her errand boy's shortcomings the whole time he had been in her employ, Sarah was not apt to pity her, but she could not help being curious about how Harry now divided his time. Fortunately, the postmistress delighted in the sharing of information, and the answer followed at once.

"Two afternoons a week I'm to give the boy up, so he might go and do whatever he likes! I pass over the nonsense of him learning navigation. Harry Barbary has no more need of navigation than of sprouting a second head. I tried to talk to Mrs. Barbary about it, but of course she said she can no more get Harry to obey her than the weather, even if she wanted to try. Useless. She even had the cheek to thank me, as if I had any say in it."

"I daresay Mr. Langworthy won't be in Iffley very long," Mrs. Barstow soothed her, "and then you will have all the Harry you can manage again. Good day to you! We had better not dally."

"I'm dying to know more," Frances said as they turned into the Upper Field. "Do you suppose Mr. Langworthy really intends to teach such a young boy—and such a one as Harry Barbary!—to find his way by the stars?" But then she shrugged. "Oh, well. If Mr. Langworthy does not tell us all about it, surely Mrs. Lamb will, the next time we see her."

"Why, Mrs. Dere, how pleasantly you have arranged things!"

This was not Frances' usual courteous flattery, but spontaneous praise drawn from all of them, and the mistress of Perryfield lifted a proud chin. "Though my uncle and I have never hosted a ball, we are prepared to do the thing nicely."

The usual fire blazed in the drawing room, and the sconces were lit, as well as a candelabra beside the pianoforte. All the furniture had been pushed against the walls, the carpet rolled up, and even a side table laid with orange wine, small beer, and a plate of sandwiches covered with a cloth.

Maria looked longingly at the refreshments, and such was Mrs. Dere's good mood that, instead of looking disapproving, she smiled at the girl, announcing, "And after the lesson we will have apple turnovers, Cook promises."

They had only looked over the music Mrs. Dere had chosen and talked through the figures while she played rapidly through the opening bars before voices and footsteps were heard. The drawing room door opened again and in walked the baron, followed by Mr. Langworthy and the four pupils.

To judge from the glowing faces and chatter, the first mathematics and navigation lesson was a great success. "—An eyeglass," Lord Dere was saying, and Mr. Langworthy chuckled, "Yes, perhaps some evening."

"We learned about triangles!" crowed Gordon, running up to his mother. "And what the lines are called, from where I stand to a point in the sky like a star or planet and then down to the horizon. And what a degree is, and the most familiar heavenly bodies: important stars, and the sun and moon and planets. Did you know the nautical almanac will even tell us where to find Georgium Sidus in the night sky—"

"Though it is so very far away that Mr. Langworthy says the weather must be nearly perfect to pick it out, even with an eyeglass," finished Peter.

The ladies were duly impressed by the heap of knowledge conferred on the boys, and the boys so eager, it seemed, to recapitulate the entire lesson for their edification, that Mrs. Dere was forced to clap her hands for their attention after several minutes.

"This is all very well, young gentlemen, but now I must insist we begin lessons equally important and sooner applicable. Come, Peter, you stand here, and Gordon, you here—no, no, Uncle, you must not think to excuse yourself, nor you, Mr. Langworthy, for you will be required to demonstrate the figures."

Sarah was sorry to see the boys' enthusiasm silenced, but the way Peter and Gordy grimaced with the effort to contain their further praises made her smile. As she took the place assigned her opposite Tom Ellis, her eye happened to catch Mr. Langworthy's, and on impulse she said, "Thank you, sir, for the lesson. You appear to have been a rattling success."

"I'll make midshipmen of them yet."

There was no time for more, as Mrs. Dere had placed Frances at the instrument and was handing out instructions of her own. "There being only four ladies to dance at any one time, I have chosen dances specifically for four couples. Listen and watch carefully, Tommies," the mistress of Perryfield intoned, for you will take Lord Dere's and Mr. Langworthy's places shortly." The specialized vocabulary the boys had so recently learned was superseded by a host of new terms: set, cast, turn single, up a double, arm left, and so forth, and the figures were taught and repeated a dozen times over.

While the selected dances involved no excessive hand-holding, and while the constant whirl of movement and the teacher's scolding prevented any awkward pauses (much less conversation), Sarah could think of no reason-able explanation for the irregularities of her pulse or the blockishness of her feet.

It's not really so odd, she told herself, *to feel uncomfortable around a person who asked you to marry him only a week ago and was refused!* Usually a refused suitor took himself off at once, tail between his legs, never to reappear again, or at least never to reappear until he had been triumphantly successful with someone else. Therefore it was no marvel she should be embarrassed by his continuing, inexplicable, contrary presence.

Things improved once Lord Dere and Mr. Langworthy gave place to Peter and Gordon and Mrs. Dere replaced Frances at the pianoforte. Romping with family members and children was long familiar to Sarah, and she regained her customary self-command, even joining in the laughter when the weaving pattern of Aye Me thoroughly confused Tommy Wardour and Gordon, ending in them not only far from their partners but paired with each other.

Beside the window, Langworthy and Lord Dere had retreated to observe the proceedings, the baron's frequent chuckles heard between the music and chatter, and he turned a face both beaming and somewhat apologetic to his guest. "Ah, Langworthy, there is nothing like a full house for delight."

"Indeed."

"It was a great joy to me, to hear from my cousin Camilla—Mrs. Barstow—a few years ago," Lord Dere continued. "I regretted her meeting with such difficulties in life, naturally—the death of her husband and of her son, your friend Sebastian—and sometimes I feel guilty that I am so glad of their coming to Iffley, when the cost to them was so high."

"Both feelings are understandable, sir."

"Do you...hail from a large family yourself, Langworthy?"

"It once was larger, but now there remain only one widowed uncle, a married cousin and her husband, and myself."

The baron drew a deep breath and patted Langworthy's shoulder. "What a comfort you must be to them, then. They must be very proud of you—and very grateful for the Peace which brings you safely back."

Langworthy's mouth thinned. Lord Dere made the mistake of judging other men by his own yardstick, it seemed. "I am...afraid we are not particularly close, sir. I used to have two uncles, not mutually related themselves, and only the…less fond one still lives. Uncle Horatio was my father's brother, and Uncle Edwin my mother's, and the match was popular in neither camp."

"Oh, dear." The baron clicked his tongue unhappily.

"But they did work together on one thing," Langworthy resumed, "for which I am thankful: they each contributed to putting me to sea, and they were not wealthy men."

"Ah. Well done! Well done on their part. And judging by your performance this morning, you must excel in your duties."

"You are too kind."

"Kind—nonsense. Only see how eagerly the boys took to your lesson! Why, you ought to be a mathematics instructor. The fact that you can provide practical applications for the lessons only adds to their charm. Perhaps teaching is not as thrilling a profession as the navy, but it is altogether less perilous."

Langworthy made no response. There was certainly nothing perilous about being a discarded peacetime lieutenant on half pay, but it would hardly do to say so, not when Sebastian Barstow had reaped all the peril Horace himself escaped.

They watched the dancers for a few more minutes before the baron resumed. "My cousin's two daughters Adela and Jane have recently married and removed some little distance to Oxford and St. Lawrence, and no doubt Frances—Miss Barstow—will marry when she is a little older, but I comfort myself that I have some years of company yet. Gordy and Maria and Bash are still very young."

"And—there is Mrs. Sebastian Barstow."

Mrs. Sebastian Barstow, whose face glowed with the exercise and who had laughed more times in the last half hour than in all Langworthy's previous acquaintance with her. Not that his acquaintance had been of any length, to be sure, but it was a striking sight. A—pleasant sight.

"Our Sarah," murmured Lord Dere. "I suspect, had Adela and Jane not married and gone away, Sarah would have been content to be the widowed daughter-in-law the rest of her days, but as the nest empties, I would not be surprised if she too would begin to consider making a change."

"You speak as if it were in her power to do so," Langworthy answered. He ran a hand along his clean jaw. "Hidden away as she is, with no money and with a young son."

The baron shrugged. "Iffley may be hidden away, but only see how her sisters-in-law managed. One married Peter's tutor and the other the curate who preceded Dr. Rearden. And now appears Rearden himself, yet another bachelor. Unmarried men seem to pop up like tulips."

"Rearden!" repeated Langworthy, unable to keep a note of incredulity from his voice. "With all respect to the worthy man, he must be twice Mrs. Sebastian's age." Realizing Rearden might also be a contemporary of the man beside him, he sputtered, "That is—er—still in the prime of life but—er—further along than she."

"Perhaps," Lord Dere said, a twinkle in his eye suggesting he guessed the cause of his companion's discomfiture. "I am no matchmaker; I only give him as an example of yet another single man added to our little community. And a well-off, respectable one, to boot. Of course, Mr. Langworthy, I do not count *you* among these tulip bachelors, as you are only passing through."

"Yes."

"It was good of you to come, however. A great comfort to the Barstows."

"Mm."

"I am certain I speak for all of us when I say we hope you will stay a good long time."

But here one of Langworthy's brows lifted, as at a private joke only he could understand. "*Are* you so certain you speak for all?" Then, catching himself, "Never mind. I thank you, sir."

Receiving such noncommittal responses, most men would have left the subject, but after a pause the baron went on. "And should you ever decide to leave off seafaring and hang your sword upon the nail, or whatever the equivalent naval expression might be, Oxford and its environs are the very place for a mathematics tutor."

Here he had overreached.

Langworthy stared at the older man—if this wasn't matchmaking on the baron's part, it was so nearly like it that he could not tell the difference! What was the fellow suggesting, but that Langworthy had better snatch up Mrs. Sebastian before some other stray "tulip bachelor" did, and trust to teaching and tutoring for income? Indeed, Dere might even be hinting he could find Langworthy a position, if asked!

Astonishing.

And despite having already made Mrs. Sebastian exactly the offer of marriage Lord Dere now proposed, everything contrary in Langworthy rose up to reject the idea. It was one thing, after all, for his dear friend Barstow to ask it of him, and quite another for every other Tom, Dick and Harry to make the suggestion in chorus.

In this rebellious spirit he replied shortly, "Thank you again, sir, but it's the navy life for me. I have no intention of 'sheathing my sword' anytime soon. Indeed, I firmly believe there will soon be more use for it than ever. Who knows, but I may return to Portsmouth within the month."

Had Mrs. Markham Dere been at liberty to overhear their conversation, and had she at all shared in the baron's unacknowledged design, she would have rolled her eyes in disgust at his clumsy execution and told him plainly that he had accomplished nothing but to drive Mr. Langworthy off. But as it was, Lord Dere was spared her scorn, and he was allowed to retreat with only his own secret sighs to bear.

CHAPTER 12

Young persons, on their first entering into service, should endeavour to divest themselves of former habits, and devote themselves to the controul of those whom they engage to serve...They should endeavour to discard every low habit and way of thinking...[and] wisely take advantage of the opportunity which Providence fortunately presents to them.
—Samuel and Sarah Adams, *The Complete Servant* (1825)

M rs. Sebastian Barstow had not guessed amiss in thinking the rectory servants Winching and Polly would object to taking on Harry Barbary.

"Polly and I have our hands full from dawn to dusk and beyond," the cook told Langworthy politely but firmly. "And the more so with so many of you." Winching happened to be holding her rolling pin as she made this speech, giving the viands on her board a good whack at the conclusion, and he thought it best not to contest the point.

"Sir," added the maid, "I know you mean to be kind, but all of us here have known that boy a great deal longer than you, and to teach him how to black boots or light a fire is more than my life is worth."

"Very well," replied Horace. He might have dropped the whole matter then, if he hadn't thought how Mrs. Sebastian would find satisfaction in being proven right. Therefore he continued, "But I hope the two of you will suffer him to be around the rectory a couple afternoons a week, that I myself might train him to do a few things."

Winching gave the pork chops another whack. "That's your business, Mr. Langworthy. But I don't doubt some of your food and belongings might find their way into that boy's stomach and that boy's pockets if he's left to himself for any length of time."

"I am forewarned," he answered solemnly, "and will consider any losses the tax I must pay on this whim of mine."

Had Horace Langworthy been raised a landed gentleman, he might be helpless to teach an aspiring footboy anything of use, but as a navy man he was stuffed with humble skills. Thus Harry eventually learned to clean and polish boots, knives, and brass. To brush and dry Langworthy's hats and coats. To wash and clean his gloves. To mend shirts and stockings. To oil the wooden furniture, remove ashes from the fireplace and build a new fire, clean the looking glass with spirits, and prevent the lamp from smoking. To lay a table (though the accoutrements were merely drawn on a slate, to leave Winching and Polly in peace and ensure none of the silver disappeared). And while Mrs. Lamb had already taught him to run errands and deliver messages, he never did it for her with the same alacrity as he did for his new master.

All this time, as Harry brushed and oiled and polished and sewed and scrubbed, Langworthy talked to him of the same things he did the other boys. He spoke of lines, points, angles, ratios, heavenly bodies. And like the other boys, Harry drank up the learnings and clamored to know more. Nor had Harry lied about being good with figures—he could calculate sums as quickly as Tom Ellis, who was twice his age, and do so without writing anything down. He could grasp concepts which Tommy Wardour and Peter Dere still frowned over. And where Harry's social betters hung on stories about naval life as Shahriar must have hung on Scheherazade's Arabian tales, Harry Barbary not only paid attention but occasionally slipped in specific questions.

"How old were you when you went to sea?" "How old was the youngest boy on the ship?" "If you have to pay to be an officer, how were there other boys on the ships, ones who weren't gentlemen?" "How old was the youngest volunteer?"

By the second week of this, when Harry finally asked, "When will you go back to sea, sir?" Langworthy eyed him beadily. "I can't say. But one thing I can tell you, Harry, is that I will not be making the trip with you stowed away in my trunk."

To this Harry only shrugged and went back to blacking Langworthy's boot.

The next time he came, when there had been a half-hour lull in conversation and Langworthy sat reading a letter from his uncle Horatio, Harry broke the silence with, "You'll go back to Portsmouth sooner, rather than later, I expect."

Horace glanced up, his thoughts still far away. Harry continued to scour the plate cup in his hand with the whiting powder, adding casually, "Because a man your age withouten wife or family has nothing to keep him tied anywhere."

Langworthy's gaze sharpened. "Who told you that?"

"I hears things. Some guess you had a sweetheart who died or broke your heart, and you come here because you've naught else to do. But you could do better back in Portsmouth even if the war don't pick up again, I think. In Portsmouth there'd be more ladies to marry and p'raps improve your fortunes." Giving the cup a few more swipes, he admired its surface. "Here in Iffley, there isn't much to choose from. The richest lady is Mrs. Markham Dere, but you've no chance at her because she loves her position more 'n anything, and she'd have to give it up to marry you. Then there's the ladies at Iffley Cottage, and I suspect they'd take you, but they 'aven't any more brass 'n you do."

"Suppose I married one of them anyway?" asked Langworthy. This was the mischief at work because he knew well he should tell the boy to hold his tongue. "Who needs 'brass'? I could turn highwayman to support a wife."

That suggestion brought the same leaping glow to Harry Barbary's eyes that the tales of adventure on the high seas had, and Langworthy held up his palms with a laugh. "*That* was a joke, and if you repeat it, I will deny it utterly."

"I can keep secrets," declared Harry. He set the cup down and picked up a candlestick to give it the same scrubbing. "But if you pick a Barstow lady, the best one is already taken. That was Mrs. Merritt—Mrs. Egerton now."

"Mm," grunted Langworthy. "'More dregs than water' left at the Cottage, you say?"

"'Cos the first Mrs. Barstow is too old for you," explained Harry. "I suspect she's older than Mrs. Dere by twenty or thirty years." (However good Harry was with numbers, he had the tendency of youth to overestimate the age of his elders, and Langworthy hid a smile.) "And Miss Maria too young. Miss Barstow isn't bad looking, but she's hand in glove with Mrs. Dere, and then you're back at the start because Mrs. Dere wouldn't approve of you."

After a pause, Langworthy said, "There's Mrs. Sebastian Barstow, I suppose."

"Oh, aye, but she's still sweet on her dead husband and never looks at anyone, though some as think she'll take Dr. Rearden if he were to ask."

Langworthy snorted. "A little old for her, wouldn't you think?"

But Harry looked very wise. "I've heard it said the gennelman's age makes no matter. If he has money enough, he can marry as pretty and young as he likes."

Though Langworthy suspected the boy was only repeating what he overheard from Mrs. Lamb and company, it irked him all the same. "Well," he rejoined, "it's one thing for a gathering of hens to cluck about who should marry whom, and quite another for such things to come to pass."

"Why that's just what one old biddy said, only not in so many words," marveled Harry, "but Mrs. L—er—another one—stood to her guns and said if Mrs. Sebastian don't prove a goose, or if she has any friends who care for her, she'll reckon what side her bread is buttered on and get to work on him, like it or not."

"Good luck to them all," Langworthy said with a shrug. "And that's enough on that candlestick, or you'll wear right through it."

What was it to him if provincial gossips thought old, bewhiskered Rearden a good match for Mrs. Sebastian?

Nothing.

Not one single thing.

And yet, Langworthy could not help thinking of a sure way to thwart such a match ever coming off, should the need arise. *Not* that there was a need. It all had absolutely nothing more to do with him. Whatever slender thread Sebastian Barstow had attached to his friend on one end and his widowed wife on the other had snapped at the first tug, leaving both parties at perfect liberty to go off in whatever direction they chose, Langworthy's duty done and the life buoy tossed to Mrs. Sebastian by her dying husband utterly scorned.

And yet—

It was Mrs. Sebastian's fault, really. Or the Iffley Cottage maid Reed's. Because on the occasion of the third navigation class, when Rearden happened to accompany Langworthy to Perryfield to see the baron's insect collection, that was the very day the maid had a toothache, and Mrs. Sebastian was obliged to bring her young son along with her to the dancing lesson.

This time, when Langworthy and his pupils descended from the second-floor schoolroom, in addition to the sound of music being practiced, delighted screeches rent the air, and they entered the drawing room to find little Bash Barstow toddling and tumbling behind the sofa and chairs while the curate romped after him on his hands and knees.

"Oh, Dr. Rearden," Mrs. Sebastian was gasping with laughter, "do be careful! You will surely hurt your knees or rend your—your inexpressibles."

"Pah!" cried the curate, waving away this warning. "It would be one thing if the carpet had been rolled up." And he lumbered again toward Bash, who retreated with another round of shrieks. Even Mrs. Dere was smiling, which surprised her son, but Langworthy failed altogether to notice.

By heaven—was there any truth to the gossip? Look at the woman's eyes shining and the way her amusement revealed a full set of even little white teeth! Look at the color in her face and how the tips of her slippers peeped from beneath her skirts as she shook. (Admittedly, the tips of her slippers had nothing to do with anything, and he did not know why they should catch his eye, but they did.)

If Mrs. Sebastian did not want to marry him, Horace Langworthy, all well and good—he did not want to marry her either. But it did not therefore follow that she should be permitted to fascinate poor, defenseless Rearden.

There was nothing to be gained by putting the curate on his guard, however. Ten to one it would plant an idea in the man's mind which would not enter it for some time, if ever, were the matter left alone. Not that the matter could be trusted to be left alone, if Mrs. Sebastian set her mind to it, and if the likes of Mrs. Lamb and Harry Barbary were going to be proclaiming it from the house-tops.

No.

He must put into motion his own scheme after all.

At least Rearden's frolicking and Mrs. Sebastian's overlavish pleasure were here cut short by Mrs. Dere calling for their attention. "Welcome, boys, Mr. Langworthy. Now that you are here, you may help us prepare the room. And Dr. Rearden, you must catch your breath, for as long as you are present, you certainly must stay to see how the Tommies progress, and I hope I might prevail upon you to make one of the set. No, no, I insist."

With hidden impatience Langworthy waited while their hostess arranged and explained and instructed. With hidden impatience he partnered maladroit Tommy Wardour, grateful when the boy managed to remember his steps and get where he needed to be at appropriate times. With hidden impatience he suppressed the urge to speak with Mrs. Sebastian whenever their paths crossed in the figures, or to catch her eye knowingly. And with hidden impatience (and a stern set to his jaw) he said and did all that was expected when they gathered for refreshments and Mrs. Dere announced to general delight, "Now that Candlemas has passed, the baron and I have decided that the long-awaited children's ball will be held here at Perryfield, and we propose the last Saturday of the month."

For this long forbearance, Langworthy was rewarded by Mrs. Dere assigning Mrs. Sebastian as a partner to him when the lesson recommenced. To this was added another piece of luck after the two of them had traveled up the room and were waiting for their turn to rejoin the set: Tommy Wardour chose that moment to become completely addled, letting not his left foot know what his right foot was doing, so that he made an utter bungle of it, and all came to a standstill.

"Poor Tommy," murmured Mrs. Sebastian. "Perhaps Mrs. Dere should have left things as they were, for he didn't blunder so when he danced with you."

"Perhaps. But he can't go the rest of his life dancing only with me, so he had better begin trying other partners now. It wouldn't even be right for me to claim more than two of his dances at the children's ball, you know—think how people would talk."

Seeing the corners of her mouth curl, he felt absurdly pleased with himself, though in truth a half smile could not compare with her hilarity at Rearden's antics. But he would take care of Rearden.

"Speaking of people talking," he began again, "despite my short tenure in Iffley, I unexpectedly find myself among the village's best informed."

Though she said nothing, her eyebrows clearly asked, "What can you mean, sir?" and he gave an abbreviated bow in response. "I have you to thank, madam, for my plunge into Iffley undercurrents, for it was you who introduced me to Harry Barbary and suggested I give him what instruction I could—"

"I said nothing about instruct—"

"—And I have learned as much from him as he from me, I daresay. But pardon me, Mrs. Sebastian—" (with another little bow) "—I interrupted you interrupting me."

Knowing she would not deign to ask what Harry Barbary was teaching him, he helpfully added, "Perhaps because of his fellow employer Mrs. Lamb, nothing passes (or threatens to pass) unnoticed in the village. Which is how I learned some felicitations may shortly be due to you."

She took the bait, her eyes sparking. "*What* felicitations?"

But Tommy Wardour had at last grasped the subtleties of the hey and made it through the pattern without stumbling, drawing Langworthy and his partner back into the figures. Five full minutes passed, in which she moved through the steps correctly and even gracefully, but the instant they arrived at the bottom of the set and waited once more, she repeated, "What felicitations?"

He made a face of mock surprise. "Need I elaborate?"

"As I am unaware of anything for which I need to be congratulated, you had better," she said tightly, *sotto voce*.

"You cannot be unaware!" A plaintive sigh escaped him. "I suppose, when once a lady finds herself in high request, the names and faces must begin to blur."

"To my knowledge, sir, my name has only ever been paired with the man who was my husband."

"Though even your husband paired it with *one other*, if you will forgive my mentioning it."

"It is hardly likely I would forget it," she replied, her hands clutching each other with marble rigidity, "and for someone who was refused, you allude to it with surprising frequency. May I therefore request that you refrain from mentioning it ever again?"

He swept a gloved finger across his lips, as if brushing something away, but she saw the infinitesimal hesitation halfway along, the universal sign for secrecy.

"Fortunately," he whispered, in the whisper which was not quite a whisper, "I need not mention your rebuff of me again here, distasteful as it is to you. Rather my embryo congratulations concern you and someone else altogether. That is, I hear from Harry, who heard it no doubt from the mistress of the Tree Inn, who heard it from—but I see you 'sit upon hot cockles' till my tale be told, and I will cut short my ramblings—in brief, they say you grow weary of widowhood and now aim for our new curate."

If she had been tinder she could not have gone up in a more satisfying blaze, and Langworthy did not even try to resist tossing further fuel on the fire.

"No one criticizes you for it, naturally," he resumed. "For thinking him a worthy object, I mean. A prudent and respectable one, despite his—er—seniority and—well—the...extravagance of certain features." (This last he delivered with fingertips splayed by his jaw, like a man trying to remember a word which escaped him, or like a man imitating the wave of luxurious whiskers.)

And though her eyes were fire, Mrs. Sebastian had recovered enough self-command to reply, her voice shaking only the tiniest bit. "I will thank you to tell Harry Barbary and—and—whosoever might follow in that chain of gossip—that I utterly deny making *that person* or, indeed, anyone else my 'object.' It is a complete invention, a fabrication from beginning to end, born of minds which have too little to occupy them, and to say I resent it cannot be stated too strongly. Nor need you shrink back like that, as if you felt the rebuke," she added, her hands clenching and then—with an effort—unclenching, "when you know very well you are enjoying the whole situation."

She had him there.

Because Langworthy was undeniably enjoying the whole situation. Not only for the success of his scheme (he would offer odds to all comers now that she would not accept Rearden if he were the last man on earth), but also because the sight of Mrs. Sebastian ablaze did much to warm the cockles of his heart.

Even better, upon re-entering the dance, when young Miss Maria peered in her sister-in-law's stony face she blurted, "I'm sorry, Sarah! Was your hand supposed to be on top?"

"What? No, dearest, you did nothing," answered Mrs. Sebastian, turning even redder. "It's—a toothache."

But that only made matters worse, Langworthy imagined, for at once the music and dancing halted, and Mrs. Sebastian was engulfed in kindly concern, subjected to a half-dozen questions and a full account from Dr. Rearden of past remedies he had used in his own case, along with their relative efficacy.

Yes, altogether a good day's work, Horace congratulated himself, and he trusted Harry Barbary would keep him apprised of the aftermath.

Whistling merrily as he and Rearden walked back to the rectory with the Tommies, the parson gave him a nudge of the elbow and murmured,

"What did I tell you, Langworthy? Nothing like a change of scenery and new friends to lift the spirits. I'll wager you didn't think once all morning of having a broken heart."

CHAPTER 13

Aye vow and protest that ye care na for me,

And whyles ye may lichtly my beauty a wee;

But court na anither, though jokin' ye be,

For fear that she wyle your fancy frae me,

—Robert Burns, "O Whistle, and I'll Come to You, My Lad"

(1793)

He had not, he realized, thought of his broken heart for some days. But soon enough he had reason to. For the next time Harry Barbary skipped to the rectory, it was a day before he was expected, and he carried an equally unexpected letter.

"From H. Langworthy, Nobbs Lane, Portsmouth," the boy read, dragging a none-too-clean finger across each line of the direction. "That part was plain enough. And so was this 'Mr. H. Langworthy.' But from there things went wrong. Doesn't this look like 'Ilkey' to you? 'Iffley Rectory, Ilkey'? Is there an Ilkey in England, sir?"

"I have no idea," he replied with a grimace, fishing out a coin for Mrs. Lamb the postmistress. "But if there is, I think this letter has been there first. It's from my uncle, you rapscallion. And he's a dry old stick, so there'll be nothing in it to interest you. Be off, and see that Mrs. Lamb gets paid."

Langworthy spoke no more than the truth—his namesake uncle was in truth a dry old stick—but he neglected to add that letters from Horatio Langworthy the elder were rare enough to be noteworthy in themselves, and he quickly slipped away to his room to read this one.

Because of its detour to the possibly-mythical Ilkey, the letter had taken almost a week to reach him. But his uncle, at least, after the equivalent of some preliminary throat-clearing, came straight to the point: "You have been away from Portsmouth nearly three weeks, living among strangers, forgetting your career, and no doubt 'sponging' upon this new curate acquaintance in a way best known only to yourself. I pass over this in silence but feel it my duty to inform you that the town rings with talk of the resumption of hostilities, and some recently come down from London report that the Commons House daily expects a message from the king on the matter. I need not point out that, should you wish to secure another appointment, it would be more easily done in Portsmouth than in some lubberly, landlocked hamlet. Only send word, and a room shall be got ready for you."

His uncle had signed the letter after reading him this lecture, only to add a hurried postscript.

"Before I could send this, I received a most surprising call from Miss Mary Pence, accompanied by some ancient companion who, if she had not been wearing a dress, I would not have known for a female. And, yes, Miss Pence assured me she was still Mary Pence and not yet the bride of Captain Colley. After some beating about the bush, in which I said little and let her die away into silence, she at last said she hoped you were well and expressed surprise that she never chanced to see you at the dockyard or walking the ramparts or even at the garrison chapel on a Sunday. I explained that you had been away visiting a new friend met in London and that I did not know when you would return. This brought on more indirection from her until she could discover this 'new friend' was male and not female and where he and you could be found, and then, finding no more excuse to linger, she and the ancient companion took themselves off. Make of this what you will. H.L."

Here were two pieces of news!

Hostilities expected to break out shortly and Mary Pence still unmarried!

Langworthy read the missive again, his uncle's barbs glancing off him through long practice, but none of the words on the page said anything different the second time.

War imminent.

It had not begun at least while the letter in his hand wandered the kingdom, though perhaps it was that many days nearer.

With a shake of his head, Langworthy set this thought aside for the present because the second loomed larger.

Mary Pence.

Mary Pence, who was still Mary Pence, and not Mary Colley.

She was no fool. With the renewed threat of war, she must have calculated that Langworthy might yet make his fortune; whereas the half pay of one-legged Captain Colley would never be more than that.

For a moment he indulged himself in the vision of arriving back in Portsmouth, commander of a captured French vessel, gold louis d'ors spilling from his pockets to roll and chink in the gutters when he went ashore. An admiral came forth to greet him with the news that he had made post. Mary waved a handkerchief damp with her tears and wailed, "If only I had chosen *you*, Horace!"

It was a fantasy so extravagant even he had to laugh. Very well—the odds of his vision coming true were a hundred to one, but they were not nil.

It was clear what his uncle thought he should do: drop everything in Iffley (all his courting of strangers and his sponging upon the unfortunate

Rearden) and return at once to Portsmouth, there to court instead influential navy people and the still-single Mary Pence.

Solid, sound advice, even if his uncle's manner of imparting it grated upon him.

Yes, indeed. Solid, sound advice.

Then why did he still sit here? Why did he not leap up at once, hallooing out the window for Harry Barbary to take a letter by return post? Why did he not fling open the lid to his trunk and begin to toss things in?

"Portsmouth may expect war to break out any moment," he muttered, "but the fact remains it has not, even here a week later. Would there be any harm in waiting a little longer for the king to address the Commons? If—when—he does, I might return within a day if the announcement comes. And as for Mary..." He stretched his arms up and folded them behind his head to contemplate the ceiling.

As for Mary, if Captain Colley's luster had faded, and she had jilted him, all the better. But would she not think less of him, her former beau, if he were to fly back and throw himself at her feet? Would she not think it was a case of "O whistle and I'll come to you, my lad"?

On the one hand, of course, the business which brought him to Iffley was completed. He had done everything Sebastian Barstow asked of him. He had seen with his own eyes that Barstow's widow and Master Bash were safe and relatively secure. He had gone so far as to make his dutiful offer for Mrs. Sebastian, only to be roundly rejected. He was free to go at any time.

But on the other, knowing Mary's whims, it would be good to hold himself aloof for a spell, during which his absence might continue to make her heart grow fonder.

This latter conclusion agreed with his own desires, it happened. For if he remained in Iffley, he might continue the pleasant activities of giving navigation lessons and of exacting small measures of revenge upon Mrs. Sebastian for her coldness and ingratitude.

No, no—that wasn't right. "Revenge" was too strong a word for his little pranks, he decided. He had merely annoyed her, teased her a little. Touched the invisible fuse of her temper with the match of his mischief and enjoyed the explosions. Explosions he liked all the better for her attempts to hide them.

If he were to leave Iffley now, all this must be given up. And for what? To grovel for Mary Pence's renewed favor? If Mrs. Sebastian had wronged him in small ways, Mary Pence had wronged him in the extreme, for which the best vengeance would be to ignore her. To let her stew in uncertainty. What more could he lose by such a tactic than what he had already deemed lost?

For some minutes the mill-race of his mind ran, with no new revelations breaking upon him, and at last he threw up his hands, rising so suddenly from his chair that it toppled backwards. "We'll leave it to fate," he said aloud. "Unless the king summons us back to war, I will stay in Iffley until the children's ball. Then it's back to Portsmouth for me. And I'll tell Rearden as much."

That quickly, peace settled upon him again. He bent to snatch the overturned chair from the carpet and set it upright, unconsciously beginning to hum "O Whistle and I'll Come to You, My Lad."

A two-minute walk from the rectory, Mrs. Markham Dere was calling at Iffley Cottage to discuss the selfsame children's ball, completely unaware of how near she came to losing one of its chief attractions.

"It may be a children's ball, but I intend it to be a glittering affair," she declared. "I have told the housekeeper Robson to hire and train a few additional footmen wherever she can find them and to purchase cakes and other refreshments from Oxford."

Frances clapped her hands, and Maria gasped at the notion of boughten sweets, but Mrs. Barstow regarded her doubtfully. "Mrs. Dere, it sounds delightful, and we very much look forward to it, but are you certain you must go to all this trouble when we have already informally gathered twice to practice?"

Mrs. Dere drew herself up. "Of *course* you don't suppose the ball will only be us and the rectory people, Mrs. Barstow?"

"Won't it, though?" asked Frances. "For a children's ball, it's already more grown-ups than children, but what other children are there in Iffley to invite?"

"Harry Barbary," suggested Maria with a giggle. "And Jimmy and Anna Cramthorpe."

But Mrs. Dere turned a quelling eye on the girl, and Maria shrank under it. "There will be no mixing of classes at the Perryfield children's ball, Miss Maria. But as we certainly would like to have at least a few more children than adults, I have spoken with Mrs. Lane and Mrs. Chauncey, and both of them say they would be pleased to summon a few grandchildren—only those well able to dance, naturally—and Mrs. Chauncey also suggested she might accompany us, that I might dance. Therefore I count at least nineteen or twenty people, depending on the grandchildren, which means we certainly must do the thing right."

Although Frances and Maria, greatly excited by the increased numbers, peppered Mrs. Dere with additional questions and remarks, and Mrs. Barstow asked what Iffley Cottage might contribute to the food or decorations, Sarah said nothing. She continued with the work in her lap, countenance serene but mind busy. And just as Horace Langworthy's thoughts had gone swift as horses that morning, so too did hers.

It was good, very good, that the children's ball would be crowded. More people would mean a greater variety of partners, and a greater variety of partners would mean fewer chances of being paired with Mr. Langworthy. Better yet, it being a children's ball, Sarah would be free to approach all the children and ask them to stand up with her, which meant she might even escape dancing with the man altogether, unless he made an effort to snap her up.

Would he?

Most likely he would.

Because, for whatever reason, pique or pride, ennui or entertainment of time, above all activities Mr. Langworthy delighted in nettling her.

Feeling the needle prick as she drew it through the muslin in her hands, she hastily put the wounded fingertip to her tongue, lest any blood fall upon the cloth.

Yes—he delighted in nettling her. And if Sarah were to give any appearance of avoiding him at the ball, it doubtless would only make him the more determined. Therefore that scheme must be abandoned. She would neither seek him nor flee him. If a child was at hand, she would ask the child to dance, but if not, she would not run after one only to escape Langworthy.

Moreover, her original plan, of pretending his words had no power to rankle, had failed thus far.

Completely.

She knew it and so did he. And each time he succeeded in vexing her, he gained even more the whip hand.

She must try another method.

"...At the very least I hope the children will gain new friends," Mrs. Markham Dere was saying. "When the time comes for university or entering more widely in society, friends prove invaluable."

Frances heaved a sigh. "Mrs. Lane and Mrs. Chauncey didn't mention having any older granddaughters, did they? Sarah and Maria are all very well, but I wouldn't mind making a friend my age."

"Have patience, my dear," their patroness smiled upon her. "I may not be your age, but I am your staunch friend and will do what I can when it comes time for you to take a larger share in the world."

"When will that be, I wonder?" Frances might have rapped back, had Mrs. Dere indeed been her age (or had she not considered her more of a benefactress than friend). But knowing on what side her bread was buttered, Frances refrained, and the call soon came to a close.

Mrs. Dere's words had given Sarah a new idea, however. And one which made her rather eager to see Mr. Langworthy again than otherwise. For supposing she were to befriend him? If he could be persuaded to consider her a friend, would he not then leave off his constant picking at her? He did not appear to spend time picking at Dr. Rearden, for instance, nor at any of the boys in his charge. And if Sarah could make a friend of him, would that not equally satisfy the pique or pride or ennui or need for entertainment which at present drove him to act as he did?

Yes. It might.

It *must.*

"Would anyone like to go for a walk before dinner?" Sarah suggested some time later. Her new plan made her restless, and she could only think she must see Mr. Langworthy as soon as she could, to put it into practice.

Frances made a face. "But it's raining!"

Maria likewise shook her head. "Didn't you hear Mama promise Mrs. Dere a jelly for the ball? I want to help her and Reed make the trial one."

"We may as well take advantage of the cold weather," Mrs. Barstow agreed. "We can see how it keeps overnight in the shed. Mrs. Glasse in her *Art of Cookery* has a receipt for a 'French Flummery' I would like to try."

"Oh, Mama," protested Maria, "mightn't we put a little of it aside in a glass to eat with our tea this evening?"

Laughing, Mrs. Barstow yielded. "You assume it will be worth eating, dearest. But better we learn now, than I bring a disaster to the children's ball to set beside the other sweets. You won't mind walking alone, will you Sarah? Take the umbrella and no one will trouble you."

No one would trouble her, but neither could she pay a call at the rectory by herself. Still, perhaps Mr. Langworthy might take it into his head to go for a walk, and a serendipitous meeting would be the best beginning.

If Mr. Langworthy had any such thought, however, he sensibly did not act upon it, for it was wet and slippery out of doors, with just enough wind that Sarah's umbrella threatened to turn inside out more than once. She made a circle of the village, keeping away from the muddy meadows and fields and creeping the length of Church Lane, but there was no sign of him. Indeed, the only person Sarah met was Mrs. Lamb, who spied her passing the Tree Inn and darted out to greet her, a newspaper held over her head.

"Good day to you, Mrs. Sebastian. Imagine you taking a walk on a day such as this! Why don't you step inside for a cup of tea? I can tell you the news about the footmen and Mr. Langworthy's letter."

All unknowingly, Mrs. Lamb had said the magic word, and, mumbling something about warming herself by the inn fire for a minute, Sarah followed her within. As soon as Mrs. Lamb ushered her into the coziest parlor and shouted for Harry to bring a cup of tea, the hostess drew up a chair beside Sarah's, fairly quivering with eagerness.

"What a treat, Mrs. Sebastian! I so rarely see any of you Iffley Cottage ladies by yourselves, and when I do, my hands are full and there is no time for a comfortable coze. But with this rain—!"

Sarah knew she need not prompt her hostess; Mrs. Lamb could be depended on to divulge whatever she had to share, but she still had to bite her lip lest she ask, "What was that letter you mentioned?"

Mrs. Lamb considered the letter of secondary importance, unfortunately, for she began with, "I suspect you know about Mrs. Markham Dere wanting a couple more footmen because Mrs. Robson came from Perryfield while her mistress was calling upon you Barstows."

"Yes, she did say—"

"And wouldn't you know it, but Mrs. Robson had no better sense than to tell me this when that dratted Harry was loitering about, so of course after she goes he straight off tells me he wants to be one of the footmen, and he can do it because Mr. Langworthy has been showing him servants' tasks. As if blacking the sailor's boots and brushing his coats and polishing his tinware would be any preparation for donning livery and waiting upon the baron and his niece at Perryfield!"

"I could do it!" came a bellow, the parlor door banging open to reveal Harry, Sarah's tea spilling from the cup he carried. "Mr. Langworthy said I do a good job for him, and Mrs. Robson said they want two or three fellows, and I don't see why I can't be one of them, if you don't go crying me down to her."

"Look at you, boy, and the mess you're making! Give me that—" Mrs. Lamb snatched the tea from him and presented it with a grimace to Sarah without even pausing in her scolding "—And wipe this up. Mrs. Robson said nothing about wanting any shabby little footboys, so you just put that out of your mind."

Harry glowered at his employer as he dashed at the floor with a rag, and then he jumped to his feet and stamped away, slamming the door after him.

"Lordy Lordy," groaned Mrs. Lamb, applying two fingers to her temples. "He'll be the death of me, you mark my words."

"*Will* there be any difficulty in finding Mrs. Dere additional footmen, do you think?" asked Sarah.

"Oh, I do hope not. Mrs. Robson sent a message to her cousin at the Angel Inn, to see if he knows of anyone, but with the Hilary term under way I suppose they're already using everyone they know of. But I'll close the inn and serve 'em myself before I let the likes of Harry Barbary run wild there."

"I suppose Mr. Langworthy must…think more highly of him than you do," suggested Sarah.

"Pah! What's that to do with it? I can promise you Mrs. Markham Dere holds to higher standards than a navy lieutenant, though he seems a pleasant man. It don't matter anyhow because he got a letter from his uncle, and Harry said he looked right stern about it. Wouldn't be a bit surprised if Mr. Langworthy had to quit Iffley even before the ball took place. Poor folk are ever at the beck and call of those with money," she sighed. "Ay, it's the way of the world. Oh, but I forgot he was a special friend of your husband's, wasn't he? Still, there's no denying he's yet to rise as high as he probably hopes to—what—wait—must you go so soon, Mrs. Sebastian?"

"I had better," said Sarah, setting her cup down and reaching for her umbrella. "They will wonder what became of me. Thank you, though. Could you please add this to the Iffley Cottage account, Mrs. Lamb?"

"Add it to the account? This?" sputtered the good lady. "There's no charge for this cup, Mrs. Sebastian. This was a friendly visit. My compliments to your family—oh! How quickly you young people zip about. Good-bye! Good-bye!"

CHAPTER 14

Bid her have good heart:
She soon shall know of us, by some of ours,
How honourable and how kindly we
Determine for her; for Caesar cannot live
To be ungentle.
—Shakespeare, *Antony and Cleopatra* (c.1607)

Sarah received nothing for her walk in the rain apart from a bad cold, which confined her to her room, to be sustained by Mrs. Barstow's (successful) jelly and occasional sips of broth.

"You're awake! Hurrah!" cried Frances on the fourth day, when she entered with a tray to find her sister-in-law pale and tousled but blinking at her. "Everyone will be glad to hear it."

"What day is it?" It emerged as a croak.

"Monday. You've missed our final dance lesson—Tommy Wardour was as disastrous as the first day and had to be paired with Mr. Langworthy throughout, for everyone's safety—and then you missed church and a half-dozen callers. The Deres, of course, and the Lanes and the Chaunceys. And then Dr. Rearden and Mr. Langworthy came yesterday afternoon."

Still drowsy, Sarah yawned and murmured, "He was in my dream."

"Who was? Did you have a nightmare about Dr. Rearden smothering you in his whiskers. Because when I peeped in once, you were tangled in the coverlet, and your forehead hot."

"No. No, it was—the other one. Mr. Langworthy. He was—on a ship." As full consciousness returned, she just managed not to add, *He was sailing away, and I felt...bereft.*

"Isn't that curious," said Frances, "because sadly he very soon *will* be on a ship, he says. Or at least he hopes so. His uncle writes that the country—and the navy—must prepare again for renewed hostilities, so Mr. Langworthy says he will likely go again shortly after the children's ball." She lowered her voice conspiratorially. "Mama shed a few tears about it—I think she wished he might stay for much longer—so please don't mention his departure, if you can help it."

Sarah shook her head weakly, grateful that any tears which inexplicably threatened her own eyes would be attributed to her cold.

But Frances was too preoccupied to notice and fairly buzzed with eagerness. "How do you feel? Do you think you could sit up and take something? Mama says you will get better ten times faster with something substantial in you. And I have a full budget of news which I am dying to share, if your head doesn't ache too much to hear it."

"Help me sit up, and I will eat and hear your budget," replied Sarah. "Where is Bash? Can you call him to join us?"

"That is the first item I have for you, I'm sorry to say. I'm afraid Bash has caught your cold. No—don't try to get up—he's a good, strong boy, and Mr. Travers has already seen him and says his fever is so slight he expects it will be altogether gone tomorrow. Mama has taken him into her room, where he has been sleeping as much as you have, and we have all been peeping in at him and hovering over him as much as even you could."

Even if Sarah didn't believe her, her effort to rise was so unsuccessful that Frances easily pushed her back.

"Oh," Sarah sighed, "but I would feel better if I could see him."

"You will, you will, if you will only eat and drink and not tax yourself," insisted Frances. "And you simply must get better because you are already going to miss something today, and I don't want you to miss another tomorrow."

Dutifully, Sarah took hold of the teacup and managed a sip. "What am I going to miss today?"

Frances gave a delighted wriggle. "Why, Della invited us all to Keele's this afternoon because the pupils have prepared speeches and scenes from *Antony and Cleopatra*! Mr. Weatherill thought it would lighten the winter days and bring alive both their Latin studies and Mr. Keele's Egyptian stories."

Sarah almost wailed. "That's for today? I should very much like to go. What time is it? Perhaps if I dress very warmly—"

"Pooh! And make yourself sick again? You know nobody would let you. But I promise Maria and Gordy and I will do our best to reproduce it all for you later. Besides, if it is a wild success, they might even be persuaded to recite again."

"Is everybody going? Surely the Deres are, to see Peter." What Sarah meant, if she would only admit it to herself, was, *Were the rectory people invited?*

"Certainly the Deres will be there," answered Frances. "They're coming in the coach for us. But I don't know who else. I suppose whichever of the pupils' families are nearby."

Despite her disappointment at missing the performance, Sarah had no difficulty attacking her toast. She found she was ravenous. "Very well," she said, covering her mouth with her hand while she chewed, "that is the thing I must miss today. What is the other? The one tomorrow? I refuse to be deprived of it, even if you must wheel me there in a chair."

Frances clapped her hands and bounced on the bed as if she were as young as Maria. "Mrs. Dere has invited us to dinner tomorrow!"

"What's so wondrous about that? We go all the time. I would far rather miss *that* and see the Keele's pupils instead."

"It's not any old dinner," protested Frances. "It's a *special* one."

Remembering Mr. Langworthy's announcement that he would leave Iffley soon, a fear clutched Sarah. Could it be a farewell dinner? One they must have now, if he were to leave directly following the ball?

Frances soon relieved her. "It's a special dinner because Mrs. Robson's cousin at the Angel Inn has sent Mrs. Dere the two new footmen for the ball! And he told her—Mrs. Robson's cousin told Mrs. Robson—that they will have to do at this short notice because he can't spare anyone, and she should consider herself fortunate that these two recently applied to the Inn for employment. But Mrs. Dere declares they are raw and unskillful, and she suspects neither one has ever been in service before, despite the glowing testimonials they presented, which she thinks must surely be forged!. She says she dare not let them serve at the children's ball unless they have proper training. So we are going to dine there tomorrow, to give them practice!"

Sarah laughed at this, and Frances was glad to see some color return to her face. "Only you could think it delightful, Frances, to be the subject of Mrs. Dere's experiment! All it means is that we will likely have soup spilled upon us, or those of us at one end of the table will not taste the dishes at the other until they are cold."

"Pooh!" said Frances again. "It will be amusing, and it cannot be that hard for them to learn service, or why would Mr. Langworthy say he thinks Harry Barbary already acquits himself well? When we told Mr. Langworthy yesterday about Mrs. Dere's plans, he said she would do better to enlist Harry than two incompetent strangers, even if Harry is only eight or so. But you know Mrs. Dere will never hear of it, be the strangers ever so incompetent."

Her first meal in days gave Sarah enough energy to dress and come down, where she was fussed over, asked solicitous questions, and re-told Frances' news a few times. But when she had assured herself Bash was on the mend, she let them place her before the fire, with blankets tucked about and books near at hand, and promptly nodded off the moment the family had gone.

A soft scratching awoke her.

Blinking slowly, she noted the winter sunlight had grown fainter, and Reed must have come in at some point to light the lamps.

The scratching continuing, Sarah shifted, leaning past the wing of the chairback to discover its source.

And there at the little desk sat Horace Langworthy, of all people, his pen scratching as he wrote!

She must have made a sound because he looked up.

"Ah. You are awake." Gesturing before him, he added, "Reed said you were sleeping, and I didn't want to disturb you, so I was writing you a note."

For the second time that day, she spoke without thinking. "I hear you are going."

"Going where?"

"Going—leaving Iffley. Frances said—" she broke off, conscious of her face warming. Swallowing, she changed the subject. "Er—what are you writing?"

He stood, sliding Mrs. Barstow's dainty chair back in and holding up the sheet of paper. "'Mrs. Sebastian,'" he read, tucking the other hand in his waistcoat and throwing back his shoulders as if he were a candidate delivering a speech, "'I am glad to hear you are feeling more the thing and—'"

Her lips twitched in spite of herself. "And...?" she prompted.

"And...that's as far as I got."

Then Sarah did laugh, eliciting that boyish grin from him.

"Would you like anything, Mrs. Sebastian? I can call the maid. A cup of tea, perhaps? Or the fire built up?"

"Thank you, no." Then, with an effort she forced down her shyness to say, "I am surprised to see you. I thought you might be in Oxford." She blushed because that sounded like she had been thinking of him and picturing where he might be. "Er—that is—I thought everyone was gone to Oxford this afternoon. For the students reciting Shakespeare. The Keele's students, I mean. But—er—obviously not. Because here you are. Won't you—won't you sit down and—chat with me?"

Her babbling received the punishment it deserved, for he lifted one eyebrow in the teasing way she had come to expect. (*As if I had said something quite improper!*) Then, tossing aside the unfinished note, he took hold of the nearest chair, placed it directly opposite hers, and dropped into it.

"Chat with you? If you insist, Mrs. Sebastian."

Here we go again, she thought, bristling at the word "insist." *He picks at me, and I respond.*

But this time she flattened her palms against her lap, the wool blanket tickling her skin. This time she was determined to change the tune of their conversation. *If he intends to leave after the children's ball, I will not let any hard feelings remain between us. We will part as friends. Not only for Sebastian's sake, but for our own.*

For the sake of the living.

And if this *rapprochement* were to take place, she must begin it at once because so little time and opportunity was left! Whether he had vexed her first or she him did not matter—if it could even possibly have been determined or agreed upon.

She folded her hands, the fingers of the left invisibly clutching the thumb of her right. "Mr. Langworthy," Sarah uttered, "perhaps 'chat' isn't exactly what I mean. In fact, I know it isn't. I wouldn't ask you to 'chat' with me, much less insist you do so. What I wanted to say was that—"

She faltered as his eyes narrowed in curiosity. Or puzzlement. Or both. Then, with another swallow, she pushed ahead. "Ahem. What I wanted to say was that I—owe you an apology."

When he straightened in his chair, blinking rapidly, Sarah felt a dart of pleasure. Ha! For once *she* had caught *him* off guard.

"I cannot think what for," he answered warily.

His trepidation contrarily gave her confidence. So much so that she would have patted his knee, if it had been permissible. "Because, Mr. Langworthy, you did not need to come and see Bash and me, but you did. And you certainly did not need to offer to tie yourself to us for the rest of your life, but you did. My husband Sebastian never spoke to me of any of this—his...the demands he placed upon you—which means no one but yourself would have known if you had chosen to ignore his requests. But you did not choose to. Never mind that what he asked of you was so...excessive. So unreasonable. Therefore, I apologize. Because I was...affronted. Short with you. When really it was Sebastian who lay at the bottom of it all. Sebastian, who should have been the object of my anger. I vented my feelings on you, however. And therefore I was dismissive of your offer, instead of recognizing what it must have cost you."

She had practiced this speech in her mind—before she caught cold, at least—until she could deliver it thus, without qualifications and with evident sincerity.

A silence fell, one so complete that even the fire refrained from crackling, and no sounds carried to them from either kitchen or street. Throughout it, Mr. Langworthy stared so long into the uncrackling fire, his brow furrowed and eyes in shadow, that Sarah began to doubt herself. Had she accidentally said more than she intended to? Had she interpolated something which he received with offense?

She could not guess that her companion's reserve stemmed from his own mental struggle. For he was like a fencer who stood with foil upraised, expecting to ward off a thrust to the head, only to have his opponent slip beneath his guard and pierce his heart.

For she *had* pierced it. With her honesty. With her clear, frank gaze. With her willingness to humble herself.

She asked for his pardon, as if he had not himself, at every opportunity, done what he could to vex her. To repay her for her rejection.

A hit, Langworthy. A very palpable hit.

What else could he call it, when she proved herself the more generous person? The better person?

At last he turned to look at her again, and Sarah could not tell if he flushed, or if it was merely the reflection of the fire which made his face glow.

"Mrs. Sebastian," he said, in a gentle voice she had never heard from him before. "You quite shame me."

Her eyes widened and lips parted. "Shame you? Sir, that was not my intention."

"Of course it was not, which is precisely why I am ashamed. I have behaved badly to you."

"Mr. Langworthy!" Sarah breathed, her hand lifting—again with that urge to touch him, heaven help her! She let it drop back to her lap. "If you think to beg *my* pardon, which it certainly sounds like you are about to, I must insist you wait your turn."

"Very well," he agreed hurriedly. "If you persist in thinking it necessary, I admit I did come away from our first interview with my self-regard bruised—"

"Yes," she agreed. "I was quite curt with you."

"—So I accept your apology and thank you for it. But, Mrs. Sebastian, I hardly offered for you in a winning manner. In fact, I suspect, had I asked a dozen ladies to marry me that day in the way I asked you, not a one of them would have treated me differently."

To their mutual surprise, she chuckled. "Indeed, if there had been a dozen ladies and they knew of each other, they might have treated you more and more shabbily as the day went on. Because worse than being someone's second choice for a bride is being someone's third or fourth or twelfth."

"While I did arrive in Iffley embittered over Miss Pence's defection, it is not true that you were a *second* choice, Mrs. Sebastian."

"You are very right, Mr. Langworthy," she answered, "for one would be hard put to call me your 'choice' at all. If you only knew the scold I would like to give Sebastian over the whole matter! Never mind my personal feelings, to discover he 'assigned' me to another—but to be *you* would be even worse! To be the person so peremptorily saddled with someone else's wife and child!"

"No, no, I must contradict you there," he returned, beginning to smile. "Considering how often and how tiresomely he boasted of you, I am certain he thought he was doing me the greatest of favors."

Something odd was happening to Sarah's insides, something between a tremor and a flutter, and it was not only from hearing that Sebastian had been so proud of her. If only it were! But no, she feared Mr. Langworthy's charming grin also played a part, and that suspicion made the trembling grow.

To her dismay, an involuntary sound escaped her throat, which she instantly exaggerated into a cough, taking refuge in her handkerchief and thanking Providence for her recent cold.

He did not wait for her to quieten before saying, "Villain that I am, I will take ruthless advantage of your incapacity to argue my point again. Mrs. Sebastian, having granted you your share of the blame in our earlier estrangement, I pray you will do as much for me. As I was saying, I behaved badly on that occasion. When you made me understand you did not share

Barstow's...vision for the future, I'm afraid I thought myself ill-used. I did not ask myself if it was unjust to resent you, whom I knew not at all, and who did not know me, or if I came to Iffley already predisposed for resentment, having been cast off by one who had given me her word and whom I had known half my life."

"Oh, Mr. Langworthy," said Sarah helplessly, "I am sorry for it. For your broken engagement."

But this made his eyes gleam in amusement. "There! What are you doing? You've apologized again, when we agreed it was my turn."

"Well, what am I to do, I would like to know, if you insist on telling me such a pathetic story?" she heard herself say teasingly. But as soon as she spoke, awareness checked her again. What was happening? When she decided she must defend herself from Mr. Langworthy by befriending him, she had not supposed she might actually begin to like him. (Never mind that everyone except she herself already liked him.) And she most certainly never dreamed she would say anything to him in what some might deem a flirtatious tone. Had Frances been there to hear, for one, Sarah had no doubt Frances would call it flirtatious.

Heavens.

"Are you finished with your apology, that I might accept it?" she blurted.

"Quite finished," he replied with mock meekness.

"Good. There. That's done, then. You have forgiven me, and I have forgiven you, and we may now drop the subject of who wronged whom."

"And become fast friends," he suggested. "Which, if not the blissful union your husband hoped for us, would surely strike him as the next best thing."

Fast friends? This caused another terrible ripple through her midsection, and it must have been self-disgust at this which prompted her to say, "Mm. Then, as one of my first acts of friendship, Mr. Langworthy, I wonder if it might ease your heart a little to—speak of Miss Pence. She must have been—must be, rather, a—remarkable creature."

"Remarkable, yes," echoed Langworthy, a shadow crossing his features. "Mary Pence. Spritely. Mischievous. Dainty."

So much for Sarah's regrettable flutter. It smothered under the weight of these adjectives, for it would be difficult to think of three words less applicable to herself. But why should that matter? Why should it matter if, in comparison, Mr. Langworthy must find her spiritless, dull, and, if not oversized, certainly not "dainty."

It did not matter.

It should not.

"She was as quick and changeable as...as the flames here," he continued. "One never knew what she would do next."

"Even after knowing her half your life?" asked Sarah. "You still found her so? But I suppose that is because you did not predict she would break her engagement to you. Her letters gave no hint of it, perhaps."

This drew a grimace. "She was not the most reliable correspondent. No, Mrs. Sebastian, when I say we knew each other half our lives, that would be as years are reckoned. But if you added, end to end, the hours we have spent in the same place in all those years, it would be less. Much less. You, of all people, will understand, having been married to Barstow and knowing how often and for how long he was away."

"Yes. I do understand that."

He rose restlessly to poke at the Mary-Pence-like fire. "Nor have her surprises ended with our engagement."

"No?" prompted Sarah, when he did not continue.

Jabbing at the log, he broke it into glowing embers. "No. For my uncle tells me she has not yet married the one-legged captain."

She could only look inquiringly at him as her throat seemed to close up. Thank heavens he was not looking at her!

"She was asking about me, it seems."

"Oh!" Her mouth formed the word, though no sound emerged. Sarah Barstow and Mary Pence might be chalk and cheese, but Sarah was woman enough to understand all: Mary Pence had changed her mind. Mary Pence had come to her senses and wanted her dashing betrothed back.

Well, then.

Perhaps it was his stirring of the fire, but all at once the world was with them again. The fire crackled; Reed murmured to Irving in the kitchen and set something heavy down; sheep baaed outside in the lane, following the hollow-clanking bellwether. And reality punctured the quiet little bubble which had contained them.

"I had better be going," he said reluctantly, rising to his feet. "This has been a long call (and a worthwhile one), but I would not be much of a new friend to you if the first thing I did was to start tongues wagging."

Sarah gave herself a mental shake. He was going? But—

But before she allowed him to, she would say what was right to be said, once and once only, cost what it might. And it would cost, now that she had seen a little way into her own unreasoning heart. Yet if she were truly his friend, she could not leave it unsaid. Sebastian would not have, in her place.

"A moment, Mr. Langworthy," she breathed. "One word in parting—"

"You may have as many as you like, Mrs. Sebastian."

"You—asked me once for advice, though you did it in jest, I know. That is, you asked me how you might increase your chances of having your offers of marriage accepted…"

"Just one," he chuckled softly. "One acceptance would suffice."

"Yes. Well. Then, now that we are friends, I am prepared to give you that advice." She was on her feet as well now and took a deep breath, one hand pressed to her midsection. "I advise you to…put aside your pride. If Miss

Pence has—repented—of jilting you, forgive her as you have forgiven me and go back for her. Why would you tarry here?"

"Why? I—have my obligations," he muttered. His gaze raked her and then flicked away.

"None that you would not be excused from, if you explained," she pressed. "You will regret it if you do not go. People can be lost, Mr. Langworthy. I speak from experience, as you know. Love can be lost. Do not let yours be."

Again his eyes met hers, and again he looked away.

She thought he might speak, but he did not.

With a last nod, he saw himself out.

CHAPTER 15

FOOTMAN WANTED in a Gentleman's Family, A steady Man. He must have been used to waiting at table, and the business of a family.
—Advertisement, *Ipswich Journal* (1795)

Sanity returned with the rest of the Barstows, and Sarah thanked heaven they were so full of enthusiasm for *Antony and Cleopatra* that her mention of Mr. Langworthy's call elicited no more than a sighing "I'm sorry to have missed him, when time is so short" from Mrs. Barstow.

"I *told* you not to remind her!" Frances hissed, widening her eyes at Sarah behind Mrs. Barstow's back before saying loudly, "You should have heard Gordy recite Enobarbus' speech about 'the chair she sat in like a burnished throne,' Sarah! It was far better than that little boy what's-his-name squeaking, 'Let Rome in Tiber melt.'"

Sarah of course prevailed upon Gordon to repeat his triumph, and Mr. Langworthy was safely forgotten.

Except by Sarah.

It doesn't matter, she told herself as she fell asleep that night. *It doesn't matter if I think now I might have learned to like him well enough to—*

Well enough to marry him? replied the darkness.

It did not matter.

He would be going soon. By the children's ball, or even sooner, if he took her words to heart.

Though the following day was dry and clear and Sarah another day better, Lord Dere would not hear of them walking to Perryfield and sent his coach. At the foot of the baron's note Mrs. Dere added in her elegant hand: "Please pay no particular attention to the new footmen, but rather treat them exactly as you would Wood or any of the others."

"That's like being told not to look at a person," remarked Frances. "What can one do then but look right at him?"

"And Peter says they're perfect bunglers," put in Gordon, "which makes me especially want to look."

Her thoughts elsewhere, Sarah alone was uninterested in the new servants, but when the coachman Ogle helped her descend at the great house, his muttered "Ah, Lord a mercy" caused her to glance at him and then to follow his gaze to the front door being opened. A head poked around it, which was the next instant whipped away again, to be replaced by Wood the footman, his usual impassive countenance marred by a cross expression.

When the Barstows entered, Wood's stiff bow and pressed lips made it impossible not to peep at the two apprentices he had been assigned. They wore livery as he did, wigs as he did, but they could not have looked less like him. One was tall and stooped and ancient, with a square, slack face, and Sarah could only wonder at such an aged person still needing to learn the duties of a footboy. He must be incompetent indeed. The second was as young and lithe as the first was old and decrepit, and in him Sarah recognized the pert features which had first peeked around the front door. Pert features dominated by two pale eyes as keen as ever Harry Barbary's had been. Could he possibly be a relation?

"Wrigley and Blodgett," grunted Wood. Not bothering to indicate which was Wrigley and which Blodgett, nor waiting for the infirm one to creak upward from his bow, Wood stamped past both, leading the Barstows to the drawing room.

"Mrs. Sebastian, how good to see you up and about again," Mrs. Markham Dere greeted her. "We feared your illness would prevent you attending the children's ball, and you were much missed as a partner at our last dancing lesson."

"Thank you, madam. I am glad not to miss the ball."

"We missed your gracefulness," spoke up Lord Dere, when he saw that his niece considered her show of concern complete. "Perhaps Mr. Langworthy in particular, since poor Tommy Wardour's feet seemed beyond the boy's ability to control, and our naval friend bore the brunt of them."

"If we were learning clog dancing, Tommy would excel," joked Frances.

"Why, Uncle, you speak as if Mr. Langworthy were Mrs. Sebastian's particular friend," said Mrs. Dere with a brittle laugh, "instead of being a friend of *all* the Barstows. Besides, whatever Mr. Langworthy's sufferings, they are nearly at an end." Regarding Sarah with a thin smile, she added, "I'm certain your family has told you, Mrs. Sebastian, that we are soon to lose the man back to Portsmouth?"

Sarah bowed her head in acknowledgement but was spared making a response by the younger footboy suddenly giving a shriek and beginning to dance about the room, as if inspired by the idea of Tommy Wardour clog dancing.

"He's caught fire!" cried Gordon and Peter in unison, while Maria screamed and pointed helpfully at the tail of the footboy's coat.

In a blur both Wood and the baron sprang forward, but Wood seized the little fireplace broom first and laid about him until the footboy was flattened on the carpet, wig askew and posterior extinguished.

"Little fool!" hissed Wood. "What did I say about standing further to the side?"

"Now, now, Wood," soothed Lord Dere, "he has already received his punishment, in mortification, if not injury. You all right there, young Wrigley?"

On the contrary, young Wrigley looked about to burst into tears, but he managed to unscrew his features enough to squeak, "Yes, milord." Clambering to his feet, he gave his wig a tug to straighten it, covering a stripe of ginger hair.

The kindly baron took pity on the unfortunate lad and stepped in front of him to block him from view of the gathering. "Mrs. Sebastian, did you make Gordon give you his Enobarbus speech yesterday? It was very well done, indeed. Quite the hit—"

"As was Peter's delivery of Octavius' 'She shall be buried by her Antony,'" interposed Mrs. Dere.

"Very true, Alice," he agreed. "Both boys did marvelously."

"I would have liked to see them at Keele's," Sarah answered. "Gordon did recite for me later, and perhaps I might prevail on you too, Peter, after dinner?"

Peter agreed, of course, and Mrs. Dere was appeased, and Wrigley the footboy had time to recover (if one ignored the occasional gulping and sniffling heard during the pauses) before Wood led him and Blodgett away to carry up the dinner, but then Sarah was sorry to see the subject of Mr. Langworthy renewed. In fact, she somehow found herself on contested ground, with the baron inexplicably wanting to talk up the wonders of the man to her and Mrs. Dere equally determined to take him down a peg.

"It is too bad Mr. Langworthy will leave us soon, or we might have managed some theatricals at Perryfield," began Lord Dere when they were seated for dinner. There being only eight of them, the leaves of the mahogany table had been stowed, and it was possible—indeed, inevitable—to hold one general conversation.

"I don't see what his presence or absence would have to do with it, Uncle," returned Mrs. Dere. "It is not as if he performed at Keele's."

"But he might indulge us in a private setting if we proposed it," said the baron. "And he is such a talented fellow that we would all enjoy it. I can vouch that even Langworthy's reading of the nautical almanac holds everyone's attention, wouldn't you agree, Peter and Gordon?"

The boys nodded vigorously, Peter adding, "He's splendid! I wish we could go back to sea with him."

"And I!" chimed in Gordon, "if only for a little bit, to test what we are learning."

"So that we might take readings and chart our course accordingly." Peter's chin lifted as he employed his teacher's terminology.

"And have a limb blown off for your troubles, should your ship come under attack?" demanded Mrs. Dere.

Here the poor footboy Wrigley, who had been assigned the position behind Mrs. Dere's chair, dropped the cover to the soup tureen. It hit the floor with a hollow *dong!* before rolling away into the corner, Wrigley scrambling after.

Mrs. Dere shut her eyes briefly, leaving it to Wood to scowl at the hapless lad while the cadaverous Blodgett creaked forward with the fish, his knees popping like musketry fire.

"None of Mr. Langworthy's limbs have been blown off," objected Peter.

"*Yet*," retorted his mother ominously.

The baron hastened to recall their attention. "Mrs. Sebastian, you see how fortunate it was for us, that your late husband's friendship with Mr. Langworthy brought him to Iffley. And if Mr. Sebastian Barstow was at all like him, they must have been quite the pair."

With all eyes upon her, Sarah was forced to reply. "For years I only knew of Mr. Langworthy from Sebastian's letters, but my husband made him out to be a—memorable character. I have been glad finally to make his acquaintance for myself."

"Sarah has such an even disposition that his coming has not ruffled her, but I cannot say the same for myself," said Mrs. Barstow, one hand to her bosom. "For me it has been a true comfort and pleasure to become acquainted with him, and I wish he might stay in Iffley forever! I grieve this terrible war which threatens again."

"This 'terrible war' might be the means of making his fortune," Mrs. Dere answered briskly. "And you ought therefore to be pleased for him, Mrs. Barstow, for there's no denying he's otherwise penniless and without prospects."

Sarah's face darkened. Apparently in Mr. Langworthy's case, Mrs. Dere thought the chances of gaining prize money at sea outweighed the cost of possible death or dismemberment! Thus provoked, all the even disposition in the world could not stop her then from leaning around Wrigley, who was ladling soup into her bowl, to say, "I share Mrs. Barstow's regret, Mrs. Dere. Though—though I have not known Mr. Langworthy long *in person*, I—feel what I have learned of him only—accords with my late husband's high opinion. And though I wish him fortune for his own sake, the price at which it may come—that is, the loss of life or limb—strikes me as—as far too high."

She was certain she went all over crimson as she spoke, as if she had blazoned her newfound fondness for the man in the public square, but fortunately the baron read her outburst differently.

"Of course you feel that way," he soothed in his gentle tones. "How could it be otherwise, when your husband was already called upon to pay the highest price? There is Christian resignation, but one could hardly welcome being called upon to practice it again."

He neither addressed nor looked at his niece as he said this, but she must have received it as a reproof, for Mrs. Dere swelled like a toad, setting down her spoon and almost roaring, "Watch what you're doing there, boy!"

Boy?

Sarah's confusion was dispelled the next instant when Wrigley dropped the ladle he was holding, spraying droplets over the cloth, and having already dribbled soup from the tureen to Sarah's dish.

Wood lunged forward with apologies and a towel from the sideboard. "Take the covers to the kitchen and don't return until you can pay proper attention to your tasks!" he growled at Wrigley, a command the boy obeyed with alacrity, but in the speed of his flight he clumsily juggled the soup and fish covers so that they clattered like castanets.

Maria's and Gordon's shoulders were shaking with suppressed mirth by this point, a shaking which increased in violence when Blodgett (who had continued to serve out the fish, oblivious to everything around him) reached Sarah's place and, with a wet slap, deposited the fish head on her plate.

Mrs. Dere sighed. "It is enough to make one despair."

"At least the children's ball will be a buffet of cold foods," Frances tried to comfort her, "with no waiting at table nor covers to remove. I myself would be happy to make the tea. The—er—new servants will only need to clean and polish before and after, and perhaps take charge of the wraps and hats and such."

"They might have to answer the door," suggested Maria.

"And take away the dirty dishes," added Gordon. "Without dropping them."

"But we will all be friends gathered, my dear Alice," the baron reassured her.

Rubbing at her temples, Mrs. Dere said only, "At this rate I might as well have enlisted Harry Barbary."

The rest of the dinner passed off without mishap. Wrigley returned, if not chastened, at least making no more loud mistakes; Wood directed and corrected with subtle tilts of the head, grimaces, and lifted fingertips; Blodgett shuffled around wearily.

And it might have been Sarah's imagination, but she thought Wrigley blamed her for his earlier disgrace, as if it were Sarah's fault that he dropped things and slopped things. In any event, he seemed to serve her grudgingly, reserving the smallest portions for her, dropping them higgledy-piggledy on her plate, and sparing the sauces as if he feared they would run out. Moreover, when they retired to the drawing room and tea was served, Wrigley gave even Maria, Gordon, and Peter their cups before carrying one to her!

Mrs. Dere failed to notice this irregularity, being occupied with showing Mrs. Barstow and Frances how she proposed to set the refreshments in the little adjoining parlor. "Then we will only require a few chairs around the edges of the room for observers, and a path might be left for those who wish to refresh themselves, without having to wait for a dance to end."

Perhaps noticing Sarah's discomfiture, the baron came to sit beside her.

"How I look forward to this children's ball, Mrs. Sebastian, do not you? I am only sorry dear Mrs. Terry will not be in attendance, since this was her own idea a few years ago."

"If the Terrys return in the spring, perhaps we might have another," Sarah suggested. She took a hasty sip of her tea, noting from the corner of her eye that, like a sleep-walker, Wrigley already began to collect the cups.

"Yes, but then we would not have Mr. Langworthy."

"Or Dr. Rearden, I suppose, because Mr. Terry will be home to take up his duties again."

Lord Dere regarded her shrewdly. "Would you mind, particularly, if Dr. Rearden went away?"

His question was so uncharacteristic in its pointedness that Sarah blushed. Could Mrs. Dere have planted the notion in his mind?

"Er—as much as I like Dr. Rearden, there is no substitute for Mr. Terry as our clergyman," she fumbled, refusing to acknowledge that the baron could be hinting at any other construction on the matter.

"At least, unlike Langworthy, Dr. Rearden holds so many profitable posts that he need not risk life and limb to make his way in the world."

"Mm." Sarah took another sip as Wrigley rattled up with the tray and snatched Lord Dere's empty cup from the side table.

"More, sir?" mumbled the footboy.

"Thank you, lad, no."

Sarah thought Wrigley would move on, but instead he lingered, arranging and rearranging the wares. The baron, long used to the omnipresence of servants, paid no attention to this loitering and returned to his topic.

"Mrs. Sebastian," he said softly, "I pray you will forgive an old man his presumption, but I would be remiss in my care for your family if I did not ask you this question."

Sarah's breath caught. What question?

Oh, mercy. May it not be about—

"My dear, it has been brought to my attention that—your sisters-in-law's situations notwithstanding—that we do not often meet with eligible single gentlemen in Iffley. Now one of them will be leaving us shortly, but if he is not going with your heart already in his possession...?"

He paused, but for love or money Sarah would not, could not, reveal the state of her heart. Not even to the Barstows' kindly benefactor. Because however kindly Lord Dere was, Sarah was certain Mrs. Markham Dere would not hesitate to beat the truth out of him.

He nodded as if she had spoken, going so far as to pat her arm. "I have made no secret of the fact that I find him an admirable young man, and if you had told me you liked him and thought one day of marrying again, there are many things an intelligent, active fellow like Langworthy might do for income, with some assistance from friends. Many *safer* things."

Tears threatened at his quiet generosity, and Sarah took a last, hurried gulp of her tea before signaling to Wrigley. "I'm finished, thank you," she coughed.

The footboy frowned at her.

"The cup," she rasped, holding it out. "Here—take it."

For a boy with such keen, watching eyes, he could look awfully stupid at times. This being one of the times. He pointed. "There's still some in there."

"Nevertheless." Sarah had almost to thrust the item into the boy's hand and curl his fingers around it. But at last he took it and backed away.

Turning back to the baron she murmured, "Thank you, sir. If—it should ever come to that, I'm sure he would be appreciative."

It was too ambivalent a reply, for Lord Dere evidently saw more than she intended.

"Do you not, then, rule out the possibility?"

"What? No. I mean, yes, I rule it out. I only meant to say, sir, that I'm certain Mr. Langworthy would value your goodness as we all do, if—ever there were occasion for it. Nothing more than that."

"Then *you* do not wish for him to be encouraged...?"

The bud of panic within her bloomed. "No!" she whispered. "Please, sir. *No*. Leave him be. I know you mean nothing but kindness, but I wish we may not talk of this more. *Please*."

It was a case of the lady protesting too much, Sarah would think later when she was free to rehearse the conversation in her head, but thank heavens the baron was too gentle and retiring a man to insist.

CHAPTER 16

She toke me by the hand and led me a daunce.
—John Skelton, *Deth Edwarde IV* (c.1563)

The day of the children's ball arrived at last. Sarah sat before the looking glass in the green bedroom while Frances curled her hair. It was agreed Sarah's would be dressed first because she could be trusted not to romp about in her excitement, and Maria's last, knowing even then it might be in disarray by the time they arrived at Perryfield.

But though Sarah might be outwardly calm, inwardly all was in uproar. How soon after the ball would Mr. Langworthy depart? Would he ask her to dance, even with Mrs. Dere's surplus girls invited?

Surely, surely he would. At least once. They were friends now, after all. She had seen him twice since their talk, but the first time only in passing in the street and neither time alone, and though he had smiled at her and addressed her generally, it had not been enough.

It had been nothing.

She had found herself imagining how she might seek him out, draw him apart, but she was ashamed of these schemes and too timid to try them.

But if he did not speak to her tonight—she must make the attempt. She could not let him go away without another word.

That determination led, as always, to its corollary: what precisely would she say? What was there, indeed, still to be said? She had already apologized. She had already thanked him. She had already offered friendship. The only thing which remained was the thing which could never be said.

That she had come to like him. To care for him.

In spite of herself, and in spite of him, and in spite of all.

Could she ask if they might correspond, when he went away? No—no—absolutely not. But Mrs. Barstow might ask it with impunity. She might ask him, as a sort of surrogate son, to write to her, and Sarah would have to content herself with hearing about him secondhand and entreating her mother-in-law to add a line from her or to send her compliments.

Alas.

It would be better than nothing, she scolded herself. *You will forget him—or certainly you* ought *to forget him. Because after he marries his Mary Pence it would be* sinful *to continue to think of him.*

And so on and so on.

"There," declared Frances, setting down the iron and clasping her hands in satisfaction. "I have outdone myself, and you will be the belle of the ball."

Sarah grinned. "Yes. There to put all the nine-year-old would-be belles in their place. Let Mrs. Chauncey's granddaughter beware! But thank you for your efforts, dearest, even though no one will be looking at me."

"Oh?" asked Frances archly. "I can think of one person who might be looking."

Feeling her face heat, Sarah said as evenly as she could, "What nonsense you talk."

But she was reassured the next moment when Frances cackled and held up her hands to wave beside her cheeks in the accepted sign for the whiskered curate.

"Silly girl," Sarah chided, too relieved to be annoyed. "All right, then. I am ready to charm Dr. Rearden."

She would do, she supposed. Her smooth light-brown hair shining. The dark blue of her gown emphasizing her eyes and luminous skin. Briefly she wondered what Mary Pence had looked like. "Dainty" she could understand, but what of "spritely" and "mischievous"? Her brain could make no more of it than Harry Barbary in a dress, which was hardly likely.

It being a children's ball, it began in the afternoon, with the Perryfield coach coming first for the Barstows.

"Charming, charming," beamed Lord Dere as Wood announced them. "How well you all look." The baron and his niece were as elegant and proper as if it had been a regular ball, and Peter was altogether another boy with pomade in his hair, pale blue gloves, and a silver brocade waistcoat. Awestruck, Maria took in the hothouse greenery and the blaze of candles reflecting from every polished surface. She had kept herself neat for the occasion, not allowing the dog Poppet or cat Outlaw to sit upon her and regretfully telling Bash she could not gambol about with him, and now she was rewarded. She looked ready to cry with delight.

Frances, who at eighteen had attended an assembly or two as well as the previous year's Greenwood Ball, bore the wonders with equanimity, however, being far more interested in Mrs. Dere's servant woes. "Where are they?" she demanded of the hostess. "Never say you have already dismissed Blodgett and Wrigley!"

Mrs. Dere's lovely features twisted in a grimace. "They are here still and managed to carry the food to the little parlor without mishap, but I prefer they have as few dealings with the guests as possible. Therefore I have told the creeping Blodgett to remain by the refreshments throughout, refilling the trays and taking away the used dishes. And as for Wrigley, here he comes. He will be Wood's lieutenant, heaven help us. Let us hope the boy can stir the fire and replace candles without burning down the house."

The footboy's first duty was to carry away their cloaks and wraps. (He dropped Sarah's and trod upon it. Mrs. Dere patted the back of her hair and pretended not to see.)

Before they could do more than admire the variety and placement of the decorations, Wood reappeared to announce the arrival of the Chaunceys and Lanes, or rather Mrs. Chauncey and her two granddaughters, ages ten and eight, who looked so like each other they might have been twins, and the Lanes with a great-nephew and granddaughter both Gordy's age. The children all made the polite greetings expected of them, trying to hide their stares of curiosity.

"Here we are," said the baron with a welcoming smile, "now only waiting for the party from the rectory. Come, Miss Amelia and Miss Kate, Master Harold and Miss Anna, was it? Tell us which dances you have been learning and if you have any favorites…"

"Lord Dere's coach," Langworthy heard the maid Polly announce. He waited for the Tommies to pound down the stairs in their usual manner, but this time his ear caught only Tommy Wardour, who paused halfway to leap the final few steps. The older Tom Ellis trod carefully, no doubt aware of his finery. In this household of men, only the boys had accepted Polly's offer to spruce them up; Dr. Rearden was too shy of female assistance and Langworthy too used to fending for himself.

Every other day of his life he had shaven, run a comb through his hair, brushed his teeth, and then rested on his oars, so to speak, satisfied with the person he presented to the world. Why it should be any different on this day disturbed him.

But the fact was, not only did he find himself spending more time than he was wont on his appearance, but now that the children's ball was upon him, the artificial end date he had set for his stay in Iffley, he found himself not wanting to go. And yet nothing could be more important to his career or his future at this point.

Why should Mrs. Sebastian Barstow say her first friendly words to him, and suddenly his plans were in disarray? Should it not rather confirm them, as a sign that his work in Iffley was complete?

"Don't be a fool," he muttered to his reflection, raising a fist to rub at a streak Harry Barbary's ministrations had left. "What would you do? Stay, delay, idle about at another's expense? Lose the good opinion you have gained?"

No. The ball was upon him. And a day or two hence he would pack his trunk and go.

Reaching for his gloves, he went to join the others.

As Frances Barstow had recently said, the one reliable way to ensure one looked directly at a certain person was to be told *not* to look at that certain person.

If Sarah Barstow and Horace Langworthy doubted the truth of such a declaration, they would have had to concede it on this occasion. For each had instructed himself not to look at the other in any significant fashion (if at all), yet each found himself doing precisely that, from the moment the rectory party arrived at Perryfield.

Though Sarah's glance lasted the merest eyeblink, it was enough to make her color rise. She wondered how she had never before noticed what a trim, good-looking man Mr. Langworthy was, from his burnished hair to his defined jaw and lean, vigorous person. As for Horace Langworthy, though his glance equaled Sarah's in brevity, a shiver ran his length. Had he really once thought her nothing remarkable?

"You are all welcome to Perryfield," said Mrs. Markham Dere graciously when the whole company stood in her drawing room. "Now that we have gathered, as your mistress of ceremonies I have a few announce-ments. Firstly, Mrs. Chauncey has kindly offered to provide our music this evening." (They broke into polite applause as the lady took her seat at the pianoforte.) "Secondly," she continued, "Mr. Langworthy is not the only expert in mathematics! For I have done some calculations myself. You will see we have enough for nine couples, which means we may do a few longways dances for three couples, perhaps one or two round dances for three-couple sets, and mix in a few for as many as will, so the children may practice progression. Moreover, that we need not fuss over choosing partners each time, I have taken the liberty of drawing up a diagram, that for each dance you may see whom you have been assigned."

With a flourish she indicated a sheet of paper which had been propped upon a music stand, and though every child wanted to rush over and inspect it, they hung back until Peter led the way, followed at once by Gordon and Tommy Wardour. The adults must disguise their anticipation, but they were soon enlightened by Peter taking it up and reading it out.

While Tommy Wardour could hardly be foisted upon Mr. Langworthy in this setting, Mrs. Dere did the next best thing, which was always to put Tommy in the same three-couple set so Mr. Langworthy could set him right. And by orchestrating the sets and partners, Mrs. Dere ensured Sarah would always be found going through the figures with, or in the vicinity of, Dr. Rearden.

It is better thus, Sarah told herself. *Mrs. Dere can't make me marry Dr. Rearden, nor make him marry me, but it is just as well I do not dance with Mr. Langworthy.*

Still, though they belonged to different sets, it was impossible for him not to float in and out of her vision, being so much taller than the children in his group, apart from gangling Tom Ellis. And by virtue of his height, it was just as impossible for Langworthy not to see Sarah. There being only one ticklish part of The Black Nag—the three-person hey near the end of the pattern—Langworthy was lulled by Tommy's early lack of errors. He let his eyes wander Sarah-ward, with the unfortunate consequence that he missed his own cue and Tommy collided with him, bouncing off to stumble into Harold Lane. Down they both went. Tommy and Harold's partners shrieked, causing Mrs. Chauncey to fumble a chord and lose her place in the music.

The dance halted.

"My new stockings!" cried Harold, pointing. "Tommy's buckle tore them."

Mrs. Dere threw Tommy such a withering glare that the boy shrank and Langworthy felt it his duty to come forward. "It was my fault, madam. I was—distracted—and failed to vacate the place Tommy was meant to occupy."

Of course she could neither glare nor bellow at him, so instead she snapped at the footman. "Wood! Where is the housewife? Let us put a few stitches in Master Harold's stocking so we may proceed."

Wood in turn snapped his fingers at Wrigley lurking in the corner, and the boy darted out, unrolling the housewife as he came.

Mrs. Dere's lips parted, probably considering whether she wanted a bungler like Wrigley wielding a needle anywhere near her young guest, but to her surprise the lad knelt nimbly, pinched together the ragged sides of the tear and whipped the rent shut with stitches so tidy and expert that the mistress of Perryfield was not the only one to blink in amazement.

The task done, the footboy backed away, stooped in a half-bow with head lowered, rolling the housewife up. In this humble posture Wrigley's backside narrowly missed knocking down a flower-filled vase, but it *did* miss, and the dance could resume.

Millison's Jig followed The Black Nag. After which came The Boatman.

As the dancers found their feet, they began to enjoy themselves. The children started to laugh and tease and make faces. Little mistakes became cause for good-natured amusement, rather than embarrassment. Even Mrs. Dere relaxed into smiles, not even noticing when Wood had to tell Wrigley twice to crack open one of the casements for air because the footboy was shuffling his feet to the music. Indeed, Sarah began to think she might be the only one present who still felt any anxiety.

Because she did feel anxious.

There was Mrs. Dere, nodding at her encouragingly, whenever Sarah and Dr. Rearden shared a word. There was Dr. Rearden himself, excessively amiable to her (it seemed to her stretched nerves), his cheeks warm with exertion and his whiskers in full froth. There was the baron, serene and untroubled, as if he had forgotten all about asking Sarah whether she might like Mr. Langworthy—but how *could* he have forgotten? And there was Sarah herself, contrary and troubled.

Indeed, the only other dancer not enjoying an exuberance of high spirits seemed to be Mr. Langworthy, but because she could only steal peeps at him and because the figures kept them in constant motion, it was hard for Sarah to be certain. Only once did his gaze cross hers, though that once it crossed and held. He gave a tiny shrug, and his mouth twisted in—what?—derision? Ruefulness?

Nowhere on Mrs. Dere's diagram was Sarah paired with him, but when it came time for the first longways duple minor dance The Indian Queen, her heart began to hammer. He might not be her partner, but as he and Mrs. Barstow stood some ways below Sarah and Tom Ellis, they would progress up the room while she and Tom went down, culminating in one or two blissful (or wretched) times through the pattern when Mr. Langworthy would be her corner. When they would face each other and take both hands in a turn and pass each other in rights and lefts. She was pitiful to look forward to so little, and yet she did, even praying Mrs. Dere would let them dance it through twice! At a ball with twenty couples it would take too long, but with nine...?

Too quickly it passed. She thought perhaps he gave her hands the merest squeeze in taking them, but, no, Dr. Lane held them just as firmly when he was her corner. And little Harold Lane positively wrung them in comparison.

But she had not imagined the intensity of Mr. Langworthy's eyes when they met hers for that fleeting encounter, had she?

Yes, she must have, she decided later, after Master Harold gave her a dead set with his eyes, like a magician working a complicated enchantment. Either the boy's dancing master had emphasized the importance of meeting one's partner's gaze or Harold Lane was embarking early on a career as a lady-killer.

When The Indian Queen ended, Mrs. Dere clapped her hands for attention. "Let us step across the passage for a little refreshment and to give Mrs. Chauncey a rest, please."

"There's tarts and a jelly and sandwiches and chocolate and syllabub," cried Peter to the other children, and the baron laughed and told them to lead the way.

"Mrs. Sebastian?"

Sarah turned to find Dr. Rearden offering his arm, and she forced a smile. Impatience was rising within her, overpowering her uncertainty. This might be one of the last times she saw or spoke with Mr. Langworthy, and she was wasting it! Wasting it in politeness and self-reproach and timidity! What did it matter if Mrs. Dere disapproved? What did it matter if the baron guessed at her heart? The ball would end; Mr. Langworthy would return to Portsmouth; and Sarah would have no more than memories the rest of her life, and not even many of them.

She would not let it be so.

She had lived more than two years on memories already, and even though there were so many of them, and even with the physical existence of Sebastian's letters to remind her, and even with Bash—dear Bash—memories were no longer enough.

She would speak to him. The moment she could do so, short of thread-ing her way across the parlor to his side, shoving everyone else out of the way.

"Can I fetch you something, Mrs. Sebastian?" asked Dr. Rearden.

"Yes, please," she answered promptly. "Something to drink. Anything."

Heaving a breath to have got rid of him so easily, she tried to peer past Dr. Lane and the baron and the ancient Blodgett, who was creaking around with a dish of tiny mince pies, only to hear her name called.

She turned, and there was Mr. Langworthy.

"Mince pie?" he asked.

"Yes, please," she breathed through suddenly numb lips.

"Ah." To her surprise, he extended an arm over Blodgett's shoulder and plucked a pie from the footman's plate. "Have you a handkerchief to hold it?"

"Er—" To have him all at once beside her, when she had been thinking she must go and seek him, deprived her of speech. Mutely, she shook her head.

"Better just—pop it in, then," he said. "It's not much bigger than a thumbnail, and no one's looking. Here—open up."

To her own amazement, she obeyed, her lips parting as if he had spoken the *Open Sesame*. It must have surprised him as well, for his own mouth curled in a delicious grin.

"There we go," he murmured. "How very, very inviting."

As gently as if touching a soap bubble, his fingers carried the savory dainty to her lips, which opened wider to receive it, her face flushing and her own fingertips rising to prevent anything tumbling out. They brushed his; her scarlet deepened. She could not tell if the drumming in her ears was the children running about or her own wayward heart.

"Sarah," he whispered.

CHAPTER 17

**Some mallice has corrupted your opinion
of that we call the Ball.
—James Shirley, *The ball, a comedy* (1639)**

Mind you! Make way!" shrilled a voice, and the next instant the footboy Wrigley dived between them, a brimming dish of chocolate held high. On Mr. Langworthy the collision had no more impact than Tommy Wardour had earlier, but Sarah was nearly flung to the floor, the bowlful of thick chocolate oscillating, overtopping the rim of the cup to spatter her dress.

"Why, you great bumbling bungler," Langworthy snapped, his temper getting the better of him. "Off with you! Are you all right, Mrs. Sebastian?"

"Yes," she replied quickly, biting her lip to hide her dismay at the blobs running down her skirts in spreading stains. Mortified and annoyed as she was at Wrigley's clumsiness, it would only make matters worse if it drew Mrs. Dere's notice.

Too late.

"What is *this*?" cried the mistress of Perryfield, her guests parting to either side before her like the Red Sea before Moses's rod and outstretched hand.

"This mutton-fisted clod ran into Mrs. Sebastian and me, spilling chocolate on her," explained Langworthy through a tight jaw.

"If you weren't standing so close to her I wouldn't have!" piped Wrigley with an indignant flash from his blue eyes.

The flash was met with utter stillness on Langworthy's part, as if he had turned him to stone, the only movement his own eyes widening in a look Sarah could not understand, and then narrowing in fury the next second.

But so overcome was Mrs. Dere by this show of uppishness from a servant—and a temporary, incompetent one at that—that she seized Wrigley by the elbow and marched him away, hissing, "Go and get water and a cloth from Mrs. Robson and come back with them at once!" Then, turning back to her guests, she pasted on a smile. "My goodness, what a to-do. How hard it is to find reliable servants! But we must not let things like this spoil our fun. Shall we resume our dancing? Poor Mrs. Sebastian will have to miss The Queen's Jig, but surely she will be set to rights by the dance following it, Christchurch Bells."

"Should I wait here with Mrs. Sebastian, madam?" asked Tommy Wardour, his eyes sliding toward the remaining little cakes. "I was to be her partner for The Queen's Jig."

"How gallant of you, Tommy," she replied. "However, you will still be able to observe, if you cannot participate. Blodgett, fetch a chair for Mrs. Sebastian. And Uncle, if you would lead the way..."

Sarah watched them go, feeling abandoned. Not by the children, per se, but by Mr. Langworthy. He had no choice but to follow, of course, yet still she envied whichever person would dance with him or beside him next.

Her view of the departing fortunate ones was blocked by Blodgett lumbering up, chair in hand, and Sarah hastily made to take it from him, lest he collapse in placing it for her. Which was how she did not see Mr. Langworthy slip back until he was directly before her.

"Mrs. Sebastian."

"Mr. Langworthy." She was glad of her seat then, for her pulse resumed its ridiculous unevenness again.

"I—hope the stain will come out."

She nodded.

"I would—stay and help, if I could."

This brought a smile. "Help? Do you mean you would scrub and soak, sir?"

But no answering amusement gleamed in his eyes. Rather he looked troubled. "I—have my doubts about that clumsy footboy."

Then Sarah did laugh, though she glanced Blodgett-ward. Blodgett merely shuffled away toward the refreshment table, however, beginning to load used dishes on a tray. "You are not alone in your skepticism, Mr. Langworthy," she said in a low tone. "If you could have seen young Wrigley the other night! I believe, if Mrs. Markham Dere ever chooses to host another ball, she will likely prefer to borrow other people's servants than introduce ones altogether unknown and untried."

"How *did* she find these ones? I would be on my guard against—the younger one—"

"Do you suppose he will dump the basin of water over my head, now?" she teased. "Come now—he is young and inexperienced, and his fingers seem to be all thumbs—"

"It is not that," he interrupted, "though that is bad enough. But I suspect—"

"Mr. Langworthy!" called their hostess, reappearing in the doorway. "We wait on you, sir."

His fine, broad shoulders sagging an inch, he gave Sarah a final, mystifying, concerned glance and turned to follow Mrs. Dere.

He suspected *what*? Sarah wanted to demand, cursing Mrs. Dere's timing.

From the drawing room, Mrs. Dere's instructions to the dancers reached Sarah's ears indistinctly, and they were soon drowned in Mrs. Chauncey beginning again to play. A few minutes onward, while Blodgett stood like a sleeping statue and Sarah tried not to fidget, Wrigley reappeared with the requisite items and a wild expression.

Would he, in fact, dump the basin of water over her? Sarah wondered. Because whatever hostile looks Wrigley had given her at the dinner were nothing to the face he wore now. A trickle of trepidation ran down her spine. But how could the boy possibly blame her for this mishap, when he would never have spilled chocolate on her had he watched where he was going?

With a final heave, Wrigley set the basin at Sarah's feet. Then he knelt, wetting the cloth and beginning to soak the stained portions. Uncomfortable, and wishing she were the sort of young lady who could ignore a servant's existence whilst being attended to, Sarah studied the top of the boy's wig. It took her a few minutes to recognize that, as when he sewed up Harold Lane's torn stocking, Wrigley showed unexpected skill in blotting the excess chocolate and applying Windsor soap. Though Sarah would have to finish the day in skirts discolored with wet blotches, if she gave the dress to Reed at once, perhaps the stains would not set.

"I know who you are," said Wrigley curtly, startling Sarah with an abrupt lift of his head, his keen eyes meeting hers with astonishing directness. "Who you are and what you're bent on."

"I beg your pardon!" Sarah might not be the haughty sort, but no servant she ever encountered had addressed her with this sort of insolence, much less accused her of anything.

A wave of something passed over Wrigley's countenance in a series of clenches and grimaces. Then he lowered his head once more to his task, but he muttered, "You heard me. I know you've set your cap for Mr.

Langworthy, thinking you've a right to him because you were his friend's widow."

Gasping, Sarah tugged her dress from Wrigley's clutch and leapt to her feet. "Who are you? How dare you speak thus? How do you know Mr. Langworthy?"

The boy twitched. Glanced at Blodgett (who bore the look with sleepy equanimity). Then he folded the cloth, hung it on the side of the basin, and rose. They did not stand eye to eye—Sarah was perhaps two inches taller—but the very act—its audacity—put her at a disadvantage.

"I'm a servant of Miss Mary Pence of Portsmouth, sent here by her to find out what's what," said Wrigley. "As is that one there." (Pointing at Blodgett.) "I daresay you've heard of Miss Pence?"

Sarah swallowed, using every ounce of resolve not to take a step backward, not to reveal anything on her face. "I have," she replied.

"Mr. Langworthy is my mistress' intended husband—"

"Was," she interrupted. "Mr. Langworthy *was* once engaged to Miss Pence."

Wrigley's Harry-Barbaryish eyes glittered. "Was," he conceded. "But it was her choice to jilt him, and not his. Because he's wild in love with her and always has been. Always. It crushed him when she broke it off."

What sort of young lady tells her servant these things? marveled Sarah. She could not imagine confiding in Reed or Irving at Iffley Cottage, and they were miracles of discretion compared to this Wrigley!

"Only then," resumed the footboy, "when he was beaten down and in the depths of despair, did he remember his dead friend asked him to pay a visit here, and so he came, all...suffering and—and tender-like, and what do we see but he got himself taken advantage of."

"Poor helpless creature," Sarah said dryly, despite her distress. She wrapped her arms about herself for courage. "I take it, if she sent you to spy upon him—upon all of us—your mistress has changed her mind about jilting him?"

"She might have," returned Wrigley. "But one thing is for certain: it's despicable to try to steal other girls' beaux and twice as much so for those who already had their turn and got a husband and a baby from it. Those ones ought to content themselves with their widderhood like the Scripture says, or, if they can't stand it, keep their chasing after fellows to ones like that old Dr. Rearden."

"Stealing other girls' beaux"? To stand and be told to mind the Scriptures? Goaded, Sarah's urge to argue with the maddening servant warred with the knowledge that she should not dignify such slander with a response. But, oh, how she wanted to! That this snip of a would-be footboy should be allowed to make such speeches with impunity, even if bidden to do so by his mistress! Her arms tightened around herself, and she knew she was red as a brick.

But it was not pride alone which silenced Sarah; it was that Wrigley's arrows had struck home. For what did it matter if Mary Pence was fickle and possessive, or if she employed low, unworthy tactics and low, impudent servants like Wrigley, if in truth Mr. Langworthy was "wild in love" with the girl and always had been?

Of course he didn't love me *when he offered for me*, she thought. *How could he, when he had only just met me?* And he had made no secret of coming to Iffley straight from Mary Pence's rejection of him. Sarah remembered how tetchy and changeable Mr. Langworthy had been at their first meeting. There was no denying he had been troubled in spirit. There was no denying that, however offensively Wrigley put it, truth lay beneath the boy's words.

But that did not mean Sarah ever had designs on the man—how could she, when, until Mr. Langworthy told her, she had no idea of the commission Sebastian gave him? It was so unjust to accuse her of trying to steal Mr. Langworthy's heart! So very, very unjust!

Especially because, all to the contrary—

Especially because he had somehow stolen hers.

Wrigley watched her, unblinking.

Releasing herself slowly, Sarah gave her dampened skirts a twitch and then smoothed them. She could not bring herself to thank the boy for his services—not when it was obvious that he had interfered with her on purpose—but she gave one crisp nod to the wall over his shoulder and started past him.

"Wait!" Wrigley called after her.

Though she did not turn, Sarah paused.

"Are you still going to try to catch him, then?"

Swallowing carefully through a tightened throat, Sarah said only, "I had not been trying in the first place."

Her return to the drawing room was greeted with enthusiasm, and Mrs. Barstow and Frances hastened to assure her that the stains were much improved and would be gone altogether once Reed had done with them. She felt, rather than saw Mr. Langworthy's eyes upon her, but Wrigley's accusations still rang in her ears, and she could not bear to look at him.

"I'm your partner for Christchurch Bells," declared Peter Dere, bounding over to claim her and sweeping her a bow which made her smile in spite of all. "This is my favorite one, Mrs. Sebastian, because of all the galloping and clapping."

The dance did involve a great deal of galloping and clapping, besides constant turning with one's partner and one's corner, so even had she wanted to talk to Mr. Langworthy or to observe him furtively, to determine if he too thought she had set her cap for him, the whirl of Christchurch Bells made it impossible.

But though she would not look at him, Sarah was terribly conscious of his approach as she and Peter progressed up the set. And of the blank of his face turned toward her whenever he passed through her field of view. And then Mr. Langworthy was on her corner, taking her hand for the turn. He pressed it.

"Look at me. What happened?" he uttered through unmoving lips. At least, that's what she thought he said, but then he must release her to turn with Maria, and more clapping and galloping ensued before away they went.

She did not have long to puzzle over what he might or might not have said because only a few times later through the pattern, when she and Peter were in the galloping circle with Anna Chauncey and Tommy Wardour, galloping, galloping, a cry came from further down the set, and there was Mr. Langworthy grimacing and hobbling away.

The music jangled to a halt, and a clamor arose. "Mr. Langworthy, have you injured yourself?" "Mr. Langworthy, did I tread on you?" "All right there, Langworthy?"

He sank into a chair along the wall, holding up a hand. "It's nothing, it's nothing. I only turned my ankle or something. Forgive my clumsiness, Miss Maria, and do go on, everyone. I will just slip away to rest it a minute and see if I can—untwist it. Pardon me again, Miss Maria." And with that, he limped from the room.

Mrs. Dere snapped her fingers for Wood to follow him, and the set re-formed for Christchurch Bells, with Maria left to observe. "We will begin from the beginning, Mrs. Chauncey," said Mrs. Dere.

Their accompanist cheerfully played the introduction again, and the company set off once more into their galloping and circling. Nor was Sarah sorry for the repetition because she had not a thought to spare for the steps.

He recognized Wrigley. Mr. Langworthy's twisted ankle is a pretense to seek him out and ply him with questions about Mary Pence.

But what questions?

How in love with Mary Pence did Mr. Langworthy remain? Perhaps he was passing a message to Miss Pence via her servant, telling Wrigley, as he had Sarah, that he had obligations in Iffley to fulfill before he could return to Portsmouth. Or, contrarily, that he meant to return almost on the instant. Perhaps he had taken Sarah's advice to heart and hinted to Wrigley that he was prepared to forgive and forget.

In any case, she should be glad for him. For the resumption of his naval career and the resumption of his suit.

And how much better for him if there were no delay in either.

But Sarah thought she might choke on her own attempt to be generous. She imagined Mr. Langworthy again in his lieutenant's uniform, his spritely, dainty, mischievous bride on his arm, beaming up at him as his fellow naval officers cheered—and felt only desolation.

At last, when every couple had progressed the length of the set, Mrs. Chauncey's pace slowed, signaling the end of the dance, and Wood reappeared in the doorway.

"And how fares Mr. Langworthy?" Mrs. Dere asked. "Will he be able to rejoin us?"

"He sends his deepest regrets, madam," answered the footman, "and wished me to tell you how much he enjoyed the occasion, but he thought he had better go home and rest."

"Go home?" she echoed. "Did you tell Harker and Ogle to bring up the carriage?"

"I offered, but he said no," explained Wood. "He said the walk would do him good. Stretch his ankle out, or something of the sort."

"Whoever heard of such a remedy for a sprained ankle?" she demanded, frowning at the servant as if he had proposed it.

Wood bowed. "He said Wrigley might assist him. Act as a crutch."

This was too much for Mrs. Dere. "Wrigley is more likely to break his ankle off altogether!" she snapped, ire darkening her lovely features much as "thunders and lightnings, and a thick cloud" wreathed the heights of Mount Sinai when the Lord descended upon it. "If Mr. Langworthy was capable of walking back to the rectory, he was capable of walking through the figures of a few more dances, I daresay, rather than to so inconvenience his remaining partners."

"Now, Alice," soothed the peacemaking baron. "If Mr. Langworthy required assistance making his way home, I hardly think him capable of dancing. Nor could Wrigley help him there. If anything, it showed consideration toward us, to only avail himself of Wrigley's help."

There was no denying Perryfield could spare the incompetent footboy better than any of the other servants—indeed, removing the lad might even be deemed a favor. Seeing all her guests uneasy and waiting for her instructions, Mrs. Dere threw up her hands. "I suppose if Mr. Langworthy chooses to abandon us and subject himself to Wrigley's ministrations, that is on his head," she huffed.

But her *che sera sera* dismissal only succeeded in rousing Lord Dere's further concern. "Perhaps I had better send Harker after them with the gig," he suggested, "for they will make slow progress."

Her bosom rose and fell in silent wrath. *Another* servant to be wasted and inconvenienced by this inexplicable behavior? Not to mention the trouble of hitching up the gig, when soon there would be guests to drive home? Moreover, there would be delay, with the horse having to be unhitched from the gig and re-hitched to the coach and—heavens, what a nuisance!

But she beat all this down with the good manners engrained in her.

With only a tight smile she said, "Very well, Uncle. Mrs. Chauncey, shall we have Childgrove next?"

CHAPTER 18

Appearances were all so strong,
The World must think him in the wrong.
—Swift, *Cadenus and Vanessa: a poem* (1726)

"What on earth are you doing here?" asked Horace Langworthy, in a low, shaking voice at which those on deck who had served under him would have blanched.

"Why shouldn't I be here?" Wrigley answered, not the least bit daunted.

They had made their way wordlessly down the long Perryfield drive, Langworthy's hand on the footboy's narrow shoulder as he limped. But once they were out of sight of the house, shielded by the stone half wall, both the hand and the supposed lameness fell away.

"There are a thousand reasons," he rejoined, "beginning with that disguise which wouldn't fool a child."

"I beg your pardon," retorted Wrigley, "but this disguise has fooled several children already and an equal number of adults."

In reply to this he said only: "Mary."

A giggle burst from Wrigley, his nose wrinkling in fun and his hand reaching to remove his wig. But Langworthy's own hand flashed up to stop him.

"Don't, you little imp! Do you want to be discovered?"

"Ha! There, I told you. If you didn't think my disguise was convincing, why would you object to my removing it?"

"Because, feeble as it is, it is essential. Now is neither the time nor the place for you to metamorphose into a young lady."

His erstwhile intended bride grinned up at him unrepentantly, executing a little twirl. "Aren't you going to tell me how charming I look in livery? The color suits me, don't you think?" But she pouted when, instead of him smiling ruefully at her, fighting to hide his admiration, she saw his eyes had narrowed to glittering slits.

"Mary," he bit out, "what can you possibly be thinking, taking such a risk to come here?"

"If you have a thousand reasons why I shouldn't be here, I have a few of my own why I should," she returned roundly. "And as I am my own mistress, why should I not do as I please?"

In answer, he began to stride away, following the road which ran along the wall.

"Where are you going?" she demanded.

"I am going to Oxford," he said simply, "where I will put you on the evening coach to London and thence to Portsmouth."

"That's a half-hour walk!" she protested, chasing after him. "And how can I possibly take the coach unchaperoned?"

This drew an incredulous snort. "As you noted, you have your impenetrable disguise."

"But I can't just leave poor Blodgett! She will have no idea what became of me, nor any notion what to do."

"Good Lord," he groaned, not slowing. "I suppose I should have guessed. That poor ancient creature is female?"

Another giggle. "Of course she is. Though Tibby does have rather a square jaw and hulking person."

"And you involved your companion—for I suppose this Miss Blodgett is your companion—in this wretched scheme?"

"*You* always did your mischief with a companion," she reminded him. "It was always Sebastian this and Barstow-and-I that."

He ignored this. "However did you persuade her to the ruse?"

"Tibby Blodgett is not an opinionated person and will do whatever I ask because she adores me. As you once did." She threw this last bit down like a gauntlet, but again he did not take it up.

"Can't we walk a little more slowly?" she wheedled after another minute. "Your limbs are much longer than mine and it's growing darker. I wouldn't want either one of us genuinely to wrench an ankle. May I take your arm?"

"Why would I be arm in arm with Wrigley the footboy?"

"You really are angry with me, aren't you, Horace? I thought you would be glad to hear I didn't marry Captain Colley. I thought you would come back at once when your uncle wrote to you. And when you didn't, well, I had to see what delayed you."

"I have obligations here," he said gruffly. They had reached Wallingford Way, but no wagons or carriages were in sight which might be stopped and asked to carry them. They might indeed have to walk all the way.

At least in the exercise and the brisk air, Langworthy could feel his initial shock beginning to ebb, along with the fierce fury which attended it.

He marveled at his blindness now. Despite denigrating the effectiveness of her disguise, he had neither noticed nor recognized Mary Pence in Wrigley the footboy until she threw herself between him and Mrs. Sebastian. But how could he possibly have recognized her, so wholly out of place, where she was not only unexpected, but possibly even the last person on his mind? Little wonder, then, that sheer perplexity—unbelief—had almost paralyzed him.

Mary Pence—here? In Iffley? At the Perryfield children's ball? Dressed—heaven help him—as a young man in livery?

And then the first thing to follow, breaking through his fog of astonishment, was nothing he would have guessed. For, upon seeing again the young lady he had known half his life and wanted to marry nearly as long, the young lady who had so recently broken his heart, he felt neither elation at her reappearance, nor any passionate desire to take her in his arms and call her his own again, nor even a flicker of amusement at this latest prank. A prank to top all previous pranks.

No, indeed. The first thing to flood him was dismay.

Alarm.

Horror, even.

Because what would happen, if she were discovered?

What Mary Pence considered a romp, a lark, would be for him the end of all.

The end of his time in Iffley. The end of his friendship with Mrs. Sebastian. The end of his liberty. For what could he do under the circumstances, but rescue Miss Pence from the consequences of her own reckless actions? And what form could such rescue take, to silence scandal, other than to claim her before all the world as his bride?

These were the hideous fears swirling through him when Mrs. Dere summoned them back to the drawing room, leaving Mrs. Sebastian in Mary Pence's custody!

Oh, the dread of those minutes, waiting for them to reappear, while he moved like an automaton through the figures with his partner. What would Mary say to Mrs. Sebastian, he wondered, arming right with little Kate Chauncey. And, then, as he wound around Mrs. Lane in the figure eight: What would Mrs. Sebastian think and do? Whatever her opinion of Mary Pence and Mary Pence's outrageous conduct, Langworthy knew he would be tarred with the same brush. Would she possibly think he endorsed it?

Perspiration broke out on his forehead, causing the baron to say, "This is a lively one, eh, Langworthy?"

And then, when the dance ended and Mrs. Sebastian at last re-entered the drawing room alone, subdued and avoiding his gaze, he thought he would go mad with the uncertainty.

One thing had become clear to him as crystal, however, in the midst of his distressful minutes. The sudden apparition of his former beloved, like the parting of nighttime clouds to reveal the stars, allowed Langworthy all he needed to calculate his new position with perfect accuracy.

That is, he needed only that glimpse to understand.

When he had come to Iffley, he considered himself rudderless and adrift, leagues and leagues from all familiar landmarks and without any fixed destination. But somehow, in spite of his circumstances and in spite of all expectations, he had been carried along by friendly, unseen currents. He had come, after all, safe to harbor.

He had come home.

And home bore the shape of a woman with light brown hair and blue eyes, outwardly quiet but with fire beneath the surface.

Home was now Sarah.

"To *what* obligations do you refer?" Mary Pence demanded, breaking into his thoughts. Unknown to him, she had observed the softening of his profile, the easing of tension from his muscles, even as he kept to his deliberate pace. In the exact proportion that Langworthy's ire faded, hers increased. "It seems to me your obligations here have been fulfilled. I know Sebastian Barstow wanted you to make sure his wife and child weren't starving in the hedgerows, but it's quite clear they have fallen upon their feet—petted friends of a peer, no less! Dining and dancing and being waited upon. So that's taken care of."

"I have taken up teaching the baron's great-nephew, along with some other boys, in mathematics—"

"As if such as Lord Dere, a stone's throw from Oxford, could not find ten dozen mathematics tutors," she scorned.

Further defenses died in his throat because, truly, had he not all but announced the lessons would end with the ball? He might be following Mary Pence and her companion Blodgett back to Portsmouth within the week. Not that he wanted to tell his companion that bit. If he knew Mary, she would insist he come with her now. Or she would insist on waiting for him, that they might travel together.

"They have enlisted me, at any rate," he replied. "For pay. And I have found I enjoy the work."

"*You*, Horace Langworthy—a schoolmaster?"

He knew from experience that, if not checked, there was a point at which her temper would fizz and pop like a sackful of lit fireworks, a display which would do neither of them any good. It was this realization which allowed him to master his impatience. He had one goal now: to win Mrs. Sebastian Barstow, and he would pay in whatever currency was necessary to secure it—in patience, in hard work, in time, in pride.

The mere thought of Sarah calmed him now. His new love had a temper of her own, he knew, but with her greater maturity, she fought against giving in to it—never willingly indulged it—the way Mary would. Only think how Mrs. Sebastian had won him from hostility to admiration through her apology and friendly overtures. In her generosity, she had even encouraged him to lay down his self-regard in order to reclaim Mary Pence!

But what if he no longer wanted her?

All he wanted from Mary now was that she not throw up obstacles for him in his pursuit of Mrs. Sebastian. Because just as she had destroyed his previous hopes, Mary Pence alone had the power to destroy his new ones.

He must tread carefully.

Extricate himself from his past ties to her without stirring desires for vengeance on her part.

His pace slowed perceptibly. "Mary—Miss Pence, I should call you now—"

"Call me Mary! Ones who have known each other so long and so well should not balk at Christian names. Or do you want to forget our past intimacy because you would rather *someone else* not know about it?"

When she saw he would not be baited into replying, she was forced to press further. "Do you like that Mrs. Sebastian Barstow now? From what I saw, she's doing all she can to catch you."

"She's doing nothing of the kind," he said, unable to prevent himself.

"And looks like your new friend the baron would be in favor of the match."

He said nothing.

"I would never have thought you so changeable. To forget me and your family and Portsmouth and—everything. All forgotten in a couple months' time!"

"Mary," he said through a hard jaw, goaded at last, "if I might remind you, you were the one to end things between us. Should you be surprised I would go as far away as I could and try to surround myself with new people and new memories?"

The ghost of past heartbreak she detected in his words was enough to soften her. "Well, you need not fear me anymore," she told him. "You may come home now."

Her use of the word jarred him, having just applied it in his own thoughts to—the other one, and then he did speak rapidly enough.

"—Tell me what has become of Captain Colley," he urged. "The last time I saw you, you told me in no uncertain terms that you preferred him to me, and I was to set you at liberty."

She pursed her lips coyly and lifted a roguish shoulder, which, in Wrigley's costume had more a grotesque than a charming effect. "I was harsh with you, was I not? I confess to you, Horace, that he quite captivated me in your absence, being ever so handsome and every bit as daring as you. Perhaps even more so, now, now that you turn up your nose at this little escapade of mine," she added with a sniff. "You, who used to love a joke better than anything!"

"But to return to the handsome, daring captain," he said inexorably. Had she always danced around the point thus in conversations? Always flirted so? "What became of him?"

There was a pause. Mary kicked at the stones in the road, scuffing the fine slippers which surely belonged to Perryfield and Lord Dere and must be returned forthwith. (Another item added to the list of tasks he must see to, to conclude this affair.)

"I sent Captain Colley to the right-about," she answered at last. "Just as I had you."

They were nearing where Wallingford Way joined the causeway, and soon the Pettypont would be in sight, marking the entrance to the town. Langworthy's pace slowed another degree. This matter must be settled now. And if Mary Pence could not be brought to reject him, once for all, he must determine how best to bring it about himself.

"Did you break your engagement with him because you had changed your mind?"

"I am not so inconstant!"

"But—certainly Captain Colley had not the right to end it."

Her small form sagged, and then the Mary Pence who looked up at him was not the mischievous, teasing miss of Langworthy's adult years, glorying in the discovery of her beauty and power, but, in her disguise, more like a schoolboy caught in an awkward predicament.

"I will tell you, Horace, but you mustn't laugh or fling it in my face, though I did treat you so badly."

A fortnight earlier—less, perhaps—he would have wanted to do just that. (Had he not spent the last many weeks dreaming of revenge on not only her, but all womanhood?) But that was before Sarah Barstow. Sarah Barstow, and her disarming kindness to him.

Therefore he did not have to dissemble to say gently, "How long have I been your friend? I won't. I promise."

"Very well." She heaved a sigh, barely audible over the sound of their steps. "Captain Colley did not end my engagement with him, but he did ask if—if I would do him that favor. Because—" breaking off, she pressed her lips together a moment, striving for mastery. "—Because a-a-a young lady he had once loved had been recently widowed, and-and-and he told me he...could not help it, but he thought of her still."

Although the sun was setting, its lingering beams caught the two tears rolling down her cheeks.

"Oh, Mary," he echoed her sigh. "I'm sorry." And he was for her.

"I have my pride," she sniffled, extracting a handkerchief from an inner pocket. "I refuse to marry a man whose heart belongs to another, so I told him of course I released him and wished him every joy, though in truth I wanted to run him through with a rapier or push him off the nearest dock."

Langworthy understood that as well.

He said nothing, only making a sympathetic sound in his throat. And perhaps it was her disguise as Wrigley the footboy, but he made the move he would have done with any fellow man: he clapped a compassionate hand to her shoulder and gave it a squeeze in the universal unspoken expression of *Brace up, my lad*.

It was imprudent of him, to say the least.

For Mary Pence turned at once to face him and metamorphosed as quickly from Wrigley into Mary Pence. "Oh, Horace!" she cried. Throwing her arms about his neck, she collapsed against him, giving way to a storm of tears. "Oh, Horace, who has ever loved me like you have?"

"Mary! Mary, hush," he pleaded over her noisy laments. "They will hear you in the next county!" They had reached the Pettypont Bridge, and if traffic had been nonexistent before, here the London and Henley roads met, and both vehicles and pedestrians were sure to come along.

"If I didn't have your love, what would I do?" she wailed, even more loudly, and such was the flood of her weeping that he felt his breast dampened as if he had spilled soup upon himself. Nor was it any use trying delicately to detach her—that only made her cling the harder to him.

"You will always have my friendship, Mary," he hissed, "but you must release me. Remember where you are!"

"I am with you, my darling Horace," she sobbed. "Faithful, steadfast Horace! Forgive me! Take me back! Say I am yours again!"

Before faithful, steadfast Horace could say anything, however, his former intended bride tugged his head downward and fastened her lips to his.

They had kissed before—over two years previously—once, when she accepted his offer of marriage, and again the next day, when he took leave of her to go again to sea. And though those kisses had dimmed in his memory, he could have sworn they were nothing like this one. Indeed—what kiss ever had been, where the young lady adhered to the man like a barnacle to a ship's hull, though the victim tried, through the pushing of his hands and twisting of his neck, to get away? Moreover, despite her crooning and crying and muffled endearments, Langworthy's cocked ear caught exactly the sounds he dreaded. A carriage was coming!

"Let go!" he cried, no longer trying to be gentle. Seizing her wrists, he tugged, his own body twisting and writhing to break free.

"Ooh," gurgled Mary Pence, a mixture of tears and overexcitement making her voice husky. "How you navy men do like your rough play."

"Lad! Lad!" shouted a voice. "Is that man attacking you?"

Without waiting for an answer, even if one had been forthcoming, the driver gave a grunt and a "whoa, Blackie." The vehicle halted, and the driver jumped down, holding up his lantern. What its rays illumined almost caused him to drop it.

"Can that be you, *Wrigley*?" he asked, dumbfounded. "With Mr. Langworthy?"

CHAPTER 19

**And contrarie the remedy of the one evill
is the occasion and commencement of an other,
as in Scilla and Charibdis.
—Francis Bacon, *Essayes* (1597)**

Langworthy made rapid calculations. Flee? Deny? Take the bull by the horns?

Flight was pointless. Having already been identified by the coachman, running away would do nothing but make him appear more foolish than he already did.

Equally unavailing would be an attempt to deny what Harker had seen—without knowing exactly what he *had* seen, Langworthy would have to try to ferret it out, putting himself on the defensive and adding to his guilty aspect.

Take the bull by the horns, then. But which bull? The bull of Wrigley the footboy or the bull of Miss Pence, young lady in disguise? Would it be better to be thought assaulting a servant or assaulting a lady disguised as a servant?

The former, he decided. Absolutely the former. Whatever the consequences of wrangling with Wrigley, they would be nothing so bad as the consequences of tussling with a young gentlewoman, not to mention what it would mean for Mary, to be found in such costume!

Not that the choice of interpretations lay with him, he realized bitterly. On the contrary. It lay entirely with his companion in calamity, Mary Pence.

These conclusions were the work of a moment, taking place in the instant it took for his hands to release her. Hands he then held up in the lantern light, to show he meant no harm. For Mary's part, her own still clutching him and all the tighter in her alarm, her head whipped to take in the coachman, the surprise of Harker's appearance at least serving to dry her tears.

The threesome stood frozen in their tableau until the restless Blackie whiffled and tossed her head at being made to stand.

Mary turned back to Langworthy. "Here's a predicament," she whispered, lips twitching. "If I threw off my wig now, you would be forced to marry me, sir. But I scorn such measures."

"Are you all right, Wrigley?" called Harker again, uneasy at their silence.

"I am," answered Mary Pence in the footboy's voice, pushing Langworthy away and wagging a finger at him. "And that'll teach you, Mr. Langworthy, to accuse me of stealing from you!"

"*What?*" he mouthed, perplexed.

She widened her eyes, as if to say, *I have provided the excuse, now your story must run with it.*

When he continued to stand there, mute as a stock, she hissed, "What's wrong with you? You used to be better at this." And then, in carrying tones, "I told you, I don't have your ring, so it was no use—er—shaking me like the dickens until I cried."

Belatedly he took up the thread. He didn't like the thread, but he took it up.

"My mistake," croaked Langworthy. "I beg your pardon."

"You lost a ring, sir?" asked Harker doubtfully.

"Er—perhaps. Perhaps not. It might just be in my trunk at the rectory."

Blackie danced again, and Harker had to murmur reassurances to her. "I had better get out of the road, sir, but...begging your pardon, weren't you on your way to the rectory in the first place? Lord Dere sent me after you and the lad here, saying you'd turned your ankle and might appreciate a lift."

Langworthy grimaced. *Blast. That was right—his ankle.* Here he'd been standing, weight evenly distributed, legs solid as two tree trunks. Not that it would have helped even if he had remembered to affect an injury—he would still have to explain how he'd got so far in this wrong direction. *Double blast.*

"Very kind of the baron to send you. Very thoughtful. You see my ankle is much improved. So much so that I was able to accompany young Wrigley here on this longer walk."

Mary made an impatient noise in her throat. "We were going back to the rectory, see," she explained, "but then I says, 'Sir, your ankle! You're not lamed anymore.' And he says, 'It was a ruse, me lad. I just wanted out of the dancing and away home for some peace and quiet.'"

Langworthy swallowed his own exasperated scoff, stepping in front of Mary before she could introduce further troublesome features to this Banbury tale. "Yes," he admitted. "I—developed a headache and lied about my ankle to excuse myself. I would entreat your discretion on that matter, Harker, after all the effort and goodwill the Deres put into the occasion."

The coachmen gave a curt nod, though whether in agreement with Langworthy's request or only acknowledgement that a request had indeed been put to him, Horace couldn't be certain. Asking *anyone* to keep such stimulating details to himself was likely useless, and to bid Harker assist them in covering the matter by telling lies to his employers was out of the question.

"But then you noticed your ring went missing, Mr. Langworthy," Wrigley reminded him, hopping up and down to peer over his shoulder, "so we didn't go to the rectory at all."

"That's right," he agreed heavily, thinking this was the stupidest, least plausible set of lies he had ever been forced to go along with in his entire life. "I noticed my ring was missing, and I thought the boy might have taken it."

"Taken it from the rectory or from your finger?" frowned Harker.

"The rectory," piped Wrigley, at the same moment Langworthy said, "My pocket."

"But—you said I must have taken it from the rectory," sputtered Mary, giving him a wild look. The girl was on the verge of laughter, and he could have shaken her for it.

"How could I have said that, Wrigley, when you *have never been to the rectory*," he countered icily. "What I said was, there was no use in *going to the rectory*, if you had taken the ring from my pocket, and if you would only confess and return it, I would put you on the next coach to London, no questions asked, and would never speak a word of it to anyone."

"Oh, right," nodded Wrigley. "I remember now. That's how it went."

Heaven might have placed Charlie Harker in the role of a coachman, but he would have done just as well as an examiner, for he cocked his head and said, "But you say you didn't steal his ring, Wrigley?"

"Not a bit of it!" the footboy declared.

"Then what are you doing here on the Pettypont Bridge, over a mile from Perryfield, if he's not intending to put you on the first coach to London?"

It was obvious to Langworthy that only engrained deference prevented Harker from putting these questions to *him,* their story being so riddled with inconsistencies.

"I—did take the ring," blurted Wrigley, Mary Pence obviously having come to the same conclusion. "I did take it. So he was taking me to the Angel Inn."

Which made no sense either, given that Harker had just come upon them locked in either a struggle or an embrace. Langworthy had the passing wish that he might dive over the balustrade and let the River Cherwell carry him far, far from this ridiculous scene. Either that, or just start over and tell the whole truth. But how could he, if telling the whole truth would end in him being shackled to Mary Pence for life?

No. The story was contradictory and nonsensical, but they had no choice but to go forward with it. Indeed, Langworthy's only saving grace in the situation lay in the protection his rank afforded. As a servant, Harker could hardly accuse a gentleman—and the Deres' friend and guest to boot—of lying. Moreover, if Langworthy gave him orders, Harker would have to carry them out—at least until his employers released him.

But Langworthy chafed at this advantage. It felt like a dodge, an evasion, and he hated to use it. Beggars could not be choosers, however, so use it he must and would.

With a silent sigh he said, "Harker, we are talking in circles here, and you had better leave this to me. I am going to accompany Wrigley here to the Angel Inn and would appreciate it if you would ask Mrs. Dere to send Blodgett and the belongings of both of them along as well. I believe their duties ended with the ball in any case."

"Sir." That it was a bitter pill to swallow was obvious from the swelling of the coachman's chest and the reluctance of his movements. But he climbed up again and, after Langworthy refused his offer to take them all the way into

Oxford, told Blackie to "back," expertly reversing the gig until he could turn around in the open space of St. Clement's.

Mary waited until the vehicle was out of sight before giving a triumphant whoop. "That was a near thing! Do you think he was fooled? I think he might not have been."

"Of course he wasn't fooled in the least," growled Langworthy.

"Oh, Horace. How cross you are. I thought it great fun. Though it is a very good thing I do not require a character from Mrs. Dere, if now I am to be known as a thief!"

"If I am cross, it is because you have landed us in this rare mess, and I know not how to be lifted out of it."

Planting her fists on her hips, she rolled her eyes. "What does it matter? You'll be returning to Portsmouth almost on my heels—though I had hoped we might travel together. Who are these people, whom you have known not even two months, that you should care so what they think of you? You will never see them again."

"They have nevertheless become important to me," he replied, "as has their good opinion. A good opinion which, barring some miracle, is now lost."

"I don't understand you, Horace. What has happened to you? The Horace Langworthy I knew cared for nothing but the navy and me and good fun. But you—"

"The Horace Langworthy you describe," he interrupted, "dates from two years ago. Before I was a prisoner of war. Before my closest friend died. Before I was turned ashore on half pay. Before you jilted me."

"Ah," she said, softening, her voice dropping to a purr. "Poor darling. But the remedies to all but Sebastian Barstow's death are either given to you or near to being reversed. You have your freedom, the war will began again at any moment, and...if you will have me, I am yours again."

Her hand stole to rest on his forearm, but he evaded it. "Mary, we will be seen! Would you repeat the performance we have just given?"

Instead of being abashed, she hugged herself. "Hurrah! You called me Mary again! Come now. Say you have forgiven me, Horace. For the jilting, at least, if not for running you into a little predicament here."

"Let us continue walking."

Obligingly she fell into step beside him again, but he knew from the glances she gave him that she would not let him go without an answer. He forgave her for the past, of course—

"Of course"?

There had been nothing "of course" about it until the day he woke to find his bitterness gone and Mrs. Sebastian Barstow occupying Mary Pence's place in his affections. But he knew instinctively no young lady would appreciate forgiveness being granted at such a price.

The streets of Oxford were never empty, especially on a Saturday evening during Hilary Term, and for the first time Langworthy was glad of Mary's disguise. A young man in livery attracted no interest at all, whereas sprightly, red-headed, pretty Mary Pence would have drawn admiring looks and possibly even remarks before they reached the Angel Inn.

As it was, they found a table in the coffee room, and after ordering her some refreshment, Langworthy could leave her there while he secured places for her and Blodgett on the evening flyer.

Then it could be postponed no longer, the necessary, plain-spoken truth.

He returned to find her drinking her chocolate, one shapely little leg swinging carelessly as she studied the other patrons.

"It's too bad I was so unpromising a footboy," she said when he sat down across from her, "because I rather like the freedom of being a young man. No wonder you will not say when you will return to Portsmouth. It is one thing to bind oneself to a girl when one is mostly at sea and need only see her from time to time, and quite another to be trapped at home with her day after day."

"That is not the reason I did not answer you earlier…Wrigley," he said quietly, shooting an uncordial look at the waiter clearing the next table who peeped over. "It was because we were standing in the street where we could be seen and overheard, as indeed we were by the Perryfield coachman. But believe me now when I tell you, it is not for love of my liberty that I do not wish to restore our engagement."

Color washed over her elfin features and her chin lifted. "Then it's because you're still angry with me."

"I was indeed angry," he confessed. "And hurt. I do not deny it, nor think I was unjustified in feeling so. But neither is that the reason."

"Then what?" She picked up her cup of chocolate, swirling the beverage about. "Do look at this. I will share it with you, if you like. I was quite envious of you all at the children's ball, with your delicious drinks and sweets."

Her ability to make such a remark at such a time reassured him that there would be no repeat of her outburst, if he could only keep her calm. She had always loved dramatic moments, and he supposed she had not been able to resist the emotion which moved her earlier.

"Listen to me—Wrigley," he urged, ignoring her giggle at the name. "We were good friends for years and were once very fond of each other. Fond enough to decide to marry. But when Captain Colley came along, you preferred him to me, for whatever reasons. No—wait—let me finish." When she shut her lips again, pouting a little, he went on. "And had the captain not asked to be released, I do not doubt you would prefer him still."

To this she shrugged, but the gesture further encouraged him. It was not a denial.

"Mar—Wrigley, rather, let us be sensible. Marriage is too important an enterprise to be undertaken with one's second choice because the first is no longer available."

"You're not my second choice," insisted Mary. "I know your pride is hurt, but you were my first choice from childhood, Horace. Captain Colley did draw my attention away for a time—I do not deny it—but now that he has disappointed me, I see your true worth."

Was it true? Once he would have been tortured by the question, wanting desperately to believe her, yet fearing she only kept him in reserve for such an eventuality. Now...well, he was curious, but no more than that.

Clasping her hands together, she leaned forward earnestly. "Forgive me, Horace. Do!"

"Sit up," he hissed. "What footboy ever behaved thus?"

"I'll sit up if you say you've forgiven me."

"I have. Truly. I do and I have."

She straightened then and grinned at him. "Does this mean we are engaged again?"

"What? No! Look here, Mar—Wrigley, I mean. It is time to leave our former relationship behind us."

Her nostrils flared indignantly, and Langworthy braced himself for another explosion. "Remember yourself!" he mouthed.

It was touch and go at that point, he would think later, for her bosom began to heave in an even more un-footboy-like manner, half in anger and half in humiliation, but it was the hovering waiter's reappearance which forestalled an encore to the earlier scene.

"Is everything all right here?" the waiter asked, lifting the lid of her chocolate pot and peering in.

"Perfectly," said Langworthy shortly.

"Perfectly," echoed Mary.

The waiter moved on again, but he might not have been out of earshot before she clutched the sides of the deal table and whispered, "Is it because of that cunning Mrs. Sebastian that you no longer want me? Tell me! You owe me that much."

"Do—not—mention—her—here," he bit out ominously. But seeing her brows draw together, he relented, adding in complete honesty, "I do not want to renew our engagement because we have outgrown each other. You said it yourself—I have changed, and you have as well. You would not have loved Colley if you hadn't."

"But we could change back, I know we could, if we wanted to," she persisted. "You're probably right—you have grown serious, and I grew…tired of waiting at home for you to return, but now you have returned, and if we are together again, I can make you forget about the two wasted years and your lost friend and how I hurt you! I could, I know I could."

"Wrigley—" He felt doubly a fool for having to address her thus and for holding this conversation while she was in that preposterous disguise, but there was no alternative. "What's done is done. Besides, I will be going away to sea again, as soon as I can find an officer's berth."

"Yes—to sea!" she nodded, her eyes brightening as a new idea struck her. "If only—say! Suppose we didn't start with being engaged again. Suppose I were to go to sea with you as—as your cabin boy? You see what a good boy I make. What larks! What adventures!"

He stared at her in thorough amazement. "Have you—lost your mind? You cannot be serious."

"Why can't I? Why must men have all the fun?"

"*Fun?* Mar—Wrigley, this is *war*—not a—not an excursion to Ramsgate! It's certainly no place for a la—for one like you. All dangers aside, if you knew the conditions—the close quarters, the hard work, the rough company, the language, the food, the smells! For—one like you—there is scant privacy aboard ship—"

"Wouldn't the cabin boy share your cabin?"

This drew a raised brow. "I'm a lieutenant, Wrigley, and heaven only knows how senior I will be. Whatever 'cabin' I am assigned might more accurately be called a closet. And even if it were larger, the cabin boy is generally stuffed into the smallest compartment which will fit him, nearest the mess, so he can rise early to serve meals and be at everyone's beck and call."

"Oh." She drooped with disappointment. "That doesn't sound very delightful."

While naval life was not devoid of delightful things, Langworthy forbore to mention them here. "Wrigley, for your own safety and for your friends' and family's peace of mind, promise me you will return to Portsmouth and to your…station in life."

"You have no right to exact promises from me."

"I ask as your friend."

"Will you come and see me in Portsmouth as soon as you return?"

The hesitation gave her her answer, but instead of bristling, she sighed this time. "I will go home. I don't see as I have any choice, though it would serve you and everyone right if I took Blodgett and disappeared to London."

"Ah, but then you would miss all the navy men, young and old, rich and poor, handsome and plain, pouring as we speak into Portsmouth, and they would miss you."

It was true, as far as those things went, but he knew there was *one* who would not miss her. Who would never miss her again.

And when Mary Pence and her ancient companion Miss Blodgett were seen safely off on the evening coach, Langworthy made his thoughtful way back to Iffley.

CHAPTER 20

For they have sown the wind,
and they shall reap the whirlwind.
—Hosea 8:7, *The Authorized Version* (1611)

Though the day following the children's ball dawned overcast and mild for the end of February, a metaphorical whirlwind soon engulfed the village.

The first hint of the storm arrived when the Barstows were at breakfast. On this occasion, Mrs. Lamb of the Tree Inn had stood manfully to her post, and Irving returned to the cottage bearing no letters from the postmistress but a full budget of news.

"If you please, Mrs. Barstow, the Tree Inn was in uproar this morning, so I'm late with building up the fire."

"It's all right, Irving," she answered. "What was the fuss about?"

"Mrs. Robson—the Perryfield housekeeper—her cousin had taken a cart from Oxford. He's the one who works at the Angel Inn, madam. Fellow by the name of Brears. A waiter there, in the coffee room. I didn't know him from Adam, naturally, but he got to the Tree Inn just as Sealy the Perryfield gardener boy came for the post." Irving was a slow speaker at all times, but in this instance he was also busy sweeping the ashes and scraping them into his bucket. Having become familiar with his roundabout, dilatory storytelling, however, no one pressed him to come to the point but merely went on with their meal. "Mrs. Lamb says, 'Look here, Mr. Brears, Sealy can take you on to Perryfield,' and Brears says, 'Thank you, but I know the way well enough, Mrs. Robson being my cousin,' and Sealy says, 'Then are you the one who sent those wretched servants to us, what got everyone in a pother?' And Brears says, 'It's about one of those servants I'm going to see Maggie. Make my apologies to her because I would never have sent 'em over, if I'd known how queer they were, the one more than t'other.'"

Irving had their attention now, not that he noticed, as he had begun to lay the fire and took great pride in doing it just so, so that it would catch at once and require very little poking or encouragement to burn steadily.

"Then Mrs. Lamb puts in her oar and says, 'What's this about queer? Don't you two go walking off before you tell me. People depend on me to know what there is to know.' Nor did she have to ask twice because Sealy says straight off, 'That's right they were odd ones. The footboy goes to help one of our guests go home yesterday, and his lordship sends Harker with the gig after them because the guest fellow lamed himself dancing or some sort, but then Harker takes longer than he ought, so that he isn't around to help when the other guests are going, and when he does show his face again, the mistress commences to scold him good, but he throws up his hands and says, 'Madam, what could I do? I couldn't find them where they were supposed to be, but instead I catch them on the Pettypont Bridge, a-kissing or a-fighting or I don't know what, and Mr. Langworthy tells me to send on Blodgett and their things because he—Blodgett—and Wrigley are making off by the late coach—'"

"Kissing?" gasped Frances, the only one who managed to speak a word in response to this astonishing account.

"—And you might have beat her down with a feather after Harker tells her this, Sealy says—Mrs. Dere, you understand. And he says she turned right to his lordship and says, 'What is this? What is this? Have we hosted under our roof a liar and a who-knows-what-all sort of ruffian?' and his lordship tries to tell her to calm herself, says Sealy—but then Brears the cousin-waiter says, 'I knew it! I knew there was something odd-like between those two in the coffee room at the Angel'—between Wrigley and—"

"Thank you, Irving," Mrs. Barstow cut in, her face pale and hands fluttering. "That will do. If you will leave us." It was probably a case of shutting the stable door after the horse was stolen, to judge from her family's expressions (and the clamor which erupted after the door shut), but she could not think what else to do.

"What is he talking about?" demanded Gordon. "Mr. Langworthy kissing or fighting with that footboy? What can Irving mean?"

"I don't know. I don't know. There must be some mistake, and Irving told it in the most confusing manner."

"What was that about Mr. Langworthy's ankle?" asked Maria. "I'm glad Harker came along, because suppose the footboy attacked Mr. Langworthy, and he could not defend himself because of his ankle?"

"That makes no sense at all," Frances told her quellingly. "If Mr. Langworthy's ankle still troubled him, what were they doing away over on the Pettypont Bridge?"

"None of it makes any sense," rejoined Gordon. "Ankle or no ankle."

None of it made any sense, but that did not prevent the Barstows discussing it at great length, turning the little they knew this way and that, as if clarity would come with much handling.

Sarah alone said nothing. She could not have spoken if she wanted to, over the hard little knot in her chest.

"I wish you had let Irving tell us all he knew, muddled though it was," Frances said for the third time. "But since you didn't, I intend to walk straight to Perryfield and have it all out of Mrs. Dere." Gordon and Maria immediately begged to accompany her, and even Mrs. Barstow bit her lip and said she would go. Mr. Langworthy was such a favorite with her, she could not bear to think of any mystery or disgrace attaching to him, even if it turned out to be just in her neighbors' imaginations.

"Are you coming, Sarah?" demanded Frances.

Sarah shook her head.

"Yes," agreed her mother-in-law. "You had better not. After your cold, the ball must have knocked you up, for you are quite wan. You rest here, and we will get to the bottom of this tittle-tattle."

The house was very quiet when they had gone. Even the dog and cat snoozed in their baskets. Though Bash was mostly recovered from his own cold, he still tired easily and was content to sit with her, the two of them examining illustrations of insects in a book the baron had lent to them. Sarah was glad of the occupation, though it was not demanding enough to distract her. Because what exactly had taken place, and what could it all mean?

Whatever it was, it had nothing to do with her, she told herself, though she remembered with uneasiness Wrigley's hostility and his accusations. Could he possibly have repeated those humiliating claims to Mr. Langworthy? Said that Sarah was trying to steal him from Mary Pence, or that she ought better to be a good little widow and leave the young men alone? Could it have been warnings against Mrs. Sebastian and her cunning traps which angered Mr. Langworthy, if he had indeed been angry?

She could make those pieces fit Irving's ramblings plausibly, but then what about the possible kissing?

Poppet's head snapped up, and a second later Reed opened the parlor door and peeked in. "It's *him*, Mrs. Sebastian." From the way the maid widened her eyes as she made the announcement, it was obvious to Sarah that Irving had shared the morning's bombshell with her, directly after leaving the breakfast room.

"Him?" repeated Sarah stupidly. She was scarcely audible because all at once her heart was beating a mile a minute.

"Mr. Langworthy!" hissed the maid. "Coming up the walk!" Poppet went to sniff the servant's ankles, and she picked him up, throwing a glance back along the passage, as if their infamous caller might suddenly appear at her shoulder. "What should I do? Turn him from the door? I will call Irving to do it."

"You will do no such thing," croaked Sarah.

"But the village is ringing with his doings!" squeaked Reed in a most un-Reed-like manner. "Shall I say you are not at home, then?"

"But I am. At home." She wound her fingers through Bash's hair, tugging at it for comfort, and for once he did not pull away. "And I will see him. Take the dog with you, please."

Reed hung fire, eyeing Sarah as if uncertain if she were of sound mind, but then she shrugged and shook her head, backing from the room. Over her racing heart Sarah could still hear the maid's steps which followed, the front door opening and closing, Poppet barking and voices murmuring, steps returning. She rose unsteadily to her feet by the time the parlor door opened again.

"Mr. Langworthy, Mrs. Sebastian." Although Reed's sour face could not be seen by the guest, the sourness of her voice was easily detected.

He entered, hat in hand, making his bow, to which Sarah returned a teetering curtsey, nodding at Reed to dismiss her. For all the maid's disapproval, she resented being sent away, and Sarah did not doubt she would only go so far as to fetch Irving, that the two of them might tiptoe back and listen at the door.

"Won't you sit down?"

"I—did not expect to find you alone. I mean—you and Master Bash. Is Mrs. Gordon Barstow not here?"

"No. She has—they've all—gone to call at Perryfield."

He seemed to grow handsomer each time she saw him. Everything pleased her now, from his crown of red-brown hair to the lines drawn by weather and humor at the corners of his eyes, to his agile, trim person. After two months in Iffley his tan had faded, but this morning there was color enough in his face. And in her own, she suspected.

They took their seats, an awkward silence falling, both anxious to begin and at a loss how to do so.

Bash rescued them. He held up the insect book to show their visitor, uttering, "Scawb."

Langworthy leaned closer to peer at the illustration. "So it is," he said. "A scarab."

Before Sarah knew what he was about, the little boy reached a plump hand to pat Langworthy's face. "No oosker."

"I'm sorry," he replied. "I know I don't have Dr. Rearden's luxuriant whiskers. It's a terrible shortcoming of mine."

To her own surprise, Sarah laughed, and then Bash laughed to see his mama laugh, striking Langworthy's cheek a second time to see if it would elicit the same result.

"Oh, don't, darling," she reproved, unable to hide her smile. "Naughty. Mustn't slap people."

"I've had worse," Langworthy answered, but then he could have bit his tongue out because she went red.

He straightened, watching her, the happy little moment over. "You've heard something then—about yesterday evening—I take it."

Despite not knowing if she had anything at all to do with Mr. Langworthy and Wrigley's imbroglio, Sarah could not prevent feeling guilty and embarrassed, but whether it was more on her own behalf or his she could not say.

"News travels fast," he went on with a grimace. "I daresay we are somewhat insulated at the rectory, but if Polly goes for the post in my absence that should complete the circle."

She raised her clear eyes to his, wishing it were permissible to say, *Then you tell me what happened, and I will believe you.*

But it was not. She had no right to demand the truth from him, even if courtesy allowed it.

With a grunt he shoved himself from his chair to pace the room, not that the crowded parlor allowed a very lengthy circuit to relieve his feelings. Sarah and Bash watched him trace a path, however, to the window, the door, the desk, the bookcase, along the back of the sofa, to the mantel. There he paused, regarding her, his lips parting and then closing again before he made another circumnavigation.

"What did—Wrigley—say to you, when you were left alone with him at the ball?" he asked at last, when he stopped again by the mantel.

Another wave of color flooded her face. She swallowed.

"He said that—he was a servant of—of your Miss Pence." This last made her wince. Should she have said "his" Miss Pence?

He overlooked this, if he even remarked it. "Is that all? Nothing else?"

She noticed he did not confirm Wrigley's claim, but neither did he deny it. Folding her hands in her lap, she repressed a sigh. And what emerged next, she later admitted to herself, sprung more from offended dignity than from any noble motive: "After he revealed his identity, Wrigley then...upbraided me for...pursuing you." There! She said it.

Muttering something under his breath, he turned away to hide his expression. When he faced her again, his voice was tight, anger humming below it. "I hope you will not hold Wrigley's nonsense against me, Mrs. Sebastian. We both know that—we both know that it was I who came to Iffley to offer for you and who chose to linger here, even after I was refused."

There was balm in hearing him say it, nonetheless, and a smile spread across her features. "Thank you," she said. "And in return I will defend you, by reminding you that Sebastian is to blame for you coming in the first place, and therefore to blame for it all, from start to finish."

"Sa-ba-chen," said Bash, pointing to himself.

"A different Sebastian," Sarah assured him. She looked at Langworthy again, waiting.

He tapped a finger on one of the corner scrolls in the mantel's plaster-work, not looking up. "Mrs. Sebastian, since you are proving so agreeable in answering my questions, I cannot refrain from pushing my luck. Tell me—what rumor concerning me did your family hear this morning, which sent them rushing to Perryfield forthwith?"

"Would you rather not tell your side of the matter first?" she questioned, her heart sinking at his wariness.

"I'm afraid not." But seeing her dejection, his hands clenched. "You see, it is not entirely my own story to tell. Therefore I must learn what is said and determine what, if anything can be done about it. Though I fear little can be done."

"Ah." If it was not his story to tell, it must somehow involve Mary Pence, Sarah guessed, and it made her sigh inwardly to think the young lady still held such sway over him. Fortunate, fortunate Mary Pence! To have treated him so and still to be loved.

She was relieved to see Little Bash close his book and yawn at this juncture, for she would rather he not be present if they were going to discuss Mr. Langworthy's public incident. One never knew what little mouths might repeat! Therefore she bent to whisper to him. "It is time for your nap, sweeting. Colds make one quite sleepy. Go and find Reed in the kitchen, and she will give you a little milk and take you upstairs."

He made a half-hearted protest but then slid from the sofa, giving the visitor a farewell wave, which Langworthy solemnly returned.

Sarah rose to open the door for her boy, and when he had toddled away, she returned to her chair, conscious of Langworthy's steady regard.

"Where were we?" he prompted. "Oh, yes, you were about to divulge all."

Reaching for her basket, she drew some work from it, that she need not look at him. "You will think we are very gossipy, sir, when I tell you what I heard this morning, but I assure you our man Irving takes a long time to say anything, so we are sadly in the habit of not attending carefully, which is how he managed to say as much as he did before any of us understood half of the—nonsense—he spouted. Truly, as soon as my mother-in-law did realize, she stopped him and—and we were left to wonder what precisely—"

"Let us have it, Sarah," he interrupted. "That is more beating about the bush from you than I have ever heard before." A ghost of a grin fleeted across his features, so distracting her that she failed to upbraid him for using her Christian name.

"Very well. Irving returned from the Tree Inn this morning, where it seemed there was a veritable conclave in process. The undergardener from Perryfield, Mrs. Robson's cousin from the Angel Inn—"

"Angel Inn!"

His guilty start did not improve matters, but when he said no more Sarah was obliged to continue. "Apparently that fellow, Briars or Beers or something, is a waiter there. Anyway, the undergardener said Harker said to Mrs. Dere—you see how muddled it is! All hearsay, and all secondhand—"

"I do see. Pray go on, Mrs. Sebastian."

Her stitches were suffering, and if she did not pick them out later, the cloth would have a ripple and not lie smoothly.

"Very well," she agreed. "In short, sir, it seems Harker reported seeing you supposedly either—embracing—or struggling—with Wrigley on the Pettypont Bridge, and Briars or Beers further reported a—a certain *oddness* between you both when he saw you in the coffee room. Mrs. Dere is horror-struck that you might be a viper nourished by the Perryfield bosom, as it were, and she required calming by the baron. That is it. The sum total of what I heard this morning before Mrs. Barstow recovered enough to send Irving from the room." Finally she looked up at him, her brow clouded.

He said nothing, though he ran long fingers through his hair and tugged at his locks even as Sarah had tugged at Bash's. Then he heaved a sigh and resumed his seat, leaning against the back of it as if exhausted.

When she could bear it no longer, she prodded, "Well...? Is there nothing you feel at liberty to add or explain? If you do not, who knows what construction idle tongues will put upon it." *For pity's sake,* she wanted to plead, *can you not even say whether it was kissing or fighting?* But how could it have been kissing? There were some sailors who preferred or who resorted to—other sailors while at sea. Sarah vaguely understood this, though it was a subject Sebastian had certainly never raised in his letters. But could Mr. Langworthy possibly be such a person?

As if he divined her thoughts, he at last made reluctant response. "It was...an argument, of sorts which Harker witnessed. A physical altercation, though no one was injured. Wrigley—when Harker came upon us—Wrigley gave Harker an explanation for it. It was...hardly adequate. And if you find that people are not...persuaded by the reason he gave, I can only say it was not, in fact, the true one."

And it appeared the true one he could not, or would not, share.

"What...will you say, when you are questioned more closely?" she asked after another pause.

"I will not be questioned more closely."

"But—but—"

He sat forward in his chair, leaning toward her so that their knees nearly touched.

"I am going away. This very morning. Rearden will send my trunk after me. After I leave here, I'm walking into Oxford and taking the next coach out."

CHAPTER 21

**Friendship is the Noblest and
most Refined Improvement of Love.
—Robert South, *Twelve sermons preached upon several occasions* (1694)**

Her mouth made a wordless O. To Sarah it seemed as if the ground beneath her opened up, and she was sinking. Sinking into a black, yawning vacancy. She knew he would go—had known it—but to have the time suddenly upon her and overshadowed as it was by this mystery and incipient scandal—

Reaching, he tugged her sewing from her numb grip and set it aside, to take both her hands in his, the warmth of his skin perceptible even through his kid gloves. She should have pulled away—it was most improper—but somehow she was immobile. Turned to stone, if stone could breathe and pulse and inwardly tremble.

"Mrs. Sebastian," he said slowly, "you know why I came to Iffley. With what carelessness, what perfunctoriness I fulfilled the obligation your husband placed on me. You know as well the outcome, and how well I deserved your rejection of such an offer. And yet, in the following two months, I have come to recognize your...great worth. Barstow did not exaggerate."

By this point Sarah's tremble was no longer merely inward, but Mr. Langworthy did not rally her for it, thank heaven. On the contrary, his hold on her hands tightened.

"He spoke of your beauty, to be sure, but also of your good sense and calm (though perhaps I saw less of that than Barstow, given my enjoyment of provoking you). But I discovered and experienced other qualities for myself. Your ability to rise above the weaknesses in my character—I speak of when you were so generous, apologizing to me when you yourself were probably the more deserving of such."

"Oh, Mr. Langworthy," she managed at last, panic rising. This was how it would end? With him saying these marvelous things to her, things which she knew she would pore over in her mind every bit as sadly as she pored over Sebastian's letters after she lost him? If only she could go back in time to that January day, when Mr. Langworthy made his "careless and perfunctory" offer! She would accept him—oh, in an eyeblink!

Then there would follow no period of antagonism, no mystery with Miss Pence's servant, no terrible parting. Indeed, had they been engaged, Mr. Langworthy would have revealed all to her. He would have told her in detail what he was doing on the Pettypont Bridge, where he was not supposed to be, struggling with (or kissing) a person he was not supposed to be struggling with (or kissing). He would have told her all, because that was how he told his tales—too broadly, with nothing held back.

And yet, even as she thought it, Sarah knew it was impossible. She would never have accepted him that day, and had she done so, he would probably have resented her acceptance.

No. Their rapprochement had only come about in spite of, and perhaps because of, their bad beginning.

"I will leave here having made a number of friends and acquaintances whom I will remember fondly," he went on, one thumb now lightly rubbing the base of hers. "Rearden, the baron, the Tommies. Even Harry

Barbary. But your family will hold pride of place in my affections, Mrs. Sebastian. And you—your friendship will be most precious of all."

Her friendship? He would hold her friendship precious?

What bloodless, mealy offering was this?

Despair strove with pride as Sarah fought not to tear her hands from his, nor to surrender to tears.

And yet, she reminded herself, her breath coming shorter, *he considered my Sebastian just such a dear friend, and you see what lengths he went to, in the name of that friendship.*

His friendship is not nothing.

It was this conclusion which gave her the strength to retain her seat. To leave her hands pressed in his. To nod and to say quietly after a minute, "Thank you. I too will remember you and your friendship."

"And you will try to think the best of me, whatever is said after I am gone?"

She shut her eyes briefly, praying she could keep this promise.

"Yes."

Drawing a deep breath, Langworthy gave one last squeeze to her hands and lifted them gently to his lips. Then he replaced them in her lap and rose.

"I had better go. I have overstayed my time as it is, but I had not expected to find you alone. I thought I would bid a general good-bye and ask Mrs. Gordon Barstow if she would be kind enough to write to me..."

"I'm sure she would," Sarah assured him hastily, afraid of the constriction of her throat.

"Thank you. Rearden has my uncle Langworthy's direction in Portsmouth. And—perhaps you might also add a line to her letters from time to time?" he asked.

A nod. She could speak no more. Impossible.

He sighed. "Very well. I wish we had more time." When still she said nothing, a trace of his old humor returned, though it was rueful. "This would be the appropriate moment for any friend of mine to wish me, among other things, Godspeed, health, safety in battle, heaps and heaps of prize money, don't you think?"

Another nod, this one with her lips pressed together.

"Right then. We'll take it as read. Good-bye, my—Sarah."

And then he left her.

She had precisely twenty-two minutes alone in her closet chamber to throw herself across the bed and give way, before the inevitable sounds of the Barstows returning forced her to sit up and repair her appearance. Nor was the process complete before she heard Frances tripping up the stairs to knock on her door. "Sarah? What are you doing in there? Come down at once, if you can at all manage it. We are *dying* to speak with you."

When Sarah entered the parlor again, Mrs. Barstow leapt up from the very chair in which *he* had been sitting to demand, "Is it so, Sarah? Mr. Langworthy called in our absence?"

"You've been crying," Maria observed.

"I have. A little," Sarah replied, her voice thick. She cleared it. "Yes, madam," she addressed her mother-in-law. "He called to say he was going away. At once. And he begged you might write to him."

"Of course! Of course I will," Mrs. Barstow said, her eyes filling. "I am sorry I was not here to see him off. How he brought Sebastian to mind, with all his stories! We will miss him. For those reminders and because he was so pleasant for his own sake." She took Sarah in her arms, murmuring just for her own ears, "I know how hard it is, dearest. I would break down myself, but we must help each other be strong."

Clearly everyone assumed Mr. Langworthy's departure affected Sarah for the same reasons it affected Mrs. Barstow, and she would have been grateful for this misapprehension, if she could have brought herself to care.

"Well, Mama and Sarah, we had better confine our crying over Mr. Langworthy to the walls of Iffley Cottage," Frances warned. "Because, Sarah, if you could have seen Mrs. Markham Dere this morning—! Suffice to say, she is one person glad to see the back of him."

"When he called did Mr. Langworthy say anything to you—about what Irving was talking about?" asked Mrs. Barstow, all too aware of her children's eyes upon her and their listening ears.

She shook her head. "He did not. That is, I told him that there seemed to be a deal of—talk—flying around this morning, and he wanted to know what sort of talk, but he did not...offer his own explanation," she answered. "Indeed, he only said what was likely to be told was untrue, but it was not—he did not feel at liberty to say more. Because he declared it was not entirely his own story to tell. I can only guess he referred to the young lady who jilted him—Miss Pence—because yesterday, when he was cleaning my dress after spilling chocolate on me, that person Wrigley confessed to being Miss Pence's servant."

This revelation led to a hundred questions, naturally, which Sarah answered as quickly as she could, knowing her replies would bring no more satisfaction to the other Barstows than they had to herself.

"You have played your cards awfully close," Frances accused. "You might have said something about Wrigley before this."

Sarah put a hand to her temple. She couldn't, *couldn't* say why again. Not with everyone about. "Tell me what happened at Perryfield," she urged instead, turning the subject.

"Mrs. Dere was turning the place upside down," crowed Gordon. "Because Wrigley told Harker that Mr. Langworthy accused him of stealing a ring! He said that's what they were fighting about."

"And Mrs. Dere had all the servants running around, to see if anything had been stolen from Perryfield," Maria put in breathlessly, jumping in her eagerness. "They were opening every drawer and inventorying the plate and counting the candlesticks—"

"And Peter told me that his mother was so angry with the housekeeper Robson—because it was her cousin who recommended such incompetent, thieving servants—that she threatened to dismiss her!"

"Poor Mrs. Robson, who had been at Perryfield since the baron was a young man!" Maria added.

"It was Lord Dere who intervened, of course," Frances said, placing a hand on either shoulder of her younger siblings to calm them. "And Mrs. Robson is happily reprieved. But I'm afraid Mrs. Dere has transferred the indignation to Dr. Rearden and—and to us."

Sarah stared. "But what have Dr. Rearden or we to do with the matter?"

Mrs. Barstow sighed, dropping again into the chair Mr. Langworthy had occupied. "She said what were good gentlefolk to do, if others were to bring such people to Iffley—"

"She was referring to *us* with that bit, you understand," explained Frances. "Because Sebastian told Mr. Langworthy to come."

"—And then when people like the curate, utter strangers to the neighborhood, should invite them to stay," finished Mrs. Barstow.

Grinning, Frances reared back and put a hand to her bosom in her best Mrs.-Dere imitation. "There are standards to be maintained, Uncle! I know you were taken in by Mr. Langworthy, just as Dr. Rearden was, but I had my suspicions all along. Even his reasons for coming struck me as flimsy: to ensure Mrs. Sebastian and her son were well? How concerned could he have been, if he waited so long to come? No, mark my words. He came when he had no more funds and no more excuse for not carrying out his friend's request. And we were his dupes—all of us—providing shelter and employment and amusement!"

Then Frances bowed a little and held up placating palms in the baron's fashion. "Now, now, Alice, you are distraught. Mr. Langworthy was an unexceptionable houseguest and teacher and was in no way responsible for the unsatisfactory servants sent by the Angel Inn."

"Oh, no?" (Again in Mrs. Dere's manner.) "Then if nothing has been stolen from this house, how can we possibly make sense of that *fable* we were told? That *nonsensical* fable about a stolen ring, which, come to think of it—why would Wrigley admit to such a thing? What motive would he have for explaining away Mr. Langworthy's conduct? What possible reason did Mr. Langworthy have, to pretend to injure himself at the ball, and why should he be walking with Wrigley to Oxford, much less wrestling with him in public?"

Flouncing down in the chair beside her mother's, Frances threw up her hands. "Well, now we know Mrs. Dere was right. Mr. Langworthy *did* have a connection to Wrigley, though I am not going to tell her about it if you aren't. And she was right about the stolen-ring business being a Banbury tale, for that matter, since Mr. Langworthy told you that himself, Sarah. Goodness! What will happen now? Mr. Langworthy is gone, and so are Wrigley and Blodgett, so maybe it will all die away. There remain only us and Dr. Rearden to punish for whatever just happened, and the curate must fend for himself. It used up every cent of credit I gained through two years of flattering and managing her, I fear, to persuade her to forgive us Barstows for even knowing Mr. Langworthy."

Sarah was rubbing her forehead with both hands by this point. "Did she come to no final conclusions, then?"

Frances and her mother exchanged glances, which told Sarah that she had, but not conclusions which could be discussed before Gordon and Maria. Nor did those two show any signs of wanting to take themselves off, it all being too exciting to be missed. Gordon, in fact, mourned Mr. Langworthy's departure all the more, surrounded as it was with such a swirl of rumor. Even when Mrs. Barstow suggested Frances and Sarah assist her with plucking capons and sorting through the remaining pippins and pomwaters, Gordon and Maria showed unwonted eagerness to help.

I will steal Frances away on a long walk this afternoon, Sarah plotted.

But her ruse proved unnecessary, in that, when the Barstows were still at work in the kitchen, feathers flying and Gordon and Maria juggling and rolling the spoiled apples in races, Irving appeared, cap in hand.

"Mrs. Markham Dere is here, asking if you would like to go for a drive with her, Mrs. Sebastian."

"I?" wondered Sarah. Though they all stared at this unprecedented request, she hastily untied her apron and followed him out, snatching up her cloak.

The day had grown windy, and Sarah had to clap her bonnet to her head when she went out the front gate to where Mrs. Dere sat in her cart, Chauncey the pony standing patiently. On any other occasion Sarah would have suggested they return indoors, but nothing would stop her now from learning what Mrs. Dere had to say of Mr. Langworthy.

Nor did the good woman beat about the bush. With a chuck to Chauncey they were away down Church Lane, gathering what speed the pony could, so that when they passed the Tree Inn and Mrs. Lamb came scurrying out in hopes of an informative exchange, Mrs. Dere merely lifted her whip in greeting and rattled by.

"I am glad you agreed to come out with me, Mrs. Sebastian," Mrs. Dere began, "because you were not of the party which called this morning."

"No." Sarah thought about lying—about pleading Bash's recent cold as an excuse—but she held her tongue.

"But I will assume you know at least as much as your family did of recent events."

"Yes." She had to say it twice because of the noise of the wind and the cart, and her monosyllables did not seem to please her companion. They gave Sarah time to make a decision, however, and she made it.

"It was probably just as well that I remained behind, Mrs. Dere," she said, raising her voice to be heard, "because Mr. Langworthy called at the cottage to take leave of us. If I had been at Perryfield, there would have been no one to receive him."

Having left the inquisitive postmistress behind, Mrs. Dere allowed Chauncey to slow to a plod, slow enough that Sarah could see the earliest snowdrops and crocuses pushing up through the bare patches in Iffley Meadow, and slow enough that Mrs. Dare could turn to study her without danger of putting them in a ditch.

"Mrs. Sebastian," she said, her sculpted features a trifle stonier than usual, "tell me plainly: did you stay behind in hopes of seeing Mr. Langworthy alone?"

Sarah drew a sharp breath. "No!"

"I rejoice to hear it because, as you will remember, I did caution you against fostering particular hopes or feelings for the man, penniless and without prospects as he was, and now he has proven far more problematic than even we could have guessed by his circumstances."

"I do not see that that has been proven," Sarah returned stiffly, holding her companion's gaze, "whatever my feelings—or indeed anyone's—toward Mr. Langworthy."

Mrs. Dere gave an incredulous scoff. "Do you not? Then you require far more evidence than I, Mrs. Sebastian. That man pretended to have twisted his ankle, that he might speak privately with that impossible footboy Wrigley. He then lied about where they would be going and was discovered by Harker on the road to Oxford, where Harker witnessed some—activity—between them, which Wrigley tried to explain as an altercation over a stolen ring, an explanation Harker suspected was trumped up and which I too have come to believe was false. Therefore, I am now persuaded that, if the two men were not fighting, it must have been...contact of another sort."

Sarah's throat seemed to twisted into a knot as she listened, but she shook her head with vigor. Twice.

And here, glancing up and down to ensure no traffic would come upon them, Mrs. Dere drew Chauncey to a halt. "You disagree, Mrs. Sebastian. Perhaps when Mr. Langworthy called at Iffley Cottage, he provided his own version of the story?"

What could Sarah say or do? Mr. Langworthy had decidedly *not* provided his own version of the story! In fact, he had warned her that the story she would hear was patently untrue, just as Mrs. Dere and Harker supposed.

Again she shook her head, but this time it was a rueful motion. How could she defend him, when he would not defend himself?

Sarah's dejection had the benefit of softening Mrs. Dere, however, the latter choosing to interpret it as an admission of reluctant agreement. Her features softened accordingly, and she went so far as to take hold of Sarah's forearm and give it a comforting squeeze.

"If he provided no other explanation, Mrs. Sebastian, I begin to think I have guessed why that may be. Indeed, this is why I asked you to drive with me. I thought it better to share this word with you privately."

To Sarah's mingled amazement and dismay, Mrs. Dere blushed as she spoke. Actually blushed! Why, Sarah could not think of a time she had seen the elegant, self-possessed mistress of Perryfield look this uncomfortable, and she did not like to see it now. If only she could climb down from the pony cart and flee from whatever lay ahead!

It got worse.

Mrs. Dere reached and took Sarah's two hands in both her own, exactly as Mr. Langworthy had hours earlier. Then, steeling herself, she plunged ahead.

"My dear Mrs. Sebastian, I suppose you heard that one other possibility for what Harker saw was that Mr. Langworthy and that wretched Wrigley were—were *embracing*. No—please—let me say what I need to say. Indeed, I only feel at liberty to speak to you on this matter because you have been a married woman and married, moreover, to a navy man. I do not know how much—if at all—Mr. Sebastian Barstow might have spoken to you of such matters, or whether you can possibly be still unaware of something—er—which has been mentioned in the public papers with some frequency, but there are *certain things* which might and do take place between men at sea which really cannot be talked about in polite society."

Now Sarah's own face was as scarlet as Mrs. Dere's, and she wanted more than anything in the world to be far, far away in her little closet bedchamber, the coverlet pulled over her head.

Yes, she understood what Mrs. Dere hinted at, though a Sebastian Barstow who did not share the rougher aspects of crossing the equator with his wife had never, never come within a mile of this particular topic! But she understood as well that what Mrs. Dere now ascribed to Horace Langworthy was no more true than the ridiculous tale of the stolen ring. How could it be, the way Mary Pence nearly broke his heart? Or the way he held Sarah's hands and lifted them to his lips in farewell?

Of the latter proof—if it proved anything at all, and how could it, when Langworthy himself spoken only of friendship?—nothing could be said, but what could be said *must*, and Sarah roused herself to do so, urgency loosening her tongue and making her curt.

"I believe you are mistaken, madam. I have no better explanation to supply, but I do still believe you are mistaken. Entirely. If you will remember, he came to Iffley after being jilted by his intended bride. It was part of his delay in coming."

Mrs. Dere did nothing so vulgar as snapping her fingers, but the toss of her head served the same purpose. "That is what the baron said, as if anything could be deduced from it. Is it not equally possible that this is why she jilted him? Are engagements so commonplace to be thus tossed aside? You are welcome to your own opinions, Mrs. Sebastian, but I tell you again it is a good thing you heeded my warning. Iffley is well rid of such a person, and I would not be a bit surprised if, in coming days, we were to read something in the newspapers which vindicates me."

If Sarah had never before seen Mrs. Dere blush, it was a day for firsts. Because neither had Mrs. Markham Dere ever seen quiet Mrs. Sebastian look so...obstinate.

Ah, well.

No one liked to be told she was wrong and another person was right. The important thing was that Mrs. Dere had spoken her mind for conscience's sake and would be guiltless, whatever might come after. Mrs. Sebastian might not recognize it, but Alice Dere had been a true friend to her.

The mistress of Perryfield clicked her tongue to wake Chauncey.

"Come now, Mrs. Sebastian," she said, smiling serenely, "let us get out of this wind. I will take you home."

CHAPTER 22

...For thy Children dead I'll be a son to thee!
—Wordsworth, *Lyrical Ballads* (1800)

I don't believe it," whispered Mrs. Barstow to Sarah. "Not a word."

"Nor do I," Frances uttered.

The three ladies had their heads together, having seized the first opportunity in the days which followed, Gordon having gone to school and Maria occupied with her lessons.

"And even if it were so, it would make no difference to me," Mrs. Barstow added staunchly. "He was nothing but kindness to us, no matter what happened at the children's ball or afterward. Nothing but kindness to Sebastian and nothing but kindness to us. I consider him—a son. Or as good as one. He asked me to write to him! Is that not proof he considers himself bound to us?"

"Certainly," Frances agreed. "But now I rather wish he would marry the girl who jilted him. Or marry somebody. Because even if it is *not* true about him, there are such dangers even to have rumors of that nature floating about. It might injure his career—or worse!"

"How would the silly rumors in Iffley ever reach Portsmouth?" asked Sarah, trying to sound dismissive. Her insides were roiling to hear Frances wish a bride—any bride—on Mr. Langworthy.

"That's right," said Mrs. Barstow, her chin lifting. "Of course they won't. Now that he is gone back, there is no connection anywhere between here and there to betray him."

"Don't say 'betray,' Mama!" Frances scolded. "'Betray' implies that we believe he did something wrong. I mean—besides lying about having turned his ankle and where he was going. I suppose the only possible connection between Iffley and Portsmouth would be Robson's cousin, the waiter at the Angel Inn. But why should the waiter speak of Mr. Langworthy to anybody?"

This was hardly reassuring, considering how the man had raced over to the Tree Inn the morning afterward to do exactly that, but seeing her mother's and Sarah's distress, Frances quickly added, "But of course the gossip would have to go by way of Newbury or London just like the coaches, and at least in the latter case, there are already so many reports and slanders flying about in town about so many people that one more counts for nothing."

"True, true," her mother nodded, determined to be persuaded. "Still, I may in my first letter to him advise him to tread carefully. We know, from the amusing stories he told us, that he is not by nature a...cautious man."

No, Horace Langworthy was not a cautious man.

It was one thing to say she would write to him, however, and another actually to sit down and record such thoughts as these in black and white. And though Mrs. Barstow thought much on the matter, the days passed with the task yet undone. Until she began to say, "Perhaps it would be best if he wrote to me first. You gave him permission to, Sarah, and he might take offense if the first thing I wrote to him was, 'Take care, for people are talking about you in Iffley'!"

And they were.

Not out in the open, perhaps, but behind doors and hands. At church the following Sunday, some went so far as to congratulate Dr. Rearden on being quit of such a guest, this message delivered with a knowing raise of the eyebrows and received with mumbles and sheepishness.

Thankfully, Mrs. Dere did not stoop to stir the coals. Having said her piece to the family and to Sarah in particular, she was content to let the matter be forgotten. "He was a charming man," she told the parishioners gathered in the churchyard after the morning service, "though sadly not as forthcoming as one would wish. We will never know his relation to the servant Wrigley, I suppose, but whatever it was, no lasting harm has been done."

"That's very magnanimous of you, Mrs. Dere," said Mrs. Lane huffily, "but it is only by the grace of God nothing seems to have been stolen, nor any of the youth corrupted."

Mrs. Dere inclined her lovely head a few degrees in acknowledgement, but such was her ascendancy over Iffley society that those around her must give way, and the conversation might have turned to other subjects, had the baron not spoken up.

"I, for one, will refrain from drawing any conclusions about Mr. Langworthy, given the paucity of evidence," he said in his soft way. "But I would hate to think him anything but a fine young man. A worthy young man."

His niece by marriage gave a tight smile, but his cousin Mrs. Barstow looked as if she would like to kiss him for this speech, going so far as to loop her arm through his. "Thank you, sir. I cannot think ill of any friend of my lost son. And if I were to learn Mr. Langworthy was guilty beyond doubt of—any number of crimes—I fear I might love him still."

Such a declaration met with indrawn breaths, uncomfortable throat clearings, and a click or two of the tongue, but the rest of the Barstows thought variations of *Hurrah! What a gem Mama is,* and, Sarah, emboldened, said, "Yes, I agree. My husband Sebastian thought Mr. Langworthy the best of men, and therefore I cannot do otherwise."

Gordon told her later that the Tommies shared the Barstows' opinion, "and they say so does Dr. Rearden, only he knows what side his bread is buttered on and doesn't care to cross Mrs. Dere or his other congregants. And Peter is torn, but I don't hold it against him. A boy has to be loyal to his mother, even if his mother is impossible."

Thus, over the course of a fortnight, the uproar gradually died away, starved of oxygen.

Mrs. Barstow began to talk again of writing to Horace Langworthy because, though neither said it aloud, she and Sarah were each secretly saddened by each passing day with no word from him. "Perhaps now I need not refer at all to the circumstances in which he left," she mused as they sat over their work in the parlor. "If no one talks of it *here* any longer, after all, why need I mention it in a letter? I might simply talk of other things."

Much as Sarah yearned for news, her doubts had also grown with each passing day. Why did he not write to Mrs. Barstow? Was he, in fact, waiting for her to begin the correspondence? Or, in returning to Portsmouth, had he so quickly forgotten them, swept up in his old life—finding a naval berth and taking up again with Mary Pence?

Sometimes Sarah thought she had imagined the scene between them in the cottage parlor. Other times she concluded she had invested it with far more meaning than he intended. The friendship he had offered, unsatisfying as it had been to her, had still meant more to her than to him.

News came soon from other sources which only put the Barstows more strongly in mind of Mr. Langworthy: the papers reprinted His Majesty's Message to Parliament in early March, calling for the nation to be returned to a war footing, and the Commons responded by voting for those preparations.

"'£603,500 was then voted for wages of the 10,000 seamen for twelve lunar months,'" the baron read aloud to them after another Perryfield dinner, "'£290,000 for victuals, £330,000 for wear and tear of the ships, and another £27,000 for ordinance.'"

"Ten thousand seamen? That's so many!" cried Peter, but alas—only one of the ten thousand occupied the Barstows' thoughts.

He will find his new berth now, Sarah thought as she lay in bed that night. *Oh, Lord, keep him safe!* She did not care if he ever won a penny of prize money or an ounce of glory—only let him live! Please. *Please.* Let Mary Pence have him—

Only let him live.

"What do you think, Sarah?" her mother-in-law asked, holding out a sheet of paper. "I hardly knew what to say, but if war might be declared at any time, I thought I would not delay longer, lest it not reach him before he ships."

The letter was brief, more of its apparent length due to Mrs. Barstow's emendations than contents. She wished him and his uncle well and hoped his return to Portsmouth had been everything that was pleasant...the Barstows were well...Lord Dere read to them of the coming preparations for war, and it was natural to think of their dear friend Mr. Langworthy and what effect this might have on his prospects, etc.

"It will do very well, madam."

"Is there anything I should add? It seems so cold, so formal, but I hardly know what more to say when there is so much which must be avoided."

Sarah's pulse sped. "What if—would it be friendlier, if the children were to add a sentence in their own hand? Or a little diagram or drawing, if they wanted. As a remembrance of each of them."

"What a splendid idea, Sarah! And why only the children? Would he not then wonder why you and Frances could not be bothered to greet him?"

"Very well. You are right," Sarah agreed, her spirits soaring. But a half hour later, after a fair copy had been made by Mrs. Barstow, and after Frances, Maria, and Gordon each appended a cheerful tit-bit, the sheet was passed to her, and her mind went blank.

He had spoken to her of friendship almost in the same breath that he encouraged her to "add a line" to Mrs. Barstow's letters, and whatever she wrote here would be seen not only by him but also by the other Barstows on her end and by who knew whom on Mr. Langworthy's. Nor could she spend overlong at the desk, unless she wanted the children to wander over, inquisitive.

Like a child being forced to take a spoonful of medicine, Sarah screwed up her features in resolve and set pen to paper.

At a small table wedged into the corner of the Dolphin's front room, Horace Langworthy fingered the letter which had reached him that morning. His namesake uncle had shown no curiosity about it, seeing it bore no naval connection, but Langworthy stole out soon afterward to this inn in the High Street, a safe distance from Keppel's and the George, which were so popular with navy men.

He could have laughed at himself for the way his hands trembled—if he had not been the one trembling.

He had not written to Mrs. Gordon Barstow first because how could he? Fleeing Iffley as he had, under such a cloud, as if he were the thief or ruffian they imagined him! He had wanted to write. Every day. Every hour.

But he had not.

Moreover, he tried to school himself to resignation. Iffley was lost, and he must put it behind him. Put *her* behind him.

Not that he had any intention of forgetting about Mrs. Sebastian Barstow. About *Sarah*. Quite the contrary. But his wishes for her must wait. Wait for the memory of his disgraceful exit to pass and wait for favorable opportunities. One weighty French prize, with him receiving his allotted eighth, and he would be on the next coach to Oxford. If only war would be declared! He had his appointment to the *Gazelle* (formerly the French ship *Triomphe*) which lay already at Spithead awaiting the proper conditions, but even if hostilities recommenced that day and they had the good fortune to sail out and capture the first French ship which crossed their path, he would see no money until the prize had been adjudicated, which might take as long as a year.

One whole year.

And that was if Fortune favored him. Surely it must, however, when he considered his time as a prisoner of war. Must not Lady Fortune turn her wheel? Unless he was still on the downward swing and death or dismemberment awaited.

Just let it not be death, he bargained. If Mary Pence would take Captain Colley with his missing leg, Mrs. Sebastian wouldn't balk at one, he was certain. And he could still serve with an arm or leg missing, if need be—look at Nelson!—until the necessary, large-enough prize was won.

Having made these determinations, he bore up and opened the letter, and it was well that none of the other Barstows knew how quickly he scanned it for portions written in a different hand. He would read it all, of course, several times, but first—

And there it was. "Mr. Langworthy, we remember you fondly and hope you have been well. Do write to us about whether you have succeeded in securing your next appointment. Mrs. S. B."

It was not much, and yet it was everything.

After skimming the rest of the letter and reassuring himself that, whatever the scandal left behind in Iffley, at least no warrant for his seizure had been issued, Langworthy returned to the postscript, sitting through a second cup of coffee to ponder how much encouragement he might take from it. He could hardly say she expressed anything more than her mother-in-law had, but still she had taken the time to say it. Could her fondness be more fond than general fondness? (It was almost disheartening that both Miss Barstow and Miss Maria also mentioned fondness in their notes. Perhaps, uninspired, Mrs. Sebastian merely copied their sentiments...?) Well, what about her interest in his next appointment, then? That might be a hint that she, too, wished him to be buried in prize money, enabling him to marry. On the other hand, Langworthy admitted Gordy's contribution had been, "Hope you get a first-rater!" beside a sketch of a rudimentary ship bristling with guns.

No, altogether he could not find anything of lasting comfort in Mrs. Sebastian's two sentences beyond the fact of their existence and the thought that, if she had made such a beginning she must certainly go on thus. Every subsequent letter which came from Iffley might yield more.

He would march straight back to his uncle's house in Nobbs Lane and reply to Mrs. Barstow, answering all her questions and asking a dozen of his own. With any luck they might get up a regular correspondence before the *Gazelle* put out to sea and letters became long-awaited treasures dependent on time, tide, and passing ships.

Tossing a coin down, he rose and threaded his way through the tables toward the door, only to have it open just as he reached it and a voice call out, "Langworthy!"

It was Stolles, the surgeon of the *Gazelle*, sweeping in with a rush of fresh air and raindrops. "Are you going? Stay and have coffee with me, and I'll tell you about my stroke of luck. I found us a new cabin boy, to replace little Lord Measles."

Eager as he was to be on his way, news which so nearly concerned his future could not be ignored, though he convinced Stolles to accompany him back to Nobbs Lane.

"Little Lord Measles" had been the nickname bestowed on eleven-year-old Archie Lordmaison, the *Gazelle's* cabin boy who was not, in fact, a lord, but rather the youngest grandson of one, and a most unpromising boy even before he was stricken with measles.

"You know we despaired of replacing Measles at the eleventh hour," Stolles reminded him, as they strode up the High Street. "The space allotted would have hardly held *him*, much less any small seaman we could press into service. Nor was there time to send to the Marine Society in London for a replacement. But fortunately I heard my landlady rating some lad for stealing something she had cooling on a windowsill, and he whined back that he was hungry and would be willing to work for it, if she had any work."

"You have enlisted some unknown street waif who was robbing your landlady?" marveled Langworthy. "What will Captain Waller say?"

Perhaps because of his profession this behavior was not unprecedented in Stolles. He was known for taking in strays of all kinds, though heretofore these had been of the animal variety. A shade of uncertainty crossed the surgeon's features. "He's really not so bad, Langworthy. A little rough-spoken, maybe, and no little gentleman like Lord Measles, to be sure, but he has other qualities. He can read and write and even work figures! He showed me." But when the *Gazelle's* second lieutenant merely raised a skeptical brow the surgeon's confidence crumbled, and he bit his lip. "I say—let us stop at my boarding house, and you can meet him. It is on the way to Nobbs Lane."

"You've left the little thief in your room?" he laughed. "He's probably made off with all your valuables and some of your landlady's, to boot."

"If he has, then I am no judge of character, and it is just as well," insisted Stolles. "But if he has not, and you like him, you can join me in persuading Waller."

Langworthy grimaced, remembering the letter he wanted to write and having no desire to stumble at the threshold with his new captain, but he gave in with a shrug. If the child was a disaster, better that he be sent on his way before the captain even knew he existed.

The child was indeed a disaster, but not of the sort Horace imagined.

For when Stolles led the way up the narrow staircase of his boarding-house (making sufficient racket, Langworthy guessed, to warn the boy if he was up to no good) and threw open his door, the two men discovered the urchin just where the surgeon had left him. He sat on the wooden chair beside the fire, polishing Stolles' boots to a respectable gloss, and from the looks of it he had already finished the buckles and brushed the surgeon's coat.

"You see? I was right," Stolles crowed, gesturing toward the boy with the air of a conjurer who had transformed his rod into a serpent. "*Voilà*! Is he not a happy discovery?"

Langworthy stared.

The boy stared back.

The boot dropped from the lad's hands, and he swallowed audibly.

"Can it possibly be?" Langworthy croaked. "*Harry Barbary?*"

CHAPTER 23

Strike up our drums, pursue the scatt'red stray.
—Shakespeare, *Henry IV, Part II* (c.1596)

With her shiftless and wandering husband, her numerous children, and the freedom to roam she granted her eldest child, two full days passed before Mrs. Barbary stirred herself to report Harry's disappearance. And it might have been even longer, had Mrs. Barstow and Sarah not been delivering the shirts and gowns they had sewn for the village poor.

"Did you see my boy Harry at the Cramthorpes?" asked Mrs. Barbary, holding up one of the new gowns against her second youngest child.

"I'm afraid not," replied Sarah as her mother-in-law assisted a third one into a new shirt. "Just Jimmy and Anna."

The faded woman grumbled, frowning. "That boy! He'll be the death of me, see if he isn't. Just like his father—does whatever he pleases, and never mind if he puts me out of my way."

"How long have you missed him?" Mrs. Barstow asked.

Mrs. Barbary shrugged narrow shoulders. "A day or two. He did this last summer and called it 'going abroad.' But now it's March and dirty out."

"Perhaps Mrs. Lamb has seen him," suggested Sarah. "He still works for her, does he not?" Especially now that Mr. Langworthy was gone, she could have added.

As if she had heard the thought, Mrs. Barbary sniffed. "And not happy about it, either, he has made it plain. Ever since that navy man of yours left—"

"Not *my* navy man, Mrs. Barbary," interjected Sarah helplessly. She quite remembered the woman's malicious streak and what cruel things she sometimes would say to Jane and had no desire to draw her ire, but she could not allow this to pass unprotested.

But the maddening woman lifted a dismissive hand. "Didn't he come to Iffley because he knew your husband? Oh, yes, I know what's what, even though I have all these tiresome children and can hardly ever stray past my doorstep. I know he's the special friend of you Barstows, and he's drawn the wool over my Harry's eyes as well—not a one of you bothered by his carryings-on—"

Hearing Sarah draw breath, Mrs. Barstow shot her a warning look and said lightly, "So Harry was as sorry as we were, to see Mr. Langworthy go, then?"

The redirection worked, for Mrs. Barbary wadded up the new shirt in her hands, complaining, "Sorry? Sorry isn't the word for it! He's been moping and cross, with not a good word to say to anybody and talking big about what he'd do, if we lived somewhere better than Iffley."

"What's wrong with Iffley?" asked Sarah, recovering somewhat.

"It's not on the sea! Whoever heard the like? I blame that Mr. Langworthy, putting such thoughts in Harry's head."

"Thank heaven Harry is a clever boy with many interests," Sarah said. "He will surely find something new to absorb him, especially now that—Mr. Langworthy has gone away."

"And we will keep our eyes open for Harry," Mrs. Barstow assured her, rising to go, "and tell him to come home and set your mind at ease when we see him."

When they emerged from the Barbarys' cramped home, the two women shared a relieved look, the elder saying under her breath, "There's that duty done for another month!"

But Mrs. Barstow was mistaken, for the very next day Mrs. Barbary appeared at the kitchen door of Iffley Cottage, with two of her children clinging to her skirts. Irving had procured a bucket of birch sap, and Mrs. Barstow was assisting Reed to boil and skim it while Sarah measured out the sugar and lemon peel.

"Mrs. Barbary—what a pleasure," said Mrs. Barstow, wiping her brow with her sleeve before passing the skimmer to Reed. "You find us making birch wine. Won't you and the children step in?"

"I don't know about pleasure," retorted their visitor, her pale blue eyes reddened and watery. "I waited and waited but heard nothing, though you said you would speak with Mrs. Lamb, so I had to go to the Tree Inn myself. And me with all these children and no one to help me! But that's how it is—no one looks out for others' concerns."

Mrs. Barstow and Sarah both knew they had made no promise to walk up to the Tree Inn, but there was nothing to be gained by arguing this point. They both felt a little conscious, however, for not having been anxious about Harry. But who could keep a willful imp like him always in sight? Not even Mrs. Lamb had managed it.

Tears began to leak from Mrs. Barbary's pale eyes.

"Oh, dear," murmured Sarah, handing her a cloth when no handkerchief seemed forthcoming. "Did—Mrs. Lamb know where to find Harry?"

Mrs. Barbary shook her head and pounded a fist on Reed's kitchen table. "That wretched woman said she couldn't say for certain, but that if she knew one thing, it was that, a couple days earlier when Harry was last there, coins went missing from the till and bread and a pie from the pantry, and when she saw him again she would take a broom to him!"

"Oh, dear," said Sarah again. She could not, with any convincingness, pretend she thought the charge an outrage, but she wished Mrs. Lamb had not made it all the same.

Maybe Mrs. Lamb regretted it too, for Mrs. Barbary added sullenly, "But since no one came for your post this morning, she gave me a penny to deliver this and said she would add the postage to your account." (Slapping a letter on the same kitchen table next to the lemon Sarah had peeled.) "I can't read like my Harry, but Mrs. Lamb said it's from your *friend* in Portsmouth."

Portsmouth!

It need not be said how eager Mrs. Barstow and Sarah were for the Barbarys to be gone, but even if courtesy did not require them to hide this, it was equally plain that Mrs. Barbary had no intention of hurrying away.

With a grim face, Reed left Mrs. Barstow to stir the sap while she supplied the visitors with stools to sit upon and some little snacks, which were devoured as quickly as the maid could produce them. But when her appetite was satisfied, Mrs. Barbary nodded toward the still-untouched letter. "I wish my Harry were around to hear that. The likes of Mr. Langworthy don't correspond with boys like my poor Harry, but he'd want to hear the news all the same." When this hint drew no more than a polite smile from Mrs. Barstow, Mrs. Barbary descended to wheedling. "You needn't read it to me, naturally, but only think how happy my Harry would be when I see him again and can tell him something of his idol!"

Short of outright refusal, then, there was nothing to be done, and Mrs. Barstow gave in with good grace, giving Reed the skimmer once more, and removing to the window with the letter in hand. Sarah willed herself not to watch, knowing that if she did, she would do it with as greedy an expression as Mrs. Barbary, studying every fleeting expression which crossed her mother-in-law's features and straining to hear what murmurs might pass her lips.

No. She did not watch. Instead she sliced another pippin for the children, squeezing a little lemon juice over.

"Tart, isn't it?" she said to Herbert (or was his name Albert?), a boy just breeched and proudly wearing his new shirt.

Before Herbert/Albert could answer her, however, Mrs. Barstow gasped, her hand flying to her mouth, and their unwanted guest demanded, "What is it? Bad news? Has something happened to the gentleman?"

So much for Sarah's assumed indifference. She flew to Mrs. Barstow's side, her heart in her face, if anyone had cared to notice. Fortunately they were all staring at her mother-in-law, who quickly answered, "No—Mr. Langworthy is well, I assume. It's just that—Mrs. Barbary—your Harry has been found! He is in Portsmouth, of all places."

The fond mother gave a shriek to shatter glass and then began to wring her hands, crying, "Portsmouth? However could he have got there? Kidnap! It's kidnap, I tell you! My Harry has been kidnapped! He'll be impressed into the service! He'll be drowned! He'll be blown up!"

The children began to scream in sympathy, Herbert or Albert jumping from his stool to throw his arms about his mother and Molly tumbling from hers, only to break her brow on the corner of the table. Wails were added to the cacophony, and such was the noise that Frances and Maria and Irving came running, Frances with Bash in her arms.

"What is it? What is it?"

"Kidnap! My Harry has been kidnapped!"

"Careful of the hot sap! Mrs. Barbary—Mrs. Barbary—Harry is not kidnapped—"

"Molly's head is bleeding!"

"Who kidnapped Harry?"

At last Sarah was driven to beat a spoon against one of Reed's copper pots, surprising them all into silence. Even Molly left off her wailing.

"Mrs. Barstow has received a letter from Mr. Langworthy," Sarah explained to the newcomers, "in which he says something about Harry." Mrs. Barbary sucked in a breath, preparatory to another outburst, and Sarah quickly added, "May we hear it, please, madam?"

"Thank you, Sarah. Mrs. Barbary, this will ease your mind somewhat. Your Harry has been found. It seems he ran away to Portsmouth. He was not kidnapped. Mr. Langworthy did not even realize Harry was there until the ship's surgeon told him he had found them a new cabin boy, and that boy turned out to be Harry!"

"He was pressed, then!" shrilled Mrs. Barbary. "The press-gangs got him!" She looked in danger of swooning, and Reed firmly pushed her back onto one of the stools.

"Do they impress such little boys?" asked Maria.

"But how did he get to Portsmouth?" Frances wondered.

"Mr. Langworthy explains all," said Mrs. Barstow patiently. She patted Mrs. Barbary's arm so that the woman did not spring up again and then plucked away the cloth they had given her and passed it to Molly. "Hold this to your head, dear." When they were settled, she resumed. "I will read you exactly what he says. 'Harry astonishingly claims he made his own way to Portsmouth, riding outside on the coach—'" (a muffled whimper from Mrs. Barbary) "'—and then made himself useful at both the inn and the dockyards, doing whatever odd jobs came to hand. Here he ran across a Mr. Stolles, a man already known to me because we are both due to sail in a matter of days on the *Gazelle*, he as surgeon and I as second lieutenant. It happens that the *Gazelle's* cabin boy has unfortunately succumbed to the measles, and Stolles instantly recruited Harry as a most enthusiastic replacement. I'm afraid I am popular with neither Stolles nor Harry at the moment because, no sooner did Harry tell me all this, than I insisted his mother must be informed of his whereabouts.

"'Dear Mrs. Barstow, will you take this task upon you? I know you will say yes, but I had better remind you that if Harry's mother commands him to return to Iffley, I can pay his fare, but he will again be traveling alone, as neither Stolles nor I can leave Portsmouth at this juncture. If, in the unlikely case she approves of his going to sea, I will of course keep an eye on him, but I cannot promise there will not be times of danger and possible injury or worse. He would not be the youngest boy who ever served, if you can believe it, and in his favor he has always been as clever as some twice his age.

"'Please reply as soon as possible. In the meantime, I have housed Harry with friends, and I have made it clear to him that, should he abuse their hospitality, I will put him on the first coach home and not wait for an answer.'"

Calmly Mrs. Barstow folded the letter, and all eyes turned to Mrs. Barbary. Sarah was not the only one who expected the decision to be instant, after the woman's (understandable) fears and protests, but it was not. Perhaps it was the idea of Harry traveling back alone which gave her pause, for she perched on the stool now, silent, mouth working wordlessly.

Sarah knew one thing: if Harry been her own son, she would have fetched him back herself, even if she had to beg, borrow or steal to do so. Harry was younger than Gordy, for heaven's sake! How could he be a cabin boy, even under the protection of Mr. Langworthy? Sebastian Barstow had been twelve when he first went to sea, and Sarah knew Mrs. Barstow had thought even that age too young. If Harry had survived his trip to Portsmouth and a day fending for himself, it was a miracle, not proof he should embark on a naval career! Indeed, had Harry Barbary ever been on so much as a raft on the Thames?

But if Harry had inherited unreliability from his father, perhaps from his mother came the gift for surprise. For contrary to Sarah's expectations, Mrs. Barbary's demeanor underwent a definite change. After all, she had not been the recipient of village charity for over a decade without learning a thing or two about how to make the most of her benefactors' generosity.

"I would not want the boy to have to come back all by himself," she said at last.

"Would you want to go and fetch him, then?" asked Mrs. Barstow, bemused.

"Me fetch him?" wondered Harry's mother. "And how would I do that, with all my little ones? No'm. I only meant I'll be beside myself the whole time. To think of that little boy by himself on the outside of a coach, at the mercy of wind and rain and cold and highwaymen and kidnappers! Ah! It will be the death of me."

"If only we knew someone else in Portsmouth we could ask to accompany him," Mrs. Barstow said.

"No, no—I wouldn't want him with a stranger!" protested Mrs. Barbary, as if Harry had not just spent the last few days among strangers. "I would want him brought back by friends! Friends who could be trusted." With that she turned suddenly to address Sarah, her hands clasped to her bosom. "Friends like you, Mrs. Sebastian! You know both my Harry and Mr. Langworthy. It should be you to go to Portsmouth for my boy."

"I?"

"It is owing to you, you know, that my Harry ever made the acquaintance of this navy man and got such ideas in his head," sighed Mrs. Barbary. "He told me so. It's always been you Barstows. Teaching him to read and figure. Puffing him up, like—like—I don't know. Like he could be somebody. If Harry has done this, you should feel it was your doing. Only please go, Missus. *Please.*"

It need not be recorded here, the fussing and discussion and back-and-forthing which followed. It was not that Sarah was persuaded to accept responsibility for what Harry had done, and she doubted Mrs. Barbary even believed half of what she said. But neither did Sarah believe the burden laid upon her was altogether false. She *had* effected the introduction, after all, instead of telling Harry to go away and leave the gentleman alone.

No. If anything, Sarah resisted the demand to go and fetch Harry Barbary because she did not trust herself.

You secretly desire this excuse to see Mr. Langworthy again.

It was true.

She wanted to see him again. Of course she did. Though she had told herself he had gone forever from her life, hope refused to be extinguished. It was mortifying, but there it was. Given another chance to steal a moment with him, how could she possibly refuse?

Mrs. Barstow had her own wishes to consult. The news that Mr. Langworthy had found a berth and would be sailing so soon into unknown dangers, possibly never to return—!

"You must go, Sarah," she urged. "As soon as the coach for Newbury goes tomorrow. You can take Frances with you, and I am certain my dear cousin Lord Dere would be willing to pay for the trip." Her opinion settled matters, silencing Sarah's feeble objections and filling Frances with glee. It also succeeded in dislodging Mrs. Barbary and the little Barbarys from the Iffley Cottage kitchen before the birch sap was ruined.

Only when they were gone, and a note had been dispatched to Perryfield, did Mrs. Barstow add, "And you will deliver a message to Mr. Langworthy from me when you see him, Sarah, if you please. I would have said it myself, but he left in such a hurry and under such a cloud."

"What message would that be, madam?"

She lifted her chin. "That I wish, whenever he is on shore, he will consider Iffley Cottage his home. He never sounded as if his uncle was glad to see him, and as long as he is not married—"

"Wherever would we put him, Mama?" demanded Frances. "I like him as much as the rest of you do, but *honestly!*"

Her mother waved this away. "We can work out the details later, if we ever need to. The important thing is that he know it. That he has a home. You must tell him, Sarah."

"Perhaps you should write it down," her daughter-in-law suggested, coloring at the idea of making this earnest offer to him. It would be as good as begging him to come back to them!

But Mrs. Barstow rose from the desk and took hold of Sarah's arms. "No—please. Please tell him, Sarah. I know you—it's different for mothers, I suppose—but not a cold letter! It was so lovely to have him here—like having a piece of Sebastian back. Or another piece, I should say, for of course you are a piece, and darling Bash is another. But Mr. Langworthy had to leave so abruptly, and I suppose I am being silly, but—in a way it's like losing Sebastian all over again. Oh, there—I've made you cry too. I'm sorry! But how I would hate for something to happen to him without my having said what I could. You will tell him, won't you? For my sake?"

CHAPTER 24

Our lost, but now found Comrade.
—Defoe, *The life, adventures, and pyracies, of the famous*
***Captain Singleton* (1720)**

Mrs. Barstow's faith in her cousin proved justified, for not only did the baron willingly pay Sarah and Frances' coach fare, but he insisted on accompanying them, something Mrs. Barstow hoped for but had not dared ask.

"He must have done battle with Mrs. Dere over this," whispered Frances when Harker and Ogle the Perryfield coachmen drew the landau up at the cottage gate. "She, for one, wanted never to hear the name of Horace Langworthy again. Only imagine if she learned of Mama's proposal that he come regularly to Iffley!"

The two young ladies were handed in beside Lord Dere, their portmanteaux stowed in the trunk-boot, and the door about to be shut upon them when a now-familiar voice screeched, "Mrs. Sebastian! Mrs. Sebastian!"

Peering out, Sarah's heart sank to see Mrs. Barbary galloping up the lane to slide to a halt beside them. The woman made an awkward curtsey when she saw the baron within before hissing (as if then only Sarah could hear her), "Just one thing, Mrs. Sebastian. I have given more thought to this, and my Harry being how he is..."

"Yes?"

"Yes. That is—if, when you get there—you find he will not obey you and come back, I will understand. That is—supposing everyone thinks he would make a good cabin boy and will pay him for it, and Harry can't be persuaded to give it up, I will understand."

"But, Mrs. Barbary, are you saying I—we need not go?" Sarah asked. "Because I suspect if I even told Harry you would consider letting him stay, there would be an end of it. We would have to kidnap him indeed, to get him to return to Iffley."

"You don't know that," Harry's mother returned contrarily. "And I said he would have to be paid as well. And some of that pay would have to be sent home—because what would such a young boy need with it anyway, all that prize money?"

"Er—Mrs. Barbary," interposed Lord Dere, leaning forward to address her, "forgive me, but I could not help overhearing, and I think it imperative upon me to say the taking of ships and winning of prize money is no certainty."

"What? Are you saying it is or it isn't certain?" she demanded. "I don't follow your lordship."

"Isn't," he replied meekly. "Isn't certain."

"Well!" she sniffed, sounding rather put out. Perhaps she thought one so fortunate as Lord Dere of Perryfield begrudged those at the bottom of the ladder trying to hoist themselves up. "Well! That may be, sir. Only God knows."

Having put him in his place, she returned her attention to Sarah. "Mind you remember, Mrs. Sebastian." Giving her own forehead a tap and raising her eyebrows, Mrs. Barbary stepped back and let the mission proceed.

After a night spent in Newbury, they were off again following an early breakfast, the miles lurching and rattling away beneath them. The roads were dry; the weather was fair; no axles broke; no passengers caused undue delay at the successive stages; and they reached the outskirts of Portsmouth before sunset. The town had grown since Sarah last visited, but that had been before Bash was born, and the new construction amazed her. Only when they had passed the drawbridge and entered the older town did she see more familiar sights, and drawing up to the George Inn was like seeing an old friend.

They had already decided it would be too late to call at Mr. Langworthy's uncle's home, even if they were not weary with the journey. Had Mrs. Barbary continued frantic, they might have made the effort, however tired they were, but as it was they came down the following morning, refreshed.

"That's better," said the baron, smiling. "I like to see the roses in your cheeks, my dear Barstows. I need not ask if you slept well. Come. Let us see if the George's breakfast is as comfortable as their suppers."

It was, but with the departures and bustle of the morning coaches, it was some time before they could be served.

Sarah had put especial care into her appearance. There could be no flowers or curled hair, but she wore the dark blue dress which made her eyes almost violet and used Sebastian's cameo brooch to pin her linen fichu.

Frances looked well herself, her dark blonde hair and brown eyes complemented by a dress the color of wheat, and they drew admiring looks as they set out on either side of the baron up the High Street, Frances' head on a swivel trying to take in the sights.

"Perhaps after we see to this Harry Barbary business there will be time for a walk to the dockyard," Lord Dere suggested.

"Unless the sight of the ships and sailors makes Harry the less willing to go," said Sarah ruefully. "If he escapes us there, there will be no catching him."

There was hardly time for more, Nobbs Lane being a mere five minutes' walk from the George. The home of Mr. Langworthy's namesake uncle was a narrow building halfway along the street, with even narrower steps leading up to the door. Sarah and Frances waited on the pavement while the baron went up to knock, and after a long pause, the door was opened by a wizened servant with silver hair tied back in a queue.

"Good morning. I am Lord Dere of Perryfield with Mrs. Sebastian Barstow and Miss Barstow, here to call upon Mr. Langworthy."

Squinting at them, the servant retreated into the passage to admit them and led them into the nearest parlor. "I'll fetch him." When the door shut behind him, they heard his slow footfalls recede down the passage's creaking floorboards.

One thing was certain, Sarah thought as she inspected the austere room with its worn furniture and single framed picture of a ship under all sail. Whatever Mr. Langworthy's feelings toward the Barstows or Iffley in general, Iffley Cottage at least *looked* more home-like.

"It's so quiet in here," ventured Frances. "I feel I have to whisper. I see why Mr. Langworthy chose to keep Harry at his friend's house, rather than here."

"Although the atmosphere might have succeeded in silencing even Harry," murmured Sarah.

Presently they heard heavy steps in the passage—not the servant's because they were quicker—and Sarah had only time to sit straighter and ball her fists before the door opened.

It was not Mr. Langworthy.

That is, it was indeed a Mr. Langworthy, but it was Mr. Horatio Langworthy, their friend's uncle, a long, dour man as narrow as his house. He paused in the doorway before making a rickety bow.

"You must be acquaintances of my nephew, Mr. Horace Langworthy. I myself am Horatio Langworthy."

"We are," agreed the baron. He repeated their names for the elder Langworthy. More courtesies followed, but then, before Frances could fidget with impatience, Lord Dere asked, "Is your nephew not at home? We hoped to speak with him about the boy Harry Barbary."

"Boy who?"

Sarah thought possibly he was hard of hearing, but he added the next moment, "Never heard of any Harry Barbary. But I can tell you where Horace is. If he's not at the Dolphin or the George with fellow naval officers, he's at the Pences' in Highbury Street, not three minutes from here."

Hardly feeling Frances' elbow nudge her, Sarah required all her efforts to keep her face impassive. She must have succeeded, for when the baron turned to consult her, she saw no alarm there.

"Would you like to leave a note, Sarah?"

But the thought of sitting under Mr. Horatio Langworthy's cold eye while she wrote out Mrs. Barstow's kindly, heartfelt plea was too much for Sarah, and she shook her head. "Time presses, sir. We had better go and find Harry." Although her voice did not falter, her heart did. For was it not likely, then, that the friends with whom Mr. Langworthy entrusted Harry must be the Pences? Had his good footing with them been restored?

It was impossible to ask the uncle, however, if his nephew was again engaged to Miss Pence, and as quickly as it could be managed, Lord Dere and the Barstows took their leave.

"At the Pences'!" exclaimed Frances when they were again in the street. "Sarah, wasn't that the surname of the girl who jilted him?"

"It was."

"Do you think that means...?"

"Possibly."

"Mm...I don't suppose poor Mama will see him very often then, if ever again. Unless we can manage to charm this Miss Pence when we see her. Then he might persuade her to come to Iffley once or twice."

"You will certainly charm her," Lord Dere assured them. "And because Highbury Street is nearer than the Dolphin (and we know he is not at the George), shall we call there first?"

The walk might have been only the three minutes Mr. Horatio Langworthy predicted, but Sarah was glad of the baron's arm, for she felt a little unsteady. What would meet them in Highbury Street? The "sprightly, lively, mischievous" Mary Pence, glowing with triumph as Mr. Langworthy looked on, lost in adoration? Oh, mercy—then they must take Harry and go at once. No—no—there was Mrs. Barstow's message to be delivered!

I will tell Frances I feel faint, and she will deliver it, she decided. If that was cowardly, then, well, she was a coward.

She was also petty and jealous, Sarah realized, when they stood before the Pence home. A home as charming as Mr. Langworthy's had been uninviting. Despite being almost as narrow, the Pence home boasted bright curtains at the windows, drawn back on the ground floor to display vases of flowers on candlestands. Of course a sprightly and lively girl would hail from such a place! It was not that Iffley Cottage was less charming—it was that what Sarah hoped might be an advantage was here equaled and nullified.

This time the steps were wide enough to allow the trio to ascend, and therefore it was all three of them who were thunderstruck by the servant who answered their knock.

Tall and stooped and ancient with a square, slack face—

"M-Mr. Blodgett?" gasped Lord Dere, only to turn crimson because how could it be the old temporary footman Blodgett if he stood there in a dress, shawl and lace cap? But how could it *not* be him, unless Blodgett had a sister who resembled him in every particular except the particular of sex?

Any doubt that they faced one and the same person was dispelled the next instant, however, when Blodgett blundered backward in confusion, with the familiar sound of knees popping like gunshots.

"It is you!" exclaimed Frances. "But what is happening? Who *are* you, Blodgett?"

Head spinning, Sarah clutched the baron's arm all the tighter. Blodgett was a woman? But why would Wrigley have been accompanied to Iffley by a *woman*? A woman dressed as a man! Why, indeed—unless Wrigley had also been a woman? A woman, dressed as a man.

Wrigley, a woman!

In yet another blow, Sarah remembered Harker's claim that he had seen Mr. Langworthy and Wrigley either kissing or struggling or both. In some sort of entanglement which Mr. Langworthy had called a "physical altercation," and which Mrs. Dere had ominously called "things which might and do take place between men at sea which really cannot be talked about."

But it seemed neither grasped or told the truth.

For if Wrigley was female, as Blodgett was, then there might very well have been kissing on the Pettypont Bridge, whether Mr. Langworthy admitted it or not. And would he not have all the more reason to dismiss it as a "physical altercation," if he were trying to protect a woman's reputation?

Did Mary Pence know Mr. Langworthy carried on a dalliance with her servant? And if she did, did it make her as miserable as it did Sarah?

At least his kissing (Miss) Wrigley ruled out the sort of kissing Mrs. Dere feared, thought Sarah unhappily. Because this would have been plain old, ordinary kissing, such as took place between any pair of young lovers.

Lovers?

These thousand tangled thoughts passed in the seconds it took for the Barstows and Lord Dere to follow the retreating Blodgett inside, but before Sarah could overcome this shock there came a second.

"Who is it, Blodgy?" came a playful, rallying voice. "Are they back?"

"Blodgy" made a wordless gurgle in her throat.

"What did you say?" A head popped into the passage, a bright, red-headed one with keen, pale eyes and a charming grin.

A grin which metamorphosed into an O of astonishment before it was covered by her hand.

Now, the entire purpose of outfitting one's servants in wigs and livery is to render them uniform and indistinguishable, and thus as invisible as possible. Lord Dere, therefore, could be forgiven for not drawing an immediate connection between the young lady before them and the footboy Wrigley from Perryfield, Blodgett or no Blodgett. But Frances had been seated beside Mrs. Dere at dinner, with Wrigley behind Mrs. Dere's chair, and she at once straightened, her eyes widening. And Sarah—

Sarah had to put a hand to the wall to steady herself. Well!

That answers that question, she thought. *Miss Pence would not, in fact, object to Mr. Langworthy kissing Wrigley, unless she objects to Mr. Langworthy kissing her very own self.*

It explained more than that. It explained Wrigley's animosity toward her at the children's ball—even Wrigley's presence in Iffley in the first place! She had come to see for herself.

Did this revelation make things better, or worse? Was it worse to think of Mr. Langworthy kissing Miss Pence's hoydenish servant, or Mr. Langworthy kissing hoydenish Miss Pence? (For what other word could describe a young lady who dressed up as a footboy and traipsed across the country with only her aged companion?)

Miss Pence.

By far, it was worse that he had kissed Miss Pence.

He would not be obligated to marry a servant, if he kissed her. Moreover, though it would undeniably reflect poorly on his character, troubling servants was sadly common behavior and would carry no consequences beyond that. But kissing Miss Pence—surely they must be engaged again. What of the ensuing struggle, then?

Ah, it made her head hurt.

Her head and her heart.

Miss Pence, however (perhaps because she was far better versed in mischief), was the first to regain her composure, her eyes darting back and forth as she made her own swift calculations.

"My word," she said cheerily. "Won't you come in? I'm sorry my mother is not at home. But I see you have met Miss Blodgett. Sly Miss Blodgett. What adventures she has been on! Blodgy, do come and introduce the guests to me. I suspect they are in search of Horace—that is—Mr. Langworthy—and his little friend. Am I right?"

"Er—yes," said the baron.

"I thought so. He has told me all about his Iffley acquaintances, and when this Harry Barbary showed up, he said he would write to—some of you—at once. Come in, come in. If Horace—Mr. Langworthy, I mean—has not told you about me, I am Miss Mary Pence."

Her self-assurance, so complete, disarmed reproof. Neither Frances nor Sarah found it possible to fly at her with accusations or even to pose challenging questions, and they numbly followed her into her cozy parlor. Miss Blodgett played her role in this farce as stolidly as she had played her footman role in Iffley, leaving the guests with no alternative but to play theirs. Because Lord Dere only had to stuff down his confusion over Blodgett, he was the least agitated, but Frances took the seat beside Sarah on the sofa, full against her, that she might relieve her discomposure by nudging and poking her sister-in-law almost continuously.

"You see me working on linens for Harry," said Miss Pence, holding up various items. "He can hardly go to sea with only the clothes on his back. And boys grow so fast I thought I had better make them a trifle larger than necessary."

"You—think Harry ought to go, then?" blurted Sarah. "To sea, I mean."

Miss Pence seemed glad of an excuse to look at her, and it was an effort for Sarah to sustain her gaze. At least the hostility which had characterized Wrigley seemed absent, but Sarah marveled that a girl in Miss Pence's predicament—in danger of discovery and scandal—should be so cool.

"Oh," Miss Pence answered with a shrug, "I don't think he ought to go at all, at his age. But he seems quite determined. And who can blame him? That siren call of adventure, you know."

"What a lovely home you have here," said the baron, in an attempt to smooth the unspoken currents in the room. "And in the heart of the town."

"Thank you." With a saucy smile she added, "If you've already been to Mr. Horatio Langworthy's home, you know it's in the heart of the town as well. Though perhaps it is a little less comfortable than ours."

He gave a half-bow of acknowledgement. "It has been kind of you and your mother to keep Harry."

"Ha! Well, Mr. Langworthy did not want to ask his uncle to do it because Harry is so harum-scarum. And Mr. Stolles couldn't, because he's in a shared room at the George. But tell me—what does Harry's mother say? I suppose she must want him to come home, if she has sent such a force to recover him!"

Before Mrs. Barbary's inconsistencies on the matter could be made intelligible, the street door banged open, and Harry Barbary and Mr. Lang-worthy were the next moment in the room.

CHAPTER 25

Tolde with tongue of barbary In rude maner.
—Stephen Hawes, *The pastime of pleasure* (1517)

Langworthy had his hands full with Harry Barbary, to say the least. He had spent the past few days doing what he could to dissuade the boy. He talked of Harry's age, his inexperience, his cruel abandonment of his mother, the perils of life at sea in wartime, the perils of life at sea at *any* time, the unending hard work, the cramped quarters, the dangerous pranks, the inevitable bullying officer, the poor diet, the stretches of sameness and ennui. Not only did these truths fail to move the boy, but Harry countered with truths of his own.

"I will only get older, and I'm as big as a ten-year-old." "I learn fast—you've said so yourself." "Mama has so many children she will be glad to have me gone, when she forgets the shock of it." "I don't need much space. At home I share a bed on the floor with two brothers." "I won't mind the food. At home it's bread and ale, bread and ale, ninety-nine times out of a hundred."

"What of the dangers, Harry?" he persisted. "We will soon be at war. You might have a limb blown off. You might *die*."

But what person as young as Harry Barbary ever thought he would die? The boy only shrugged. "That's what the coachman said when I sat on top with hardly a thing to cling to. He said, 'Don't you fall asleep up there, or you'll tumble straight off and crack your head open and then be crushed under the wheels.'"

Great heavens! Suppose Mrs. Barstow wrote back to him saying he must return the boy to Iffley at once, and here was money for a servant to accompany him? (This solution would only lead to another problem because he could not imagine his uncle's ancient Coots managing to keep Harry under control, even if his uncle would spare him. Wouldn't Harry just run away from Coots and come straight back to Portsmouth? By then the *Gazelle* might have sailed, but Harry would simply haunt the dockyards again for another opportunity, this time with no friends or supervision.)

As a last resort, Langworthy proposed taking him out in one of the *Gazelle's* boats to where the ship lay at Spithead. The stiff breeze, at odds with the current, would make a chopping sea, and perhaps seasickness would succeed where arguments failed.

It did not.

Because when even Langworthy had to stare at the horizon to keep down his lurching stomach, Harry continued to bounce and exclaim and point. And to actually see the *Gazelle* and walk her decks—! Well, let it suffice to say it might have been Horace's worst idea yet.

It was this excursion they returned from that day as they turned into Highbury Street, Harry still chattering in his excitement and Langworthy still grim.

Knowing there was only old Blodgett to answer the door, and knowing as well how slowly the servant moved, Harry did not bother knocking but instead burst in, Langworthy on his heels, muttering a reprimand.

The words died on his lips.

For there sat—or rather, was hastily rising to her feet—Mrs. Sebastian Barstow.

There were other people in the room, of course. It was just that he didn't see them straight off. He saw Sarah, and then it was as if he were peering through a spy-glass at the first sight of land after months at sea. He could not look away.

But if she was his promised land, his glimpse was too soon overclouded. Because she stiffened; her lips parted and then shut again; her eyes dropped.

"No!" shouted Harry Barbary, jarring Langworthy from his shock. "No! Take yourselves off! Go it—budge! I won't go!" The boy spun around, meaning to leap for the street door, only to plow into Langworthy. The latter nearly doubled over, his breath expelled from him, but he retained enough presence of mind to throw out his arms for Harry.

"I won't go! I won't!" protested the boy, writhing and twisting to break Langworthy's grip. "You can't make me!"

Then everyone in the room was rushing forward and speaking at once, and Harry was taken by the arms and hands and coat. Both Lord Dere and Langworthy positioned themselves before the door, and Miss Pence guarded the windows, and poor Harry suffered himself to be led by Frances and Sarah to an armchair. He threw himself into it, scowling mightily and grumbling all manner of shocking oaths and imprecations under his breath.

"Harry," Sarah addressed him softly. She smiled ruefully to think how she welcomed the violence of his response, because she too had been struggling against an urge to throw herself at Mr. Langworthy. She, too, wished she could cry and curse and flee far away from this man who was breaking her heart. "Harry," she coaxed, "your mother has been fretting about you. You did not even leave her a note."

"Why should I?" he demanded thickly, giving the padding of the chair a punch. "She couldn't have read it even if I had."

"Someone might have read it for her."

"What difference would it make? I would still be gone, and she would still fuss about it."

Sarah tried another tack. "Are you all right? You haven't come to any harm since leaving Iffley?"

Harry shrugged, as much to say, *I am as you see me.*

Lord Dere sighed and shook his head over these discourtesies, but Sarah persisted. "I'm glad you're well. What an adventure you've had. Won't you like to come back with us and tell your brothers and sisters and the Cramthorpes about it? They will be amazed. And perhaps in a few more years, if you still think you would like best to go to sea, you might do it with your mother's blessing."

"If you take me back, I will only run away again," he declared, not a jot moved by these efforts any more than he had been by Langworthy's.

"Come, lad," said Lord Dere. "How can you speak thus to someone whose whole family have been your friends?"

Jerking his chin toward Miss Pence Harry retorted, "She's a better friend than the Barstows have been. She's making my linens for me."

"What?" blurted Langworthy. "We spoke about this, Mary. That is—Miss Pence."

"So we have." She took the clothes she had displayed to the visitors only minutes earlier, rolled them into a ball, and stuffed them in her workbasket. "Too bad, Harry. You will have to obey your elders. I feel for you."

Astonished at the rapidity of her desertion, Harry fired up. "That wasn't how you talked to me before. You said life was full of dull dogs and silly rules, and it was better to do what I liked, for the fun of the thing."

Frances cleared her throat and lifted her eyebrows at Sarah, which her sister-in-law easily understood as *Miss Pence would know all about that, wouldn't she?*

"Oh, pooh, Harry," Miss Pence replied with a toss of her head. "You're just disappointed that you have to go home."

"Will you come with us, Harry?" Sarah asked. "There will be other opportunities, in good time."

The boy shook his head vehemently, but there were tears of frustration in his eyes. And perhaps it was her own downcast state, but Sarah could not help pitying him. She supposed if she had all Harry's quickness and spirit and nothing to look forward to but a hovel shared with Mrs. Barbary and countless siblings, she would be dejected as well...What would become of him, even if they could drag him back to Iffley and manage to prevent additional flights?

With a sigh, she turned to the baron. "Sir, may I have a word with you in the passage?"

Harry perked up, but she was careful to keep her face impassive. No need to raise the boy's hopes, if they might only be dashed again in another minute.

When she had shut the door behind them she said in a low voice, "What is your opinion, sir? He seems very set on being a cabin boy. There would be no question of it, of course, except that Mrs. Barbary did seem to waver at the last minute."

"If he would be paid wages," Lord Dere reminded her. "And presumably if some of those wages were remitted to her." He chewed his lip thoughtfully. "A lad from his station in life hasn't many chances in Iffley to better himself..."

"Yes, that's what I thought. Harry loves to learn, and half of his mischief—if not more—could be attributed to idleness. If he were to be the *Gazelle's* cabin boy, he would see some of the world, and, if he proved able and did not come to harm, he might even rise. Become an able seaman. Possibly find work in the merchant marine afterward, if the war doesn't last."

The baron's eyes were gleaming by this point. "Let us discuss this with Mr. Langworthy, Sarah."

"With Mr. Langworthy? Why?"

But Lord Dere had already opened the parlor door to summon him. Wringing her skirts with her hands, Sarah tried to collect herself. *He is engaged to Miss Pence again. He kissed her. He called her "Mary."*

"Sir?"

The passage seemed suddenly too confined. Langworthy's sleeve brushed Sarah's, and each tried to back away, only to be prevented by a wall sconce at her back and a hat-stand at his.

Succinctly the baron summarized the situation for him, concluding with, "So we have two questions for you, Langworthy. First: you taught and trained the boy yourself in Iffley—do you think he could learn to be a passable sailor? And second: is there any pay granted to cabin boys beyond the food and shelter allotted them, or would Harry have nothing to send home?"

"In short, yes, and yes, sir."

Langworthy in turn described his failed attempts to dissuade Harry, including the morning's rough-seas experiment. "I confess he fared better than I in the chopping waves, though I managed not to humiliate myself. When Harry wants to learn and wants to please, I would back him against any boy the Marine Society might send us from London. And as for pay, he would be one of the captain's servants and receive up to £3 per annum, though some of this would go for his clothing and such. It isn't much, I admit."

The baron nodded thoughtfully. "Mrs. Barbary would be spared Harry's keep, however, in addition to the pound or so he could send home, which means she might make a small gain of, say, seven or eight pounds."

Sarah had not known the baron the past three years without learning something of his character, and she was not surprised when he said, "I wonder, Mr. Langworthy, if you would participate in a little kindly deception...?"

Unfortunately Mr. Langworthy is no stranger to deception, she thought with a smothered sigh. *Kindly or otherwise.*

But his sleeve brushed hers again, and when she glanced up, he was watching her. Even as he answered, "Say on, sir."

"Well, suppose we were to tell her Harry would be able to send home a pound per month? That's a nice, round number. I suspect Mrs. Barbary would feel quite satisfied to have her son embarked on a profession, young as he is, for a pound per month. Instead of paying for an apprentice-ship—which she would not have been able to do without help—she will herself be paid!"

"You propose making up the difference, sir?"

"Er—yes," admitted the baron. "In these times, it would almost be my patriotic duty, to train up another sailor. I have never made a gift to the Marine Society, though they do such important work, giving boys with no prospects a possible career, and this will atone for that. What do you say, Langworthy? I might advance the money to you, and you might in turn ensure Harry sends it to Iffley whenever letters get through."

"But—" Sarah hesitated as both men turned at the sound. "But it might be that Mr. Langworthy—that *you,* sir—would prefer not to be responsible for Harry on board. As Miss Pence observed before you came in, he is quite 'harum-scarum.'"

With the door to the parlor shut, the passage was dim, but Sarah thought he colored.

"He...is certainly that, Mrs. Sebastian," he murmured. "I think we would all agree. But I would not be alone in watching the boy. I have warned him, *ad nauseam* I daresay, that his lowly position would render him answerable to the *Gazelle's* full officer complement, and, if he were to be found wanting, there would be nothing I could or would do to protect him from the consequences. Nor would there be anything to be done if there were such a one aboard as that Lieutenant Beeton I told you

Barstows about. And there always does seem to be a Lieutenant Beeton, unfortunately. Still, Harry persists in wanting this."

"But what if we are making a bad decision for him, in giving him his head, and he ends in hating it?" she persisted.

Langworthy's mouth twisted in rueful awareness. "Then let us say he would not be the first young boy who ever deserted. If he turns up again in Iffley, you will have your answer."

All this while, Sarah had simultaneously been casting about for how she might pass Mrs. Barstow's message to him, and her heart drummed faster at this reference to turning up in Iffley. Would Mr. Langworthy himself ever turn up in Iffley again? Suppose those on the *Gazelle* were granted leave, and Mr. Langworthy thought Harry should see his mother?

Who knew. There was no telling what the future held.

But one thing was certain: if they were all agreed now that Harry would remain in Portsmouth, their mission was ended, and the Barstows and Lord Dere would likely leave the following morning.

"Come," said the baron. "Let us tell Harry the good news."

Mr. Langworthy opened the door, stepping back to let the baron and Sarah precede him. And just as Sarah steeled herself—*I must tell him I require a word with him!*—he lifted a hand a few inches from his side to arrest her.

"Mrs. Sebastian," he uttered, so low it might have escaped ears which were not tuned to every note of his voice. "I must speak with you."

Her hand flying to her throat, there was no time to do anything but nod, once.

There, then.

He might only wish to explain himself, defend himself, but if he was determined to do so, at least he would make his chance before they were gone. And when he had done so, she would say what she needed to say, and they could be quit of each other.

Dear heaven, thought Horace Langworthy, *settling Harry Barbary's fate was the easy part!* But he felt the tightness in his shoulders lessen a fraction, to know that she would hear him out. Whatever she made of Mary Pence, and whatever Mary had already said, and whatever was going to happen when they re-entered the parlor, Sarah would hear him. He would have the final word, and not Mary. If only he and Mrs. Sebastian could march straight out the street door at once and not have to return!

He could see immediately that Mary was in a state. She and Miss Barstow must have had an awkward time of it while the rest of them were out of the room, because Miss Barstow expelled a relieved breath and smiled widely at them. "Have you reached a verdict?" she asked.

"We have," said the baron. He smiled at Sarah. "Will you tell it, my dear?"

"Harry, we have decided you may stay and go to sea as the cabin boy on the *G—*" That was as far as she got before the boy erupted in a whoop, jumping up and hurtling to throw his arms about her. "Hurrah! Hurrah! Hur*rah*! I'm going to sea! I'm going to sea!"

"Goodness me, what a hullabaloo," Miss Pence said crossly. "I can't say I think much of your judgment, if that's what you decided, sending such an infant into who knows what peril!"

Confusion checked Harry's celebration, and he wrinkled his nose at her in perplexity. "But you said it would be great larks, and that of course I should go, Miss Pence."

She shrugged. "Did I? Well, and what if I did? I hope you don't get blown to bits an hour out of Spithead." Taking up the clothes she had been sewing, she almost hurled them at him. "Here, then. Take your linens. I won't be needing them."

Langworthy stiffened, his eyes narrowing at these words, but then Mrs. Sebastian was saying, "So generous of Miss Pence to prepare them for you, Harry, *and* to have let you stay here until you sail. You will be a good boy, won't you, and prove our trust in you is justified? And perhaps when you are at sea, you might write to your mother from time to time. If you direct your letters to me or to Miss Barstow, we will be glad to pay the postage and to read them to Mrs. Barbary."

Harry agreed to this, of course. Having got what he wanted and already dismissing Miss Pence's mercurial moods, he was prepared to love all the world and to promise all sorts of things.

Not so Miss Pence.

She invited the visitors to stay to dinner, but in such a tone that the baron needed no hint to decline, instead proposing a walk to the waterfront with Harry. "Then you might show us everything you have already discovered," he suggested.

Much as Langworthy would have loved to join them, having secured Mrs. Sebastian's promise to talk to him later he let her go now, resigning himself to stay behind to have it out with his erstwhile betrothed.

CHAPTER 26

**Rash Lover speak what pleasure hath
Thy Spring in such an Aftermath?
—R. Fletcher, *Poems in Ex Otio Negotium* (1556)**

As soon as the callers were gone, Mary threw herself across the sofa, resting her face on the cushion and staring into the fire.

"Why didn't you go with them, Horace?" she demanded. "I know you wanted to."

"We must talk, Mary," he sighed. "Did you tell them that was you in Iffley, or did they guess it when they saw Blodgett?"

"I think only the young ladies guessed it." A giggle escaped her, in spite of her sulkiness. "The dear old man was simply confused."

"But you did not talk of it?"

"No." Sitting up, she studied him. "They don't seem the sort of people who will tell anyone, for your sake, if not for mine."

"No. I don't suppose they will." He ran tired hands down his face. It was enough that they knew it. That *she* knew it. But he could still explain it away, possibly, if she would only hear him—and if Mary did not play the aces in her hand.

"You like her, don't you, Horace? Mrs. Sebastian. The widowed one who was married to your friend."

There was nothing to be gained by denying it. Someone who knew him as long as Mary had would not be fooled.

"I do."

"I suspected it, when I was there, in Iffley. That there was...something between you. And I couldn't think why, when you used to love me, and you and I were so alike, I thought."

"We did used to be more alike," he conceded. Or, at least, he used to be more like her. More reckless. More devil-may-care. It seemed a long time ago.

"You were so full of fun and mischief!" She smiled dreamily, remembering. "And I had a new adventure in mind, Horace, which the old you would have loved, but which the new, tiresome Horace you have become would likely not have approved. Can you guess what it was?"

"Did it have something to do with the linens you were purportedly making for Harry Barbary?" he asked grimly. "I did hear you say 'you' wouldn't be needing them now."

"That's it!" she shrieked in delight. "How great minds do think alike. Yes. I thought, once Harry was fetched home, I would go in his place. I would see the world! I have no doubt I could do anything a young boy was expected to do, and when I grew tired of it, I would simply put my dress back on and desert."

There were so many, many problems with her scheme—twice as many as he had ever tried to scare Harry with!—that Langworthy was at a loss where to begin.

"What—how on earth—did you not consider—"

Again he passed his hands over his face, this time in sheer amazement. If he and Mary had once been so much alike, did that mean he too had once been so utterly *brainless*?

Mercy. What next?

Inwardly shaking his head, he gave up. Let it be enough that her ridiculous plan was thwarted.

"If this was your intention, Mary, why did you act so eager for Harry to go?"

"I was throwing everyone off the scent, naturally," she plumed herself. "I even said I was making the clothing a little too big, so Harry could grow into them, when really it was to fit me."

But after a moment, her self-satisfaction faded, her shoulders sagging. "But so much for that. He will go, and you will go, and I will remain. And I suppose you will marry that Mrs. Sebastian person, and I will—I will do nothing for the rest of my life and grow old and ugly and be loved by nobody."

"Mary." Though she had wronged him so painfully, and though he still did not know if he could repair the damage done by her Iffley escapade, he could not sustain his anger. Because she was a child, he realized. Almost as much a child as Harry Barbary.

"Mary, listen to me. You have a great deal to look forward to. As we speak, gentlemen are pouring into Portsmouth. Everywhere you turn you will see new faces and meet new people. Dashing officers, and not the sad creatures on half pay such as I have been. Already there is activity, and soon there will be assemblies and battles and news of prizes taken. I would not be surprised if you accepted and jilted a dozen men before I see you again, and I will only have the satisfaction of having been the first."

To his relief, she laughed. There were tears in it, but it was a laugh all the same. "Why do you not start me off again, then?" she asked, dabbing at the corner of her eye with the heel of her hand. "Could we not be engaged once more?"

When he hesitated, her features gathered in a little pout, and her voice lost its playfulness. "I could make you do it, you know. I could shout from the rooftops that I was the root of your little scandal in Iffley, the reason you had to leave so abruptly. And then you would have to save me, in order to save yourself. Save my reputation, at the cost of your own. That Mrs. Sebastian wouldn't think much of you, then."

There they were. The aces he had been waiting for.

He nodded, knowing he would have to choose his words carefully. "Mrs. Sebastian and her sister-in-law Miss Barstow have already penetrated your secret, you said earlier. And as you also observed—and I would agree with you—they don't seem the sort to tell tales. Which means, if the story were to get abroad, it must be your own doing, and what girl would choose to destroy her own reputation? Half the fun of your pranks, I suspect, is the fear of being discovered. But if you were, in fact, discovered, that fun would end. You would be left only with the consequences. And however unjust it may be, it is also true that a man's reputation, once lost, is not beyond revival...as a woman's is."

In answer to this she scowled, her bosom swelling in vexation. Had they been ten years younger, she might have pelted him with the nearest convenient object. As it was, her little hands did clench and unclench. "*She* has a spotless reputation, I suppose. Mrs. Sebastian, whom you are going to marry."

Unable to prevent a short chuckle he answered, "She has at least lived a quieter life."

"Then you admit it, Horace?" she pressed. "You *will* marry her?"

"If she'll have me, yes."

His former beloved's features screwed up in a grimace. "She'll have you, all right. I could tell straight off that she aspired to you. Set her cap for you and her heart on you. And you think *I* am overbold."

"If she was so resolved, she had a peculiar way of showing it," he retorted, goaded at last. "Because she refused me when I asked her."

Mary's mouth fell open—there was no other way to put it. Fell open and stayed open. "You—asked her? You—you went from me to *her*?"

Again her hands clenched fitfully, and with a rueful smile he tapped the back of one of them. "Oh, Mary. Leave it be. We have been good friends. Let us continue so. I don't think you've been in love with me for a very long time, and why should you want me now, dull as I am?"

"You *are* dull," she returned, though he was glad to see a grin tugging at her lips. "Dull and staid and still as poor as you ever were. But I know the second I let you go with my blessing, you will make commander and then captain and then admiral and take a hundred prizes and be made Lord High ThisandThat, and I will gnash my teeth in chagrin!"

"If that's all it will take, won't you please do it?" he teased. "I might act on commission for you and return you a percentage."

Her grin widened, and he leaned closer to make her meet his eyes. "Come. Shall we lay this dead engagement of ours to rest and part friends?"

The wind was brisk on the saluting platform which overlooked Spithead. They had been there an hour already, but Harry and Lord Dere's interest showed no signs of flagging. The *Gazelle* must be pointed out (no easy matter with so many ships readied and awaiting orders) and distinguished from its neighbors, and Harry must share every ounce of knowledge already imparted to him.

For Mr. Langworthy's sake Sarah could also have listened for another hour, but Frances wound an arm through hers and walked her further along the wall.

"I can't wait any longer to discuss it," she apologized. "Because what do you think of Miss Pence and Blodgett? In all Mrs. Dere's conjectures, she never hit upon this explanation! Nor did I, for that matter."

"Nor I," said Sarah. Catching at her flapping bonnet ribbons, she occupied herself with retying them, so she need not look at Frances. "But it answers one question," she rejoined. "The one about whether they were kissing or fighting. As they were formerly engaged, I suppose it might have been kissing and then fighting, or else kissing and then...grappling with each other."

Frances sighed. "Yes. How very disturbing. I really do like Mr. Langworthy—not only for Sebastian's sake, but also for his own. And I wish he weren't so entangled with such a one. One who dressed as a boy! Posed as a servant! Endangered herself and him! If she could have known the suspicions it aroused and the trouble she landed him in—and to what end? All to spy on him? To win him back?" She took hold of Sarah's arm again. "Do you suppose it has worked, and she has succeeded? But if she had, wouldn't they have made an announcement when we were there?"

"We were rather busy settling Harry's fate," answered Sarah shortly. "It was hardly the time for celebrations. If it helps matters any, Mr. Langworthy did say to me in the passage that he would like to speak with me. To explain himself, I imagine. And I said yes, of course, because I have to give him Mrs. Barstow's message."

"Mm." Releasing her, Frances leaned her elbows on the platform's stone wall. "If Miss Pence came all the way to Iffley in such an elaborate disguise to catch him again, I don't expect she would be keen on allowing him another visit when they are married. Poor Mama."

Poor Mrs. Gordon Barstow, indeed.

And poor Mrs. Sebastian Barstow.

"Isn't it odd," continued Frances, "to think that Sebastian and Mr. Langworthy should marry such different people? To hear Mr. Langworthy tells stories, they were as alike as two peas, but Sebastian chose you—rational and sensible and *dear*—and Mr. Langworthy prefers that shocking creature—"

"Sebastian thought Mr. Langworthy should marry me," Sarah blurted. She had not meant to say it—not at all—never—under any circumstances, and yet out it popped. Later she would think it was because secrets never shrank for being kept; they only grew. Grew, and grew heavier. And that afternoon in Portsmouth, after such a morning and after standing so long on the platform, she simply could no longer support its weight.

"What do you mean?" puzzled Frances. "Sebastian told you that?"

Sarah shook her head. "No. I didn't know. It was Mr. Langworthy who told me when he first came. He said Sebastian had written to him after he was wounded and...asked him to...take care of Bash and me and—marry me, if—if—he happened not to marry Miss Pence."

"My goodness!" Frances breathed. "Only imagine." She turned an unseeing gaze out toward the ships floating in the sheltered anchorage, and some minutes passed before she ventured, "Then...did you—have a good laugh about it? I mean, he didn't ask you, did he, even though Miss Pence had jilted him?"

Sarah had gone too far for retreat now, even if she wanted to, and the story was soon told, leaving Frances dumbfounded and reviewing all that had gone before through this new lens.

"I wish—" Sarah began again when her companion still said nothing, "—I wish now I had given him a different answer."

"Indeed, so do I. You would have made him a far better wife than Miss Pence. But I don't see how you could have given him any other answer, Sarah. You had only just met him, and I remember you weren't predisposed to like him."

"No..."

"Mama would be very sorry to learn of this, however. Of how near we came to making him part of the family."

"You mustn't tell her yet, Frances!" urged Sarah. "We will announce his renewed engagement first, and then, when that is got over, I will tell her all. To tell her now would only sadden her."

Squeezing her hand in agreement, Frances looked like she might say more, but then she shook her head. She gave Sarah a kiss meant to express all that could not be said, and then the two of them rejoined the others.

CHAPTER 27

Happilie I have arrived at the last
Unto the wished haven of my blisse.
—Shakespeare, *The Taming of the Shrew* (c.1616)

Although Mr. Langworthy had not named a time for their conversation, Sarah had hoped he could come later that evening to the George, for not only would he and Harry be taking their leave aboard the *Gazelle* in the next day or two, but the Iffley party had no more excuse to linger, and Sarah was anxious to return to Bash.

He did not come, however.

Nor did he send word the next morning at breakfast.

Indeed, if Sarah had not told the baron of Langworthy's request, she would have been hard put to invent reasons for waiting. As it was, they walked out to see the dockyards and the garrison chapel after breakfast, certain they would return to find him in the inn's coffee room, but he was not. There were navy men aplenty, all very fine in their uniforms, but no Mr. Langworthy.

"Are you certain he is not expecting *us* to call again at his uncle's home or again at Miss Pence's?" asked Lord Dere when he caught her glancing at the clock again.

"He said nothing of it," Sarah replied anxiously.

"Should we send a note?" suggested Frances. "He might have forgotten."

If he had forgotten, Sarah balked at reminding him. *He* had asked to speak with her, so why should she be the one to give chase?

But there was still her mother-in-law's message to deliver, even if he would never come to Iffley again. And, truth be told, the thought of being robbed of this last time gave her a miserable little pang.

"Very well," she murmured. "I will beg pen and paper and send a note."

"You had better tell him Mama's invitation, while you're at it, in case he was already called away and cannot come to us," Frances said, reading her disappointment. "And in the meantime I will go up to our room and pack the presents we bought in our bags." Rising, she gave Sarah's shoulder a consoling press.

Patting back a yawn, the baron excused himself as well. "If you don't mind, dear Sarah, I will take a little nap after the morning's exercise. But if he comes, you need only send someone to knock on my door, and I will come down at once."

Even if Sarah had not been fretting over the wording of her note, she might not have noticed Langworthy when he entered the coffee room a quarter hour later. Not because she had ceased to glance up in hope whenever the door opened, but because he entered in a bustle of seamen dressed as he was, in uniform.

He had always been a fine, upright, good-looking young man, but in his beautiful dark blue lieutenant's coat with its white lapels he was magnificent. The more so because he spied her right away and came straight to stop beside her table.

Startled, Sarah looked up...and up. "Mr. Langworthy!"

His color rose, but he made her a bow, his black bicorn hat tucked beneath his arm. "Pardon me for not coming sooner—or sending word. I came as soon as I could," he said, flustered. "I had only returned to my uncle's five minutes yesterday, before Stolles—the *Gazelle's* surgeon—arrived in Nobbs Lane to hunt me up and carry me off. The crew is complete. That is—I'm ashore on duty now to see to last-minute things, but I've only just got away and haven't long before I must be back. The boat's to be off for Spithead by four—"

"Then let us waste no time," Sarah broke in, her own face hot as her heart thumped. "Won't you sit down?"

He shook his head. "Not here. If—you wouldn't object, they have smaller, more private parlors."

She did not object. Folding up the note she would no longer need, she followed him from the coffee room. Langworthy received a respectable share of nods from fellow officers, including one or two boasting gold buttons and epaulettes, and curious glances traced his companion's progress as well. Sarah was looking her best, if only because her cheeks were crimson and her blue eyes dark with apprehension.

The hum of voices quietened when he shut the door behind them, and then they were alone. She didn't know whether to sit or stand. She didn't know what to do with her hands. She didn't know where to look.

He was scarcely better off.

It must have been the smallest parlor at the George, containing only a round table and two armchairs before a modest fire. Beneath a painting of the Battle of Quiberon Bay, a clock ticked loudly on the mantel.

Tick. Tick. Tick.

"Where—where are the baron and Miss Barstow?"

"Upstairs." It emerged as a squeak, and she hastily turned to march over to the farther armchair, trying quietly to clear her throat. "They are upstairs. I was just writing to you to say we would be returning to Iffley tomorrow and that—and that we would be sorry to miss you. Frances thought maybe you forgot." She folded her hands in her lap.

"No—how could I, when I was the one who asked to meet?" Finding that he was gripping his hat too tightly, he laid it on the table. "It is as I explained. I did not forget. Indeed, I've thought of little else since I last saw you."

"Oh."

Another pause. Just when Sarah wondered if he remained standing for fear of creasing his handsome uniform, he took the other chair, his gaze dropping to her hands. She remembered him taking them in his own when he left Iffley and, afraid he would read her mind, had to resist the urge to sit upon them.

"What must you think of me, Mrs. Sebastian."

"You must tell me what to think," she said gently. "We—understand now that it was Miss Pence and—er—Blodgett—who posed as servants at Perryfield, and I would guess it was not at your suggestion."

A mirthless chuckle was her answer.

She wished she could ask if they were engaged again, but it proved impossible.

Tick. Tick. Tick.

With a whirring of gears, the hour struck.

Giving himself a shake, he grimaced and ran a hand through his hair. "I have thought and thought what I should say, but it has all floated away. Therefore I must blunder ahead, though I may regret my words the moment you are gone. Mrs. Sebastian—Mary Pence did not come to Iffley with my knowledge. You had asked me to forgive her for jilting me, and I had, and congratulated myself for it. But when I discovered her at the children's ball, I found how cheap my forgiveness was."

"Cheap?" repeated Sarah. "Do you mean because you realized you had not forgiven her after all?"

His mouth worked a moment. "No. Because I realized I had not so much forgiven her as *forgotten* her. If I had found it easy to forgive her for breaking our engagement, it was only because she had lost her place in my heart. Utterly. She had been…superseded.”

He raised eyes then so black, so bottomless that Sarah felt herself sucked in, whole, body and soul, like a ship spiraling down, down in a whirlpool.

“Sarah.”

She clung to the arms of her chair as if they were the only things preventing her from falling into him. (They were.) How she longed to give way! To let herself plummet, praying he would catch her.

Had she been five years younger—had the last several years of her life not taught her about loss and grief—had she had only herself to answer for—Sarah might here have abandoned restraint as rashly as ever Mary Pence had.

But no.

She was who she was, and who her life had made her.

And so she did not move.

There was nothing she could do, however, about what her eyes might express, without recourse to words or motion. And what he read there was enough.

“When she and I left the ball,” he went on, his low, rumbling voice sending tremors through her, “we did not return to the rectory, as you know. I took her directly toward Oxford, intending to send her straight back here. She and Colley had ended their own engagement, and Mary then thought it would be good fun to see what delayed me in Iffley. She was not…well pleased with what she found. Put simply, she saw enough to make her throw chocolate on you and to say whatever she might have said to you when you were alone.”

Even the memory of Mary Pence’s dreadful accusations that night made Sarah ill. She could not repeat them now. Could *not*. Especially when Mr. Langworthy, for all his blazing eyes, had not yet said where he stood with the young lady, nor why they had kissed, if they had kissed.

She shook her head. "I would—I would rather not—that is—I"

"That good, you say?" His faint grin made her heart turn a flip-flap like a tumbler at the fair.

"Mr. Langworthy," she whispered, unable to wait any longer, "are you and Miss Pence engaged again?"

"No."

"Oh."

"Sarah. Aren't you going to ask me what Harker saw?"

She swallowed. "I have already been told by every busybody in Iffley what Harker saw."

"A good point, Mrs. Sebastian. An important distinction. I misspoke. I should have said, do you not want to ask me what precisely went on between Miss Pence and me, that Harker witnessed?" Reaching two fingertips, he took a fold of her skirt between them and gave the smallest tug.

"I—only if you want to tell me, sir."

"'Sir'!" he protested teasingly. "Sir me no sirs. I do, in fact, want to tell you, Mrs. Sebastian, and for the first time I am at liberty to do so."

"Are you?" she whispered.

"Indeed. Not only because Mary's Iffley escapade is no longer a secret with you, but also because, following your call in Highbury Street, she and I spoke heart to heart and settled two things." Leaning closer, he gave her skirt another twitch. "Perhaps you should come nearer, so I might murmur the rest in your ear. You never know who might be about in places like this."

"We had better chance it," she managed to reply. But she did not jerk her dress from his fingers.

He sighed. "Very well. But if you should change your mind, you need only say so. Where was I? Oh, yes. Miss Pence and I spoke heart to heart, and our first determination was that we *were* not, *had not been* for several months, and *never again would be* engaged to be married."

"Oh."

"She did, on the Pettypont Bridge, become greatly excited and emotional," he continued, "but I swear to you, Mrs. Sebastian, the embrace Harker saw was no more mutual than when Bash falls upon Poppet and kisses him before the poor dog can wriggle free."

"You're a deal stronger than Poppet," said Sarah dryly, though inwardly her heart floated with joy.

"So I am," he agreed, "and had I made use of that greater strength, I could have lifted Mary overhead and flung her in the River Cherwell, but I hope you will agree that would have created another whole set of problems."

As her former fears evaporated and her spirits rose to dizzying heights, a laugh escaped her, causing his own to ring out in turn.

"Hush, Mr. Langworthy," Sarah bid him, still giggling. "Such a bellow will bring the innkeeper at a run."

"Then come here," he replied. Releasing her skirts, he made use of his vaunted strength to seize her by the arms and transfer her to his lap.

"What are you doing?" she protested, still laughing but turning to slap at his hands. "Suppose someone comes in, sir!"

"Then he too will hear the second conclusion Miss Pence and I arrived at in our talk," he said, gathering her still closer to his chest.

"Which was...?"

"Which was, that I would marry you, if you would have me. Look at me, Sarah. I asked you once before and deserved the answer I got. I asked you flippantly, in bitterness of spirit, without any effort to court or win you. But God bless you, my love, for though I remained in Iffley vowing revenge on you for your rejection, you overcame my misplaced rancor with your kindness and honesty. I ask you again now, beloved Sarah, will you be my wife? If this time I lay at your feet my heart, my person, and all that I have or will ever have to give in this world?"

She said Yes.

Of course she said Yes, even if she could not say it in words. She gave her consent with smiles and tears, and when he urged, "Then kiss me, Sarah," she gave her consent again by lifting her lips to his.

It was an hour they would recall with sighs and with longing, the many months they were apart, an hour they would occasionally be blessed to return to in dreams.

The relentless mantel clock ticked away their time, however, and the hour could not all be given to embracing (although a shocking portion of it was).

"You will write to me, Sarah?" he murmured, his lips at her ear. "Because I don't know when we will see each other again, much less marry. Ah, marriage!" This drew a frustrated groan. "I would need to get very lucky with prizes or we could never afford to until I made post captain. It might be years."

Or never.

A shiver passed through her when she remembered how Sebastian had sailed away from her that final time, never to return. "Of course I will write to you," she promised. "But Horace—if you do return to Portsmouth and are given shore leave, what will we do? You will not have time to come all the way to Iffley—oh, good heavens!" Suddenly, she remembered her mother-in-law's request and blushed to think what had driven it so far from her mind. "Dearest, I entirely forgot to tell you that Mrs. Gordon Barstow had a message for you."

When it was told, it only made her love him more to see the tears stand in his eyes. "Bless her. I've never had a mother—that I could remember. You saw what sort of house my uncle's is. Tell her—and I will tell her again when I write to her—that I will come to Iffley every chance I have."

"But Horace," Sarah said again, "if you must travel to Iffley whenever you have leave, it will cut fearfully into your time—into our time together."

"But how could I ask you and Bash and the Barstows to meet me in Portsmouth? It would be expensive and very hard on you all to travel and to find temporary lodgings whenever I knew I would be ashore, and the precise days and times can never be depended upon."

"Perhaps if Mrs. Barstow and I came and left Bash in Iffley...?"

But he shook his head decisively at this. "Absolutely not. If I am to be the boy's new father one day, I must be given the opportunities to win him." Grinning, he took her hand and rubbed it against his jaw. "I may even have to grow a fine set of 'ooskers,' so that usurpers like Rearden don't presume upon my place."

(Further embracing, but more hurried this time.)

"If we will have so little time together, you must have your likeness taken and sent to me," she insisted, pulling away again.

"And you must give me something of yours. This lock of hair? I have kissed it enough that by rights it belongs to me now."

The hands of the clock were flying now.

"Horace," she ventured, driven to boldness by him reluctantly setting her on her feet again and rising to straighten his uniform, "you know our expenses are low in Iffley—the baron is so kind. Do you suppose, now that you are receiving your full pay again, and I can continue to economize and remain where I have been, that we might not wait so very many years to marry, even if there is no prize money or promotion?"

"Darling girl!" He kissed her again on her lips and her brow. "Don't you want me to be a rich admiral one day?"

"I don't care about that, except for your sake. If you want it, I mean. If you want it, I will want it for you. But then maybe when you are wealthy and have made post-captain, you might think it would have been wiser to choose a young lady who would aid your career through her connections or fortune."

Such a statement could not go unchallenged, and Langworthy defied it in the most satisfying manner possible.

"But perhaps *you* will be the one to be disappointed, Sarah," he rejoined a few minutes onward. "Because suppose I meet with ill luck—"

"Hush! Don't say that, Horace—"

"No, sweeting, don't look like that! I didn't mean that sort of ill luck. I meant ill luck like I experienced before: capture, imprisonment, no chance of prize money or promotion—"

"I don't care! I wouldn't care!" she vowed. "Only promise me you will come back to me alive."

"Alive, yes, as much as it is in my power. But what if I had to invalid out? Or had a leg blown to bits like Mary's Captain Colley?"

"Just so you are alive," she insisted.

"Would you still like me, though, if I didn't have this very handsome uniform and had to turn schoolmaster?"

"I liked you well enough when you were hardly more than an idler in Iffley."

"'Idler,' indeed! I ought to punish you for that, and so I will."

But when the punishments had been administered he said, "Did you know, the baron tried to persuade me into the schoolmaster line permanently?"

"I wish he had succeeded, then," Sarah declared. "If he had, we might marry next month and be always together."

As it was, far too soon the moment of parting was upon them. In truth, he should have gone ten minutes earlier, and as it was he prayed Stolles had succeeded in getting Harry to the boat which would row them out to Spithead. "For if he didn't, it's too late now, and you will have to take the boy back with you to Iffley, heaven help you."

There was no time for more.

He left her at the door with one final, lingering look.

Then they parted, as miserable as it was possible for two blissful, avowed lovers to be.

Chapter 28

I am a stranger, & cannot tel
what your horse play meanes.
—Richard Harvey, *Plaine Percevall the peace-maker of Eng-*
***land* (1590)**

Has she had a letter at last?" asked Mrs. Markham Dere, where she sat in the cozy parlor of Iffley Cottage with Mrs. Barstow, Miss Barstow, the younger Barstows, and the rector's wife Mrs. Terry. It was a late autumn day in the following year, and they were enjoying an unexpected warm spell, warm enough that Reed had opened one of the windows slightly to admit the occasional breeze.

"Two of them," Frances answered. "I thought Sarah would die of happiness."

"And I must die of impatience to hear some of their contents," Mrs. Barstow added with a smile. "Though you must not suspect me of complaining. Sarah is very generous with the portions which she shares."

"Wind speed, weather conditions, ship positions…" laughed Frances.

"Don't forget that one time the entire crew had chilblains on their hands and feet," Maria suggested. "We heard about that in some detail."

"Goodness!" exclaimed Mrs. Terry. "But I suppose Mrs. Sebastian would far rather read about chilblains than battles, for the former pose no lasting danger to her Mr. Langworthy. What a good thing the *Gazelle's* orders have been for blockade duty."

"Mr. Langworthy quite chafes at it!" said Frances. "He says not only is it monotonous, but they may never come ashore, and with the French ships all bottled up, none venture out to make things exciting."

"Mr. Langworthy may keep his excitement," Mrs. Terry replied. "When Mr. Terry and I returned from the Continent last spring, we were very glad of our ship's naval escort, but it did not altogether dispel the fear that a cannonball might land on our heads at any second. It would hardly have served to go to Italy to cure my husband's cough, only to be blown to bits as we came home! But all's well that ends well. I am very sorry to have missed Mrs. Sebastian and Mr. Langworthy falling in love, however."

"There was nothing to see," Frances assured her. "They were quite secret about it. I daresay they kept it a secret even from themselves until he'd gone back to Portsmouth, and we thought we would never see him again."

"Considering the circumstances under which he left, we thought it best at the time," interposed Mrs. Dere. "You will remember, Mrs. Terry, what my coachman Harker witnessed on the Pettypont Bridge..."

"When I count the number of people in Iffley who have told me versions of the incident, I don't see how I could ever forget," answered the rector's wife humorously. "Still—Mr. Langworthy's former betrothed sending servants to spy upon him! That's such good gossip we should record it in the parish register."

"In any event, Mr. Langworthy was not to blame, and it was quite gallant of him to try to shield the young lady from talk," spoke up Mrs. Barstow, ever eager to defend her favorite. (Frances was very absorbed in her work for this portion of the conversation. She and Sarah had decided to let Miss

Pence's lie stand, even if they suspected they were being more careful of her reputation than Miss Pence herself had proven.)

"One part I cannot understand, however, and for which no two people can offer the same explanation, is why Harker could not tell the difference between kissing and fighting! Mrs. Lamb believes it wasn't kissing after all, but rather that they were butting each other with their heads. And our own Polly supposes the footman-spy was trying to bite Mr. Langworthy. I do wish Mrs. Sebastian might learn the truth for all of us—though, if she were to ask after so much time has passed, it would look less like curiosity and more like an unhealthy preoccupation."

No reference was made to what Mrs. Dere's leading theory had been at the time, but a little pause fell before Mrs. Terry spoke again.

"Well, though Mr. Langworthy left Iffley under a cloud, imagine young Harry Barbary playing, if not Cupid, at least the function of Cupid, in running away to sea and bringing Mr. Langworthy and Mrs. Sebastian together again!"

Here was a safer topic. They might all agree on Harry Barbary.

Mrs. Dere sucked in her lower lip and shook her head. "I am amazed that boy has neither fallen overboard nor set fire to the ship yet."

"Mr. Langworthy writes that we would hardly recognize him now," said Mrs. Barstow. "He says Harry has grown taller and become quite the naval know-all. Though he suspects certain pranks which befell some of the troublemakers on board might be traced back to our Harry."

"Too likely!" agreed Mrs. Terry, and even Mrs. Dere looked in danger of smiling, but she regained control of herself, saying roundly, "No doubt the boy will not be the only one changed before he is seen in Iffley again. I persist in thinking it would have been more prudent of Mrs. Sebastian and Mr. Langworthy to wait to engage themselves until matters were more certain. She knew him only three months before he went to sea, and now she has not seen him for a year and a half! And as long as the *Gazelle* must sit there and sit there eternally on blockade duty, and as long as this war goes on and on, nothing can be done. At least if Mr. Langworthy's ship had been ordered to chase Napoleon around, they might have captured a prize by now, as well as put in from time to time for repairs, but *this*—! This endless waiting!"

"'And Jacob served seven years for Rachel; and they seemed unto him but a few days, for the love he had to her,'" quoted Mrs. Terry peaceably.

Mrs. Dere said nothing to this (presumably because one cannot say, "Fiddlestick!" to the rector's wife), but she looked her skepticism.

"Come, come, Mrs. Dere," urged Mrs. Terry, placing a placating hand on her forearm. "We must let the parties involved decide what they will and will not bear. They have been wise enough, certainly, in choosing to wait for more income before they marry. Not everyone would, you know. And matches made without enough to live on founder on the rocks in greater number. I suppose Mr. Langworthy and Mrs. Sebastian have been as wise as lovers can be."

"Waiting for income is all very well," Mrs. Dere conceded. "I applaud that part of it. But waiting is harder on a woman, and Mrs. Sebastian is no girl fresh from the schoolroom."

No sooner did she make this pronouncement than the parlor door burst open, and Sarah herself appeared. And if she was no girl fresh from the schoolroom, she was a good imitation of one on this occasion, for her eyes and cheeks glowed, and her smile was so wide it displayed every last tooth.

"They—saw action—and he is safe. But he was made commander of a captured sloop and ordered to take it to Plymouth for repairs," she announced breathlessly. "He thinks it will be several weeks before it is made properly seaworthy again, so he will be in Iffley as soon as ever he might! He is coming at last!"

A week later, Horace Langworthy climbed down from the London coach at the familiar Angel Inn in Oxford's High Street. He was stiff and rumpled from travel and his face a trifle more weathered than when he had last appeared there, but he was instantly recognized.

"Mr. Horace Langworthy?" piped a voice.

Turning to inspect the young man who greeted him, his brow creased in puzzlement.

"It's Brears, sir. I'm a waiter here in the coffee room. Didn't know if I'd know you, after all this time, but it happens I do."

"Ah. You have the advantage of me, then." Lifting a hand he called, "Easy there" to the two coachmen who were lowering his trunk.

"Last time I saw you," Brears continued, unmoved by his quarry's disinterest, "you were sitting in the coffee room with a young man in livery. Little fellow. Bright eyes. Eager look."

Then he had Langworthy's attention. Warily, he took a longer look at the fellow. Confound it—was Mary Pence's ghost going to rise up again after all this time to pester him? Whatever this waiter person wanted, Horace had neither time nor interest to delve into it.

"I've been paid a sum to meet every London coach and look out for you," Brears took up again. "And it's been arranged that as soon as you were to show up, we would drive you out to Iffley."

"Iffley!" It had to be the baron's doing, and this was nothing to do with Mary Pence. Suddenly he was grinning at Brears as if at a long-lost friend. Digging in his pocket, he fetched up a coin. "Splendid. Here. Show me where I may spruce myself up, and in ten minutes I'll be at your service, Brears."

He had thought of sending word ahead while he waited at the Angel Inn, but if this watch had been set on his arrival, surely it could be dispensed with? Eager as he was to see Sarah again, he did take long to convince himself.

As was typical of his acts of generosity, however, Lord Dere had made no mention of his arrangements, and so the Barstows were taken completely by surprise.

When the strange gig drew up at the Iffley Cottage gate, Sarah was in the kitchen cutting Bash's hair with the rest of the household looking on. Now that he was breeched, she thought shorter hair was in order, though her mouth trembled a little to lop off his handsome curls.

"What a little man!" cried Frances, while Maria whooped and clapped her hands.

"I've got every last strand, Mrs. Sebastian," the maid Reed declared, displaying the sweepings, "if you wanted to save some."

"Birds like hair," said Bash. "Irving says. To build nests."

This made them all laugh, and Reed let him poke his fingers into the heap.

"But your hair might be too fine, Bashy," Frances said, rubbing some strands between her own fingers.

"It's curly, though," Gordon pointed out, tossing a little at his nephew. "That will help it stick together, even though it's fine."

"It formed knots easily enough on his head," joked Sarah.

A voice broke in on their merriment. "I must be in the wrong place. Because for my life I don't remember such a great big young fellow here before."

Everyone in the kitchen turned as one, and there was one long moment of incredulity before—"Langworthy!" shouted Gordon, hurling himself at him.

Horace managed to catch him without falling over, but when Mrs. Barstow and Sarah flew after, the whole lot of them went staggering back into the passage, laughing and crying and clamoring. It was full five minutes before any one person could make himself heard, and everyone had as much to say as if eighteen months' of correspondence hadn't made its slow way back and forth, stuffed full with every last mundane detail of life, for how otherwise could you trick yourself into thinking you were together and not missing anything?

They moved en masse to the parlor, Langworthy occupying the sofa so that Sarah could sit next to him, while the others dragged chairs nearer. Only Bash held himself apart, forgetting his new breeches and trimmed hair and maturity so far as to suck on one of his knuckles, watching his mother weep and smile at the same time beside the dread interloper, so close she was almost against him, and the strange man looking at her as if he had never seen anyone so marvelous in all his born days.

"No," said Bash at last. (Not that anyone heard him.)

Then, louder: "*No!*"

Rushing forward, he seized the intruder's hand from where it lay atop his mother's and flung it with all his might away.

"Bash!" came a chorus of horrified Barstows.

"No, it's all right," said Horace. "Of course he doesn't remember me." Then he took up his flung-away hand gingerly, as if it were in danger of shattering, and tucked it to his chest, wincing.

The little boy frowned, perplexed, his strength never before having yielded any such result when he attacked his uncle Gordon or even the smaller Peter Dere. Indeed, the only members of his world he had ever done injury to had been Poppet the dog and Outlaw the cat, but Poppet yelped in pretended pain at everything, and Outlaw always avenged herself by hissing and clawing him.

Bash glanced at his mother to see if she was angry with him for hurting her friend, but she was biting her lip, and there was an odd hum in her voice when she said, "Do forgive him, in any case, for his discourtesy."

"It's all right," the newcomer rasped out. But then he lifted the damaged appendage. "Perhaps if you were to kiss it and make it better?"

With a roar at this renewed outrage, Bash drew his little leg back (not failing to note how satisfying this was to do when one wore breeches, as opposed to a silly gown which always entangled one) and kicked the gentleman in the ankle.

"Bash!" cried one and all again, but not loudly enough to drown the man's piercing "Ooh!" Forgetting the hurt to his hand, he slid from the sofa to curl on the floor, cradling his booted ankle and rocking slightly. "Ooh!"

"That's it, Bash," cried his uncle Gordon, "we'll show him who the men of the Barstow family are!" With a *whoo-whoop!* worthy of a pack of Oxfordshire hunters, he leapt upon the visitor, and the two of them went rolling and grappling and crashing into furniture while the girls screamed and Mrs. Barstow scrambled about, trying to smack her son on the back.

It was safe to say the walls of Iffley Cottage had never contained such riotry before, unless Peter Dere used to wrestle with his father Mr. Markham Dere before the latter's death, but Sarah could not imagine Mrs. Dere allowing it. Nor could she imagine Mrs. Dere giving way to helpless laughter, as she and the others did now. How had they never thought that Gordy might miss the romping and horseplay a father or a brother closer in age would have provided? If he and Peter or their other Keele's classmates indulged in it, they did so out of sight of school or their sedate homes.

Gordon escaped the older man's hold and dodged behind his nephew, scooping him up and shaking him at his fellow contender, so that Bash's little arms and legs flapped. When one hit the man, his victim doubled over, huffing out a breath. Gordon swung him again, Bash's foot connecting with the man's shoulder, sending him crumpling to the carpet.

"Mercy!" he pleaded. "Mercy. I surrender."

Not being an unkind child, and seeing the flushed and delighted faces of his family, Bash gave a solemn nod.

"Hurrah!" cheered Gordon, setting him down again. "Let us celebrate the Peace of Iffley Cottage. Combatants, shake hands." He extended his own, and when Bash saw how it was done, he imitated the gesture.

Rome was not built in a day, of course, but over the following fortnight foundations were laid. There were walks in clear weather, Bash carried pickaback when they went as far as Perryfield, and games and reading when it rained. Just as he had with the other Barstows, Mr. Langworthy told the little boy stories about his father—nothing formal, just little lines or remembrances as they came up. He treated Bash as if he were another Gordon, and it was not lost on the child that his uncle—nay, every member of his family and all the neighbors—liked Mr. Langworthy tremendously. Only Mrs. Dere at Perryfield remained aloof, but even at his young age Bash knew she never fawned on anyone but her own son Peter.

Iffley Cottage being so modest in size, the Barstows for the first time made use of the baron's standing offer to house any guests of theirs, but Lord Dere likewise insisted that, apart from asking that he indulge the Deres with a few calls and several dinners (all to include whichever Barstows he would like), Mr. Langworthy must feel entirely free to be gone as much as he liked, an offer Horace accepted with gratitude.

"You know, my good Langworthy," the baron took him aside to say at the first opportunity, "I hope you will pardon my audacity in even saying this, and trust you will believe I mean it with the best of intentions, but you know I feel rather smug about your engagement."

"Do you?" he said with a grin. (He was grinning a lot these days.)

"Certainly. Because, if you will recall, when you first came to Iffley, I hinted at Sarah's unmarried state and how you might earn an income as a mathematics tutor."

"I remember," he answered dryly. "You also alluded to the possibility of her marrying Rearden, but you weren't so lucky there."

"No, indeed. But truly I only mentioned the curate to stir you—to open your eyes to the charm of our Sarah."

"Oh, believe me, sir, my eyes had been opened, whether or not I would admit it."

"Just so. In any event, feeling I played no mean role in bringing you two together, I cannot help putting my oar in again. You say you have a little more than a fortnight here—suppose you and dear Sarah were to marry now?"

"Now?" he gasped.

"Why not? I know the bishop of Oxford, and our permanent rector Mr. Terry is a friend of long standing. A license could be arranged easily during your stay, if you and Sarah wished."

"We—I would be lying if I said I did not wish it, sir," began Horace, his heart beating harder. "Of course, a lieutenant's pay is not much. Most men wait until they rise to post captain."

"What about the capture of the sloop *Moineau*? That will bring a little prize money in time, and you were its commander, an important step."

"If—if Sarah were to become in the family way..."

"Then she could not be better cared for than in the bosom of her family. You have waited a year and a half already, and who knows when you will be able to return. It will give you both comfort. I insist on nothing. Only discuss it with her."

CHAPTER 29

Play, music; and you brides and bridegrooms all,
With measure heap'd in joy, to th' measures fall.
—Shakespeare, *As You Like It* (c.1599)

Mr. Terry was willing, but the bishop had "whistled off" somewhere as Gordon put it, so that he could not give his approval until half of the fortnight was past. Sarah was only a little sorry at the delay, for it thrilled her heart to see her intended husband knit himself into the very fabric of the family. Though he lodged at Perryfield, he was with them from morning to evening, if they themselves were not at Perryfield. Moreover, it seemed all Iffley was as eager to welcome him back as they had been eager to discuss him and pass judgment upon his hasty departure months and months earlier. After church he was invited to a half-dozen dinners and suppers and card parties, but the baron had got to both Mrs. Dere and Mrs. Terry beforehand, and both women joined forces to insist there was not time for more than a large dinner party at Perryfield and a musical evening at the rectory, to which all those issuing individual invitations to Langworthy were invited and with which they must be satisfied.

"If he and Mrs. Sebastian are to be married in a week's time," Mrs. Terry proclaimed in the churchyard, "they must be left alone to prepare. And if they have been deprived of the sight of each other the last eighteen months, I assure you we are all of us *de trop.*"

"I am the talk of the town once more," Horace said to Sarah the morning after the Perryfield dinner. They had donned wool cloaks and braved the light frost for a walk before breakfast. "It quite swells my self-regard."

Rubbing her cheek against his shoulder, she chuckled. "You had better get used to it, because if you are only to appear in Iffley every year or two, your appearance will always make a stir. And we will always have to fight to snatch what minutes we can."

"We have our allies," he returned. "We can ask Mrs. Dere to organize a review at the beginning of every visit, in which I am paraded before the village to shake hands and exchange greetings. I will then regale them with my three best stories, told in Irving's most roundabout manner, losing and recovering the thread several times and venturing into side alleys of no particular interest. After which I will begin to repeat myself. When I catch the first yawn or glance at his watch, I will abruptly conclude, and everyone will go home satisfied and hoping not to see me again for a long while."

"Better yet," she laughed, swinging his arm, "In your absence I will call on everyone regularly and insist on reading to them portions of your letters—the dull bits—so that they do not want to attend Mrs. Dere's review in the first place and will try to beg off."

"The dull bits!" he protested, giving her a little pinch. "I'll show you dull bits!" Throwing a glance all around and finding them unobserved, he made good on his promise.

"Have I indeed bored you in my letters, my love?" he asked some minutes later.

"No! Don't leave anything out, Horace," she urged him. "Not even the wind conditions which Frances makes fun of. Unless—perhaps you have yawned over my letters yourself? Would you prefer to read less about the harvest or what Bash said or did or what the latest thing was to put Mrs. Dere in a huff...?"

"Don't stint a single word," he said with conviction. "If you knew how blue one can get, so far from home and surrounded always by everlasting men! Why, even Harry can't be got rid of, if he knows I have received a letter. Not until I've read him every last passage—except for the ones about how you adore me, you understand. (Frightfully long, those parts. I blush like a schoolgirl throughout.) It's been kind of you and Mrs. Barstow to read his letters to Mrs. Barbary, but I'm afraid nothing can be done about how little she gives you to say in response."

"Poor Harry! For his sake Frances and I will drag ourselves more often to the Barbarys, and I will try to be especially observant so I may give him news of his siblings. Is he...doing well?"

"So well I suspect he will become a pirate, if given the opportunity. I told him as much, and he replied that if he did, he would share the loot with me, as a wedding present."

Sarah shook her head, smiling. "How kind and generous everyone is being! Harry—at least in his criminal imagination—my family, the baron...Horace, you don't feel rushed into this, do you? We were going to wait, but now, this very Sunday before you must go again you will be—"

"'Cabin'd, cribb'd and confined'?" he finished for her, pulling her close again. "I wish I could be, if it were with you, Sarah. As tightly as I am holding you now. Tell me you're happy about it, too, darling, even if you must hitch yourself to someone who will abandon you again next week, for who-knows how long, and who may, unless Fortune smiles upon me, leave you poorer than he found you."

"Yes. I tell you now, yes. And so I will tell you again on Sunday when Mr. Terry asks."

It did not rain on their wedding day, though it did the night before and the night following. The bride wore her dark blue gown because it was her husband's favorite, and though he was sorry not to be allowed to wear his dress uniform off duty, no one who saw the dashing young lieutenant thought anything wanting in his appearance. All Iffley was there, it seemed, joined by the Weatherills from Oxford and the Egertons from St. Lawrence. Mr. Horatio Langworthy the uncle sent terse felicitations and an invitation that Sarah might visit him in Portsmouth, which she shuddered at but politely deferred.

The baron's wedding gift to the couple was a lavish breakfast at Perryfield and the engagement of a room for two nights at the Star in Oxford. "But I have additional plans, my dear," he informed Sarah before handing her in to his coach. Beaming, he leaned to whisper in her ear and was rewarded by her eyes growing round with amazement.

"But don't tell Mrs. Barstow," he said. "I mean to surprise her with the news at Stir-up Sunday."

"Not a word," she promised. "But may I tell Horace?"

"Of course you may! What God hath joined let no man put asunder, you know." Chuckling.

"What was that about?" asked her husband, when they were bundled in the Perryfield coach, hot bricks at their feet and a blanket across them. But then, "No—wait. Tell me in a minute. I have more pressing business."

They were nearly to the Pettypont Bridge before Sarah pushed him away, laughing, so she might remedy her appearance. "Look, Horace," she said, pointing from the window. "Is this where you kissed Mary Pence?"

"Wicked wife," he scolded.

"Wicked husband, more like."

"Too late for regrets now, Mrs. Langworthy. The deed is done, and I am yours."

"So you are," she sighed, settling back into the circle of his arm.

"And if I had heeded Sebastian Barstow's counsel sooner, my bestowed bride, we might have had two months together, instead of two nights."

"No," she replied thoughtfully, "it had to be this way. Neither of our hearts was ready when we first met. And we will have the rest of our lives, Horace, whatever happens."

"So we shall. Look here, Sarah, I have a wedding gift for you."

"A wedding gift!" She sat up and squeezed his hand. "That reminds me. You kissed it out of my head. Lord Dere told me he is going to build an addition to Iffley Cottage! There isn't room for much, but he wants to knock out a wall and enlarge the little parlor, making space for another bedroom on the first floor. I know you haven't been upstairs, but when it is done, you and I will have my little room and the larger one adjoining for ourselves. Isn't it splendid?"

"Splendid," he agreed. "A splendid gift from a splendid fellow. And you must write in great detail about the renovations, so I may experience the noise and dust and fuss vicariously. Now for my gift. It is no home, but I hope you will like it." He thrust a little velvet pouch into her hands.

Biting her lower lip, she opened the bag and shook into her palms a pair of teardrop earrings made from opaque, peach-colored stone.

"Oh, Horace." Her throat was tight.

"Do you like them? I thought you could wear them with your cameo. Did I ever tell you I was with Sebastian when he bought that cameo for you? He was trying to decide between two designs. He said blue would match your eyes, but the blush color would match your face and your spirit. I said I liked the peach myself, and so I do."

Dashing away a tear, she replaced the earrings in their pouch and carried it to her lips. "I love them. And I will love my cameo all the more, knowing it was from both of you."

Kissing him again, she placed her hand in his, and the coach rattled along the High Street, carrying them into their new life.